How to HANDLE A COWBOY

JOANNE KENNEDY

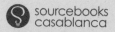

sourcebooks
casablanca

Published by Sourcebooks Casablanca, an imprint of Sourcebooks, Inc.
P. O. Box 4410, Naperville, Illinois 60567-4410
(630) 961-3900
Fax: (630) 961-2168
www.sourcebooks.com

Printed and bound in Canada.
MBP 10 9 8 7 6 5 4 3 2 1

To Carolyn Brown
Friend, mentor,
and
fellow smut peddler

Chapter 1

AFTER SIX WEEKS IN WYNOTT, WYOMING, SIERRA DUNN gave up on love.

Powering up her laptop, she logged into HeartsOnFire .com. There was her picture, all bright eyes and perky smile. And there were her dreams and desires, summed up in twenty-five words or less.

HARDWORKING IDEALIST SEEKS WORLD PEACE, JUSTICE, AND AN INTERESTING MAN FOR FUN AND ADVENTURE. NO WHINERS, TORMENTED ARTISTS, OR DEADBEAT MUSICIANS NEED APPLY.

When she was living in Denver, the ad had generated a few dates with aging hipsters who thought "fun" and "adventure" were code words for kinky sex. None of them were interesting, and all of them were whiners when they found out that her idea of fun was roller coasters and rock climbing.

Moving the cursor down to the bottom of the page, she hit the *Delete Profile* button and a box popped up, blinking frantically.

Are you sure you want to give up on love?

Yup, she was sure.

She hit the kill button then gazed out the small slice of window she could see from her office at Phoenix

House, an old Victorian home that had been repurposed as a group home for foster children. There was a hardware store straight out of a Norman Rockwell painting across the street, with a tattered awning and a bench on which old men chewed over the news every morning. A rusty pickup, mostly blue with a red tailgate, was parked askew with one wheel up on the curb. There were no window-shoppers cruising the sidewalks, no traffic backed up at the single streetlight, no taxicabs, no street vendors. And she sincerely doubted there were any interesting men.

Actually, there were interesting men in Wynott. The trouble was, most of them were over seventy-five and none of them seemed to grasp the concept of a group home. Half of them were convinced she was running a juvenile hall for delinquents, and the other half thought she was a single mom with five kids. Since Isaiah was African-American, Carter as blond as Brad Pitt, and Frankie a dark-eyed Italian, they probably figured the kids had at least three fathers. It was all a bit of a shock for a small Wyoming town.

That was probably why her call for volunteers had gone unanswered until today, when her boss had called to let her know he'd talked a friend of his into volunteering as a sports coach. The guy should be arriving any minute. In fact, he was late. Hopefully, he'd...

Blaaaaaaaaaaaaaaaaaaaat!

There might not be any men in Wynott to make her heart flutter, but the sound of the old home's doorbell never failed to make it leap in her chest. Jacob Prescott Wynn, the founder of Wynott, had built Phoenix House with every deluxe feature the Victorian era had to offer, including delicate gingerbread eaves, hand-carved wood paneling, and faceted glass doorknobs. He'd also installed a pullout doorbell that made a sound like the "you lose" buzzer on a game show. It was so loud, it scared the bejesus out of half the neighborhood every time Sierra had company. This was very helpful to the women in town, who kept the gossip grapevine growing and found Sierra's comings and goings to be fine fertilizer.

She headed for the front door, wondering what kind of sports coach Mike Malloy had come up with. The owner of Phoenix House and the son of a senator, Mike was an overgrown frat boy. His friends reminded Sierra of a bunch of overweight Labrador retrievers, falling all over the place with their tongues hanging out. They were rude but good-natured, handsome but a little soft in the gut.

Swinging the heavy wood door open, she gaped at her guest. Surely, surely this wasn't any friend of Mike's.

There wasn't an ounce of frat boy in this guy. Not an ounce of fat, either. Just to make sure, Sierra let her gaze drift downward from the brim of his battered felt hat to his broad shoulders and muscular chest, which were both hidden—unfortunately—by a plaid Western-style shirt. He was wearing some kind of fancy belt buckle too, with a picture of a horse on it. Squinting, she tried to read the lettering around the edges but found herself distracted by the very obvious bulge beneath it. The jeans fit just fine everywhere else but seemed a bit strained here.

The hat. The hat. Look at the hat. And stop staring at his—his whatsit.

She'd once heard a country song about how you could gauge the quality of a cowboy by the condition of his hat. Barstool cowboys had shiny new hats, but real cowboys had hats that had been through everything from snowstorms to stampedes.

This guy was apparently the real thing, and the battered brim shaded the hard gray eyes of an outlaw. His jaw was darkened by stubble that made him look like he'd just come off the Chisholm Trail with Kevin Costner and Tom Selleck, though she suspected he could outride and out-rope both of them.

"I'm supposed to talk to the manager," he said.

He didn't sound like Kevin Costner or Tom Selleck. He sounded like Sam Elliott, all gravelly and masculine. His voice curled into Sierra's ear and slid down her backbone, coiling up somewhere warm and making it even warmer.

"The manager?" he repeated.

Sierra sighed. At five foot next-to-nothing, with short, blond hair and dimples that popped into being if she even thought about smiling, she was rarely taken for authority. Certainly no one ever guessed she'd been a Denver cop for three years. She'd gone into law enforcement figuring she'd be helping people, but instead she'd found herself escorting the same petty criminals in and out of the revolving doors of the justice system—crime to prison to parole to crime. She wasn't sure who she was really helping.

Then, a child abuse case inspired her to go back to school, majoring in social work and child psychology. When she'd returned to Denver as a social worker, she'd worked some hard cases in dangerous neighborhoods. It had been her oversized tough-girl attitude, born from a childhood on those same streets, that kept her safe.

It was her tough-girl attitude that got her the job at Phoenix House too. These kids needed special protection, and her combination of a social work degree and law enforcement experience had made her the perfect applicant.

So where was that tough-girl attitude now?

Evidently it had taken a break to curl up in her belly with Sam Elliott's voice.

"I'm Sierra Dunn, group mom here at Phoenix House." She started to extend a hand, but he kept his fists jammed deep in his pockets.

No handshake? No problem. His paws were probably dirty anyway.

He stepped inside, glancing around the newly renovated house as if he was looking for decorating ideas, but he wouldn't find any at Phoenix House. The old place's renovation had apparently busted the state's budget, so the furniture consisted of refugees from various government offices—gray metal desks, dented file cabinets, and chrome chairs with ugly vinyl cushions.

"Name's Ridge Cooper. I'm from Decker Ranch, out west of town."

"Oh. I've heard of you," she blurted.

You couldn't spend five minutes in Wynott without hearing about Ridge Cooper and his brothers. The three cowboys and their rodeo exploits seemed to be the single source of pride for a town that had fallen on hard times. The men in town spoke of the brothers with envy, the women with admiration.

Sierra didn't get it. Riding wild horses didn't make this guy any better than Ed Boone, who ran a thriving hardware store despite the town's economic struggles, or Colt Carson, who had turned the hole-in-the-wall Red

Dawg Bar into a cross between a senior center, a soup kitchen, and a Wild West saloon. Tying up baby cows for a living didn't make him better than Phoebe Niles, who was raising an energetic granddaughter on the slim profits from a gas station at the edge of town. Ed and Colt and Phoebe were the people who kept Wynott alive. Not the Decker brothers.

"I'm looking to volunteer." He glanced down the hall, where the boys were cheering and razzing each other over a video game. The old house's high ceilings and cavernous spaces amplified everything.

"How many you got?" he asked.

"Only five right now. We're set up for more, but that's it so far."

He nodded. "No problem. I'm used to dealing with a herd. You just have to anticipate what they're going to do. Jink left when they zig, right when they zag."

He gestured as he spoke, like his left hand was a cow and his right a mounted cowboy. The left hand didn't stand a chance; it was headed off in a heartbeat.

"These are kids, not cows," she said.

"Cattle."

"Kids."

Sierra felt like she was arguing with the boys. You could go back and forth for an hour and never resolve anything.

"No, I meant that's what you *call* them. Cattle, not cows," he said.

"All right. Cattle." She narrowed her eyes. "What are you going to teach them, anyway?"

He shrugged. "Riding. Roping. Rodeo."

She should have known. He wasn't exactly dressed for soccer.

Leading him across the hall to the old walk-in pantry she'd claimed as an office, she edged past her rickety fiberboard bookcase to her scratch-and-dent desk. The cowboy dropped into the old captain's chair across from her, but rather than crossing his legs like a normal human, he tilted the chair back on two legs and draped one booted leg over the arm. Maybe sitting in chairs wasn't enough of a challenge when your day job was sticking to the saddles of bucking horses.

And that day job was a problem. She needed someone who could make a commitment. From what she'd heard, rodeo cowboys were always on the move.

"You travel around a lot, don't you?" She kept her smile friendly, but her eyes watched for signs of weakness. Volunteers for this kind of work always arrived all bright-eyed and hopeful, ready to save the world one kid at a time. But her boys were slow to trust—with good reason—and most folks gave up when they didn't get the warm fuzzies they were expecting. Gave up and walked away, just like the boys' families had.

"You'll do more harm than good if you take off on these kids once we've started."

He'd taken off his hat upon entering the house, so she got the full force of those eyes. Darkness cut through the gray, reminding her of broken crystal, and his gaze was direct.

"I'll be here," he said. "Trust me."

She decided she might as well take his word for it. Not because she'd deluded herself into thinking he was some paragon of cowboy virtue, but because he was so abrupt she figured he wouldn't bother to lie to her.

But she couldn't figure out why he wanted to do this.

He didn't seem like your typical do-gooder dad or concerned citizen. In fact, he seemed almost reluctant. She
needed to probe deeper.

"Do you have any experience with children?" she asked.

"I was one once," the cowboy said.

"Really?"

The question slipped out in a tone of disbelief.

"Okay, I don't know much about kids," he admitted.
"But Mike thought it was a good idea to teach your boys
to ride, maybe rope a little." He flushed. "Well, not *your*
boys. I know you're not…"

"That's actually how I think of them." Sierra smiled.
"They're my boys as long as I'm here. And I'm hoping
everyone else will see it that way too. If people can see
us as just another family, the boys can really feel like
they belong here."

His eyes narrowed. "In Wynott?"

"Well, sure. Why not?"

He didn't laugh. She didn't blame him. Everyone here
had probably heard the joke about a million times. Old
Jacob Wynn had had a playful sense of humor, but after a
hundred years, it was probably getting a little stale.

"This is the last-chance placement for these kids,"
she said. "They've been rejected, over and over, from
one foster home after another. They run away. They
play hooky. They steal. They fight. And they don't think
much of authority."

The cowboy smiled for the first time. "Sounds like
we'll get along great."

"I hope so," Sierra said. Ridge Cooper seemed like
an unlikely ally, but he had influence in this tiny town,
and she'd take any help she could get. "It's not the kids'

fault. Authority's never done a thing to earn their trust, and the rules have never worked for them, either. The foster care system in this state is terrible. Not just in this state. In this country." She realized she was ranting and reined herself in, settling back in her chair and smiling. "I think Wynott can help fix it."

He snorted. "How do you figure that? This town's about ready to tumble down and go back to the land, dust to dust. The folks who still live here are either too poor to leave or too tired to try."

She started enumerating the town's charms on her fingers. "Small-town setting. Isolation. Elderly population. I'll bet a lot of these old folks spend all their time watching what goes on and gossiping. Am I right?"

He nodded with a wry smile, just as she expected.

"It's small, it's safe, and there are plenty of folks to watch over the kids," she continued. "I'm hoping Wynott can become a real hometown for them. I've always thought that might be the way to go with foster kids." She ignored his disbelieving stare. "Maybe if we give them roots, they'll stop running."

Chapter 2

RIDGE COOPER TILTED EVEN FARTHER BACK IN HIS CHAIR, courting disaster. "So you think this town's going to make that big a difference for your kids?"

"I do." Sierra was starting to think he was one of those negative types who were always punching holes in other people's plans without coming up with any of their own. "Not only that, the kids are going to make a difference for the town too. It needs something to liven it up, you know? The empty streets, the sad little stores…"

He scowled. "Doesn't sound like you like it much," he said.

"Actually, I love it."

"How do you know? You just got here."

"It's been six weeks."

"So after six weeks, you think Wynott can save your kids?"

"Sure do. And I think my kids can save Wynott."

"I don't know," he said. "I'm not sure a bunch of kids is going to help any."

Sierra picked up a pencil and bounced it on its eraser. She'd thought this guy was on her side, but he acted like her hometown idea was some kind of pie-in-the-sky stupidity. Why did this freaking cowboy, with roots as deep as the Wyoming soil, think he knew anything about foster kids?

Her little guys were nine, ten years old. If things

went wrong for them in the next few years, they'd never recover. If things went right, they just might have a future. The key to that future was roots and a real home. Why should they care about anyone else if nobody cared about them?

She wasn't sure this cowboy cared. And she wasn't sure she trusted him with her boys.

She bounced the pencil on the eraser end again, almost shooting it up to the ceiling. Snatching it out of the air, she clutched it in her fist.

"I appreciate your offer but don't think rodeo's a good idea for these kids," she said.

The crystal eyes hardened to flint. "Why not? Mike said you were looking for something to keep the kids active."

She tapped the pencil on the desktop. "I was thinking soccer, maybe football—although that encourages too much violence. We're here to break the cycle of abuse, not continue it. But at least team sports teach cooperation and give them structure and discipline."

"Dang." He cracked a smile for the first time since he'd arrived. "You make playing games sound like a lot of work."

She flushed. She knew she was wound a little tight. It was just that she *cared*. She couldn't stand it if one of the kids got a paper cut. What kind of injuries might happen on horseback?

"I want the kids to have fun," she said. "I just don't want anybody hurt."

He shrugged. "I got hurt all the time when I was a kid. Bumps and bruises, cuts and scratches—it all goes with being a boy. Trust me, they won't mind."

"But *I* mind. My guys have been hurt enough."

"I know that. I get it."

"Do you?"

"Sure." He shrugged. "They wouldn't be here if they hadn't had a rough time, right?"

A *rough time*. Sierra resisted the urge to roll her eyes. The guy was trying to be understanding. But how could a man who lived a carefree cowboy life know anything about what it was like to live on the streets? What it was like to have no parents, nobody who cared about you?

He didn't have a clue.

Ridge Cooper knew he needed to get out of Sierra Dunn's office.

Fast.

The room was so small there was barely room for the two of them, and although they didn't seem to be getting along, the pheromones were flying. He couldn't stop breathing in her scent—sweet and grassy, with a hint of flowers. The woman smelled like a meadow in the sun.

He leaned closer, inhaling. It was like she'd rolled around in sage and violets and fresh-cut grass on her way to work. He probably shouldn't be standing there sniffing her like a flower, but dang, she smelled good.

Maybe it had been too long since he'd been around a woman. Not too long ago, he'd had plenty of cowgirls to choose from. Barrel racers with their strong, sleek muscles and crazy, hell-for-leather courage. Rodeo queens with sparkly clothes and attitudes to match. Even buckle bunnies, energetic and inventive, offering themselves up for a night with a cowboy and expecting nothing in return but good times and new notches on their bedposts.

The barrel racers smelled like horses and hard work. Rodeo queens and buckle bunnies smelled like night jasmine and spice, heady scents designed to spark dreams of twisted sheets and hot skin. This woman wasn't as wholesome as the ranch girls, but her scent was sweet and subtle.

And it was knocking him on his ass.

He needed to shake it off. With sixteen screws and a steel plate in his riding arm, his career was a shambles. He didn't have a thing to offer any kind of woman, and he wasn't about to inflict his moodiness and despair on anyone.

Especially not a social worker. She'd probably diagnose him with depression and tell him he needed therapy. He didn't need therapy. He had horses. Nobody who had horses needed therapy.

But wasn't there some kind of smell therapy or something? What did they call that?

Aromatherapy, that was it. He needed some of that.

He edged toward her. She seemed to move in a cloud of fragrance, clean and wholesome but sexy as hell. Sage, violets, and what was that other smell? Something fruity. He dared to sneak another sniff.

Apples.

She took a step back and shot him a glare.

"What are you doing?" She narrowed her eyes. "Were you *smelling* me?"

He started to stammer out an apology, but she held up one hand and shushed him.

"Do you hear anything?"

He heard plenty. He heard his heart pounding, his blood humming in his ears, and his breath coming fast and hard. What the hell was going on here? He'd sworn off women. For good. And yet here he was, getting all hot and bothered about a girl who probably couldn't tell a quarter horse from a golden retriever.

"Don't hear a thing," he said.

"Me neither. And that's not good. The boys are never quiet." She dropped her voice to a whisper. "They're up to something."

She put her fingers to her lips and smiled. He did hear something—a soft brushing noise, like stocking feet on hardwood floors.

"They're sneaking up on me," she whispered. A playful light danced in her eyes. "They're going to jump out and yell. Act scared, okay?"

He barely had time to nod before there was a flurry of footsteps in the hall and a stifled giggle.

And then, the door slammed shut with a loud *whap* and he heard the unmistakable *snick* of a lock snapping firmly into place.

Chapter 3

SIERRA'S SMILE FLICKED OFF LIKE A LIGHT.

"Shoot. I knew I should have done something about that lock." Lunging for the door, she smacked it with the palm of her hand. "Hey, come on, guys. Let us out."

No answer.

"Gil must have gone home. He was on day shift today." She checked her watch. "Yup. Five past five. But he's not supposed to leave without checking in with me first."

"Gil Martin? He's working for you?"

She nodded.

"Well, good luck getting him to toe the line. Gil's an old hippie. Free spirit, does as he pleases."

"I'm starting to see that. About the only rule he follows is the one about quitting time." She twisted the doorknob so hard it had to hurt.

"Breaking that off probably won't help," he said. "How good's the lock?"

"Really good." She slouched against the wall beside the door. "I just moved the office in here today. Before that, it was the supply closet. Supplies as in *snacks*. The kids have tried to jimmy that lock a dozen times." He was surprised how glad he was to see her smile again, even if it did tremble at the edges. "They had an expedition one night, all of them out here in their bare feet hunting for the key while Isaiah tried to pick the lock

with a bobby pin. Trust me, Jell-O Pudding Snacks in-
spire all kinds of ingenuity. That lock won't break."

She slid down the wall until she was sitting on the
floor with her head in her hands. "How could I be stupid
enough to spend even half a *second* in a room that could
be locked from the outside?" She lifted her head and
let it loll against the wall. "They've probably eaten all
the Pudding Snacks by now. My budget won't let me
buy more until November. How am I going to work my
reward system without Pudding Snacks?"

He frowned. "If mass-produced pudding is the
most they have to look forward to, it's no wonder
they don't behave."

"They do behave. They just…"

"They just lock you in the office and eat all the pudding."

"Exactly."

She rose to her knees and put her ear to the door. "I
don't hear anything. They're probably out running wild
in the streets."

"Just one street."

"Right. Route 35. Cars go through here at eighty
miles per hour."

"We've got a thirty-mile-per-hour speed trap right at
the town line. They'll be fine."

"Have you seen our sheriff? He rides a bicycle."

"Well, yeah. We can't afford a real cop. Our sheriff kind
of elected himself, so nobody's about to buy him a car."

"One more reason we can't let these kids run around
town unattended."

"They'll be fine," he repeated.

"No. You don't get it. They *won't* be fine." She
staggered to her feet and started to pace the tiny office.

"They're not here just because they're troublemakers. Their parents are—well, let's just say their parents are criminals of one kind or another."

"So aren't the parents in jail?"

"On and off. Once in a while one of them gets out and decides he wants his kid back."

"So this is kind of like witness protection for kids."

She nodded. "Exactly. We don't want these kids to be found."

———

Sierra hated small spaces. Hated them.

Maybe that's why she'd made the mistake of telling this guy about the kids' families. If folks in Wynott found out what kind of trouble could follow her kids to their quiet little town, they'd run her out with torches and pitchforks.

And why was she talking to the cowboy when she should be calling for help? She edged over to grab her purse and found herself pressed hard against his chest. She paused and looked up into those strange, pale eyes.

Big mistake.

They stood there a beat too long—long enough for a hot, uncomfortable awkwardness to fill the tiny space. Long enough for certain of her body parts to warm and hum like the purring engine of a very sleek and feminine sports car. His eyes held a heat that revved her engine even higher, making her want to stand a little closer. Just a little…

What the hell was she thinking? Giving up on love must have given her a hormonal surge, because there was no way she'd be going all gooey for a cowboy otherwise. She was a city girl and a survivor—no match for Mr. Rodeo Star, with his acres of land and some big house on a hill.

She squeezed past him and dove for her purse, shoving her hand inside and rummaging for her phone. Brush, lipstick, compact, gum, keys, wallet.

Her phone must be in one of the side pockets.

She poked her fingers into the purse's generous side pockets. Another lipstick, nail clippers, and *ouch!* toothpicks.

But no phone.

If Ridge Cooper sniffed her now, he wouldn't smell her Marc Jacobs perfume. He'd smell desperation.

She upended her purse onto the floor just as a picture popped into her mind of her cell phone, charging on the counter in the house's old-fashioned kitchen.

"Do you have a cell phone?" she asked the cowboy.

"Nope," he said. "We're on our own."

Just then, there was a clunk, followed by a loud crack.

And then the lights went out.

"Dang it," said the cowboy. His deep voice seemed ominous in the dark.

Unfortunately, everything seemed ominous to Sierra with the lights out. A little ball of panic escaped from her heart, winging away like a panicked bird. She wasn't afraid of the dark. Or claustrophobic. Not really. She just didn't like being trapped.

Caged, like a rat in a hole.

She reached up to find the wall so she could pull herself up and feel her way toward the door. Instead of the wall, she laid her palm on something warm.

She was pretty sure what part of the cowboy she'd just touched. Whipping her hand away with a little scream, she banged it on the desk.

"It's me." He reached down and grabbed her upper arms, helping her to her feet. "Just me."

Yeah, right. Just him, with his tanned skin and un-canny eyes, with that five-o'clock shadow and that body part she wasn't supposed to think about. But how could she not think about it when she'd just touched it?

"Well, the good news is you've got a lot less to worry about than you thought," he said.

"Sure," she said with faked brightness. "Because now we're not just locked in a closet, we're locked in a *dark* closet. *So* much better. Now I don't have to worry about the electric bill."

"Somebody turned the lights out, right? Had to be the kids. So they're still in the house."

"Maybe," she said. "Unless it was a short in the wir-ing. This place is ancient." She could feel perspiration breaking out in a few unfortunate places. "What if we're locked in here and the place burns down?"

"Then they'll find our charred bodies lying here to-gether once the fire's out."

"Lying here?" What did he think she was going to do? She should have known this guy was trouble when the sniffing started. "Why would we be *lying* here?"

His soft laugh started deep in his chest, sliding straight down into her core to join the Sam Elliott voice. "We'd be lying here because people fall down when they're dead."

"Oh, great."

She prided herself on her courage and toughness. She wasn't afraid of drug dealers or bad men with guns, or even spiders. But she was nervous in tight spaces and scared to death of the dark.

The cowboy was about to see her fall apart.

Chapter 4

THE WOMAN GRABBED RIDGE'S ARM AGAIN, NEARLY pulling him to the floor. She couldn't seem to make up her mind. Half the time she was running away from him, and the other half she was clinging to him like he was the last floating oar from the *Titanic*.

She was claustrophobic, apparently, and afraid of the dark too. She also seemed to be a little afraid of him.

It was a shame those three things had to come together in one small room, because she didn't seem to be afraid of much else. Before the door had locked, he'd noticed that she carried herself with a lot of confidence. And when she talked about the possibility of the ex-con parents coming after the kids, she seemed totally in control.

But now? Scared to death.

With horses, the first step in fighting fear was to identify the source. The second step was touch—a touch and a promise.

The promise he made to horses was that he'd never hurt them, but he couldn't make that promise to Sierra Dunn. The last time he'd had anything to do with a woman, he'd screwed up so badly, he wasn't sure either of them would ever recover. Shelley had told him the best thing he could do for her was to stay away, and he'd followed her orders with a sense of failure mixed with relief.

He'd stay away from this woman too, once they got out of here. But right now, he needed to calm her down. He could hear her scrabbling her way around the room, feeling her way toward the door. When she found it, she hammered it with her fists.

"Hey." He crossed the room in a single step and took her wrists in his hands. "It's all right. You're all right. Shh. Shh."

She hammered on him like she'd been hammering on the door and then attempted to stomp on his instep. Fortunately, it was tough for her to aim in the dark, and all she managed to do was lose her balance and fall against his chest.

"Shh. Easy."

The darkness that stole his sight heightened all his other senses, and he could feel her pulse fluttering in her wrists like hummingbird wings thrumming against his fingers. He could smell her again too—that tantalizing combination of sage and violets. Unfortunately, it was combined with his own scent—leather and horse, hay and probably sweat. He did most of his work in the morning, and he worked hard. Today had been no exception.

"Breathe," he said anyway.

She inhaled, exhaled. Her breaths were choppy at first, but gradually they lengthened and slowed. He was starting to wonder who was sniffing who. She seemed to be inhaling his scent the way he'd inhaled hers earlier.

"Mmm." She made a little sound that hummed against his chest. A sexy little sound that upped his pulse till it probably matched hers.

"Caress," she said.

Well, that was direct.

He wasn't used to women giving orders, but if that's what she needed, it was okay with him. Releasing her wrists, he stroked her hair, surprised to notice that his hand was trembling.

She caught her breath suddenly, almost choking.

"Come on, honey. Breathe." She was so close now that his own breath must be tickling her ear. After a while, the soft tempo of her breathing matched his own.

"That's good," he murmured as if he was speaking to a fractious colt. "That's good. Nothing's going to hurt you. Nothing, ever."

He felt her draw in a quick, startled breath. Still afraid.

He held her tighter, rubbing one hand up and down her back in a slow, soothing motion.

"Nothing," he repeated. "Not while I'm here."

He could feel her muscles giving and relaxing, one by one. He'd apparently calmed her down. Unfortunately, the situation was having the opposite effect on him. If she stood any closer, she'd know exactly how he felt.

This wasn't some animal he was calming. This was a woman, with breath as sweet as her scent and skin so soft he couldn't resist running his thumbs over the smoothness of her wrists. He didn't know how it had happened, but it felt as if the two of them were wrapped in a warm, fragrant cocoon. The world faded away as they swayed in a soft dance as old as time.

And then she stiffened and jerked away like a startled colt.

Whatever had just happened between them was over, but she didn't run away. Instead, she stood perfectly still, the way a horse does when it's deciding whether to give in or spin off and run.

It was then he realized that the office wasn't completely dark. There was a transom above the door, a narrow window of frosted glass that allowed in enough light for her wide, frightened eyes to glint in the dark.

"What do you think you're doing?" she asked.

"I have no idea." He cleared his throat. "You said caress, so I—well, I did."

She started to shake. Dang it, was she getting all scared again?

But then she let go and laughed. And laughed. Her laugh was crystalline and bright, the agile notes rising in the still air of the closet.

"I was talking about soap. *Caress*," she stuttered through her laughter. "That's what you *smell* like. It wasn't an *order*."

He had no idea what kind of soap he was using. Something Shelley had left behind. He pictured the box—pink with a flower on it. Yeah, it was probably called *Caress* or something like that.

"It just surprised me that you smelled so good, so I said it." She was still struggling to get control of her laughter. "Caress."

"What did you think I'd smell like?"

"What did I *think*?" She was laughing again. "Have you *seen* yourself? Your jeans are torn, your boots look like you dipped 'em in horse hooey, and your hat…" She struggled to catch her breath. "I'm sorry, but you look like you've been rolling around in a barn. Best-case scenario, I figured you'd smell like the front end of a horse. Worst case, the back end."

She leaned against the wall beside him, her tension dissolving into unfettered laughter. Most women tittered or giggled. This woman let loose with happy whoops. He wondered what she sounded like when she…

No. He gave himself a mental smack. Then he gave himself another one, because he was still thinking about what a woman that uninhibited would sound like in bed.

She finally ran out of laughter and clutched her stomach, struggling for control of her breathing. At least it was for all the right reasons this time.

Well, not *all* the right reasons. The rightest reason of all…

He wasn't going to think about that.

In the hazy light from the transom, he could just make out her face. He hadn't noticed before how delicate it was. With her slanted cheekbones, big eyes, and pointed chin, she reminded him of a fairy in some old kids' book. Although fairies didn't wear black skirts and leather jackets.

He realized he was staring and looked away. They had a problem to solve, and big eyes and cheekbones weren't going to help.

In fact, Tinker Bell herself was starting to be a bit of a problem. Whatever had just happened might have been a mistake, but it felt important somehow. He'd made her that promise—the promise he made to his animals. *Nothing's going to hurt you. Not while I'm here.*

He'd never broken that promise, and that meant he needed to do his best to help her. But he also needed to stop thinking about how good she smelled and how pretty she looked and how he'd felt when she'd rested her head against his chest. Because this was not the time for him to take up with another woman.

He was still worn out from the last one.

He struggled to think of something to defuse the situation, but he'd never been good with words. In fact, he'd said more to this woman in the last half hour than he'd said in the past month.

Fortunately, Tinker Bell took over.

"Okay, listen," she said. "We need to straighten this out."

There was a time when he'd have been relieved to have a woman take charge of the situation, but he knew better now. He'd let Shelley take charge, and suddenly she'd started going on about weddings and babies. Now would be a good time to walk away, but he was locked in a danged closet.

"I'm sorry about the *Caress* thing," she continued. "I can see how you might have misinterpreted it. Although…" She cocked her head and gave him a curious look. "Do women often order you to caress them when you've only known them for half an hour?"

"No," he said. Actually, he'd had some pretty direct requests from strange women. But caressing? Not exactly.

"Anyway," she said, "let's just forget that happened. You're not my type and I have a feeling I'm not yours, either."

"Right." All he could do was agree, but why did he feel like a liar? Worse yet, why did he feel disappointed? He should be relieved, but it was kind of a letdown to hear her say it.

How did she know he wasn't her type?

One thing was for sure: he wasn't in nearly as much of a hurry to get out of the closet.

Chapter 5

IF RIDGE HAD LEARNED ANYTHING FROM RANCHING, IT was to be adaptable. When you couldn't fix something with barbed wire, you tried duct tape.

But there was no barbed wire in Sierra's office and probably no duct tape either. Squinting into the dark recesses of the closet, he took in the sparse furniture.

"Maybe if I stood on the chair, I could reach the transom."

"And do what?"

He eyed the narrow window over the door. "Open the transom. Push you through it."

"So I could break my head open on the floor on the other side?"

"You have a better idea?"

Instead of answering, Sierra grabbed the chair and hoisted it in the air, shoving it at Ridge legs-first, like a lion tamer at the circus. Taking it from her, he set the chair down in front of the door and placed one booted foot on the seat.

"Wait," Sierra said. "Maybe this isn't such a good…"

Crack.

It was too late. He'd already shifted his weight and launched himself up toward the transom. There was another sharp crack as the chair leg closest to the book-case collapsed.

Good thing he had a lot of experience with dismounts.

Hopping nimbly backward, he grabbed a shelf for balance. The bookshelf tilted ominously, swayed, then slowly returned to its upright position.

"I forgot," she said. "I use that chair because it's broken."

"Right. And you like broken chairs because..."

"Well, I don't want one of the boys getting hurt. Sorry."

"Fine."

She stepped toward him and the light from the transom slanted across her face. The woman sure knew how to smile. The glow of her lit up the room, and the moment seemed to draw out a little, as if there'd been an extra couple of seconds added to that particular minute.

Maybe that was why he stood there, transfixed, as the bookcase groaned and tilted away from the wall in slow motion, vomiting its entire contents onto the floor like a messy drunk who'd downed too many psychology texts.

Standing knee-deep in books, he could hear Tinker Bell trying to stifle her laughter. Darn it, the woman was always laughing at him. The worst thing was, he didn't blame her. He felt like he was in the middle of some old silent comedy, where the intrepid hero tried to save the girl and met with one disaster after another.

The only way to save his dignity was to actually save the girl.

"Here." He bent at the waist, cupping his hands and lacing his fingers together. "I'll give you a leg up. See if you can get that transom open."

Cautiously, she set one foot in his interlaced hands. Her heels were liable to skewer him if he didn't concentrate, but he couldn't help moving his gaze upward, taking in the shadowy outline of ankles, calves, knees, thighs—and the little black skirt that topped it all off.

His gaze paused at a tattoo peeping out between the waistband of her skirt and the hem of her top. It was a curving tendril that might have been anything from the stem of a flower to the tail of a dragon, and he wished he could hoist the top a little higher and check it out.

Combine a mysterious tattoo with blond hair that somehow managed to be short and gloriously unruly at the same time, and green eyes that gave away every nuance of her changing moods, and you had one intriguing package. Better yet, she'd let him caress her and hadn't asked for anything in return. In fact, she'd even insisted they forget the whole thing. He wondered what else she'd let him forget about.

"Will you quit checking me out?"

"Sorry." *The foot, the foot, the foot. Only look at the foot.* "Ready?"

She nodded. Estimating her weight, he hoisted her into the air with what he hoped was just the right amount of gusto.

And bonked her head on the ceiling.

"Ow." She slid down, landing on a book that had ended up facedown on the floor. Executing a brief version of the Charleston, she wound up standing in the only clear place on the floor—which put her practically on the toes of his cowboy boots.

They were standing toe to toe, with Sierra's hands clutching his shoulders. The position brought her body right up to his, and he could feel the soft, warm give of her breasts. When she twisted against him, he wasn't sure if she was trying to get closer to him or get away.

That was the trouble with women. You could never tell what they were thinking. With men, there were obvious physical signs of attraction.

Physical signs he needed to get control of right now.

"Hold on." She popped up on her toes and nearly bopped him in the face with the top of her head. "I'm sure I can get up there if I…"

The sentence ended in a grunt as she gripped him around the neck and wrapped one long leg around his waist. Good Lord. She was going to climb him like a tree. He felt like he was going to pass out.

"Can you maybe help a little?" She had one foot still around his waist, while the other still stood tippy-toe on his boot, grinding his toes into bonemeal.

"Sure. How?"

"I don't know. Give me a boost."

"Is that the name of a soap or anything?"

"No! I mean it."

"All right." Reaching down, he palmed a butt cheek in each hand and hoisted her up toward the transom. All he succeeded in doing was bringing the panties under that little black skirt to face level.

"This isn't going to work." She seemed totally oblivious to his arousal as she slid slowly down the front of his body, clinging to him like a very attractive monkey as she went. Finally, she stepped away, scratching her head and looking from him to the transom.

"Maybe you should bend over and put your head between my legs."

"*What?*" At this point, he couldn't tell if she was trying to get out of the closet or act out the first five chapters of the *Kama Sutra*.

"Like in the swimming pool." She spoke slowly, as if he was stupid. "As if we're playing chicken."

She picked her way carefully over the fallen books to her desk and hopped on top.

"Come on. Hurry." She jigged impatiently from one foot to the other. Either she was one impatient woman, or she needed to get to the ladies' room.

Well, he sure wished *that* thought hadn't crossed his mind. Now he had more needs than he knew what to do with.

Pushing his physical troubles out of his head, he edged through the narrow pathway then turned around so she could clamber onto his shoulders.

"Okay." He started to straighten his back and she gave a little screech. He didn't realize what was wrong until he heard the now-familiar *thunk* of her head against the ceiling.

"Oops." He bent his back and struggled through the pathway to the door. "You okay?"

"Sure," she said. "I'm locked in a closet with a total stranger, riding around on his shoulders and clonking my head repeatedly against the ceiling." She waved her arms, struggling to balance on his shoulders without hitting her head again. "Who wouldn't be okay?"

Chapter 6

Sierra flailed her arms for balance, then decided it would be better to clutch the cowboy's head in both hands, so she could tilt forward and avoid the ceiling. She already had one hell of a headache, brought on as much by her concern for the kids as the repeated bashings to her brain.

Finally, they reached the transom. She could see the hallway, lit by the faint light that slanted through the front windows. How long had they been in here?

"Here, I can reach it. Stay right there."

She had no idea what she was going to do if she got the transom open. She could probably fit through the narrow opening, but there was nothing on the other side but a smooth wooden door and a hard oak floor. She was liable to get the ultimate bonk on the head if she made it through.

But at least she'd be out of the tiny, dark, stuffy closet she was sharing with this frighteningly attractive stranger. She might have given up on love, but she apparently hadn't given up on—what would you call it? Snuggling? Yeah, snuggling. With cowboys. In the dark.

But how could she help it?

Nothing's going to hurt you. Not as long as I'm here.

What woman didn't want to hear that?

If only he'd meant it. It was a shame the whole thing was just a misunderstanding, but it was. It had to be.

Reaching over his head, she fumbled at the transom. It had originally opened from the bottom, swinging out from hinges at the top. She managed to pry open a latch, only cutting one finger and breaking two nails in the process. She pounded the bottom edge with her fist.

Nothing. No give at all.

"There must be ten layers of paint on this thing. It might as well be nailed shut." She pounded it again, this time with the heel of her hand. "It's not working. It…"

Snap.

The lights flicked on.

She froze with the sense that a flashbulb had gone off and the two of them would be exposed forever like this, with her riding his shoulders.

"The kids must be back," he said.

"Or somebody." She peered right then left. There was no sign of life in the empty hallway. She lifted her voice to a shout. "*Hey! Let us out! Hey!*"

No response.

"Somebody's around," she said. "We'll have to just wait."

"Okay. I'll bend down till your feet can touch the ground then back away. Ready?"

She clung to his head and shifted her weight backward. "Ready."

He grunted as he bent his knees and lowered her to the ground. One moment she was touching the ceiling, the next she was on the ground, facing the blank and frustratingly unmoving face of the closet door.

"Okay. Now I just need to back off," he said.

He'd better back off. His head was right between her legs. If she squeezed, she could strangle him. Well, not really. If she was one of those girls who rode horses, she could, but her thighs weren't that muscular.

Unfortunately, she didn't want to strangle him. With his head between her legs and his hands on her thighs, she felt a hot rush of lust. His hands slipped down to her calves, and maybe, just maybe, he lingered there a little too long.

She grabbed his head, figuring she'd shove him to the floor if he didn't move soon. The rush of lust had turned to something stronger, and she needed to get him out of the danger zone before he realized what he was doing to her.

"Miss Dunn?" said a small voice from the other side of the door.

She froze. The knob turned in what seemed like slow motion—but not slow enough. When the door opened, she staggered and fell backward as Ridge dropped down on all fours. She writhed on his back, struggling for purchase with flailing feet.

And that's what nine-year-old Josh saw when he opened the door.

———

Ridge had to smother a laugh at the stunned expression on their rescuer's face. The kid was a puny little guy, eight or nine years old, with sandy hair and wire-framed glasses perched askew on his nose. Skinny arms protruded from the drooping sleeves of a grubby T-shirt that hung nearly to his knees. It had a picture of the Hulk's scowling face on it and said "Don't Get Me Mad" in big block letters.

The kid's nose wrinkled up in confusion as he tried

to make sense of what he was seeing. Which was understandable, since Sierra had fallen to one side and was thrashing around on the floor.

She finally scrambled to her feet. "Josh!"

The kid squinted then wrinkled up his nose again, lifting his lip and exposing his front teeth in a grimace that reminded Ridge of a cartoon rabbit. Then he shoved his glasses up on his nose with one finger and his face relaxed again.

"Josh, where are the others?"

The boy looked longingly toward the front door then returned his gaze to Sierra and made that face again. It was evidently a technique designed to adjust his glasses while keeping his hands free.

A very ineffective technique.

"The others?" Josh poked the glasses back into position and gazed at the door again then returned his owlish gaze to Sierra, eyes wide with fake innocence. "What others?"

"The other *boys*." She ran her hands through her hair, bringing it back to some semblance of order. "Where did they go, Josh?"

He continued looking at the door while he answered. "They left." He looked back at her and gave her a winning smile. "Do I get a Pudding Snack? For letting you out?"

"Yes. If you tell me where the others went."

He looked torn, as if his loyalties had been strained beyond endurance. The squinting and grimacing intensified. "They left. I don't know where." He wiped his nose with the back of one hand. "Were you scared? In the closet?"

"No, Josh, I was just *worried*. About *you boys*." Her voice was rising into a shrill, barely contained hysteria. "Where did they go?"

Joshua squinted at Ridge then returned his gaze to Sierra. "You probably weren't scared because you had him to play with."

Ridge put on his best poker face and stared straight ahead. He could feel Sierra beside him radiating tension. If he looked at her, he'd laugh as loud and long as she had back there in the closet.

He had to admit the idea of "playing" in the closet had crossed his mind, especially when he'd felt the firm, muscled tone of Sierra's smooth calves. Tennis. That was his guess. Her muscles were ropy and hard, different from a cowgirl's.

He shoved his hands in his pockets in a vain effort to forget the feel of her muscles under his palm. It had been way too long since he'd had anything to do with any kind of girl, cow or otherwise.

"I was never scared when my sister was in the closet, and we could play," the kid said.

Ridge winced, and the urge to laugh disappeared. From the sound of it, the kid had been locked in a closet on a regular basis.

Sierra gave Josh a shaky smile, as if she wasn't sure how to respond. "We weren't playing, Josh."

"Well, what were you doing, then? Because he was down like this, and his head—"

Sierra didn't wait for the description of what had probably been one of her most mortifying moments ever. "I know, honey. We can talk about that later."

Ridge grinned. Judging from Joshua's determined

squint, putting him off until "later" was not going to help Sierra avoid a conversation about what had been going on in the closet.

"Right now, we need to find the boys. Did they leave the building?"

The answer seemed obvious, considering Joshua had barely been able to keep his eyes away from the door. But the kid fidgeted, refusing to answer. Finally, Sierra crossed the hall to the front door, and Joshua, thin shoulders bowed under the weight of his secrets, followed.

Ridge, after briefly considering his options, trailed along as well. It was hardly a bronc ride, but at least there was something going on here, which made following Sierra a much better choice than heading back to the ranch. He wasn't up for dealing with his brothers right now. He'd just as soon they hit the road and leave him with only his own wrecked body for company.

Well, almost wrecked. A certain essential part was obviously working just fine. In fact, if he didn't forget the feel of Sierra's body in the dark, and if he couldn't take his eyes off the determined way she sashayed down the hall, that part was liable to work a little too well.

Chapter 7

THERE WEREN'T MANY OPTIONS FOR A PACK OF KIDS ON the run in Wynott. The town was one of those blink-and-you'll-miss-it dots on the map, marking the point where Route 35 met State Road 267. The two roads merged into one two-lane highway bordered by a bar, a post office, and a hardware store. The other side of the street boasted a junk shop bearing a sign that promised "Antiques and Collectables," a few Victorian homes clinging desperately to gentility, and Phoenix House, along with a couple of tumbledown garages whose gas pumps had been torn out years ago.

Both the quantity and quality of the houses petered out toward the east. The residents' efforts at tidy lawns and flower gardens kept things festive, but the flowers were leggy and sparse, having cooked through the hot summer. Any night now, the first frost would end their suffering.

At the very edge of town were two ramshackle brick garages, followed by a sad little park with rusty swings and a teeter-totter. Beyond the park was a gas station with a mini mart. The last few structures at the edge of town had fallen down altogether, leaving only a few piles of sunbaked boards and crumbling stone foundations. It was as if the town aged, declined, and died right in front of travelers' eyes as they headed east toward civilization.

There was no sign of a gang of boys in any direction.

In fact, Wynott looked like a ghost town, deserted and baked to a crisp, presided over by a rusting water tower that bore the legend "Why Not Wynott" in faded black lettering, a remnant of the town's more optimistic days.

When they reached the sidewalk, Sierra turned to face Joshua. Crouching down to his level, she looked him in the eye. "Where did they go, Joshua?"

His back stiffened and he folded his arms over his chest. "I promised not to tell."

"This is one of those times it's okay to break a promise."

He remained mute, staring her straight in the eye with a combination of mute defiance and fear.

"Don't make the kid break his promise," Ridge said. "We'll find them. It's not like there are a lot of places for them to go."

She ignored him. "Come on, Josh."

Ridge kicked a stone and watched it skitter over the cracks in the sidewalk. It was obvious that Josh lived by the code of the kid—which was a whole lot like the code of the cowboy but with less ambiguity. To kids, right and wrong were black and white. The world would be a better place if grown-ups had the moral fiber of nine-year-olds.

"Josh, I need to know," Sierra urged.

"Leave him alone." Ridge's tone was sharper than he'd intended. "It won't take us more than twenty minutes to find them."

Sierra stood, setting her hands on her hips and glaring up at him. "Do you know what can happen to a bunch of ten-year-old boys in twenty minutes?"

"Do you know how it feels to break your promise to your buddies?"

"I told you, these boys need to respect you," she hissed. "And you need to set an example."

"By encouraging them to break their promises?"

He answered her fiery glare with a frown then looked down at Joshua, who had fortunately been distracted by a spider in the empty window of the brick garage next door. The kid watched it with exaggerated attention, as if the bug's progress was far more important than the two adults fighting on the sidewalk right beside him. Ridge wondered how many times Josh had heard adults fight, how many times he'd pretended not to hear.

Sierra seemed to remember Josh at the same instant, and when she turned back to Ridge, she'd changed her posture and softened her scowl. But her eyes met his in a cold challenge.

"If you're going to work with these guys, you need to lead by example, and that means doing the right thing."

"And keeping your promises isn't the right thing?"

"Usually it is."

Taking her arm, he led her slightly away from Josh, who was still watching the spider.

"Do you remember being a kid?" he hissed.

"Sure."

"Do you remember how random adults' decisions were? They never seemed to have anything to do with right or wrong. It was all about convenience." He was speaking low and fast so Josh wouldn't hear, and Sierra stepped closer. His lips almost brushed the hair curling around her ear. "You're right. Kids need to be able to respect you. And that means you have to follow the rules too. So don't you think we ought to keep our promises?"

She shot him a look that was half anger and half confusion. "Not—not right now," she said.

Ridge bent down so his lips almost brushed her cheek. She took a step back, probably thinking he was sniffing her again. But he just wanted to make sure—very sure—that she heard what he was about to say. Her, not Josh.

"Do you know how many promises this kid's seen broken in his life?" he asked. "All of them—the ones that mattered, anyway. Every single one."

"How do you know?" she asked.

"Because otherwise he wouldn't be here."

⁓⁓⁓

Sierra hated to admit it, but the cowboy had a point.

Not that she was ready to admit she was wrong. But she could remember a few broken promises herself, and how much they'd hurt. A lot of broken promises, actually. When it came to her mother, it would be easier to enumerate the promises that had been kept.

"While we're standing here arguing, the boys are probably finding a dozen ways to hurt themselves. Why can't you just help me find the kids?"

Ridge didn't answer; he just stood there with his jaw squared and his eyes narrowed to slits. Joshua turned away from the spider he'd been watching and looked up at Ridge then set his face carefully in that exact same mulish expression, doubling the amount of male disgust aimed at Sierra.

Flinging up her hands, she turned away. "Why don't you go back to your ranch and rope some cows or something?"

She took a few steps away, taking a turn with Josh's

spider. She didn't know why Ridge's refusal to help felt like a betrayal or why her eyes were tearing up.

Oh, yes she did. Back there in the closet, she'd felt a stirring that told her coming to Wynott might not be a death sentence for her love life after all. And that had made her happy and hopeful, despite the fact that she'd been *hoping* Wynott would kill her love life. The little town's empty streets were supposed to be a sanctuary, not a sentence. You couldn't make relationship mistakes when there was nobody to have a relationship with.

But Ridge Cooper was different from any man she'd ever met.

Nothing's going to hurt you. Not while I'm around.

She knew she could take care of herself. But if she had a man who said that kind of thing and really meant it, she'd be able to step out into the world more confidently. She'd have backup, and that would make her braver.

Turning away from the spider, which was disgusting anyway, she joined Josh and Ridge. The man had knelt down to look the boy in the eye. He'd put his dirty old hat back on, and looking down at his broad shoulders hunched over the boy, she felt a twinge of tenderness that surprised her.

"Good job being a man, Josh." Ridge tousled the fine, blond hair. "Men keep their promises."

Joshua turned and blessed Ridge with a radiant smile, hero worship shining in his eyes.

Tears stung behind her eyes again and she wished, for the umpteenth time, that she could shut off her emotions. Most nights she went to bed feeling wrung out like an old dishcloth. She'd been in police work for three years, social work for four, and if she didn't toughen up, she wouldn't make it through the fifth.

Blinking fast, she scanned the street again. *Find the boys.* That was priority number one.

"Hey." Ridge nudged the side of her high-heeled boots with his toe. To her surprise, his mulish expression had softened. "Keeping promises matters to me. Especially with kids. I couldn't let that go."

"I get it," she said. "Let's just find them, or we won't have any kids left to make promises to."

"If I was them, I'd go to the Mini Mart." Ridge turned to Josh. "They got ice cream there?"

"Yep. And sodas." The kid turned his worshipful gaze back to the cowboy. "They got beer too, if you want some."

Sierra winced. She'd read Joshua's file, and the cowboy was dead right about the promise breaking. The kid's dad hung on longer than the mom, but he'd been a mean drunk who took out his heartbreak over his marriage on his own child. It made her burn inside just to think of it. With his pale skin, small frame, and big glasses, Joshua was about as helpless a victim as you could find.

"You think your buds are having ice cream or soda?" Ridge asked.

"Neither," the kid said eagerly. "They're down behind the junk shop, playing in the cars." The second he said it, he clapped his hand over his mouth. Tears sprang to his eyes. "I told," he said. "I wasn't supposed to tell."

"Well, I kind of tricked you, so that doesn't count." Ridge ruffled the boy's hair in an easy, fatherly way. "You did your best, right?"

"Yeah." Joshua nodded, but he looked miserable, and his Adam's apple bobbed as he swallowed. "Just stupid."

"You're not stupid. I'm sneaky, that's all." Ridge pointed a finger at the boy's shirt, just below his chin. "What's that on your shirt?"

Josh looked down and the cowboy quickly brought up his finger to flick the boy's nose. "Gotcha," he said. "See? Sneaky. Now that you know it, I bet I won't be able to fool you again."

Josh grinned, the trauma of breaking his promise forgotten. "Nope, you won't fool me again."

"I'm going to try, though."

"No way." The kid shook his head so hard the glasses seemed in danger of flying off his face. "You won't do it."

Sierra watched the boy and man walk side by side, the boy struggling to match the man's long stride, the glow on his face making the usually somber child look as happy as she'd ever seen him. As they reached the junk shop, she heard the sound of boyish voices rising from behind the fence that obscured the backyard.

They'd found them. The worst of the emergency was over. And Josh was smiling.

Maybe the cowboy wasn't so bad after all.

Chapter 8

THE JUNK SHOP WAS ONE OF THE LAST PROPERTIES ON the left as you headed east, a single-story shack with a sagging front porch. If the place had ever been painted, the Wyoming winds had sandblasted off every stroke of color, leaving the warped boards gray and parched by the sun. Old tools were nailed to the front wall: a rusted blade from a circular saw, an assortment of branding irons, and a few dented hubcaps. Standing guard over the collection was a whimsical, wide-eyed tin man welded together from car parts. In New York, they'd call him folk art. Here in Wynott, he was just another piece of redneck yard trash.

Sierra looked up into the carburetor man's glassy eyes and shivered. "Who lives here?"

"She doesn't like people talking about her," Ridge said.

"It's a woman?" Sierra tried not to buy into gender stereotypes, but there was nothing feminine about this place. "Why not?"

Why not, indeed. She was starting to think the town had been aptly named.

"Will she mind the kids being here?"

Ridge shrugged. "I doubt it. She won't be too happy about us coming around, though."

A high fence bordered the backyard, and Sierra started to reach for the complicated latch—another masterpiece of redneck engineering constructed of a claw hammer and a complex assortment of scrap metal. Whoever owned the junk shop was a whiz with a welder, but Sierra didn't have time to appreciate that kind of skill. She just wanted her boys back, preferably undamaged by the jungle of rusty metal behind the fence.

As she started to lift the latch, Ridge put his hand on top of hers.

"Wait." He put a finger to his lips then touched his ear.

She paused and heard the murmur of voices coming from behind the fence. One rang out higher than the others.

"Lookit me!" She recognized Frankie's voice. "I'm goin' to Vegas, baby!"

Standing on tiptoe, she peeked over the fence and decided she'd have to check the records and make sure all the boys were up to date on their shots. There were eighteen potential puncture wounds and a dozen cases of tetanus back there, along with rusty cars, washing machines, industrial equipment, and piles of bald tires. Grass sprouted from empty engine cavities, and unidentifiable vines obscured stacks of miscellaneous machinery. Over it all ruled a monstrous Caterpillar tractor, its bright yellow paint nearly obliterated by rust, its long, crooked arm hoisting a toothed bucket from which sprouted more weeds.

The boys had piled into a defunct Chevy Bel Air like a family setting out on vacation. Frankie was at the wheel, which was appropriate since he was always the ringleader when it came to getting into trouble. As always, he was wearing his favorite hat—an ancient fedora that had probably belonged to some staid businessman in the fifties. It was darkened by age and stained with mold, and made dark-eyed, olive-skinned Frankie look like a Little Rascal playing gangster. Isaiah sat beside him in the passenger seat, while Jeffrey and Carter slouched in the back like a couple of junior mob enforcers. All they needed was cigars all around and a body in the trunk.

"How come you'd go to Vegas?" That was Isaiah, challenging everyone's ideas as usual. He had a quick intelligence that would take him far if he ever had the opportunity to use it for something other than finding trouble. "Why don't you go to New York or LA?"

"'Cause I could make it in Vegas," Frankie said. "I could be a dealer."

"A drug dealer? Man, you're stupid," Isaiah said.

Sierra resisted the urge to do a fist pump. Isaiah's father was in prison for dealing drugs, and like most of the boys, he clung to a fierce love for his absent father. She'd been worried he'd follow his dad down that dead-end road, but maybe the system had succeeded in breaking the cycle for once.

"You need money to be a drug dealer, and you don't got any money," Isaiah continued.

Sierra's shoulders sagged. So much for breaking the cycle.

"Not drugs," Frankie said. "I'd deal cards. Blackjack, in a casino. Or I could be a bouncer."

"You're too much of a punk to be a bouncer. You'd probably be a backup dancer. For *Cher*," Carter teased. He was a big boy, not fat but large, and he probably wanted the bouncer job for himself. Jeffrey, who sat beside him, never seemed to take up any space at all. The boy was so quiet Sierra was afraid he would disappear someday, just fade away. She didn't know what kind of tragedies festered in the boy's memory, but something had stolen his voice.

"I hate Cher," Frankie said. "I want to do backup for somebody hot. Rihanna, maybe."

The boys jeered as Ridge and Sierra struggled not to laugh.

"My mom likes Rihanna," Carter protested. "We're maybe going to go to a concert sometime when she gets out of the center."

"Your mom's never getting out," Frankie scoffed. Sierra winced at the casual cruelty—although from what she'd read in Carter's file, Frankie was probably right.

"She is too." Carter squared his shoulders and thrust out his jaw. "She's really committed to her recovery this time."

Other boys knew baseball stats or rock lyrics. Sierra's boys knew the language of therapy and addiction. Sometimes it seemed as if they'd been the caretakers and their parents the children, living in an upside-down world.

Frankie draped one hand casually over the steering wheel, like a bored commuter, and turned to Isaiah. "Where would you go?"

Sierra gripped the fence, her knuckles whitening. This was an answer she wanted to hear. She wasn't sure what Isaiah wanted out of life, and that made it hard to motivate him. Pudding Snacks would only get her so far, and she was eager to hear what his dream destination would be.

"No place." His dark brows arrowed downward, turning his delicate, almost elfin face into the embodiment of a bad attitude. "I'd just drive. Drive and drive and drive. Away from here." He scrunched down in his seat and stared out the window. "Away from all of you."

"I'd go back to Millersville." Sierra glanced down at Josh, who was whispering his own answer to the question. He seemed to be talking to the fence posts, oblivious of Ridge and Sierra beside him. "I'd go help out my dad, 'cause there's a lot of work to do around the place."

Sierra felt her heart break a little. Josh's dad had done everything possible to kill his son's affection and maybe even the boy himself. But children needed to love their parents, and it was amazing how long they'd cling to a version of reality that let them justify that love.

"You all don't have nowhere to go either," Isaiah said to the boys in the car. "You're all just talk."

As usual, his bad attitude silenced the rest of the boys. Sierra glanced at Ridge, and he nodded. The heavy latch opened with a clang and she strode into the junkyard, followed by Ridge and Josh.

"Hey," Carter said. "Who's—oh, shit, guys. We're busted." He ducked back into the car, banging his head on the roof. "Damn it, Josh told. I *knew* he would. I'm going to kill that kid."

―⁂―

Ridge had once seen a rabbit caught by a coyote. At the moment it felt the beast's jaws clamp on its neck, the normally silent rabbit had let out a high, thin cry that pierced his heart. That was the sound Josh made now, as the boys turned and glared at him.

Ridge stifled the urge to put a protective hand on the boy's shoulder. The gesture would put the boy solidly on the side of the adults—a move that would make his life hell as long as he stayed with this group of boys. Instead, he shot a glance at Sierra, to see if she'd seen how much promises meant to this little gang.

"Josh didn't tell me anything," she said.

He supposed that was true. Josh hadn't told her; he'd told Ridge.

Judging from the thunderous look the black kid shot at Josh, he wasn't buying it.

"Snitch," he muttered.

Sierra gave the boys a sharp nod, and they immediately spilled out of the old Chevy—all but the black kid, who paused a moment and met her eyes with a hostile glare of his own. Ridge recognized that look. He'd had the same one in his own arsenal once upon a time.

"Isaiah," Sierra said. "Out."

Isaiah must have decided this wasn't a good time to test authority, because he quickly followed the others. He headed straight for Josh, who was doing his best to hide in Ridge's shadow.

Ridge drew himself up to his full height and looked Isaiah in the eye. That bit of body language apparently worked as well with kids as it did with horses, because Isaiah turned away and kicked at the ground, creating a little cloud of dust that settled over the toe of his running shoes. His kick uncovered an old piece of rusted metal, which he picked up and studied, those angry brows drawn down in concentration. A change of subject and he'd forget all about Josh.

"Vegas, huh?" Ridge grinned at the curly-haired kid and yanked the brim of his old hat down over his face. The kid tilted his head back and gave him a cocky grin.

"You bet. Vegas, baby! Got a gig with Rihanna."

"I'd stay away from that chick," Ridge said. "She's trouble."

A lively argument ensued over whether the singer's hotness made dying at the hands of her various paramours worthwhile. Ridge could feel Josh releasing tension beside him, like a balloon slowly expelling air, as the conversation shifted from reality to fantasy.

"So, are you a real cowboy?" one of the boys asked. "With a horse and everything?"

Ridge nodded, settling for a half-truth. He did have a horse—several horses. But he was a long way from having "everything."

He didn't have a career, for example. Or a future. Or a woman.

"So can we ride it?" the boy prodded. It was the black kid, the one who had the face of an angel until he unleashed that rebellious glare.

"No," Sierra said. "If you want extra activities, you need to show you can be responsible. You have to make good decisions. And locking the pantry door was *not* a good decision. Leaving the house without permission was an even worse one. Did anybody get their homework done?"

The response was a lot of shuffling and mumbling.

"That's what I thought."

Sierra turned and set off toward Phoenix House, the boys trailing behind her like chicks following a mother hen. They were very grumbly chicks, and Ridge felt like joining in. Boys needed adventure like horses needed hay, and she couldn't expect them to act like angels when they were cooped up doing homework on a day like this.

Fall didn't last long in Wyoming. Soon the wind would blow the trees bare and swirl a thick coat of snow on the ground. But for now, the aspens burned bright as candle flames against the sky, and crisp grass crackled under their feet. Hitcher seeds clung to socks and pant legs, and fallen leaves colored the sidewalk like spilled paint—maple red, oak brown, and aspen yellow. Autumn had splashed the whole world with bright, festive color.

It was time for touch football, for wrestling in the grass, for saddling up and riding just to feel the wind in your face. If Sierra wanted the kids to do something constructive, she should let them rake leaves. And then she should let them jump in the piles until they'd made a bigger mess than they started with.

That's what he'd do if he ran the place, or if he had kids of his own someday.

He wouldn't. He knew that. But he also knew what childhood should be and rarely ever was.

Chapter 9

"Spider-Man don't do math," Isaiah mumbled. "Spider-Man got better things to do."

"Not in Wynott, he doesn't," said Sierra.

"Damn—darn straight," the kid said. "Nothin' good to do around here, not even for Spider-Man."

The clear, high notes of Sierra's laughter rose in the still air of the quiet little town, riding the breeze like sudden birdsong. She'd let out that same careless, all-out laughter in the closet, but Ridge hadn't seen her smile in daylight, and he hadn't seen how her green eyes caught the sunlight filtering through the leaves. He felt dazed, like a kid who'd just spun around and around for the dizzy pleasure of tumbling to the ground.

He wanted to grab her hands in his and do just that, he realized. He wanted to spin and spin until the outside world didn't exist, until there was just the two of them again—like back there in the closet. He wanted Sierra Dunn, more than he'd wanted a woman in a long time.

Which was not good. He'd returned to Wynott to recover from his injury and find a new path in life now that his rodeo career was over. That path didn't include a woman, and it certainly didn't include a bunch of kids, but he could feel Sierra and her little band of misfits tearing down the barriers he'd built around his heart. The fragile walls were collapsing like a pup tent in a windstorm.

He'd built those barriers because his last long-term relationship owed more to his ex's determination and perseverance than it did to his own feelings, which had been mild at best and annoyed at worst. Shelley had been dead set on turning the two of them into a couple, with wedding bells ringing and two-point-five kids in the yard. When she'd finally given up, he'd felt relief and guilt in equal measure.

A quick mental flashback of Shelley's face, swollen and tearstained, made his gut clench.

You don't need the things other people need, she'd said. *You think that makes you strong. But it doesn't. It just makes you alone.*

She was right. When it came to women, he had nothing to offer. He'd tried, especially with Shelley. But he'd had no deeper feelings toward her than he had toward the various one-night stands that rodeo cowboys gathered along with their gold buckles and broken legs.

He glanced at Sierra, who was helping one of the boys with the snaps on his jacket. She cared so much about these kids. You could see it in her eyes—the way they'd teared up when she'd been worried about losing them, and the way they glowed every time one of them said something funny or kind. He hoped she'd find a nice guy and get married someday, have kids of her own.

But he was not that guy. Nobody had ever accused him of being nice, and if Sierra gave him her heart, he'd probably break it into a million little pieces. She deserved better, so he was backing away—now. Right now. He'd promised her nothing would hurt her, and he was probably the number one thing she needed protection from.

It was too bad for the kids, but hell, they'd probably hijack his heart too, and then where would he be?

When they reached the top of the porch steps at Phoenix House, Sierra flashed him a bright smile. "Did you want to schedule a visit, then? Maybe Saturday?"

"Nope."

"What?" She looked hurt.

He looked away, scuffing one foot in the dust. "You told 'em they weren't allowed. I think that was the right call."

"I changed my mind. You're great with the kids. And waiting for the weekend is punishment enough." She smiled again, and again it was like the sun had come out from behind a cloud. "You know how time stretches out when you're a kid. It'll seem like forever to them. And I suspect your place has a lot more to offer than Pudding Snacks. A ranch would be paradise for these guys."

"Maybe not mine." He believed in facing his fears, though, so he forced himself to look her right dead in the eye, the same way he'd face an ornery bull. "Look, you said it yourself. It's not real safe, and they're kind of young for rodeo. Now that I met them, I think you were right."

There. He'd made the break without making her feel bad. He'd told her she was right and kept her from bringing the boys into a situation she thought was dangerous.

He'd treated her well, really.

Pressing his hat low over his eyes, he jogged down the steps and headed down the cracked sidewalk, walking fast, putting as much distance as he could between himself and temptation.

Because he wanted to go back. He wanted to tell her

to bring the boys out now, to come tomorrow too. Heck, forget the boys; he wanted her to come out on her own, just her.

But he clenched his teeth and kept on walking. He was half a block away before he heard her speak.

"Bye." It sounded like a question, a slightly doubtful, bewildered question.

He didn't answer. He didn't even look back.

He just kept on walking.

Chapter 10

RIDGE SORTED THE MAIL ON HIS WAY INTO THE HOUSE. Bills, bills, and more bills. They were definitely paying out more than they were taking in at the Decker ranch these days. When all three brothers grew up and hit the rodeo road, Bill Decker had sold off the cattle. The only livestock he'd kept were a few old horses and his dogs. He'd leased enough pasture to keep the place going, but it wasn't generating any income.

Ridge knew he was lucky to have this family home. It would allow him to figure out what the hell he was going to do with his life now that a particularly high-bucking bronc had decided to roll over and kick around like a dying bug, grinding him into the dirt of the arena before righting itself and stomping him some more. When the dust had cleared that hot July afternoon, Ridge had managed to walk back to the chutes, but his riding arm had dangled from his shoulder like a dead fish hanging on a hook.

It turned out pretty much every bone in his hand was busted. There was something wrong with his neck that required a lot of hardware to fix, and he needed a titanium plate to hold his arm together. The doctors had done their best, but he'd never get his grip back—and no grip meant no rodeo. He could ride all right, same as ever, but he couldn't throw a lasso or hang on to a bronc rope.

Ridge's brother Shane was at the kitchen table, weaving long strands of rawhide together to create a lasso that would spring to life in some lucky cowboy's hands. Ridge, toeing off his boots, put his hand behind his back and tried to flex his fingers. He tested them twenty times a day, maybe more, but the end result never changed; he could barely bend them enough to grip a beach ball.

He slapped the envelopes on the kitchen counter harder than he'd intended. Shane looked up, his expression mild. It took more than a sudden noise to rattle Shane. A wild elephant could tear through the kitchen and he'd just watch it go.

"How was Phoenix House?" he asked.

Ridge shrugged and started to leave the room, but Shane hooked a chair with one foot and whipped it away from the table, blocking Ridge's route to the hallway.

"Sit," Shane said. "We need to talk."

Ignoring the chair, Ridge picked up the mail and rested a hip against the counter, pretending to be captivated by an offer for cheap car insurance.

"I said, we need to talk," Shane said. "You know, that thing people do where you look at another person and speak."

"Dee can do that." Ridge glanced over at one of the Border collies sprawled on the rug by the woodstove. "Speak, Dee."

The dog sat up and barked. Not to be outdone, her companion did the same.

"Dammit, sit." Shane reached over and snatched the mail out of Ridge's hands.

Ridge sat while the dogs, already sitting, looked confused.

"Did you even go to Phoenix House?"

Ridge should have known he'd get the third degree the minute he got home. Once Shane got an idea in his head, he was like a terrier with a bone, and he was determined to help Ridge rise from the ashes of his rodeo career and spread his wounded wings—or something like that. Shane read too much, and it showed.

"Well, did you?" He talked too much too.

"Yeah, I went there."

"Good." Shane gave a sharp, satisfied nod. "So when are the kids coming?"

"They're not."

"How come?"

Ridge turned away and tore open a utility bill. "The lady who runs the place doesn't think it's safe."

"It's not up to her. The guy who owns the place approved it. It's a done deal, and it's her job to make it happen." Shane narrowed his eyes. "You didn't even try to change her mind, did you?"

Busted.

"Look, I'm not ready for this." Ridge tore open another bill, this one for the feedstore. "I'm still trying to figure out my future, still trying to get over Shelley."

Dang, he sounded like one of the touchy-feely cowboys in the book Shelley had left behind—the one he'd been reading in the evenings. It was a Western, but the cowboy on the cover had his shirt off and was giving the viewer a slack-jawed stare that made Ridge wonder if he had sense enough to find the front end of a horse. There were some pretty sexy scenes in it, but everybody in it had *feelings*, and they spent a lot of time talking about them.

Ridge didn't see the point of digging too deeply into emotional stuff. If you ignored your feelings long enough, they'd eventually go away. Of course, so did your girlfriend. But in his case, that had been for the best. Shelley had loved him, supposedly, and he'd liked her just fine.

But when he'd looked down inside himself for more, all he found was guilt and a grudging sense of duty.

"You were over Shelley before her boots hit the highway," Shane said. "You just want to keep on sulking around here on your own, I guess."

Ridge shrugged. "That's my choice."

Shane shoved his chair back, clearly irritated. "What are you going to do with yourself, then? Rodeo's not an option. You need to move on. What's your plan B?"

"There is no plan B." Ridge felt a fierce, hot anger well up inside him, a hot, flowing mass that threatened to spill over and burn everything in its path. "Plan A was to win a championship by the time I was thirty. I did that. Next, I was aiming for the all-around title. That was the *only* plan."

"Well, it's not going to happen." Shane strode to the sink and began rinsing dirty dishes and slotting them into the dishwasher. "Every rodeo cowboy needs a plan B. You get hurt, you get old—you can't do it all your life, you know? But for you, it's always been the one thing. You're a single-minded son of a bitch."

"That's what it takes," Ridge said. "If you want to win, you've got to give it all you've got, and damn the consequences. You can't think about losing when you need to stick on the back of a bull. You can't think about failing when the calf shoots out of the gate and you need your rope right there, right..."

He'd been gesturing subconsciously while he spoke, and now he raised his hand as if throwing a loop—but the hand wouldn't cooperate. He was just flailing at the air.

He dropped the hand in his lap and it lay there motionless. Human roadkill.

"Having a plan B means that deep down, you believe you might not win," he said. "And that kind of belief makes it impossible to be the best. I've been shooting for the top of the standings since I was fourteen. Never thought I'd need another plan."

Rage rose in his throat and harsh words tumbled out. "Who are you to talk about plans, anyway?" He jabbed a finger at Shane. "Was it your plan to have a kid before you graduated high school?" He knew every word spilling from his lips was a mistake, but he couldn't seem to stop. "Was it your plan for Amber to have to go through all the shame and the whispering? Was it your plan for her to take off with the baby on the first bus out of town? You haven't seen your son since he was a month old. Don't talk to me about plans."

"I didn't say plans always work out." Shane barely bothered to look up from the suds-filled sink. It was damn near impossible to get a rise out of him. "I'm just saying you need to come up with something. Otherwise, you'll end up being the Jack Daniel's champion of Wyoming."

Shane had a point. Having his purpose whipped away overnight had left Ridge with an aching, empty spot inside, and lately he'd been filling it up with high-test whiskey.

"What are you going to do, Ridge?" Shane's tone was so gentle Ridge wanted to punch him.

"I can always train horses. I'll get Moonpie fixed up and ready to sell, maybe take in a few outside horses."

Shane grinned. "You'll never fix that horse. And I'm not sure he's worth fixing."

"You're wrong on that."

Ridge pictured the big buckskin out in the corral, kicking up his heels and snorting, endlessly raging at the confines of his new life. The horse was the result of his recent fondness for Jack Daniel's and a random impulse to attend a Bureau of Land Management mustang sale. The whiskey had heightened his estimation of his own horse-training skills, and somehow he hadn't noticed the animal's obvious character defects. It was only when he went to load the animal into his trailer that he realized he'd taken on a kicking, biting bundle of nerves.

"I'll get him fixed up," he said. "Get him so he can live in this world, at least."

"Maybe you ought to try for a grown-up goal this time," Shane said. "Something that does the world some good and goes a little beyond buckles and babes."

Ridge shoved his chair back so he could face his brother, letting the legs screech on the wood floor.

"You think that's all it was about?"

Shane shrugged. "That's all it was about for me. Why? What was it about for you?"

Ridge opened his mouth to answer and realized he didn't know what the hell it had been about. Rodeo had always felt like the most important thing in the world, maybe because it was the one thing he excelled at. But damned if he could think what the point of it was.

Great. Not only had he had his livelihood ripped away, but now his brother had taken his purpose too. At this rate, he ought to go lie down in the corral so Moonpie could kick him in the head and put him out of his misery.

An uncomfortable silence filled the room, palpable and dense as cotton wool. Shane turned back to the sink and started on the pile of bowls and plates that were stacked on the counter, but it wasn't long before he shook off his wet hands and strode over to the door.

"Brady, get in here," he hollered. "I'm tired of cleaning up your mess."

Their younger brother wandered down from upstairs with his jeans half-zipped and his hair tousled from sleep. Instead of helping with the dishes, he started opening cupboards and drawers in his endless search for victuals. He was the baby of the family but calling him that was a sure way to earn a punch on the jaw. A rookie bronc rider, he had all the attitude of a seasoned rodeo veteran and the appetite of a grizzly bear fresh from hibernation. Finding a box of Cheerios, he poured some into a soup bowl.

"I'll get to the dishes, Shane," he said. "I just need a bite to eat first."

"Got a danged tapeworm," Shane grumbled under his breath.

Brady opened the refrigerator door and grabbed a carton of milk. Gulping a long slug out of the carton, he eyed Ridge. "So it's a no go on Phoenix House?"

Ridge nodded. "You listening at doors now?"

"No. But I saw his face." He aimed his thumb over his shoulder at Shane. "Figured you'd spoiled his plan." Sidetracked from the cereal by the refrigerator's largesse, he peered into a plastic tub that contained what was left of the previous night's cowboy stew and sniffed. It must have smelled okay, because he set the container on the counter and removed the lid.

"So, Brady," Ridge said. "Why do you do rodeo?"

Brady grinned. "Buckles and babes. Why? Is there some other reason?"

Ridge shook his head. He knew better than to seek worldly wisdom from his shallow little brother.

Brady shoved the lid toward the sink. "So you're

not going after the hot chick that runs Phoenix House? Women need to be educated in the cowboy way, you know. The cowboy way of ridin', the cowboy way of livin', and most of all, the cowboy way of makin' love."

He drew out the last word as he opened a drawer and fished out a spoon then grabbed another bowl from a cupboard. But by the time he got back to the stew, Shane had clapped the lid back on.

"That's dinner."

"What, the chick?" Brady winked at Ridge. "That would be okay with me. If you're not interested, I might stop on over there and get acquainted."

Ridge felt a hot churning in his gut. He might not be interested in Sierra Dunn, but he wouldn't let her become one of Brady's many casualties. The kid mowed through women like a McCormick reaper, leaving them flattened in his wake. Ridge might not be good at relationships, but at least he never deliberately hurt anyone.

Brady didn't either, he supposed. He just expected women to have the same attitude toward sex as he did. It was a recreational activity in his eyes, no more significant than a game of pickup basketball.

Ridge shoved his chair back and stalked over to the refrigerator to investigate the stew container while Brady doused the cereal with milk until it floated.

"Well, if you're not interested, she's up for grabs, right?"

Ridge slammed the refrigerator door and spun around, jostling Brady so that the cereal bowl flew from his hand. Cheerios and milk splatted onto the floor. Brady looked down at the mess and laughed.

"Guess you are interested."

Ridge grabbed a roll of paper towels and handed it to Brady. "Clean up the mess," he said. "And then you need to do those dishes. Shane and I are sick and tired of cleaning up after you."

Brady knelt and began cleaning up the cereal, grinning the whole time. "I'm thinking you're the one who's a mess, big brother. There's finally a woman worth chasing in this town, and you've got all the time in the world to do it, but are you going to go after her? Nope. You'd rather go out there and play with that damned feebleminded horse."

"Moonpie's not feebleminded. And what I do is my business," Ridge said. "But Sierra's a nice girl. Way out of your league."

He strode out of the room, surprised and relieved that Shane hadn't had anything more to say about the volunteering issue. But when he snuck a glance over his shoulder, his older brother's eyes were on him, dark and contemplative. Something was going on in his bossy big brother's scheming brain.

Ridge headed for his bedroom. The house hadn't changed much since they were kids, so he, Shane, and Brady still had their boyhood rooms. His was a festival of all things cowboy, including old rodeo photos signed by past stars like Jim Shoulders and Jim Charles; a rope and a riding glove hanging on the back of his desk chair; and a pine bedstead that looked like it was made from a wagon wheel.

Shelley's cowboy novel lay on the bed. He thought about picking it up and giving it another try, but instead, he pulled an old-school composition book from a desk drawer. It fell open to a numbered list penned in the painstaking printing of a teenaged boy who took himself way too seriously.

He'd enumerated all his goals at fourteen, just three

months after arriving at Decker ranch. He remembered the night he'd written them out. Up to then, his only goal had been to survive each day, and he hadn't even been sure why that mattered. That night, he'd been overwhelmed with the excitement of finding something he loved, something he was good at.

The list started with learning to ride a horse "as good as Bill" and ended with winning the PRCA All-Around Cowboy title at the Wrangler National Finals, which Bill had told him was the pinnacle of cowboying. Beside each goal was the age when he meant to accomplish it and a box to be checked off once it was accomplished.

Shane and Brady were wrong. Rodeo wasn't about buckles and babes.

It was about Bill. About giving back to the man who'd believed in him when he was a skinny, rebellious kid nobody cared about. Bill was gone now, but that didn't matter. Ridge still wanted to make him proud.

He ran his finger down the list. He'd actually won two championships before he was thirty, in bareback and saddle bronc. All the items were checked off but the last one, and until the wreck that destroyed his hand, he'd been on track to accomplish that too.

Looking down at his hand, he opened and closed the fingers, opened and closed. It looked like he was barely moving, but he was giving it his all. There was no way he'd ever win the All-Around now.

His biggest accomplishment of the evening was resisting the temptation to slam his injured hand into the desk and cripple himself some more.

Chapter 11

SIERRA FELT LIKE SHE'D SPENT HER MORNING managing a herd of rampaging bull calves. It was such a relief to finally put the boys on the school bus, she thought she might melt into a puddle of exhaustion and relief right there on the sidewalk in front of Phoenix House. That would get the neighbors talking.

Not that they weren't already. Instead of assimilating into their new school in the nearby town of Grigsby, her boys were clinging together as a group, creating a city kids versus country kids dynamic that inspired talk of gangs in town. It didn't help when Isaiah encouraged the other kids to put on exaggerated "gangsta" walks and tell wild lies about big-city life. In return, the country kids teased her boys about their parents—or lack thereof. There was no doubt that hurt and made the situation even worse.

Sierra had been worried about getting the community to buy into her hometown idea, but it turned out it was the kids who refused to cooperate. Of course, the administration at school wouldn't cooperate either. The vice principal, who seemed to be the only authority figure willing to meet with her, insisted the kids would work out their differences among themselves, without adult intervention. Sierra disagreed. These weren't puppies play fighting in the backyard. These were children, and every cruel word poked a hole in their fragile self-esteem.

The massive old Victorian house felt a little spooky

in the absence of the cheerful chatter of the boys. Her footsteps echoed as she headed down the hall to her office, and she nearly jumped out of her skin when the doorbell buzzed.

She really needed to get that thing changed.

The man at the door was dressed in a uniform that somehow managed to be neither brown nor green nor gray, and it wasn't quite khaki either. He stood militarily erect and weirdly motionless. Her first impression was that he was the most respectable man she'd ever seen. Possibly the best-looking as well, but in a Ken-doll way that just didn't work for her. Sierra had taken a Sharpie to her own Ken when she was a kid, giving him a mustache and some tattoos. She didn't like perfect men.

Maybe that explained the string of failed relationships she'd left behind when she'd moved to Wynott.

"Can I help you?" she asked.

But she knew who he was and probably what he wanted. She'd seen him pedaling around town on a black Schwinn bicycle, doing his best to look officious. He was the town police—or the sheriff, as Ridge had called him—and he probably wanted one of her kids.

Shoot. The boys had been out of her sight for five minutes, and there was already a cop at the door.

What had they done? And how had they done it so fast?

Could Jeffrey have shimmied out a bus window and taken off running? Could Isaiah have gotten in a fight already? She pictured skinned knees, bruised elbows, irate bus drivers, lawsuits from angry parents.

She held the door open and the sheriff stepped inside, executed a military turn, and introduced himself.

"Sheriff Swaggard, ma'am."

———w———

Jim wondered why the woman seemed so horrified at the sight of a lawman at her door. Guilty conscience, probably. Well, he'd figure out why eventually. He was good that way. He knew human behavior like the back of his head.

He gave the woman his best handshake, manly and firm. Hers was weak, a little cautious. He was willing to bet she had something to hide.

She was a cutie, though. Tiny little thing, blond hair, pretty green eyes that looked wide and innocent. She looked more like a woman who needed protection than any kind of criminal.

He pictured himself rescuing her from a burning building. Saving her from bad guys at a bank robbery. He didn't know how that last one would happen, since Wynott didn't have a bank, but he could picture it clear as day.

"Is something wrong?" she asked.

"Well, I don't know." He arched his eyebrows. "Do *you* think something's wrong?"

That was a sure way to get at the truth—put the suspect on the hot seat.

Not that she was a suspect. Not yet.

"Nothing's wrong that I know of." She gave him a cute little Kewpie-doll smile, the kind of smile that made him hope to God she wasn't guilty of anything. It would be too bad if the first pretty girl to come to Wynott in over ten years turned out to be a criminal.

But you never knew. He'd learned that at the academy. You never assumed anything.

"I just figure when the sheriff comes to call, he's got a reason."

He smiled his best smile, showing off his straight, even teeth. He knew he checked off all the boxes when it came to male attractiveness. Broad-shouldered physique? Check. Rugged features? Check. Blue eyes, blond hair? Check. A fine suit of clothes with creases straight as a Wyoming highway running up the legs? Double check. And his shoes were as shiny as a snake's beady eye. He didn't see how any woman could resist him.

But this woman did. She didn't even smile back.

It was his business to know what went on in this town, and he knew she'd spent hours with Ridge Cooper the day before. Ridge Cooper, with his torn jeans and dirty boots. There was just no comparison.

So why wasn't she smiling?

Evidently, she liked the Western type, so Jim leaned against the wall and crossed one leg over the other, the way he'd seen that sheriff on *Longmire* do it. "You're from the city, aren't you, honey?"

She still didn't smile. And he'd even called her *honey*. What was wrong with the woman?

"I'm from Denver," she said.

Oh. Well, that explained it.

He cleared his throat. "Well, here in Wynott, the law doesn't wait until something's wrong to show up. We believe in a preventive approach." He pretended to pause on purpose while his mind scrambled around, searching for the words in the training manual he'd gotten at the academy. "It's a new concept called community policing. We make an effort to get to know the citizens we protect."

He supposed the "we" part was a bit of an exaggeration, since he was the only law in the whole town. But it sounded better that way.

"Would you like to talk in my office?" she asked.

Did he catch a little wink there, or did he imagine it? He tipped his hat, just in case. "Sure, ma'am."

It wasn't much of an office. It looked more like a closet. But she sat down behind a big, old metal desk, so he settled into the chair in front of it. The chair was broken, with one leg held together with a C-clamp. The whole place looked like a scratch-and-dent sale.

He pinched the legs of his trousers as he sat down, tugging them up over his knees to avoid straining the fabric. It was time to get down to business.

"Now," he said, "I know you've got your hands full, and I aim to help you all I can." He smiled again, encouraging her to trust him. "You tell me which boys are the biggest troublemakers, and I'll keep an eye on them."

Was it his imagination, or did she look kind of grim? That cute little smile was nothing but a memory. Evidently, keeping an eye on these kids wasn't nearly enough.

"I could give 'em a good talking to if you want," he continued. "Show 'em the jail cells in the old municipal building, do a *Scared Straight* kind of thing."

She sat back and folded her arms over her chest. It sure was a nice chest.

"I thought the jail was shut down years ago," she said.

"That's the beauty of it," Jim said. "Place looks downright spooky, and they don't have to know we don't use it."

"It would probably give them nightmares."

There, now she was getting it. "Exactly."

"You think that's a good thing?"

"Sure do. Prevention is nine-tenths of the law."

She stared at him as if she was confused. Maybe she'd never heard that expression before. He did have a way with words.

"Sheriff, I don't know what you've been told, but these are not bad kids. Their parents couldn't take care of them for one reason or another, so they ended up in the foster care system through no fault of their own. Their parents might have been in trouble with the law, but the kids are innocent."

Oh, so she was one of those. She must not have dealt with juvenile delinquents for long. "You know what they say," he said. "The apple doesn't fall far from the pear."

"The apple—what?"

"It's an expression," he said slowly. The woman seemed kind of dimwitted to be running a halfway house.

"Did you go to school here? In Grigsby, I mean?"

"Sure did. And then right to the Wyoming Law Enforcement Academy in Douglas." He crossed his legs. "But I'm not here to talk about me," he said. "I'm here to talk about your boys."

"Right. We were talking about giving them nightmares by showing them the old jail cells."

"It would be a start."

"It would be a disaster." Her voice got all hard and shrill. "Sheriff, these kids have seen far worse places than those jail cells. Their lives have already been nightmares. What they need is normalcy. And they need people to believe in them."

Another bleeding heart. He'd seen it before. "Oh, I see." He chuckled, as if they were both in on a joke. "I realize it's your job to defend the children, but if we work together, we might be able to minimize the impact of this institution on the other residents of Wynott."

"It's not an institution. It's a *home*."

"Well, whatever it's called, you should probably know, the neighbors are concerned."

She frowned. That made little lines form between her eyebrows, and lines bracketed her mouth. If she kept that up, she wouldn't be nearly so pretty in a few years.

That was the trouble with women working. It was too stressful and ruined their looks.

She took a deep breath, like she was about to say something important, and he braced himself for a lecture.

"Sheriff, I know it's important that you and I have a good relationship."

At least she had that part right. He wondered what kind of relationship she meant. He wasn't sure he liked her much, but she sure was pretty.

"If we're going to work together, I need you to believe these boys are worth saving. If we love them and trust them, they'll do their best to rise to even the highest expectations. I've seen it happen."

He doubted that, but she was on a roll, so he wasn't about to interrupt.

"My goal is to make Wynott a hometown they'll come to care about, and I'm hoping the community will help. Certainly you, as our local law enforcement, can make a big difference. I'd be very, very grateful if you'd assure folks that the kids aren't going to be a problem."

She had a point. Without his leadership, she'd never succeed in her little project. But he wasn't sure he could get on board. After all, there had to be some reason these kids' families had given up on them.

"Tell you what," he said. "I need to meet the kids, I think. See what they're all about."

Was that panic he saw on her face or just a little anxiety? In either case, he was pretty sure she didn't want him to meet the kids. His instincts were right. They were probably a bad bunch, rude and uneducated.

She smoothed her hair and got ahold of herself, flashing him a smile he could tell had nerves behind it.

"I think that would be a great idea," she said. "Someone like you could be a really good influence on them."

"Right." And it was. He was the kind of guy every boy should aspire to be. He'd been a pretty good student, even if some of his teachers were a little stingy with the grades. And he'd been good at sports—a football hero in high school and danged good at baseball too. And now? Well, now he was sheriff of a whole town. Those kids would probably be in awe of him. He'd have to find a way to help them relax around him, treat him like he was just another man like any other.

Except better.

Speaking of better…

He fidgeted with the buttons on his shirt then cleared his throat. She wasn't going to like what he had to say next, but it had to be said.

"So are you expecting Ridge Cooper to be a good influence on them?" he asked.

She had a quick, sharp answer for that. "I'm not expecting him to be any kind of influence at all."

She sounded mad. Mad or disappointed. Something had happened between her and Cooper, he was sure of it. And he wasn't surprised. It seemed like something happened between Cooper and every woman Jim had ever had his eye on.

He couldn't understand why. Back in high school, he'd been the football hero while Ridge had been a complete outsider. The guy hardly even talked, and he wore crummy clothes. Everybody knew where he'd come from, but still the girls flocked to him.

"Ridge Cooper and I agreed that rodeo wasn't the kind of thing that would be good for the kids," Sierra said.

"Phew." Jim put a hand to his chest, pantomiming breathless relief so she'd see how important that was to him. "That is the best news I've heard all day. I heard you and the children were seen with him yesterday, and I've been worrying over that like a dog with a cat."

Sierra straightened right up in her chair, looking concerned. Now he had her attention.

"What's the problem?" she asked. "I always thought cowboys were pretty wholesome."

"Wholesome?" He laughed. "I can tell you, rodeo cowboys are a wild, lawless bunch."

"So all these ranches around here, the cowboys that work on them—they're wild and lawless?"

"Not all of 'em." He hitched up his belt with an air of authority. "Old Bill Decker, for instance, was a fine upstanding man." He looked down at the toes of his shiny shoes and shook his head sadly. "Don't know why he did what he did, but it sure didn't turn out too well."

Sierra probably didn't know who Bill Decker was or what he'd done, but she looked like she was really paying attention. She was probably grateful he'd blown the whistle on Ridge Cooper. People like her just tended to trust too easily. Look at those boys. A bunch of little delinquents, but she thought he ought to trust them.

He'd have to help her out all he could.

"I know folks like you tend to think the best of people, but sometimes that can be a little naive," he said. "Maybe you and me ought to get together some evening, have a little talk about things over a nice dinner." He reached over and patted her hand to reassure her that he understood that she couldn't help how she was. "I think I can help you learn a few things about life, and maybe about some other things too."

He expected her to melt at the thought of a date with the town sheriff, but instead she leaned over the desk and struck like a snake.

"How can I be naive, Officer? I've probably seen a lot more of life as a social worker in Denver than you ever dreamed of as a small-town cop."

So she was going to pull that city-smarts thing. It was true that he'd like to be in the big city rather than stuck out here in the boondocks. But this was the job he had, and he did it to the best of his ability. That was more than you could say for most men.

She shoved her chair back and stood. "Well, I appreciate your stopping by."

She obviously wanted him to leave, and he sure as heck didn't mind. He made sure his shoes hit the hardwood floor with a sharp, authoritative sound to show her who was boss.

〜〜〜

Sierra figured she'd probably made an enemy of the sheriff. That was the only reason she could think of why he'd want to ruin her hardwood floors with the black streaks his shoes left on the finish. Either she or Gil would spend an hour on their knees getting those off.

But she still had to be nice. Damn it.

"I appreciate your warning," she said. "I'll be sure and run a background check on Ridge Cooper as soon as possible."

"You'd need access to the state databases for that." He hitched up his pants and adjusted the buckle on his belt. "But you can always ask me if you need information."

"Actually, we contract for the state, so we have access to all the information we need—arrests, convictions, warrants, the works."

"Oh." He cleared his throat and thrust his hands in his pockets. "Well, you may not find any actual arrests."

"Oh. I thought you said—"

"I'm not sure he ever actually got caught for anything."

Sierra smiled to herself. After his hasty and rather rude exit the day before, she didn't care whether Ridge Cooper was a good man or not. Really. She didn't care one bit. But it was nice to know she could trust her instincts.

This guy had some kind of beef with him, that was all. Probably a lot of people did. He was rude and curt and infuriatingly attractive.

As for the sheriff, not even his clean-cut looks and shiny shoes could put him in the "good" category. He seemed to be more than willing to smear someone's reputation, so she'd better keep him on her side.

"Well, I really do appreciate the warning," she said as

they came to the door. "Just know that you don't need to worry about my boys. They're good kids."

"I hope so." He shook his head pessimistically as he left. "I truly do."

Sierra watched him strut down the steps and waited for his pants to catch on fire.

Liar.

He didn't hope her kids were good. He hoped they'd do something wrong, so he could flex his law enforcement muscle. She'd better keep the boys in line. With people like Sheriff Swaggard stirring up trouble, it was going to take some kind of magic to turn this little town into a friendly place for them.

She was just about to close the door when he turned around.

"About that dinner, though…"

"No, thank you," she said. "I'm afraid I've sworn off that kind of thing. I'm focusing on my career right now."

She couldn't hear what he was mumbling under his breath as he returned to his bicycle, threw a leg over the back, and pedaled away—but she was sure it wasn't good.

Chapter 12

LATER THAT AFTERNOON, SIERRA WAS HUNCHED OVER her computer, inputting reports from the boys' teachers. They basically said Isaiah talked too much and Jeffrey not enough.

No news flash there.

"You want some help?" Isaiah plopped down in front of the desk and shot her a winning smile.

"No. Go do your math, buddy."

"Maybe I did it already, so I could help you with this stuff."

Phoenix House's records were mostly paperless, except for the boys' earliest reports. Isaiah grabbed for a file and there was a brief wrestling match, which Sierra easily won. She wasn't in great shape, but she could take a nine-year-old any day of the week. It was only when they ganged up on her that she was in trouble.

"The files are confidential," she said. "You know that."

"I just wanna see Jeffrey's file. I want to see what makes that kid so screwy."

She bunched up the papers on her desk and shoved them in a file drawer. She'd have to reorganize them later. Sometimes it seemed like the harder she worked, the behind-er she got.

Now she was starting to sound like Sheriff Swaggard.

"You may *not* see the file, and Jeffrey is *not* screwy," she told Isaiah.

"Kid hasn't said a word for a week." Isaiah crossed his eyes and stuck out his tongue. "Makes him screwy in my book."

He had a point. Jeffrey had talked very little when he'd arrived, but now he'd fallen completely silent. She'd hoped Phoenix House would have the opposite effect.

"Maybe that's because you do enough talking for three kids. And speaking of books…"

Isaiah shoved out his lower lip and looked up at her as if he'd just lost his dog and his best friend too.

"I wanted to help you," he said. "And besides, I need adult supervision."

Sierra smothered a smile. She could not understand how any parent could choose drugs and crime over a child as bright and funny as Isaiah, even if the kid did drive her crazy.

The phone rang and she had to wrestle Isaiah for it. When she answered, she was out of breath.

"Hello?"

There was a long silence. Uh-oh. She knew that silence as well as if the caller had spoken.

"Phoenix House," she said.

"That's better," Mike Malloy said. "You might be out in the boondocks there, but we're still professionals. Remember that."

Her boss was a fine one to lecture anyone about professionalism. She'd bet money he had his feet on the desk of his office in Cheyenne at this very moment, and she was sure his eyes were scanning the hall outside his door for any passing skirt—the shorter the better.

"I'm sorry, Mike. I—hold on." She covered the receiver with her hand. "Isaiah, go do your homework."

"But—"

"Isaiah, *now*." She resisted the urge to snap at him. "Please."

As he slouched off, she took her hand off the phone.

"What was that?" Mike's voice was sharp.

"Just one of the boys."

He heaved a long-suffering sigh, as if she'd just frayed his last nerve. "Sierra, what is one of the boys doing in your office?"

"He was offering to help. It's fine, Mike."

"I hope you're maintaining authority over these kids," he said. "You must *always* be in charge. That's the challenge of this position. You need to maintain authority at all times. If you can't do that…"

He let his voice trail off, but they both knew how the threat ended. This was Mike Malloy's management style. Sometimes she wished she'd gotten the job in Denver she'd applied for before Mike had offered her the position here.

Oh, who was she kidding. She wished that *all* the time. It had been a state job, one that would have given her the power to make and execute policy for thousands of foster children in her home state, which had a population almost ten times that of Wyoming. She could do far more good in a job like that than she could here in Wynott, stuck in the back of beyond with just five kids to care for. She tried to tell herself that the world could be saved one child at a time, but it would take an awfully big army of social workers to do it this way.

Besides, in the state job, she wouldn't have to deal with Mike.

But though she'd made it through three interviews,

the state of Colorado had chosen another candidate. Since then, she'd racked her brain trying to figure out what she'd done wrong. Sadly, her conclusion was that she might have come off as too compassionate.

"You there, Sierra?"

"I'm here. And don't worry, Mike. I'm maintaining authority."

"I hope so. You're not their friend; you're their supervisor."

Only Mike would begrudge motherless, fatherless children a friend.

There was a rustling on the other end of the line, and she pictured him dropping his feet to the floor and leaning forward, elbows on the desk. "So did my buddy Ridge stop by?"

Relief made her slouch low in her chair. Apparently Mike hadn't talked to Ridge, so he didn't know about the closet incident.

Yet.

"Yes, he was here."

"Good. You set a date to take the kids out to the ranch, then?"

"No." She took a deep breath. What could she tell him? *He caressed me in the closet and then he got spooked and left?* How could she explain what had happened when she didn't understand it herself?

But she was in charge of Phoenix House, and that made her responsible for the safety of the kids. If she didn't feel they were safe with Ridge Cooper, she just needed to say so.

Clearing her throat, she channeled Hillary Clinton, Margaret Thatcher, Katharine Hepburn, and every other strong, steel-jawed woman she could think of. "I felt it would be a mistake. Rodeo is a dangerous sport, and there are virtually no medical services in the area. If one of the kids got hurt, it would take an hour to get to a hospital. Maybe more."

"Hell, Sierra, he's not going to put them on bucking bulls."

Sierra almost giggled. When he talked about Ridge Cooper, Mike took on a John Wayne drawl. But she could hardly poke fun, since she tended to drool whenever his name came up. Drawl, drool—one way or another, Ridge Cooper was an inspiration to everyone.

"He's just gonna teach 'em to twirl a rope, maybe put 'em up on a horse," Mike said.

"Mr. Cooper and I discussed the issue, and we agreed it was best not to proceed."

Mike didn't respond. He often used silence as a weapon, but Sierra knew how to play that game too. If you let the silence stretch long enough, the other person felt compelled to fill it—and generally babbled their way into some kind of trouble. It was a little like a staring contest. If you were really determined to win, you won.

Finally, Mike spoke. She pumped her fist in the air, even though there was no one there to see it.

"Let me get this straight. You told Ridge Cooper that we don't want his help?"

Hmm. That was definitely not babbling.

"I thought you wanted to make these kids part of the community, give 'em a hometown, all that stuff. And then the most important man in the community offers to help, and you tell him no. I don't get it, Sierra."

"To be honest, Mr. Cooper himself didn't seem very enthusiastic about the idea."

There. That put her and Ridge on one side, and Mike on the other side—the losing side.

She tilted her chair back and put her feet, clad in high-heeled boots, on the desk, mirroring the position Mike always took when he barked out orders on the phone. It was silly, but it made her feel in charge.

"Cooper was plenty enthusiastic when I talked to him," Mike said. "I don't know what you did to piss him off, but it sounds like I'll have to take care of it."

Click.

So much for being in charge.

Mike would call Ridge, who would tell him all about the closet incident and about losing the kids. And then Mike would call Sierra back and say those three little words.

You. Are. Fired.

And then she'd have to go back to her job search, back to filling out applications online, back to waiting for the phone to ring and "dressing for success"—which meant wearing boring business suits she'd never wear to an actual job. She had some savings, but she had no place to live, and most of her money was locked up in her 401k.

She could always live with her mother for a while.

Yeah, right.

Sierra loved her mom. She really did. But ever since Sierra's dad had walked out on them, Marie Dunn had been determined to pound into Sierra's stubborn head the belief that all men everywhere were bad to the bone. Not only had she bad-mouthed Sierra's dates, she'd also disparaged every male teacher or professor she'd ever had and pointed out the flaws of strange men passing on the street. It was a miracle Sierra wasn't twisted for life.

Heck, maybe she was. Maybe her attraction to Ridge Cooper was a form of rebellion. Because she could guarantee that her mother would not approve of him, especially since he was possibly the manliest man Sierra had ever met.

She leaned forward and rested her forehead on the desk, barely resisting the urge to give her brain a couple of good bangs on the hard wood. She might as well just sit there, she decided, and wait for Mike to call back and fire her.

She lifted her head reluctantly when she heard shuffling footsteps in the hall. Isaiah stuck his head in the doorway.

"You okay?"

She sighed. "I'm okay."

He stood squarely in the doorway, his fists on his hips. He looked like a tiny version of a military general.

"You don't look okay."

She couldn't help laughing a little. "That's not a very nice thing to say to a woman."

"I don't mean you don't look pretty. You always look pretty. But you look sad. You got boyfriend trouble?"

She shook her head.

"You sure? I know you really liked that cowboy yesterday, and he just walked off like it was nothing. Which was weird, 'cause he liked you too."

The shrill sound of the phone interrupted their conversation—thank goodness.

"See?" Isaiah said. "There he is. I told you he liked you."

She picked up the receiver. If only life were as simple as that. If only this was Ridge Cooper, apologizing for his rudeness and making everything okay.

But no. It would be Mike.

She lifted the receiver. "Hello?"

"Hello." The voice was deep. Masculine. Definitely not Mike. It was deep, like Ridge's, but it didn't have quite the same effect. Maybe she'd become immune.

"Ridge?"

The man chuckled. Nope. Not Ridge. When Ridge chuckled, she felt it deep down inside.

"No, this is his brother. Shane King, from Decker Ranch."

His brother. Another cowboy?

"I'm calling for Ridge," the man said. "He wanted to schedule a ranch visit for the kids. We thought maybe riding lessons would be a good start. No rodeo stuff at first. I thought maybe Saturday would work."

Whoever Shane King was, she wanted to kiss him. He'd just solved all her problems in a few short sentences.

"Um, Saturday would be great."

"You know how to get here?"

"I have a GPS. What's the address?"

He chuckled again. "We don't do addresses out here. You got a pen and paper?"

"Sure." She fumbled through her desk until she found a piece of scratch paper and a pen that worked then copied down the cowboy's complex litany of directions. Apparently, navigating Wyoming's backcountry was all about landmarks: a stop sign at the first turn, a washout at the second, then a place where the road forked and turned to dirt. There was a big old cottonwood at the last turn. She wrote it all down carefully. The last thing she wanted to do was get lost on the remote country roads with a van full of kids.

"What time should we come?"

"Let's say ten o'clock," he said. "That give you time enough to round 'em up? I heard you have a pretty wild bunch out there."

"We'll be there," she promised. "I'll see you at ten on Saturday."

"Oh, you won't see me. Ridge is on his own with this one." There was still a note of humor in his tone. "Try not to spook him, okay? He's scared of women."

Chapter 13

SIERRA SLID BEHIND THE WHEEL OF THE VAN FEELING capable and competent for a change. The situation in Wynott was wreaking havoc with her self-esteem. She wanted her boys to be part of the community, but she couldn't even fit in herself. People were polite, but she saw the way they looked at her, and she'd noticed that conversations often came to a sudden halt at her approach. She knew she didn't talk right, and she certainly didn't dress right. The only time she felt truly at home was when she was with the boys.

But for once, things were going her way. She'd called Mike back and told him she'd scheduled this expedition to the ranch. He'd sounded surprised that she'd solved the problem so quickly. She could have sworn he almost let a compliment slip out, but he caught himself just in time. Still, her job was safe for the moment.

And that wasn't the only phone call she'd gotten. She had a lot to think about, and some important decisions to make. Unfortunately, this long drive wasn't going to give her any quiet moments to think. By the time she spotted the old cottonwood noted in the directions, she was hot, tired, and ready to explode if the boys had one more tussle. The ride had been long, and naturally the van had no air-conditioning. The state of Wyoming might be getting rich from energy development, but they'd cut funding for children's services to the bone.

"Man, it's like Death Valley or something. There's nowhere to go out here," Carter observed.

Isaiah nodded. "Nowhere."

Sierra figured if nothing else got accomplished today, at least the boys would realize just how far they were from civilization. If any of them had had visions of running away from Wynott, the endless bleak vistas that surrounded the town had smothered those dreams in dirt, rocks, and sagebrush.

"I'm *bored*," Frankie said.

Just two days earlier, the boys had been fantasizing about road trips to Vegas. Now they were whining about an hour-long drive.

Maybe that was because there was almost nothing to look at. Once they left Wynott behind, yellowing fields alternated with brown stretches dotted with sagebrush. Occasional cows dotted the landscape, contained by ancient barbed wire that sagged on the crooked fence posts that lined the road. Once they saw an oil derrick slowly nodding its oversized head like a wise, rusty bird—*yes, yes, yes*. That was good for about two minutes of conversation, and then the boys lapsed into default road-trip mode, which consisted of battling over precious territory in the backseat, fighting over who was breathing on whom, and arguing about every nonsensical thing they could think of.

"Aren't you looking forward to riding horses?" Sierra asked.

"No," came the chorus from the backseat.

"You're probably scared to ride horses," Isaiah said.

"Nuh-uh," came the answering shout. "*You're* scared."

She did her best to shut out the racket and concentrate

on driving. Adult intervention only made their fights worse. At least they were interacting in a way that was normal for kids their age. All of them but Jeffrey, who sat in sullen silence in the far backseat. If Jeffrey argued, she'd pound the steering wheel and cheer. Sierra knew his past had given him a million reasons to be afraid of everything. Horses were nothing compared to the dragons he'd fought.

The landscape got more interesting after a while, with rock formations rising from the ground like rugged islands and distant hills hinting at the mountains beyond. They finally passed an old, rickety homestead that looked uninhabited. The place's siding was bleached to a uniform shade of gray, and crooked windows and a sagging porch gave it a lopsided look. It stood at the foot of the rugged hills, which, on closer inspection, proved to be layers of rock lifted during some cataclysmic geological event that must have occurred jillions of years ago. The drive leading to the old place was a sketchy two-track choked with weeds. It extended beyond the house and disappeared into the rocky distance.

"Look at that old house," Carter said. "I bet it's haunted."

"Nuh-uh," Josh said. "Ghosts aren't real."

"Yeah, they are."

The tussle that followed forced Sierra to pull over until peace was restored. As she restarted the van, she told the boys to keep an eye out for the ranch.

"Mr. Cooper's place should be somewhere right along here," she said. "Keep your eyes peeled."

"Gross. Peeling your eyes," Carter said happily.

"Like grapes," added Frankie.

"Yeah, gross."

They bounced along the uneven pavement, dodging potholes and scanning the sides of the road for any sign of the Decker Ranch while the boys discussed various methods of peeling eyeballs. After ten minutes, Sierra got the uneasy feeling they must have passed the ranch, but how could they have missed it? The road was a straight shot with no turns in sight and so featureless that any buildings would have stuck out as surely as the tumbledown house.

Thank God for cell phones.

She pulled over and dialed the number Shane had given her. Ridge picked up on the first ring. She could tell it was Ridge and not Shane because he sounded so surly.

"Hello."

"Hi, Ridge? It's Sierra."

There was a long silence.

"Sierra," he finally said.

Good thing she'd gotten over her little crush on the guy. It sounded like he'd completely forgotten who she was.

But she didn't mind. Not one bit. She'd pretty much forgotten him too. She vaguely remembered the way he'd helped find the kids and the way he'd been so understanding with Josh. And, to be completely honest, she had a near-perfect recollection of the way his butt looked in those jeans.

But the caress in the closet? It was like that had never happened.

She reached up and wiped her mouth with the back of her hand.

"Sierra?" He really had no memory of her at all.

"Sierra Dunn. You know. From Phoenix House?"

"Oh. Right. Phoenix House."

"Yeah. Hey, listen. I think we're lost."

"Lost where?"

"If I knew where, I wouldn't be lost. We must be almost to your place, I guess. Or maybe we passed it."

"You're on your way *here*?"

"Yes." Where did he think she was going—the Emerald City of Oz? "Did I wake you up or something?"

"'Course not. It's almost ten in the morning. Why are you coming here?"

"For the riding lessons."

The boys, who had been bickering in the back, fell quiet as he failed to answer. She hadn't expected a warm welcome from Mr. Congeniality, but she deserved better than this. The *kids* deserved better than this. Unless…

"Your brother Shane called me. He didn't tell you, did he?"

She winced as he let loose a particularly foul expletive into the phone. "Shane put you up to this?"

She wrenched off her seat belt and opened the door of the van, signaling for the kids to stay put as she hopped out. Leaning on a fence post, she clamped the phone to her ear and resisted the urge to swear right back at him.

"Nobody 'put me up' to anything," she said. "Your brother called and scheduled a visit. Today, ten o'clock. I've got five kids in a van headed your way if we can just figure out where you are."

"Well, forget it," he said. "I'm sorry Shane did that to you, because he left this morning for Amarillo."

She grabbed the wire that was stapled to the fence and clenched her fist. Unfortunately, it was barbed wire, and the rusty twist of metal bit deeply into her hand. She stifled another curse.

"Listen, Mr. Cooper," she said. "I've got a van full of kids and a ten o'clock appointment. I might be able to forget it, but these kids won't. They're expecting to ride horses this morning, and I'm *not* turning around."

"Well, shit." He heaved a heavy sigh. "Where are you?"

She described the view from the fence—a flat-topped mesa, a cluster of pine trees, a distinctive rock formation to her right.

"You missed it," he said. "You went too far."

"That's impossible," she said. "The only building we've seen was an old house with a crooked porch."

"Yeah, that's it," he said.

That's it?

A cold, sinking feeling gripped Sierra's heart and dropped it down into her stomach. That was *it*?

The guy had looked okay. Sure, he'd been dressed, um, casually, and that hat was downright disreputable, but she'd figured that was normal for a cowboy. He hadn't looked like he was homeless, but if that house was his, he'd be on the streets soon, because the next storm that came along would blow the place down.

Maybe Sheriff Swaggard was right about Ridge. Surely no decent man would live in a place that looked like the country version of an inner-city crack house.

She patted her pocket, where she'd put her little Nikon camera. Mike had ordered her to come here, despite her reservations. She'd be sure to take lots of pictures of that house. If she documented everything, she hopefully wouldn't be in too much trouble if one of the kids got hurt.

She got back in the van and made a careful K turn, scanning the road for traffic. You could see for miles, but this seemed like the kind of road where people would drive way too fast. She could see some James Dean–type testing a shiny, new sports car on the long, straight stretch, pushing ninety, ninety-five, a hundred…

She wished she could do that. Drive away from this place at a hundred miles per hour.

Anything rather than deal with this day.

Chapter 14

RIDGE CLUTCHED THE PICKUP'S STEERING WHEEL AS he bounced down the ranch drive, steering around the potholes and washouts right into the trap his brother had set for him.

He should have known Shane was up to something. Slipping out of the Phoenix House noose had been way too easy, and now he knew why. Shane hadn't had any intention of letting Ridge escape. He'd probably gotten on the horn the minute Ridge had walked away, calling Sierra and setting up this ambush.

He pulled to a stop at the end of the drive and peered down the long road to the left, wondering how the hell she'd missed the place. It wasn't like there were a whole lot of ranch roads off County Road 130. They always gave directions the same way, telling visitors the ranch was right after the cottonwood.

Shane probably should have mentioned the old homestead at the foot of the drive, because Sierra probably didn't know what a cottonwood was. And she probably couldn't take a van full of kids up the drive to the ranch either. It was a steep, pitted road that toiled up a rocky hill then dropped into the lush valley where the ranch sat against a snow-covered mountain backdrop. There hadn't been a lot of coming and going since Bill died, so the drive was so overgrown with weeds it was practically invisible. Further up, the ruts and washouts formed by last month's rain had hardened in the hot sun, making it tough to travel with anything less than four-wheel drive.

Rolling down the window, he dangled his arm against the side of the truck. He'd spent the morning working his way out of his own rut by shoveling out stalls, hosing down the barn floor, and disinfecting water buckets. He was dressed like a hobo, in torn jeans and shirt, and he could feel straw pricking at the back of his neck, which was damp with sweat.

Well, at least the kids would get to see what a true American cowboy's life was like. No Roy Rogers romance here. This was the real thing.

He wondered if Sierra knew enough to dress right for riding. She probably didn't own a pair of cowboy boots, and those high-heeled contraptions definitely wouldn't work. That was okay, though. Irene had taught riding for years, and Bill had taken over her students after she passed away. They'd always kept spare boots for the students. Ridge and his brothers had never moved them from the place Bill had left them, lined up against the wall just inside the front door.

Hopefully Sierra would have the sense to wear jeans, and not that skinny little skirt she'd had on the other day. It had been all right for playing chicken in the closet, though. More than all right...

Down, boy. He leaned back against the headrest and closed his eyes. He had to admit Shane was right; he needed something to do, something to occupy his mind. Maybe then his imagination wouldn't have spent most of last night and half of this morning giving him guided tours of Sierra Dunn. He'd shimmied her out of that leather jacket right at the start, and then he'd plucked at the memory of the tiny buttons that lined the front of that sexy top over and over. He'd speculated on the plumpness of her lips and the firmness of her breasts all night long.

He'd better rope those thoughts and hog-tie them in some dark place, or she'd see his fantasies flaming in his eyes every time he looked at her.

As he edged the truck forward, a cloud of dust in the distance resolved itself into a white van, the kind day cares and churches used. He could see Sierra's silhouette behind the wheel and the boys slouched in the seats behind her.

He waved them to a parking area in front of the old house. Easing the van carefully over the rocks and weeds, she lurched to a stop. Immediately, the side door of the van opened and a pile of kids tumbled out.

He expected them to run around, go nuts. Kids that age had a lot of energy, and he remembered feeling so pent up on long road trips that he'd wanted to take off running anywhere, tear off to the horizon, running for the sake of running.

But these kids just stood there in a little knot, looking around with wide, frightened eyes. Ridge's border collies leaped out of his truck bed and trotted up with their tails swishing in greeting, but the kids edged even closer together, eyeing the animals warily.

City kids. How could he have forgotten what it was like? They'd probably never seen dogs like his or the kind of wide-open spaces that surrounded them today. Heck, for all he knew, they'd never seen grass that didn't have to struggle up through cracks in the sidewalk.

Sierra was right. He might not want them here, but there was no way they could disappoint these kids. The boys didn't know it, but they needed this—a chance to breathe the fresh air and run free under the big sky. Moving from the city to the country could change a boy completely. Ridge knew that for a fact.

When the dogs started a flanking maneuver and got that determined look in their eye that was unique to herding dogs, Ridge flashed a hand signal and they obediently trotted to his side.

"These are the Tweedles," he said to the kids. "Tweedledum and Tweedledee."

"*Alice in Wonderland*." Josh shoved his glasses up his nose with that characteristic grimace. "Those are the little fat guys Alice meets." He eyed the dogs warily. "Your dogs aren't fat."

"They were when they were pups, and they'd always rather play than get things done. I call 'em Dum and Dee." Ridge knelt and ran his fingers through the coarse hair over Dum's shoulders. "You want to say hi?"

Josh tentatively reached a hand toward Dum, who leaped to greet him. The kid skittered backward.

"Ha!" said Isaiah. "You're scared of a stupid dog."

Ridge noticed the boy wasn't exactly eager to pet the dog himself.

"No I'm not." Josh tried again, and this time he didn't pull back when the dog reacted. He was rewarded with a slurp of the animal's pink tongue. Not to be outdone, Dee was soon jostling for a pat. The two dogs would have knocked the kid down if Ridge hadn't let out a sharp command that made them drop to an instantaneous down-stay.

It had a similar effect on Josh, who backed away and stood with the others.

"Sorry. They're just happy to see you." Ridge set his hands on his hips and surveyed the group, including Sierra. She had indeed worn jeans—tight, skinny-legged ones, with a white tank top that hugged her subtle curves.

A white tank top and jeans—the ultimate weapon against male resistance. He was going to *kill* Shane.

"Guys, this is Mr. Cooper."

"Ridge," he said.

She looked from the old homestead to him and then back again, flashing him a tentative smile. "Thanks for having us. We're excited to spend a day in the country. Right, guys?"

"Don't have a whole lot of choice," Isaiah mumbled. "Country's all there is around here."

She nudged him with her foot. Ridge was surprised to see that the foot was clad in a pointy-toed cowboy boot. It had a stacked heel that was a little too high and was embroidered with lots of fussy little flowers, but it would work for riding.

"Let's remember our manners," she said.

The kids murmured something that might have been a greeting and edged a little closer together, bunching like cattle surrounded by wolves.

"How is everybody?" Ridge figured he'd better remember his own manners.

The boys mumbled a little more and shifted their feet, glancing from side to side as if something might leap out from behind the crooked clumps of sagebrush and attack them.

He led them across the rocky yard, past the old house. Sierra was taking pictures like crazy. He wasn't surprised; tourists often stopped to photograph the place. Apparently folks found old rattletrap houses picturesque, and he supposed the old homestead did have historic significance. It had been the ranch's original claim shack back in the late 1800s. Subsequent generations had added on to it, but no one had lived in it since the seventies.

There was a lot of history around here, including some that Sierra needed to know.

"Did you know Phoenix House was a children's home once before?" he asked her.

She nodded. "The Wynott Home for Children. I heard it got shut down." She glanced at the boys then gave Ridge a significant look. "I heard why. It's not like that anymore."

He knew that. He could tell Sierra cared about the kids. But the woman who'd run the home before had made a good impression on the public too. It had taken some brave kids and a concerned citizen to uncover what had really been going on.

He shut down those thoughts and turned his attention back to the boys.

"Why don't you guys line up in front of the house for a group photo?" he suggested.

"Great idea!" Sierra was sure enthusiastic about picture taking. It was kind of nice that she cared enough to take them. He didn't have any pictures of himself at that age.

"Give me the camera," he said. "I'll take it, so you can get in the picture."

She whipped the camera away like it was made of

gold and he was a street thief. "No, no. Let's get *you* in it with them! You stand there, on the porch. Josh, you stand in front. Isaiah, you're taller, so get back there with Mr. Cooper. Perfect. Now smile!"

He stood behind the kids as ordered. He couldn't see their faces, but he'd bet his best boots not one of them cracked a smile.

Sierra needed to get out of here. She'd had plenty of pictures to prove that Mike had gotten her—and more importantly, the kids—into a dicey situation. The photos were made even more effective by the image of Ridge glowering from under his battered cowboy hat. He looked even more disreputable than he had the other day in the closet.

Unfortunately, disreputable worked for her. Though she'd been shocked by his appearance, she was having trouble behaving herself. He was wearing what was left of a worn denim shirt. The sleeves had been ripped off along with one of the breast pockets, and most of the buttons were missing—which meant she got a tantalizing glimpse of tight abs every once in a while.

The deep tan, the way his muscles swelled from the torn sleeves of his shirt... This was the American workingman at his best.

Focus on his face. Focus on his face.

His hat was the same one he'd worn the other day, only it looked like a couple of horses and maybe a buffalo had had a go at trampling it into the dirt. His jeans were completely blown out at the knees. As a matter of fact, he wasn't wearing one intact piece of clothing.

Unless his underwear…

Focus on his face.

No, focus on the *kids*. They were roaming around now, so she should probably get them back in the van and on the road. The place was a festival of potential puncture wounds. She looked down at the cut on her hand and noticed three nails protruding from the porch rail beside it. Plus there were those feral-looking dogs, who had scared up a couple of rodents that shot out of the shrubbery surrounding the house. She was pretty sure they'd been rabbits, but they could have been rats.

She glanced at Ridge, trying to figure out how to leave gracefully, but he was stroking one of the dogs and smiling, which made crow's-feet appear at the corners of his eyes. She felt her face warm in a slow, hot blush.

What was wrong with her? She was drooling over crow's-feet. Crow's-feet were wrinkles, for God's sake.

And the man seemed to like dogs better than people. He was kind to the boys, but he'd basically ignored her since that to-do in the closet.

He stood and walked the boys over to the truck. At a wave of his hand, the dogs leaped into the bed of the truck and sat, swishing their tails and grinning. Now that they'd stopped their endless running and circling, Sierra could see they were actually handsome animals, black-and-white mirror images of each other.

"Pile in," Ridge said.

"You want *us* to ride in the truck?" Isaiah asked. "Like the *dogs*?"

"Unless you want to walk," Ridge said. "No way that van's going to make it up the drive." He gestured toward a weed-choked two-track, which curved around a rock outcropping and disappeared into the hills.

"Wait a minute," Sierra said. "Where are you taking us?"

"To the ranch." He grinned. "You didn't think this was it, did you?"

"No, I—no," she lied. "Of course not."

"This was the original claim shack. The house is back there." He gestured toward the rutted road he'd come from. Great. He could take them back there and kill them and nobody would ever know.

"The road hasn't been graded in a while, and we had a hailstorm the other night, that washed it out in a few places," he said.

"Is there another way to go?"

"North entrance is easier, but it's about a half hour out of your way," he said.

Sierra considered a half hour stuck in the van with the kids and headed for the truck. He could kill her if he wanted.

"You can ride in the cab," Ridge said. "You boys, get in the back."

Carter didn't need to be invited twice. He vaulted up into the truck bed and stationed himself at the front, his elbows resting on the top of the cab.

"Come on, guys. This is cool."

Jeffrey had climbed halfway onto the tailgate when Sierra held up a hand to stop him.

"Come on, Sierra!" Frankie clambered into the bed of the truck. "It'll be fun!"

"We can't."

Ridge shot her a disbelieving look. "Don't tell me. No seat belts?"

"Exactly. It's not safe."

He scowled. "We're not going far."

She folded her arms over her chest and glared at him. "Ninety percent of accidents happen within a mile of home."

He muttered something unintelligible and turned away, leaving her to face the five hopeful boys in the back of the truck. They offered up their best pleading smiles, no doubt honed on adults far tougher than she'd ever been.

"All right," she said. "We'll go."

Chapter 15

SIERRA COULDN'T EVEN BEGIN TO LIST ALL THE reasons she should *not* be attracted to Ridge Cooper. His rusty pickup, for one. The fact that he lived in a place that couldn't be reached with a perfectly normal Econoline van, for another. And last but not least, his insistence that the boys—for whom she was responsible—pile into the back of his truck like a litter of puppies.

Because while she'd been scowling at him, the boys had done exactly that. Carter and Jeffrey sat on a couple of hay bales toward the front, while Josh and Isaiah perched precariously on the sides of the bed. They were grinning from ear to ear, happier than she'd ever seen them. But she couldn't help picturing them tumbling off and falling under the vehicle's wide wheels.

"Get *in* the truck, please," Sierra said. "No sitting on the side."

For once, they obeyed her without a single groan.

"Honestly," Ridge said with an exasperated grimace, "it's not far. Nobody's going to get hurt."

She went to the passenger-side door and stared down at a complicated construction of barbed wire that looped around the handle and connected to the side of a toolbox in the bed. She didn't want to go, but she wanted even less to see the boys' smiles fade to disappointment.

"Oh, sorry. It's probably easier to climb in from the driver's side."

Ridge opened the door as she came around and watched, expressionless, as she did her best to climb over the gearshift with grace and dignity. It was hard to be graceful and dignified with your butt in the air, though. Especially in tight jeans.

When he eased behind the wheel, Ridge turned and slid the cab's back window open. "Ready?" he called to the boys.

"Ready," they shouted in unison.

Maybe this would be a team-building exercise. The boys rarely agreed on anything, and here they were shouting in unison.

The pickup lurched into motion, rumbling steadily until it reached the hill, where it groaned like an old man heaving his way up a flight of steps. The gears clattered like old bones as Ridge shifted down, down, down, and finally motored up the incline at a thrilling five miles per hour.

It actually *was* kind of thrilling, because Ridge hadn't been kidding about the ruts. The truck lumbered over deep potholes and nearly high centered on the weedy strip that ran down the middle of the road. Sierra clutched the edge of the window as the cab rocked and rolled, eliciting happy shrieks from the boys in the back.

"Hang on." Ridge gunned the motor as they hit a curve, and Sierra slid across the seat until her shoulder hit his. The boys were laughing now, but she wasn't; she was floundering for the door handle so she could pull herself back to the passenger's side. The cab was canted at a forty-five degree angle, and her thigh was pressed against Ridge's, her hip against his. Her shoulder—wait.

His arm was around her shoulder.

No wonder she was having so much trouble climbing back to her side of the seat. And no wonder she felt all happy and warm inside.

This would never do.

—⁓—

Ridge felt Sierra stiffen in his grip then relax by increments. Did she think he was being affectionate?

Was she starting to think that was okay?

"Just wait," he said. "The next switchback goes the other way. Don't want you to hit your head."

The next turn was a hard left, and only his tight grip on her shoulder kept her from sliding across the vinyl seat and slamming into the door frame. She hardly seemed grateful, though. Now that they weren't scrabbling for the door handle, her hands were clenched primly in her lap.

He looked down and saw the cut and the blood.

"What happened to your hand?"

"Oh, nothing." She tried to cover it up.

"There are wipes in the glove compartment and a first aid kit with Band-Aids."

"You keep that kind of thing handy?"

He nodded. Maybe now she'd realize he was a responsible adult.

But instead, her eyes narrowed. "You get hurt a lot around here?"

He sighed. "It's a ranch. Barbed wire, horses, wood fence—what did you expect?"

"I expect to keep the kids safe."

"They'll be safe enough." This woman sure didn't like to take risks. She wanted guarantees on everything, which meant she sure as heck wouldn't like ranch life. Ranchers took risks every day. That was part of the fun of it.

As they rounded the turn, the ranch came into view—a big red barn, a white house, and a network of pastures and corrals that covered the shallow scoop of a valley. Barbed-wire fences bordered plots of hay-like stitches on a patchwork quilt.

He remembered the first time he'd come here, bouncing in the back of a pickup with his brothers, just like these boys today. He hadn't shrieked or laughed. He'd sat as stiffly as Sierra, staring at the brickred barn with yellow straw gleaming from the hay window up top. The house had glowed white against the hard blue sky, and the surrounding fields had been so green he and Shane and Brady had shielded their eyes with their hands in perfect unison, as if they were saluting the place. He'd felt like he was entering the pages of a storybook, though he'd known, as well as anyone, that life was nothing like a storybook.

The house's glory had faded a bit since those days; it needed a new coat of paint, for starters. But it still had that storybook look. The steps up to the wide front porch were flanked with lilac bushes and bordered with riotous gardens from which colorful mums and a few fading coneflowers peeked out. The windows—four on top and three on the bottom—were tall and narrow, decorated with graceful tie-back curtains.

Now that Bill was gone, the house belonged to Ridge and his two brothers. Since Brady had no interest in staying put and Shane had found a lucrative job running a nearby spread for one of the so-called "gentleman ranchers" that had invaded Wyoming lately, the place was his to run.

But he'd been given that gift for all the wrong reasons. He knew his brothers figured this was about all he could do, crippled as he was.

Worst of all, he knew they were right.

"This is nice."

Sierra sounded surprised. He should probably feel insulted, but he didn't have time. The moment he pulled the truck to a stop, the tailgate clanged open and boys and dogs spilled out.

Ridge climbed out of the cab then held out a hand to help Sierra slide across the seat. Shaking her head, she made her own way, lifting each foot past the gear shift and under the steering wheel. She sat a moment on the side of the driver's seat, legs dangling, and watched the boys. They were gaping like tourists, checking out the house and gazing openmouthed toward the barn, where a few graceful horses stood idling in a paddock behind a white-painted fence.

"It's beautiful, isn't it, guys?" She joined them, putting her arm around Frankie. "Like a hidden farm, a secret one, where nobody can see us or hear us."

The boys nodded gravely.

"Are we riding those?" Carter pointed at the horses.

"Once you learn everything you need to know," Ridge said.

"I already know how to ride," Isaiah said. "I did it before. The horse was black, and his name was Thunder. I rode him anywhere I wanted."

Ridge pictured a birthday party pony, plodding around in circles. "We'll still go over safety stuff."

"That's for babies," Isaiah scoffed. "Thought you were a rodeo cowboy."

"I am."

"Well, *that's* not safe."

"It is when you know how."

Turning away, Ridge put his fingers to his lips and gave a long, high whistle. That seemed to interest the kids more than anything they'd seen so far, and they were so busy trying to imitate him, they didn't notice an ancient paint horse rounding the corner of the house at about two miles per hour.

Except for Josh. Josh noticed everything. "He comes like a dog!"

"Yup." Ridge scratched the old horse up under his mane, just the way he liked it. "This is old Sluefoot, the first horse I ever had," he told the boys. "Ain't he purty?"

The old horse cocked his head and gave them the eye. Like many white-faced horses, he'd developed eye problems in old age. He could see okay with the left, but his blind right eye made him hold his head at a peculiar angle, so he seemed to be leering knowingly. He'd had a stroke a couple years back too, and though he'd recovered pretty well, it had weakened the muscles on one side of his face. When he cocked his head to see out of his good eye, his tongue tended to flop out of his mouth. Ridge was so used to the old horse's peculiarities, it didn't faze him, but newcomers were sometimes a little taken aback.

"Look at that old horse," Isaiah said. "I bet you'd all be scared to ride that one."

Ridge had to admit Sluefoot wasn't looking his best. His mane and tail had grown long, and looked as dry and tangled as the before photo in a hair care ad. He was munching contemplatively on a mouthful of yellow weeds that stuck out of his mouth on both sides, giving him an oversized walrus moustache that matched his mane.

"That is one ugly horse," Frankie said. "Hey, Isaiah, it looks like your mother!"

"Holy crap. What's *wrong* with him?" one of the kids burst out. It was the big, blond kid. He'd make a good running back for Grigsby High's junior varsity someday if he did some ranch work and toughened up.

"He's just old." Ridge couldn't help feeling a little defensive. Sluefoot had been handsome once. His breeding was questionable, but he'd been a well-trained cow horse with a lot of flash. He'd won the brothers a slew of high school rodeo prizes, but most important, he'd been Ridge's teacher in all things equine. They'd grown up together, and he loved the old gelding dang near as much as he loved his brothers.

"There's nothing really wrong with him," he told the kids. "He's blind in that right eye, but he's gotten used to it and gets around okay. His hocks are spavined, and you can see his back's swayed, but that's just old age. He's got some arthritis, and he had a stroke. But he's fine."

The kid smothered a giggle, but Sierra wasn't so subtle. She burst into her lilting laughter.

"Yeah, he's fine." She struggled to catch her breath. "Ready for the races, right?"

So she was going to make fun of his horse. Well, Sluefoot wouldn't know the difference. Ridge had noticed over the past few months that the old horse was becoming increasingly deaf. Anything less than that high whistle seemed to pass right through him. But he ate all right, and he still nuzzled Ridge's pockets for treats at every opportunity.

In fact, right now he was trying to sniff the kids' pants in a hunt for treats. When he reached Sierra, she tried to set an example for the kids by gingerly petting his nose, which only encouraged him. As she stepped away, he reached over and nipped one of her back pockets.

With a little screech, she jumped back and waved the horse away while the kids laughed.

"See?" Ridge stroked the horse's neck. "He's fine. Nothing wrong with his instincts."

"So are we gonna ride *that*?" Isaiah didn't even bother to pretend he wasn't afraid of Sluefoot.

"No, nobody's riding Sluefoot," Ridge said. "He retired a long time ago."

Jeffrey was already halfway to the barn, his gaze fixed on the small corral where Ridge had released Moonpie that morning.

"Jeffrey," Sierra called. "Stay with the group."

The boy turned to Ridge, wide-eyed. "Can I ride that one?"

Sierra grabbed Ridge's arm. With both hands.

"Please say yes." She clung to him, her eyes pleading and wet with tears. "He hasn't said a word for almost two weeks. He just stopped talking. I don't know why. And he never asks for anything." She shook his arm then seemed to realize what she was doing and dropped it. "Please say it's okay."

Ridge shook his head. "I'm sorry." He raised his voice to reach Jeffrey. "I can't even ride that one. Not yet. He's wild as a cougar and twice as mean."

"Wild?" Jeffrey asked.

Ridge nodded. Jeffrey's gaze was fixed on the horse. Ridge doubted he saw anything else—the house, the barn, the beautiful late autumn day. All the boy could see was the way the sun caught the buckskin's yellow coat and turned it to gold as the horse trotted up and down the fence, up and down. The horse did that all day, no doubt missing his freedom.

Ridge sympathized. He knew what it was like to be fenced in when you were used to traveling with a herd.

"Yeah, he's wild," he told Jeffrey. "He needs to learn to be a ranch horse, but he's got a long way to go."

Chapter 16

Sierra had been as horrified as anyone when Sluefoot appeared, but even though she'd laughed at Ridge's summation of the animal's health, she couldn't help being touched by the obvious affection between the man and his old horse. As they talked, Sluefoot shoved his long, homely face against Ridge's chest. The cowboy staggered slightly under the weight of the animal's affection, but he smiled tenderly while he scratched the old horse's neck. Between that and Jeffrey finally talking, she had a lump in her throat that ached so hard it made her eyes water.

Oblivious to his own charm, the cowboy was herding the kids toward the house with the help of Dum and Dee.

"We've got boots in every size up here," he said. "Try on a few and see if you can find something that fits."

When Sierra stepped into the house, she felt like she was stepping back in time to the Old West. The wooden floors, scarred by many bootheels, had mellowed to a rich honey color. The hallway was papered in a yellowed but surprisingly feminine ribbons-and-flowers design, in total contrast to the rough canvas jackets, leather horse tack, and cowboy hats hanging on the hooks by the door. Below was a row of boots, ranging in size from he-man to toddler. As the boys fell on the footwear like women at a shoe sale, Sierra's stomach clenched.

"You have kids?"

Of course he did. He was probably married. Why hadn't that possibility occurred to her before? Why had she assumed he was single? Sure, he'd acted single in the closet. But her mother would have assured her that lots of married men acted like that.

"No. Irene and Bill used to teach riding lessons," he said. "They always picked up boots at thrift stores, so the kids' parents wouldn't have to spend the money."

"Oh." She couldn't help heaving a sigh of relief. It would have been awkward, that was all, what with all the accidental caressing and calf fondling in the closet the other day...

She shut down that train of thought. This was all about the boys.

Besides, the last thing she wanted was a relationship. The state had sent these boys out here to the boondocks partly so they wouldn't run away, but the truth was, she sometimes felt like she was the one who'd run away from home. Out here in the country, she didn't have to worry about anything but her work—and maybe her growing affection for Ridge. Sure, she was responsible for the boys, but there were other things—things that drained her—that she'd managed to leave far behind.

A quick stab of guilt pierced her chest. She'd just shrugged it off when her cell phone rang. She glanced down at the screen.

Speaking of things that drained her...

—◊◊◊—

Ridge just about jumped out of his skin when the pounding beat of a Led Zeppelin song suddenly filled the hallway. "Sorry. Gotta get this." Sierra snatched up her phone and clicked it on.

"Hello?" Her eyes widened. "Riley! Oh my gosh! Where *are* you?"

She spun away from him, hunching her shoulders as if to protect the phone. Despite her lowered voice, he caught a few urgent words. It sounded like she was worried about the person she was talking to.

She walked out, still hunched over the phone, and the screen door slammed behind her. He shoved his hands in his pockets and rocked on his toes, trying not to feel dismissed. He watched the boys fight over a pair of flashy black Noconas and make fun of a pair of pink girls' Justins that unfortunately turned out to be the only pair that fit Jeffrey.

Once every kid was matched to a pair of boots, he opened the screen door and gave Sierra a questioning look. She was leaning against the house, her shoulders still rounded, her posture tense.

"I can't talk right now, hon," she said to the caller. "I have to go, okay?"

Whoever was on the other end of the line apparently was not okay. Sierra straightened and cast him an apologetic look as a faint voice squawked from the phone.

"Of course I'm glad you're back! I'm just busy right now," she said. "But I'll talk to you soon. Bye." Abruptly, she clicked the phone off and shoved it back in her pocket.

Riley must not be a kid. Judging from how Sierra dealt with the boys, he doubted she'd hang up on a child.

"Trouble?" he asked.

She shook her head, but judging from her expression all was not running smoothly in Sierra land.

"Who's Riley?" It wasn't any of his business, but she seemed really upset.

"A—a friend." She knelt to check the boys' boots, pressing toes to make sure they fit then shooing them out to the porch. "I'm fine," she told Ridge. "And I'm sorry. That was rude."

He shrugged. "Gotta do what you gotta do."

"I guess." She sighed. "It's my day for phone calls."

Normally he would have grunted and changed the subject, but for some reason, he hated to see Sierra so down. That laughter, that smile—he wanted them back. "What do you mean? Something wrong?"

She shook her head. "Most people would say everything was right." She stood and leaned against the wall. "I got a job offer yesterday. A job I applied for months ago opened up again. I guess the person they chose didn't work out, so now it's mine."

As she said the last words, she looked straight into his eyes. He could swear he felt the floor shift under his feet. What was that all about? It wouldn't make any difference to him if Sierra went away. He hadn't even expected to see her again. It was all Shane's fault that she'd turned up at the ranch, messing up his mind with her tousled hair and pretty eyes.

Resting one hand on the wall for balance, he returned her gaze. Half a dozen emotions flickered through her green eyes in the space of a few seconds.

"Are you going to take it?" he asked.

She smiled, staring down at the floor. "Of course I am. It's a state job, in Colorado. I'd be setting policy for every foster child in the state, instead of taking care of just five. I'd be a fool not to take it."

"But…"

"But I don't want to." She looked up and he saw a single teardrop balanced on her lashes. "I love these kids, you know?"

"Then stay."

He couldn't believe he'd said that. He should be glad she was leaving. He didn't want her to stay. Adjusting to his new life was hard enough without her and her little band of brothers turning up every time he turned around.

"It's not that simple," she said. "There's money, for one thing. I can barely afford to live here. And my career—this would be a huge leap."

"But would you be happy?"

"I don't know." She looked thoughtful for a moment, but then a wide smile spread across her face. She nudged him in the ribs with one very pointy elbow. "Since when are you Dr. Phil, anyway?"

"Since never," he said. "Don't take my advice. You see where it got me."

He held up his hand for evidence, but they'd just stepped out the front door, and she wasn't looking at him. Instead, she was looking at the landscape surrounding the house—the long stretch of yellow prairie, the blue bowl of the sky overhead, and the sharp angles of the red barn standing in bold, sunny relief against the distant mountains.

"Seems to me you did all right," she said.

He stood with her for a minute, taking it all in, seeing it through her eyes. He needed to do that more often—take the time to appreciate what he had.

"Hey! Let's get this show on the road!"

Isaiah wasn't about to let anyone waste time in contemplation.

"You guys ready to ride?" Ridge asked.

"Yeah!"

Maybe the boots made the boys feel more at ease. They raced out to the corral ahead of Ridge and Sierra, and as the morning wore on, they started to relax. Most of them did well with the horses, though it was clear some of them were frightened—especially Isaiah. Ridge pretended not to notice and did what he could to make their experiences positive.

The last rider was Jeffrey—the boy who wanted to ride Moonpie. Like the others, he sat stiffly in the saddle, gripping the reins too tightly, holding them too high.

Usually, it was fear of the horse that made the boys tense. But Ridge sensed something different in Jeffrey. He'd flinched when Ridge boosted him up and again when he touched him to adjust his position. Once Ridge stepped away, the boy's hands lowered and the furrows in his brow smoothed out.

After a walk around the corral, Ridge unclipped the lead rope and stepped into the center of the ring, letting the boy ride on his own. It took Jeffrey a while to notice, but when he did, he grabbed the saddle horn and turned to stare at Ridge, eyes wide.

"I didn't get to do that," Isaiah complained.

"You talk a lot." Ridge was careful to state it as a fact, without judgment. "Horses like quiet people."

"Well, they oughta love old Jeffrey, then. He never says a word."

"Then he'll probably be good at this." Ridge turned to Jeffrey, who had paused to stroke the horse's neck.

"You can do that after, Jeff. Right now it's heels down, toes out, eyes ahead. Now tell him to walk."

The boy sat up and made the kissing sound Ridge had taught them. Faithful old Dusty eased back into the weary walk of the lifelong lesson horse.

"Speed him up," Ridge said. "A little nudge with your heels."

Dusty's acceleration into a gentle jog threw Jeffrey backward in the saddle, and he clutched the horn for a moment before he caught himself and straightened up. Once he caught on to the rhythm, he rode with a dignity that reminded Ridge of pictures he'd seen of Indian riders in the old days. The breeze from the horse's brisk gait swept back the tail of the boy's shirt, and as he lifted his face to the wind, a slow smile spread across his face.

At the fence rail, Sierra put a hand to her chest and closed her eyes as if struck with a sudden pain.

Ridge crossed the soft dirt to stand beside her. "You okay?"

She struck her chest with her fist and opened eyes wet with tears. "He never smiles," she said. "Never. You've given him something—something so *good*." She turned to him with a trembling, heartfelt smile of her own. "Thank you. Thank you so much."

Ridge grunted and took a step away so she wouldn't hug him or anything. Shelley would say he was being emotionally unavailable.

Shelley was probably right.

He watched Jeffrey, only Jeffrey, but he could feel Sierra staring at him. Staring *through* him.

"You understand, don't you?" she said. "You *get* these kids."

Just then, Jeffrey rose in the stirrups, making the horse swing into a smooth, steady lope. The boy leaned into the breeze created by the horse's movement, his face a study in rapture.

Ridge *got* him all right. He knew exactly what the boy was feeling—freedom and a sense of power, the feeling of being in control of some larger force as you were carried into the future. These kids had been moved from one home to another, their lives in constant flux. The feeling of control was a rare and precious thing.

Sierra stepped away to settle some dispute between the other boys, and Ridge walked back to the center of the ring. As Jeffrey circled him, running clockwise in the sunlight, dust rose around them and time seemed to spin backward. Ridge turned, keeping the boy in view, then staggered a second, dizzied. When he caught his footing, something shifted and suddenly he was Bill, all those years ago, and the boy on the horse...

The boy on the horse was him.

As Jeffrey rocked with the motion of the running horse, Ridge could feel the bond forming, boy to horse to man. Generations of men taught generations of boys how to form the unspoken connection between horses and humans in this spinning, timeless circle. It was secret knowledge, shared in dusty riding rings like this one all over the West. Not everyone could learn it, but those who did held the key to true partnership with another species. That was where cowboys came from—real cowboys.

Through the dust, he saw Sierra approaching the fence and had to shake his head to wake back into the everyday world—back to the dull ache in his arm, the doubts and fears that had plagued him since his accident.

But when he flexed his fingers, they weren't as stiff as before. The pain was somehow lessened—or at least different. It didn't feel like the end of the world anymore.

"The natives are getting restless," Sierra said. "And thirsty."

"There's lemonade." Ridge thought about telling her he'd stay out here with Jeffrey, but that wouldn't be fair to the others.

"Know how to stop?" he asked the boy.

"Whoa!" Jeffrey pulled the reins back and the horse walked a few beats then stopped. The boy leaned over and stroked the horse's neck before reluctantly dismounting.

"His name?" he asked. His voice was rough from disuse.

Ridge didn't dare look at Sierra. "Dusty."

Jeffrey put his arms around the horse's neck and rested his cheek against the sun-warmed pelt. It was a picture Ridge had seen at a hundred junior rodeos, a boy thanking a horse for a good ride, a smooth catch, a quick run 'round the barrels.

"Thanks, Dusty."

His face still shining with happiness, the kid handed the reins over to Ridge. Beside him, Sierra drew a shaky breath. As Jeffrey walked away, she put her hand on Ridge's arm.

"You have no idea what just happened, do you?"

Shoving his hands in his pockets, Ridge rocked back on his heels. "He did pretty well."

"Pretty well? Ridge, he hugged the horse. *Hugged* it." A tear formed at the corner of her eye and traced a slow path down her cheek. "He's never shown affection. He barely speaks. Never smiles. That was a miracle."

Wrapping her other hand around his arm, she rested her forehead against his shoulder. "Thank you."

He stood perfectly still, wondering what he was supposed to do now. A lump formed in his throat, a lump that ached for her, for Jeffrey, and for his old self, the boy who'd had his life forever changed by an old man and a horse.

He brought one arm around her, slowly, cautiously, and stroked her hair, just once. Okay, twice.

No matter what he did, this woman and her little band of misfits forced him to feel something he hadn't felt in a long time. Something that made his throat ache and his heart warm. Something that made his own problems seem petty and small.

It was probably just as well she was going away. Otherwise, his life was about to get way too complicated.

Chapter 17

THE SUNLIGHT SLANTING THROUGH THE PORCH railings cast wavy blue shadows over Josh's and Carter's legs. The boys were sitting against the wall of the house while Isaiah and Frankie shared the porch swing. Jeffrey stood at the railing, staring across the yard at the horses.

"You said you had lemonade?" Sierra asked. She was seated in Irene's old rocking chair, looking as natural there as if she owned the place.

"Yeah." Ridge started to rise, but she motioned for him to stay. "I'm sure the boys have questions about cowboy stuff for you, right, guys?" She set her hands on the arms of the chair. "I'll find my way to the kitchen."

Irene's old chair rocked gently in her wake, slowing and finally stopping. A mourning dove cooed its spooky hoot from the slender branches of an aspen tree that shaded the far side of the porch. The faint breeze set the tree's round leaves to shimmering like sequins.

"What's it like to live here?" Josh asked.

"It's good." Ridge wondered why he couldn't put his feelings into words. He could hardly tell these boys the ranch was magical or healing. The broad plains, the scent of sage, the open sky—the world he lived in made him whole. But how could he explain that to a bunch of kids? "It's really good."

"Isn't it weird, being out here all alone?" Frankie

asked. "With that weird horse around?" He shuddered dramatically. "I couldn't sleep with old Sluefoot out there. That thing gives me the creeps."

"Sluefoot's not a *thing*." Josh's brows lowered behind his glasses. "And he can't help it he looks weird." He started counting on his fingers. "He has eye cancer, and his hicks are spavined, and he had a stroke, and..." He looked at Ridge for help.

"That covers most of it," Ridge said. "Good job. But as far as being alone, my brothers are here a lot. Trust me, it's never dull. I've got the horses to keep me busy."

He launched into an explanation of ranching duties so long-winded it surprised him. He told them how he got up when the world was hushed, how everything was muted blues and grays until the sun came up. How birds started singing, the different kinds chiming in one by one as the sun rose and the colors came alive, golden, russet, and green.

He explained each horse's feeding regimen, how Sluefoot needed special nutrition for his various health problems and Moonpie needed performance feed.

"Is that the big yellow horse?" Isaiah asked.

Ridge was about to explain the horse was a buckskin when Jeffrey interrupted.

"He's not yellow," the boy said. "He's *golden*."

Ridge decided to forgo a lesson on color terms and let the description stand. There was no reason to get technical.

He explained how it felt when a young horse joined up for the first time and started following you around the ring. He talked about floating teeth and trimming hooves and wondered how long the boys would sit still, enraptured by what was, to him, an everyday routine. Maybe life after rodeo wasn't so dull after all. They peppered him with questions about what horses did and why, and of course Isaiah wanted to know if they ever fought and if that yellow horse could lick the brown one. Jeffrey gave him a scornful sideways glance that showed he knew the answer.

When Ridge started talking about training, about how he'd teach Moonpie to be a ranch horse, the questions came faster than he could answer them.

"Maybe you guys could come out and help sometime," he said.

Jeffrey straightened instantly. "When?"

Ridge realized he might have promised too much. "We'll have to see. It's up to Sierra."

Jeffrey drooped like a wilting flower and kicked at the air. "Oh."

Ridge's heart ached for the boy. He knew what it was like to find a bright spot in your life only to have it extinguished as quickly as it appeared. It had happened in his own childhood, over and over. And from what Sierra had said, and the hints he'd seen in the boy's behavior, Jeffrey's life had been darker than most.

"We'll try, okay?"

The boy looked away and the ache in Ridge's chest tightened and grew. What would happen to Jeffrey, growing up alone? Sure, there were people like Sierra, and there were the other boys. But there was no one who belonged to him, no one who would ruffle his hair or give him a playful punch on the arm once in a while.

A boy needed a father—someone he could depend on, someone who helped him along and listened to him and understood who he was. Someone who helped him become a man.

He remembered the circle, the flowing spiral of dust in the riding ring with the boy and the horse at its heart, and he knew it was time to pay back an old, old debt to the man who'd done that for him.

———

When Sierra walked into the kitchen, she couldn't help letting out a little exclamation of pleasure. Sunshine slanted from a wide window over the sink, glossing the old-fashioned butcher-block counters and splashing the white linoleum floor. The cabinets were painted with shiny white enamel, and their chrome handles echoed the polished faucet of the old porcelain sink. A red tin canister set, decorated with tacky but charming roosters, sat against the backsplash.

Thankfully, the refrigerator was the one thing in the room that had been updated since the sixties, and there was plenty of ice. She found some old glasses decorated with Flintstones characters in one of the cupboards. As she scooped up the ice and plinked it into the glasses, she almost enjoyed the frigid bite on her fingers. The phone call had left her feeling like she deserved it.

Riley was the only thing she worried about more than her job. As an academically successful senior, Sierra had been matched with Riley, who was considered an "at risk" seventh grader at the time, in a program that was supposed to help failing students. The plan was to reduce problems like teen pregnancy, drug abuse, and smoking through mentoring.

Riley had managed to dodge the pregnancy bullet,

but she'd worked her way through the rest of the menu and ordered every entrée. Despite all Sierra's efforts, her "little sister" had sunk into a downward spiral that gathered speed as time passed, like water spinning down a drain.

Riley had been forced to move back with her mother in Denver over a year ago. Her mother hated Sierra for "interfering" in their lives, so the connection between the two girls snapped. But Sierra still woke some nights at 3:00 a.m., expecting an emergency phone call.

Now Riley was homeless and jobless—and back in Sierra's life.

She shut the phone call out of her mind and gazed around the old-fashioned kitchen, taking solace in its homey warmth. A photo hanging by the door caught her eye and she moved in for a closer look.

It was a picture of a family, posed in front of the old house at the foot of the drive. An older man stood on the top step with a sturdy but attractive dark-haired woman. The man's broad-brimmed cowboy hat and sharp-toed boots were as much a part of him as his erect posture and strong jaw. The woman was plump and motherly, with her hair spilling from a carelessly constructed bun. From the way they stood, it was obvious they were husband and wife.

One step down stood three boys, all of them look-ing at the camera with sulky, hostile expressions. Sierra suspected someone had told them to smile and they were doing their best to disobey. They wore cowboy hats, western shirts, jeans, and boots, but the clothes fit poorly and the kids looked uncomfortable, as if they were wearing costumes.

At their feet were two border collies much like the ones that had ridden in the truck, but of course they couldn't be the same dogs. The photo had the faded brightness of Kodachrome—the grass too yellow, the sky too blue, the subjects' skin an unreal peachy color.

She squinted at the boys' faces. She was pretty sure one of them was Ridge. Unlike the rest of them, he wasn't looking into the camera. He was looking off to the side, as if working out an escape route. She didn't think anyone would have guessed the sulky kid in the photo would someday fill a doorway with his broad shoulders or wear a cowboy hat with the same ease as his dad.

The other boys must be the brothers he'd mentioned, and the man and woman his parents. His folks looked like a nice couple, with the open-faced honesty she'd noticed in some of the other people in Wynott.

But the boys looked miserable. There must have been some kind of trouble in their childhoods. You could tell the couple was a unit, but the boys seemed separate somehow. She wondered what had happened to divide them at such a young age.

There was something familiar about the picture, something that struck a chord in the back of her mind. Finally, she took her camera out of her back pocket and hit the review button.

The last picture she'd taken popped onto the screen— the group photo of Ridge and the boys. It was the same pose, and the parallels were almost eerie. Ridge stood on the top step, wearing the same easygoing smile as his father wore in the old photo. The boys stood below him, wearing expressions almost identical to Ridge and his brothers.

The only thing missing was the woman.

Sierra suddenly regretted her refusal of Ridge's suggestion that they all get in the photo. It would be nice to have a picture just like this—her and the boys, even the cowboy. Since Jeffrey had spoken, she was willing to forgive Ridge his surliness.

Switching her camera over to picture-taking mode, she focused in on the framed photo and pressed the shutter.

"You coming with that lemonade?"

She whirled to see Ridge standing in the doorway, backlit by the sun-washed fields. Knowing something about the boy he'd been made her feel different about the man, and she was starting to understand why he was so good with the kids. He wasn't good with women, that was for sure, but as she looked at the old photograph, something warm seeped into her heart and nested there, curling up and settling in to stay. Friendship, she told herself. Maybe fondness.

She flashed him a smile. "I'm on my way."

He stepped into the kitchen, and she took a step backward. The room wasn't very big, just a narrow galley with the oven on one side and the sink and refrigerator on the other.

"Why are you taking pictures in here?"

She shoved the camera in her back pocket and backed away another step, feeling like a cornered animal, and pointed to the photo. "I was just noticing how much this picture looks like the ones we just took of you and the boys."

"Uh-huh." He was the one who looked cornered now, as he glanced around the room in a desperate search for something—probably a way to change the subject.

"What's your story?" She nodded toward the picture. "I've seen that expression on the faces of a hundred boys, Ridge. You don't get it from riding horses."

He turned and those pale eyes stared out from under the brim of his hat. They were suddenly hard, his gaze sharp. She felt as if she was pinned to the wall.

"What about you?" he asked. "Why is that your family out there? Why don't you have kids of your own?"

"That's not really your business." She laughed nervously. "Okay. Point taken."

And it was. She wouldn't ask about his past again.

But she'd find out about it somehow.

Chapter 18

ONCE THE BOYS HAD GULPED THEIR LEMONADE AND helped Ridge put away the horses, Ridge hauled them back down to the van in the pickup. Sierra sat beside him, staring out the side window. He'd done it again, ruined what felt like a budding friendship by being rude and defensive.

Why did he feel he had to defend himself against Sierra? She was a nice girl. She clearly cared about people. If she chose to give her life to these boys rather than marrying some jerk and having her own, it wasn't his business.

But he couldn't help resenting her plan to take that new job, to leave Wynott for good. It didn't matter to him, of course. But she'd break the boys' hearts. They were used to that kind of thing, but being used to having your heart broken didn't make it any easier, and they clearly loved Sierra.

Fortunately, it was all about the boys again when they got to the van, so he didn't have to talk to her or even look at her. As the vehicle rolled slowly out of the rutted drive, small hands waved from every window, making the vehicle look like some sort of slow-moving insect with wildly waving antennae.

Sierra didn't wave, and he could understand why.

He might have screwed up with her, but he'd been able to make a bunch of boys happy today. Isaiah had loved being out in the sunshine and having more space to boss people around. Carter and Frankie had made no effort to hide their joy, and Josh's smile and his shy "thank you" had been heartfelt and sweet.

And Jeffrey? Sierra seemed to think the kid had had some kind of breakthrough, and Ridge agreed. He'd seen the flash of triumph and understanding he'd experienced himself the first time he'd ridden a horse. It had been the defining moment of his life, the moment he moved from lost to found.

Since his injury had made rodeo an impossibility, he'd felt lost all over again—but watching Jeffrey, he thought he just might have found a new purpose.

He didn't have to worry about making a living. His rodeo winnings would pay for a full makeover on the ranch house, and horse training would pay the bills when that ran out. The problem was finding something to do, something that mattered. Helping kids like the ones he'd worked with today could be just what he needed.

Heading back into the house, he glanced down at the boots that were lined up, largest to smallest, beside the front door. Last in line was a pair of black Converse sneakers, sitting neatly in the spot where Jeffrey's pink girls' boots should have been.

Ridge smiled. Jeffrey might not talk much, but the fact he'd worn those boots home spoke volumes.

He rinsed glasses and cleaned counters while images from the day flickered through his mind. Out of habit, he got a glass out of the cupboard when he was done and reached for the bottle of Jack on top of the refrigerator. Taking a handful of ice from the freezer, he clinked it into the glass then let a stream of amber liquid glug from the bottle.

He anticipated the bite of the alcohol, the slow burn down his gullet that would coil in his stomach and spread warmth through his veins—warmth and a dull, slow feeling that was as close to contentment as he could find these days. When he lifted the glass to his lips, the sharp, medicinal scent seemed to slow his senses before he even took a sip. Pausing, he swirled the ice in the glass. Over the past few weeks, drinking had been the only thing that came close to filling the empty space inside him.

But the emptiness was gone, at least for a while. The boys' rambunctious arguments had brought back memories of him and his brothers, and Sierra's gentle tones had reminded him of Irene's voice as she'd gentled their high spirits. He'd half expected to hear Bill come in from the barn, stamping the mud off his boots. That had been the signal for him and his brothers to hush. The petty arguments would stop and they'd gather around the table, right-minded and respectful, to discuss the day's work. Bill had treated them like men even when they didn't deserve it, and they'd all done their best to live up to his high opinion.

The old man had made all three of them believe in themselves and taught them there was nothing they couldn't do if they worked hard enough. And he'd done it without a word of lecturing or a hint of preaching. He'd simply shown them, day after day, how a good man lived his life.

They'd all wanted to be like him, but Ridge knew he had a ways to go yet. His injury was a problem, sure, but he was sulking over it like a kid who'd been denied his shiny toys. With no buckles to wear, no trophies to show, he didn't know how to live a life that mattered.

He knew Bill had never won any kind of trophy. He'd simply lived his life with a clear eye and a kind heart. Ridge was starting to see that living like that and never wavering—and finding a way to pass on that wisdom—might be a harder task than riding the rankest bronc that ever hit the chutes.

Striding into his bedroom, he grabbed the old composition book and carried it into the kitchen along with a stubby pencil. As always, it flipped open to his list of goals, his planned route to the championship.

But for the first time in a long time, he turned the page. Tapping his pencil on the table, he decided to stick to the same format. With its dates and specific goals, that list had told him exactly what he needed to accomplish and when.

1., he wrote.

And that was it.

The excitement drained out of him as fast as it had built up. He didn't have any idea how to do this. Who did he talk to? Where did he sign up to change his life? Kicking a random boot aside—one of Brady's, probably—he gazed around the chaotic room. Bill had always kept it orderly. *A place for everything, and everything in its place*. Ridge had groaned at that phrase throughout his teens, but the old man had a point.

Clean house, he wrote.

It would be a start.

He glanced at the feed company calendar that hung crookedly by the door. It was September third. At three days per room, the cleaning would take three weeks. Add an extra day or two for tough spots like the kitchen and Brady's room, and the goal would be accomplished by the 26th. He put that date by step one.

2., he wrote.

What the hell was step two? What he wanted to do wasn't easy. There would be rules, regulations, and red tape to sort through. There would be complications, and he needed a guide.

He only knew one person who understood the state bureaucracy that held kids in foster care.

2. Talk to Sierra.

She'd know what to do next. No doubt there would be complications, lots of bureaucratic barriers to leap and rivers of red tape to cross.

Since he didn't know what else was involved in the process, he left steps three through six blank. That ought to be enough. He wrote the number seven and felt a surge of excitement. No, not excitement. Just a feeling of rightness, as if he'd finally found his purpose.

7. Adopt first foster son.

There. A clear goal, the start of his new life. He knew what he wanted, what was right for him and for the ranch.

He also knew which boy needed him most and which one had caught his heart. But you couldn't pick out boys like you chose a puppy, could you?

Well, you had to pick them somehow. And instinct seemed like the way to go.

After *Adopt first foster son*, he wrote *(Jeff)*.

He read through the list one more time. It felt good to have a goal again, and if he knew one thing about himself, it was that he made every goal he'd ever set his sights on—until his body failed him.

He looked down at his damaged hand, bending the fingers reflexively. For once it didn't bother him that they wouldn't clench into a fist. He wouldn't need his hands for this project. He wouldn't have to grip a rein or rope a calf. All he needed was a strong heart, and he didn't think anything could take that away from him.

Returning to his task, he picked up the pencil that had rolled off the table and wrote in capital letters across the top of the page:

Plan B.

———

Sierra slouched in her desk chair, giving herself a few minutes to recover from the day. Thank goodness for the night shift. Pat Morgan, an older woman who worked days as a cafeteria lady at the school in Grigsby, had already arrived to take over the reins and was watching *SpongeBob SquarePants* in the dayroom with the boys. She and Gil's wife, Jessie, who was Phoenix House's cook, were taking care of dinner and bedtime, so Sierra headed upstairs to her tiny apartment on the top floor. It was a relief and a luxury to leave behind the sound of SpongeBob's annoying laughter and relax.

Unlocking her apartment door, she stepped into the bare-bones sanctuary she'd created out of two rooms at the top of the house. The rooms weren't air-conditioned, so they were sweltering on hot days. But from the two gabled windows at either end, she could see anyone who arrived at the house. It was like the crow's nest on a ship—she could spot trouble a mile away.

She tried to eat downstairs with the boys most nights to give them a sense of family, but she needed to eat out tonight. A girl needed to have a life of her own—although having a life was a challenge in a town like Wynott.

If she couldn't have a life, she could at least have a Red Dawg burger. But first she needed to call Riley back. Her stomach had been clenched like a fist ever since they'd talked.

Grabbing her purse, she fished for the phone then remembered she'd shoved it in her back pocket at the ranch. Slapping her backside, she flinched.

No phone.

She checked the other pocket then rummaged in her purse again.

Still no phone.

A picture flashed in her mind: Ridge, showing the boys how to care for the horses. Tapping Sluefoot on the leg so the horse obediently picked up his foot. He'd talked about the tender center of a horse's foot, called the frog. The boys had laughed about Sluefoot having frogs in his feet until Ridge scowled them into serious-ness and showed them how to clean the animal's foot with a hoof-pick. She'd bent over to see, and her phone had almost fallen out of her pocket. She'd set it on the edge of the stall for safekeeping.

It was safe, all right. As a matter of fact, it was *still there*.

Darn it, Riley was probably trying over and over to call her, which meant her rock 'n' roll ringtone was en-tertaining all the horses in the barn. Ridge had told them Moonpie went ballistic around loud noises. He'd told them how the horse kicked down his stall door the first night he had him just because Shane called him in to dinner. It had taken Ridge and Brady three hours to get the horse to calm down.

Somehow, Sierra doubted Moonpie was a Led Zeppelin fan.

Should she call Ridge on the landline and let him know the phone was there?

She remembered the look in his eyes when he'd asked her why she didn't have a family of her own. She didn't know why he'd lashed out, but it was obvious he was trying to keep her from bridging the gap between his private life and the rest of the world.

She'd just as soon respect his wishes. Her own car, a little Jeep Liberty, wouldn't have any trouble making it up the ranch road. If she was lucky, she'd be able to dodge into the barn, grab her phone, and go.

With any luck, he wouldn't even know she was there.

Chapter 19

THE ROAD TO DECKER RANCH SEEMED LONG AND lonesome in the lengthening shadows of late afternoon. At least Sierra's Jeep took the curves better than the bulky van, and she didn't have two backseats full of fighting boys. Still, by the time she reached the ranch, daylight was giving way to dusk, and the old house at the bottom of the drive looked spooky and desolate.

Hitting the rocky two-track at a healthy rate of speed, the Liberty tackled the challenge with gusto. Sierra clenched her teeth and downshifted as the climb grew steeper then slid back into third as the road leveled out.

A huge washout loomed ahead. She managed to gun her way through it, but just when she thought the worst was over, there was a hideous clunk and a sudden lurch to the right, toward an abrupt and unprotected drop-off.

Opening the door, she stepped out to discover that her right rear tire was in the washout, her front one in a pothole. If she'd kept accelerating, the car would have steered its way straight to oblivion.

She surveyed the situation, pondering her choices. She could put the car in neutral and try to shove it out of the potholes, but there was a slope to the road and she wasn't sure it wouldn't back up instead and flatten her in the dirt. The other option was to try to back up a little bit and gun it over the obstacles, hoping the car would bounce left rather than flying off over the drop-off.

Neither option was very attractive. She really wished she'd called Ridge.

Maybe she could summon him somehow. She wasn't far from the house, and it was awfully quiet out here. A few birds indulged in some evening chatter, and a chorus of crickets chirped a hesitant accompaniment.

Putting her fingers in her mouth, she let out a high, long whistle. Almost immediately, she heard something crashing through the underbrush, accompanied by heavy breathing.

Seconds later, the brush parted and two black-and-white blurs streaked out, headed straight for the car. Tongues lolling from exertion, they flung themselves at her with joyful abandon.

"Tweedles!" She ruffled the hair around their grinning faces as they lunged to lick her face. "Hey, Dum. Hey, Dee. Where's your boss?" She knelt and cupped Dee's furry face—or was it Dum's?—in her hands. "Please tell me he's right behind you."

The dog barked, but no cowboy appeared. It was obvious Dum—or Dee—was just telling her what she wanted to hear.

"Go get him!" she told them, pointing toward the house. "Go on, guys! Go get Ridge!"

They stood side by side, grinning at her, obviously entertained by her histrionics.

"Go!" she said, stamping a foot. "You're collies, right? Aren't you supposed to be smart, like Lassie? Go get him."

The dogs leaped and swirled around her, panting. They seemed willing to help but utterly clueless as to what she wanted. Maybe if she got in the car, they'd give up on her and go find Ridge.

She opened the door and was nearly knocked over by two dogs who evidently loved a car ride even more than they loved sloppy kisses. Shouldering her aside, they leaped into the Liberty's tiny backseat and sat expectantly, side by side, panting.

"Oh, shoot," she groaned.

Each dog let out a happy bark as they shimmied their skinny hindquarters deeper into the upholstery.

"I'm not taking you for a ride," she said. "I'm not even taking *myself* for a ride. Now get out of there."

The dogs grinned, panted, and stayed put.

Sighing, she got in and turned the key, so she could roll down the windows and keep them from overheating. The panting increased in speed and volume as their grins widened.

She stepped out of the car and opened the back door. "There you go, guys. Good trip, huh?"

They weren't that stupid.

She considered the vehicle again, making a slow circuit around it. She probably couldn't push it forward, but maybe she could push it back. There was a rock she'd had to carefully surmount farther down that would be sure to stop it. Then she could make another try.

She got in again, much to the dogs' delight, and put it in neutral, then exited to a chorus of whimpers and stepped around to the front. Throwing herself at the front grill, she shoved with all her might.

Miracle of miracles, the car rolled backward.

And rolled. And rolled some more. Gaining speed, it rollicked over ridges and dips and bounced right over that rock. The dogs burst into a volley of barks that faded as they and the car bounced down the gentle slope of the road.

At least the ruts slowed it down. Sierra figured she might have a chance to catch it if she could run flat-out, but the uneven terrain worked against her. She kept slipping in and out of ruts. Once she twisted her ankle, but apparently she twisted it back again because it stopped hurting after a while.

Fortunately, the ruts slowed the car down too, and after much tripping and stumbling, she finally grabbed the handle of the driver's side door. She felt her ankle give and twist again inside her oh-so-Western cowboy boot, but she would *not* let go.

She lunged into position and yanked the door open, figuring she'd slide into the driver's seat and hit the brake. But the dogs were faster, scrambling over the seat back and shoving her aside, as eager to jump out of the vehicle as she was to jump in. Their determination knocked her flat.

Rising to a sitting position, she watched her car roll out of sight. The dogs stood at her side and barked furiously, as if that was any help. Though the headlights were blank and sightless, she could swear the Liberty wore a helpless, frightened expression.

Good-bye, car. How was she going to explain this to her insurance company?

She supposed she should run after it, see where it landed. But her ankle was killing her, and what would she do once she found it? Take pictures?

Turning, she began the long trek up to the ranch house, the dogs trotting companionably beside her.

—∿∿—

By the time she reached the barn, Sierra had reached her peak of annoyed, sweaty exhaustion for the day—and on this day, that was saying something. She suspected her ankle had swollen enough to fill the cowboy boot. She could have taken the boot off and checked, but she probably wouldn't be able to get it back on. Besides, she really didn't want to know.

For some reason, her spirits had risen with the uphill trek. She told herself the car had probably been stopped by a rut or a pothole, not a tree or a rock. Once she got her phone, she could probably just drive it home.

And apparently, she'd be able to do that without Ridge even knowing she was here. She'd already made enough noise to scare all the birds into the next county, and he hadn't shown up. Maybe he wasn't home.

The dogs shot ahead of her, bouncing toward the house with so much joy and grace she half expected them to sprout wings and fly. It was more likely that they'd bark, of course, and then she'd be busted.

"Dum! Dee!" she hissed, standing as tall as she could. "Shh!"

The dogs looked startled then hurt, and she felt a little sorry for them as they skulked up to the porch and laid down in what were apparently their usual spots at the top of the porch steps. Their sad, watchful eyes made her feel guilty as she headed for the broad barn door, which stood wide open.

In the dim light from the dusty windows, horses stood like ghosts, rustling the straw whenever they shifted their weight. It felt peaceful somehow, and Sierra took the time to just stand there and breathe in the sweet scent of straw and the earthier odor of animals. She was surprised to realize the odor wasn't unpleasant; it was warm and somehow comforting. She felt like the interior of the barn was an oasis in time, standing safe and unchanged as the rest of the world bustled around it.

She moved stealthily, edging down the row of stalls to the second one on the right. Sluefoot the Butt Biter was ogling her with that weird sideways leer again. She knew it was some kind of medical condition, but she couldn't help thinking the horse looked like he had some kind of dirty secret.

"Hello, Sluefoot." She cautiously stroked the animal's nose while she craned her neck to peer past him.

No phone.

Ridge had probably found it and taken it into the house. She was surprised he hadn't called the landline at Phoenix House to let her know. Maybe he had, while she was chauffeuring his dogs on a quick trip to nowhere.

She really wished she'd thought this through.

Sluefoot edged closer for another pat and she heard a crackling sound under his feet. When he shifted his weight, she saw that Ridge hadn't found her phone after all.

Sluefoot had. He'd found it with his big old feet, and he'd crushed it to bits.

"Sluefoot, no!" She felt like crying. She was barely making it financially as it was, with her student loans eating up half of her measly paycheck. She'd opted out of insurance on the phone, figuring she'd just be careful.

So much for that gamble.

She put her hand on the latch, and Sluefoot turned to face her, nosing the air in search of treats. To get the phone, she'd have to bend over, and she was sure the greedy animal would snuffle her back pockets for treats. She was liable to get nipped again.

Confirming her suspicions about his intentions, he

gave her that sly sideways look. She tilted her own head and gave him the eye, along with a grimace as gruesome as his own.

This was ridiculous. How had she ended up here, making faces at a horse? She swung open the stall door just enough to slip inside.

Slinging his head around, the horse lunged forward, shouldering her aside. Barely missing her feet with his hooves, he trotted through the door with surprising agility.

"Sluefoot, no!"

She grabbed for his halter, but he whirled and gave her backside a sharp farewell nip before galloping out the barn door.

Chapter 20

KIDS WERE EXHAUSTING. RIDGE DIDN'T KNOW HOW Sierra dealt with it day after day—especially since she seemed so emotionally invested in the boys. He remembered her tears over Jeffrey's progress. It was sweet that she cared so much.

But he was exhausted, nodding over his book. He flipped a few pages, searching for a spicy part to take his mind off his throbbing shoulder and aching arm. Just two months away from his sport, and he was already getting soft. He could barely stay awake.

He wasn't sure why he bothered to try. Chores were done, so he might as well take a nap, like some old guy—some old guy who couldn't rodeo, living all alone on a ranch.

He really had to do something about that last part. He wasn't exactly a party animal; in fact, he suspected a lot of the other cowboys on the circuit found him terse and unfriendly. But even if he hadn't joined in their raucous conversations and practical jokes, he'd been entertained. Living alone wasn't nearly as pleasant as he'd expected. He was starting to understand why Bill had liked having him and his brothers around.

He had no idea how much time had passed when a distant bark from one of the Tweedles jerked him back to the world. Glancing around the dim room, he caught a flash of white through the window. What the hell?

He rose to see old Sluefoot careening across the yard at a high-spirited trot. Dumbstruck, he watched the horse snatch up a mouthful of Irene's daylilies on his way around the corner.

Another flash of color attracted Ridge's attention, and he turned to see a woman racing across the yard in hot pursuit of his renegade horse.

Sierra.

What the hell was she doing here? She'd left hours ago with the kids.

As he watched, she put on a burst of speed and rounded the corner then tripped on a hillock of grass and went flying, hitting the ground with a stupendous, skidding belly flop.

He didn't know what was going on, but it looked like fun. By the time he got outside, Sierra was on her feet again, pursuing the horse. The Tweedles had joined her, barking a joyful chorus as they frolicked around her ankles, threatening to send her flying into another belly flop.

Pausing to tear up another mouthful of foliage, Sluefoot watched her approach then dodged away just before she grabbed his halter. She snatched at it again and again, but the wily old horse stayed just out of reach.

Putting his fingers to his lips, Ridge blew out his patented Sluefoot whistle. The horse stopped, spun around, and jogged docilely up to Ridge. He immediately began nuzzling at his master's pockets, looking for treats.

"Sorry, bud." He gently pushed the horse's nose away and scratched the animal's bony withers as a consolation prize. "No snacks this time." He grinned at Sierra, who was glowering at both of them. Her face gleamed with exertion, and her hair was a wild, spiky mess.

"That animal." She narrowed her eyes and shot Sluefoot a withering look.

Tilting his head at his usual rakish angle, the animal blew a loud raspberry.

The woman had obviously lost her sense of humor. She shot the horse a killing glare, and Ridge could swear there was steam coming out of her ears. If he could just stop laughing, he'd get the horse back to the barn.

"You mind telling me why you're out here chasing my livestock?" he asked once he'd recovered and started toward the barn.

"I forgot my cell phone." She glanced warily at Sluefoot. "I came back to get it and got stuck in your driveway and then the horse got loose, and—well, and here I am." She held up an iPhone encased in pink plastic. Huge cracks radiated across the screen.

"It's broken," he said.

She glared as he led Sluefoot into his stall. "Your damned horse stepped on it. After your driveway ate my car."

He latched the stall door carefully. Sluefoot had been known to lift a half-fastened latch and turn up at the front door, begging for treats. He was surprised the old guy hadn't figured out how to ring the doorbell. "Maybe it's just the screen that's broken on your phone."

"I'd better check. I have to call Riley. It's been hours."

She poked at the screen, sighing with relief when it lit up.

"Excuse me."

Turning away from him, she hunched her shoulders

just like she had before. Whoever this Riley guy was, she needed all kinds of privacy to talk to him.

"You okay?" he heard her say.

Then, "I'm really sorry. I lost my phone, or I would have called." There was a pause. "I know. I'm sorry."

She walked out into the sunlight, giving him an apologetic shake of the head, and muttered another apology into the phone. Riley kept her on a short leash. That meant he was controlling. Maybe abusive.

Maybe Sierra needed rescuing.

Yeah, right. Ridge was hardly the knight-in-shining-armor type. It would be out of the frying pan and into the fire. He might not be controlling, but according to Shelley, he was cold, uncaring, and incapable of commitment.

When Sierra returned to the barn, she looked frazzled and hot, as if her day had taken a turn for the worse. What could be worse than getting lost, losing her phone, and getting her car stuck? Riley had to be bad news.

Maybe he couldn't rescue Sierra, but she could probably use a friend. And while he hadn't been able to give Shelley what she wanted, he always stuck by his friends.

"Why don't you come on inside and have a drink?" he asked. "I've got some of that lemonade left." He grinned. "Or you could have a beer."

"I can't." She glanced down the drive. "My car. And my phone. And…" She stopped and stared at him a moment. He did his best to look harmless, and apparently it worked, because he could almost see her guard drop as her posture relaxed.

"Oh, forget it," she said. "Yes. Yes, I'd love to have a beer."

Sierra leaned against the kitchen counter and watched Ridge take two beers out of the refrigerator. The kitchen wasn't nearly as tidy as it had been earlier in the day. The packaging from a couple of microwave dinners was scattered across the counter; maybe he'd had company, but she doubted it. More likely, it took two or three dinners to fill him up. The lemonade glasses and pitcher were still on the counter too, and she realized she should have helped him clean up. She'd been in such a hurry to get the boys together that she hadn't thought of it.

"Where'd your car end up?" he asked.

She described the spot where she'd bottomed out.

"You walked from there? No wonder you're tired."

She smoothed her damp hair and wiped the sweat from her forehead. "What makes you think I'm tired?"

"I just—um…"

He looked stricken, and she was tempted to let him try and talk his way out of the insult, but she took pity on him.

"You're right. I'm absolutely wrung out." She collapsed onto one of the breakfast nook's benches and gratefully downed a draught of beer then lifted it in a toast. "Thanks."

He joined her, sliding onto the bench across from her. His long legs tangled with hers for one awkward moment, and she suppressed a wild urge to play footsie.

"I'll take you down in the truck," he said. "We'll get you turned around."

She shrugged. "I can do it." She glanced over at the dogs, who were cooling off on the cold kitchen floor. "Your dogs were very helpful."

"Were they?"

"They got in the backseat and wouldn't get out."

He threw back his head and laughed. Apparently, she'd caught him in a good mood.

She nodded toward the picture she'd noticed earlier. "So are those your parents?"

He nodded.

"And your brothers?"

"For all intents and purposes."

She scanned the picture again—the blond boy, the dark-haired one, and Ridge himself, with his unruly mass of wavy, brown hair. "You're all so different."

"We're alike where it matters."

She wanted to ask if they'd been adopted. That would explain how different they looked. But the question seemed too personal. Despite his easy good humor, Ridge seemed guarded about his personal life.

"Are they rodeo cowboys too?"

He nodded. "Functioning rodeo cowboys. Unlike me." He downed another sip of beer and set the bottle down a little too hard.

"What happened?"

"Got thrown."

"I'd imagine that happens a lot."

"It does."

His sharp tone was a clear indication that he didn't want to talk about his injury, but she couldn't hold back her curiosity.

"Is it bad?"

"Yes." He stood up from the table and busied himself with the dishes, squirting soap in one side of the double sink and cranking on the hot water. Either he was embarrassed by the mess, or he didn't want to talk about his injury. Or both.

She stood and crossed the room, nudging him aside with her shoulder. "Here, let me. I should have done this earlier."

"No." He nudged her back, a little too hard. The man didn't know his own strength.

"Yes." Impulsively, she scooped up a handful of bubbles from the sink and swatted at him. Most of the white foam wound up on his chin, but a generous dot stuck to the end of his nose. It should have looked ridiculous, but the hard glint in his eyes shut down the giggle that welled up in Sierra's throat. He scooped up some bubbles of his own and swatted at her, leaving a trail from ear to chin.

A playful smile tilted his lips, but it was clear he wasn't accustomed to losing games. She suspected a lot of bucking horses had seen that same narrow-eyed grin, and wondered if their big hearts had pounded as fast as her little one.

Dodging back to the sink, she scooped up another handful of bubbles. He needed some on top of his head to complete the look.

She should have gone for something less ambitious, because when she hiked herself up on her toes he grabbed her hand and held fast to her wrist. Her giggle exploded as the two of them wrestled. He was strong, even stronger than she'd expected. His grip on her wrist wasn't painful, but it was powerful. There was no way she could escape, no matter how she twisted and turned.

Inexorably, he forced her bubble-laden hand toward her own face.

"Want some bubbles?" he teased. "Mmm... bubbles."

They were standing still now, locked in battle. She was resisting as best she could, but her arm muscles were starting to tire.

"Yum," he said.

Her hand shook with the effort of holding him back, but it stopped just inches from her nose—and only because he stopped pushing.

"Say 'uncle.'" He grinned, his eyes on hers, and she almost forgot to resist.

"Never! *Ooh!*"

She said the last word through a face full of foam. Sputtering and blowing, she dove toward the sink and scooped out another handful. She couldn't win on strength, so she went for speed, splashing his chest with water as well as bubbles.

The fight was on. Dodging around him, she managed to soak the front of his shirt and the back of his jeans before he splashed what felt like half the sink down her front. She dove for the sink again and he grabbed both her wrists, pinning her with her back to the counter and her front to—

Him.

Oh.

Their bodies were pressed together and she had nowhere to go. She wasn't sure she'd have moved if she could, because his muscular body, damp and slick with soap, was pressed against her equally wet and slippery torso. Pressed *hard*.

She looked down in shock and surprise. She hadn't realized just how wet she was or how thin her flimsy bra was. No wonder he was turned on.

She might as well be naked.

Chapter 21

"Oops." Sierra tried to lift her hands to cover herself, but Ridge had her wrists, and he wasn't letting go. Panting with exertion, she looked up at him and this time she really did forget to resist. Her hips were pressed to his, and a strange weakness seemed to be flowing from the pressure of his arousal, taking over her body and mind.

This had gone way beyond playing. His eyes were locked on hers with an intensity that made something leap inside her, something graceful and fluid as a fine horse taking a fence. She felt all the fetters of everyday life fall away, and when he bent his head to kiss her, she responded without a thought for the future. There was only now.

This minute, this man, this kiss.

She hadn't felt this good in years. Maybe she hadn't felt this good *ever*. His lips were firm but pliant, his kiss gentle but masterful. She felt like he'd pushed a button that released all the day's stress and strain, and as it drained from her body, she gave herself to the moment. She wanted to remember this: her first kiss with Ridge Cooper. It would probably be her *only* kiss with him, but that only made it matter more.

It didn't feel like a first kiss. It felt like they'd been together forever. He seemed to know when she needed him to take and when she wanted him to give. Somehow they'd skipped all the awkwardness of courtship and the tentative dance of seduction, and gone straight to something more—something way beyond a quick stolen kiss in the kitchen.

He released her wrists—obviously he didn't need to pin her down anymore—and set his hands on her hips. She reached up and nested her fingers in the curls at the nape of his neck, and the kiss deepened.

His hands moved gently up her torso and down again, pressing the wet soapy shirt to her skin. She shivered, partly at the touch of the cold fabric but mostly at the feeling of his hands on her. Without breaking the kiss, they spun slowly away from the counter and moved across the kitchen in a sweet, swaying waltz. When they reached the doorway at the far end of the room, he pressed her to the doorjamb. After pressing his lips to hers as if sealing her to him, he stood back to look at her.

She should have been shy about the wet shirt and the way her nipples had risen to the occasion. They were begging for his touch, but it wasn't like his body wasn't tattling on him too. She was surprised the zipper held.

"What's happening here?" His voice was hoarse with need.

"Something good," she said.

He kissed her again, cupping her denim-clad butt and hoisting her against him. Shamelessly, she hooked one leg around his waist and buried her face in his neck, right at the curve where it met his shoulder. Breathing in the scent of him, hay and sun and leather, she had an urge to bite into the cord of muscle there. But then he rocked against her, and all she could do was moan, pressing her heel into him to push him closer.

"You want to take this to the bedroom?" Caught up in the thrill of his breath fluttering in her ear, she barely heard what he said. Something about *did she want*?

She didn't know what she wanted. She wasn't normally the type to fall into bed with men she barely knew. She knew that kind of thing usually didn't end well—unless it ended quickly.

Which this would. She was leaving, after all. Why not enjoy herself while she was here?

Hmm. Ridge had asked a question. What was it?

Did she want…

Oh, yeah. She wanted.

Whether it was wise to take what she wanted was another question, but right now, walking away would be impossible.

He took her hand and led her into a bedroom decorated in Early American Fuddy-Duddy. It must have been his parents' room, because no man would choose the flowered wallpaper, the delicate china lamps, or the fussy crocheted bedspread. Lace curtains fluttered at the windows, and a worn rug hooked with cabbage roses warmed the bare floorboards. It seemed wildly out of character for Ridge, but the contrast only highlighted the rough, masculine nature of the man. As he pulled her toward the bed, she forgot about the decor.

Ridge was nothing like the guys she'd dated in college or the men she'd worked with in Denver. Those men had been in shape, buffed up from hours spent in the gym. But Ridge's muscles were long and sinewy, formed by hard work and long hours in the saddle.

She'd never thought of herself as repressed, but the feelings rushing through her were so far beyond anything she'd ever felt that she almost didn't recognize herself. It was like she was *made* of lust. Heat and longing rushed through her veins, taking over every cell of her body, and images of the two of them together—together and naked, twisting in the bed—flickered in her mind like a silent movie reel.

There was still a little bit of the old Sierra left—that little voice that looked to the future and planned things out. The voice told her to tense and turn away. It told her to apologize, maybe laugh at her own foolishness, drop him a compliment or two to make up for leading him on, and walk out. It told her to go back to her car, back to her apartment, and back to her ordinary life.

But she didn't want to.

She wanted to stay here, with him, and take a break from being a good girl. Heck, she wanted to be bad as she could be. She wanted to strip off her clothes and give herself to him, and damn the consequences.

She wanted to be impulsive, just this once. And he looked like he'd be happy to help.

―⁂―

Ridge eased his foot back and nudged the door shut, but the cool air streaming in the window gave it a little extra oomph. It slammed, and both he and Sierra started like guilty teenagers.

She dropped his hand. He thought he'd lost her as her gaze moved from lace curtains billowing like ghosts in the evening air to the framed Charlie Russell print of a cattle drive over the bed; from the pile of jeans and shirts he'd tossed on the old pressed-back rocking chair in the corner to the handmade quilt on the bed. Last, she fixed on the old wood-framed mirror above the dresser, where the two of them stood framed by ornate carved oak leaves. In the fading sunlight, they looked washed of color, like an old-fashioned sepia photograph.

Except they were both soaked. Their little game with the dishwater had been fun while the foam lasted, but now they were both chilled and damp. Her hair was spiky and wild, and her green eyes warmed as she looked him up and down.

"You're wet." Her gaze was fixed on his chest. He was wet, all right. The shirt was freezing cold and stuck to every inch of his skin.

His eyes on hers, he shucked it off in one swift gesture then dropped his eyes to her breasts. She had world-class breasts, small but perfectly formed, and the soaked fabric of her shirt made their outline unmistakable. Seeing how aroused she was gave him the confidence to keep looking, to press his hips a little closer to hers, to stoke the flame rising between them.

She followed his gaze and looked down at her body as if she'd never seen it before, and then, slowly and deliberately, she tugged at the hem of her shirt. It stuck to her skin as she peeled it off, revealing the slight swell of her stomach over low-slung jeans, the graceful curve of her waist, and finally, the answering curve of her breasts, swelling from the barely there confines of a thin, stretchy bra, white with tiny pink flowers. When the fabric lifted to reveal her face, he didn't see the professional of his first visit or the cowgirl she'd been this afternoon in the corral. She was all woman. Eve, Salome, Delilah—a temptress, moist-lipped and breathless and sexy as hell.

He stepped closer and cupped her chin, fixing his eyes on hers. She answered his unspoken question with a come-hither look as her tongue flicked out, pink and kittenish, to moisten her lips. That was all the signal he needed. Sweeping his hands down her neck, he eased the straps of her bra down her shoulders then crossed the stretch of elastic to the delicate hooks that held it together. With a quick flick of his fingers, the clasp released. The damp fabric stuck to her skin but finally gave way to gravity, falling away in slow motion to reveal her one perfect inch at a time.

As the scrap of fabric fell to the floor, he caught the weight of her breasts in his palms. His thumbs stroked the pink buds of her nipples and he leaned in to kiss her, deeply this time, with unmistakable intent.

For a woman who'd seemed so uptight hours before, she returned his passion with a fervor that surprised him. Their slow-motion waltz changed to a sexy samba as he unbuttoned her jeans, and she fell back onto the bed and kicked her legs up in a gesture so joyful and abandoned that he almost lost his focus. Timing was everything, and as she rocked back, he slipped the tight denim over her taut backside, tugging it down her legs to reveal a pair of matching flowered panties as thin as the bra.

There wasn't much left to his imagination at this point, but still his animal mind was riffing on the possibilities, picturing a dozen positions that would show off that graceful body to best advantage. But when she rolled up onto her hands and knees, the view was like nothing he'd ever imagined. Smiling, saucy, wanton, she glanced over her shoulder and offered herself, scanty panties and all.

—ᴠᴠᴠ—

Sierra didn't know what had happened to her. She seemed to have lost all inhibition, urged by the testosterone aura that surrounded Ridge, to shed her pretensions and offer herself with glorious abandon. She'd never felt so beautiful, so wanton, or so willing. It wasn't just her skin that warmed to his touch; the heat shot straight to her heart.

Which was a little troubling. This wasn't the man for her. There was no future she could see that showed them working together toward any kind of happy ending. She was no cowgirl, and she couldn't see Ridge helping her save kids in the inner city.

But not every relationship had to have a future. This could be a special feature, for one night only. Ridge was so different from any man she'd ever known. He was a throwback of sorts, and being with him was like traveling back in time, to the Old West of the movies.

She wanted him, and she wanted him *now*. She wanted him whatever way he'd have her, hard and fast or long and slow. She pushed away sensible Sierra and let animal Sierra take over. Animal Sierra didn't have any warning bells to keep her safe. She was ready for anything, open to the elemental lightning streaks of passion that were arcing between her and this man.

Pure sex. Now.

Fortunately, he caught on quickly. Grasping her hips, he pulled her against the hard bulge of his crotch and rocked against her. She dropped to her elbows and widened the spread of her legs as he leaned forward and cupped her breasts. They hung in his hands, aching and heavy with longing, and she thought she'd explode when he worked them with his fingers, squeezing, pinching, tormenting her nipples until they burned with the rough touch of his fingers as she panted and clung to the sheets with her fists.

He let go long enough to unfasten his jeans and jerk them down over his thighs, and she gasped. There was nothing underneath those jeans, and his thick cock sprang out and lay in the cleft of her buttocks.

The world that had been spinning in a riotous arc stopped and slowed as he held her steady, breathing hard. Hooking his fingers in the elastic of her panties, he slid them slowly down. Now she could feel him there, right there, and she thought she might die of wanting him.

"Sierra," he said. "My God, Sierra."

His voice was hoarse and low. She'd done that. She'd brought him to the edge.

He framed her hips in his hands and flipped her over so she lay sprawled on the bed, spread out and shameless and wanting him so badly she felt open and empty and aching. Never, ever had she wanted a man like this, with a need so primal she wanted to scream like a cat in heat and claw him to her.

But he stopped, panting, squeezing his eyes closed like a man enduring the ultimate torture. He drew in a long, shuddering breath, and she almost swore aloud. Was he going to get all conscientious *now*? Didn't he know she was past caring, past any kind of scruples?

He knelt, and for one horrifying moment, she thought he was going to apologize, which would have been unbearably embarrassing—especially since he'd be apologizing not to her face, but to her unmentionables, which were *not* listening.

So when he reached up and set his palms on her thighs, gently parting her legs, she almost fainted with relief and gratitude. And when she felt the warm wet touch of his tongue, she let out a cry of joy and closed her eyes, giving herself up to pleasure.

———

Ridge had been wanted by women before. Lots of women. Women who were pretty frank about their sexuality, women who prowled the rodeo grounds and the beer tents trolling for cowboys as intently as fishermen tossing their nets.

But he'd never been wanted like this. And he'd never felt this answering need before, a tug at his vitals that drew him to make love to Sierra in spite of every barrier he'd thrown up in the past week.

Because he'd wanted her from the first time he saw her. He could admit that now, since there was obviously no hiding it, from her or from himself.

And the wanting had only grown as he'd gotten to know her. Watching her with the boys, the dogs, and even witnessing her ridiculous pursuit of his ancient old horse had only confirmed what he'd known instinctively from the start: she was different from the others. If ever he wanted to take what a woman had to offer and not stop taking, this was it.

He felt like he was kneeling at some altar of perfect womanhood. She was offering a honeyed peach glossed with nectar so sweet he knew one taste wouldn't be enough.

He stopped thinking and gave himself over to instinct. Evidently his instincts were good, because he had her moaning and bucking in a heartbeat then clenching and crying out as she tossed in the throes of orgasm. It was all he could do to resist taking her then, wet and trembling, but he stroked her and held her until the aftershocks passed in long, rippling shudders that stretched her taut and made her moan all over again.

But as she recovered her senses, she opened her eyes and looked at him like she was seeing him for the first time. He could see the reality of the situation dawning in her eyes, and she stiffened slightly and drew away.

"It's all right," he said. "We're all right." He stroked her hair and cupped her cheek, doing his damndest to kiss her doubts away and cussing his own scruples as he wondered if he'd missed his chance. Resisting the urge to rush, he smoothed away her resistance with gentle hands and felt her skin warming, her passion reviving. Stroking, caressing, he brought it back to life until she closed her eyes and surrendered again.

It was a risk to stop, to reach for the nightstand drawer for the condom and take time to slip it on, but she waited, watching with sleepy, hooded eyes. When he turned back to her, she slid beneath him, her legs parting. He wasn't taking any chances this time; he entered her in a smooth, long stroke and let out an animal growl of satisfaction.

They moved together in perfect counterpoint, slowly at first. He felt her relaxing bit by bit, and then the wild woman was back, clutching his back while he rocked them both back to sweet oblivion. The world flew away as he closed his eyes and rushed down a

tunnel of flickering lights to a pounding, rocking, out-
of-control climax that shook him so deeply he thought
he'd never recover.

He collapsed beside her and must have slept. When
he woke, she'd curled into him. Her head was nestled in
the crook of his neck, and one delicate arm was draped
over his body. She'd thrown a leg over him too, and he
lay perfectly still, staring up at the ceiling and wondering if he'd ever feel this perfect again.

Chapter 22

SIERRA BLINKED AWAKE AND STARED AT THE CEILING. In the dim light of dawn, something looked different. This wasn't her ceiling. She wasn't at Phoenix House. She was…

A stuttering slideshow of memories flashed through her mind. Naked muscular limbs. Gray eyes fixed on hers. The world spinning then stopping. The feeling of flying off into space, launched by the inner combustion of ecstasy meeting passion—igniting, exploding, and finally fading into a warm glow that was with her still.

One hell of a dream. Tugging the sheet to her chest, she idly rubbed the fabric between her fingers. It was crisp, a little coarse. Coarse?

This wasn't her sheet, and that wasn't a dream.

Those naked limbs? Ridge's. Those eyes? Ridge's. That ecstasy?

Hers, all hers. The inevitable result of having screaming, flailing sex with Ridge Cooper.

Ridge. Her boss's friend. She wondered if he'd tell Mike, if they'd trade jokes about her.

Worse yet, he was a volunteer, working with the kids. Maybe they could pretend it didn't happen. Maybe if she left quickly, stole out of the house, he'd think it was a dream too.

She gathered her clothes, which had somehow been flung to the far corners of the room: her jeans on the rocker in the corner, her panties draped over the headboard, her bra—well, she didn't know where her bra was.

She was tugging on her still-damp T-shirt and hunting for

her boots when Ridge stirred. She stood still as a deer scenting a hunter, praying he'd turn over and fall back asleep, but he blinked and sat up, stretching and yawning. He opened his eyes and started like he'd seen a ghost. Apparently he wasn't happy about what he'd woken up to, either.

"Hey," he said.

"Hey."

"You okay?" His eyes were wary.

"Fine." She held herself stiffly erect, trying to telegraph the message that she *wasn't that kind of girl*. She might have been, for a minute there, or maybe a few hours, but she wasn't normally—not in real life.

Because what had just happened definitely wasn't real life. It was some kind of fairy tale, where the prince awakened the sleeping princess in the forest. Or, more accurately, where the prince awakened the princess's sleeping sexuality in the bedroom. Or the cowboy—she didn't even want to think about who they really were.

He grabbed his jeans and slipped them on. "I'll come down and help you with that car."

"You don't have to."

"I know." He pulled open a drawer and got out some socks. White athletic socks, with red stripes around the tops and—hey, did all cowboys wear tube socks? She thought those went out with Gloria Gaynor and *Knight Rider*.

He grabbed the T-shirt he'd shed the night before, his eyes avoiding hers. He was probably worried she'd want to stay for breakfast, want to stay the day, or, heaven forbid, want to stay forever.

"Look, Ridge, you don't have to worry."

"I just want to make sure you make it to the highway."

"No, I'm not talking about the car. I'm talking about

us. I mean, not *us*. There is no us. That's what I'm trying to say." She shook her head, irritated by her own
awkwardness. Why couldn't she just say, "Thanks, see
ya, that was fun but it won't be happening again"? Lots
of women had sex for fun, no strings attached. For all
Ridge knew, she was that kind of woman. For all he
knew, she wasn't freaking out inside, feeling impossibly
compromised and vulnerable and screwed up.

Screwed up, screwed down, screwed sideways.

She sucked in a deep breath, hoping the cool autumn
air carried some courage along with the scent of sage
and fresh-cut grass. This might be okay if Ridge was just
some random guy. But his connection to her work made it
essential that she wipe this problem out of existence. She
had to address it *now*, before it got any bigger and flared
up beyond her control.

Actually, it wasn't the problem that was out of control.
It was her libido. Maybe she needed Ridge to help protect
her from herself. Her stupid, impulsive, sex-starved self.

"I just want to make sure we're on the same page,"
she began.

He'd just shoved his arms into the T-shirt and was
about to pull it over his head, but now he froze.

"I'm not looking for a man. I doubt I ever will be."

He ducked his head and yanked the T-shirt on, so his
face was hidden from her. "Somebody break your heart?"

"Not really," she said. "I'm not sure I have one."

He pulled the T-shirt over his head. For half a second,
he looked startled, but then he shook his head as if he
needed to rid his brain of something unpleasant. "I've
seen you with those boys. You've got plenty of heart."

"Yeah." She couldn't help smiling, just a little. "Maybe

that's where it went. Along with my desire to get involved with anyone who's not…"

She swallowed the word *stable*, but he filled in the blank. "Perfect?"

Bingo. "It's just that I've seen a lot of bad relationships and the collateral damage. I'm not going to get involved with anyone until I'm ready to settle down and do it right. And I'm not going to be ready for that for a long time." She laughed self-consciously. "I gave up on love a while ago."

"Wow, the perfect woman. You mean you're not looking for a little white house with a picket fence?"

She shook her head. "Nope. The boys are all the family I need. Sometimes I think I'll never get married. I mean, why bring more kids into the world when there are so many out there who need you?"

Turning, she gave him a smile. "So thanks, it was great, but let's forget it happened, okay? It was just momentary madness."

"Hey, it took more than a moment."

She laughed, swinging out the bedroom door with what she hoped was a carefree wave.

"Look, just give me a minute. I'll drive you down to your car, and we'll see if it's okay."

"It probably is. And if it isn't, I'll call."

"It's a long walk."

"Which will be a pleasure." She nodded toward the window, opened just a crack. The sun was just coming up, and birds were tossing out tentative notes that sounded like an orchestra tuning up.

Something in her tone must have been strong enough to get through that hard head of his, because he stopped trying to talk her into anything and sat back down.

Passing through the house, she smothered a faint stab of regret as she entered the pretty kitchen waiting in the dim light of dawn for a family to bring it to life. Sometimes she envied her friends who had married and had babies, but then she'd remember the casualties of the fractured families she'd worked with and felt her good sense return. That kind of commitment was too much of a risk to take unless you were sure—really sure. And she'd never had good judgment when it came to men. They seemed to grow horns and a tail the minute she started to trust them.

As she stepped onto the porch, she faced a world painted in shades of blue and gray, hushed by a morning mist. She knew the sun would chase off the shadows to reveal an endless blue September sky, and hoped last night's mistake would clear up just as easily.

Behind her, the screen door squeaked open.

"Hey," he said.

She turned to see him slouched in the doorway, holding something behind his back.

Please don't let it be flowers. A cup of coffee might be okay, or a doughnut. But she'd rather just go.

He held up a pair of battered Converse sneakers.

"Jeff's," he said.

"Oh." She took the shoes and bounced them in her hands, wondering why he had the boy's shoes. Finally, it dawned on her.

"The pink boots," she said. "He wore them home."

Ridge nodded, grinning. "Guess they weren't so bad after all."

"I'll bring them back," Sierra said.

He shrugged, splaying his hands. "Let him keep 'em."

"Okay. Thank you." She paused. She really should go, but she was curious.

"Why do you call him Jeff? It's always been Jeffrey."

He shoved his hands in his pockets and looked out at the corrals. "Sometimes an abused animal connects its name with the abuse. If you change the name, they're not so scared to trust you."

"That's good," she said. "Thanks. I never thought of that."

She started down the steps. Halfway across the yard, she dared to take one last look back. He was still standing in the doorway, and she felt that lightness rising in her chest again, that soft warmth flowing through her veins.

This time she knew enough to turn away before any stray urges overwhelmed her.

Picking her way down the rutted driveway, she waved off the Tweedles, who were following like she was a Fourth of July parade and might start throwing candy at any moment.

"Go home, guys."

When she reached the car, it was clear there would be no turning around. The front wheels were poised at the edge of a deep washout, and moving so much as an inch forward would make the Jeep bottom out. It was supposed to be a four-wheeler, but it didn't have the clearance to tackle the Decker Ranch road.

Climbing in, she started the engine then shifted into reverse. Craning her head over her shoulder, she backed up as quickly as she dared, bouncing over ruts and slamming into potholes.

The engine made a high, keening noise as the miles unwound. If only she could throw her life in reverse this easily, unwind the past couple of hours, and start again at the bottom of the driveway.

Chapter 23

A WEEK LATER, SIERRA WAS STILL JANGLING WITH nerves—partly about Ridge, but mostly about Riley. She'd left her friend several messages and still hadn't gotten a call. She'd tried to calm her mind with some deliberate drudgery, like cleaning the supply closet and reorganizing the kitchen cupboards. She'd also caught up on the reams of paperwork that were required to chart the progress of each of the boys. At least she had progress to chart, thanks to Ridge.

Ridge. Every time she thought of him, her brain shut down and smoked like an overheated engine. What had happened between them that night? Why had she lost control? And most important, why hadn't it *felt* like losing control? It had all felt so right, so natural. With other men, she'd never been able to truly let go. But with Ridge, she'd been able to ride that crazy rocket ship of ecstasy straight into space. It had been countdown, launch, and straight into orbit, for the first time in her life. And through the whole trip, she'd never doubted for one moment that she'd have a safe landing.

When the boys got home from school, she helped them with homework, then played video games a while before mandatory reading time and bed. After lights out, the house grew quiet. She sipped a cup of tea as night air carried the sounds of the small-town night through the open window of her third-floor room.

She was used to the cacophony of downtown Denver—the hum of traffic, the bleating of car horns. Here, passing cars were rare, so each traveler seemed more enigmatic. Who was the stranger behind the wheel? What business carried them through this remote place?

When the peace was interrupted by the roar of an especially loud engine, she glanced down to see a battered old delivery truck parking at the curb out front. The lettering on the cab was obscured by peeling paint, and the metal box on the back was streaked with rust. A spider web of cracks marred the passenger side of the windshield.

The truck looked like trouble, and so did the man who stepped out of the cab. Bald-headed and muscle-bound, he had heavy brows and a grim set to his mouth. Sierra hoped he wasn't one of the boys' fathers. Nobody needed a scene—not the neighbors, not Sierra herself, and certainly not the boys.

She could sympathize with the desperate parents who occasionally stormed the system to try and claim their kids, but cutting off parental rights was nearly impossible in the state of Wyoming, so the abuse had to be heinous before the state would step in. And only the worst cases—with the most dangerous parents—ended up at Phoenix House.

Every one of her boys had been through hell. And it was her job to make sure no one put them through it again.

Walking quickly and quietly, staying back from the windows, she made her way through the darkened house to the office. Opening the safe hidden in the floor under her desk, she pulled out a hard plastic case and twirled in another combination to reveal a compact nine-millimeter

Glock. Another case yielded two loaded magazines.
She considered them a moment then shoved one into
her pocket, leaving the gun unloaded. She could load
fast enough, and she wasn't about to risk an accidental
shooting. The gun itself she slipped under her belt, at the
small of her back.

She'd never gloried in the power guns gave her, but
right now being armed felt right. Nobody was going to
hurt her boys if she could stop it. And she was more than
capable of stopping it.

Returning to the lounge, she moved slowly but pur-
posefully along the wall until she was next to the window.
A tilt of her head allowed her to peep out at the driver,
who was still surveying the sleeping town. She tapped
her back pocket, making sure she had her cell phone. She
really couldn't see Sheriff Swaggard taking on Delivery
Truck Man, but she needed to keep all her options open.

She leaned out from the wall again to watch the
stranger. As she watched, the passenger door of the truck
opened and revealed a familiar form—a slim, pale figure
with wispy blond hair so light it looked silver in the dark.

Riley.

Sierra's first impulse was to run out and hug her
friend. But then she looked back at Delivery Truck Man
and frowned. Who was he? And why had he brought
Riley here now? Wynott was more than three hours from
the city. And it was the middle of the night.

Something was wrong. Really wrong.

Riley Sue James had been born with the beauty of an
angel, but she'd done her best to erase the gifts heaven

had given her. Her hair, so light blond it was nearly silver, was dull with the effects of constant dying and had recently suffered a homegrown haircut that did nothing to complement the delicate beauty of her face. A dozen silver hoops, placed so close together they looked like a zipper, decorated her eyebrow. Fortunately, these were the only remnants of the piercings that had decorated her nose, lips, and even her tongue back in the bad old days.

But the tattoos remained. Right now, all that showed were the flowers twining around her right arm. The tattoo was beautifully done, but disturbing once you noticed the lurking spiders and leering elfin faces hidden in the foliage. Riley said it showed how pretty things could hide evil deep within, and Sierra had always wondered if that was how Riley saw herself.

Riley had tried every fashion fad from Goth to punk, but she couldn't stop her inborn beauty from glowing through every disguise. Her eyes were a clear, Caribbean blue, and her skin was China-doll white. No one would ever guess she was twenty-one years old; she still looked fifteen.

Sierra couldn't help thinking of her as a kid. Maybe that's why she was so relieved to have her safe inside Phoenix House—even though her über macho chauffeur strolled in behind her.

Don't let him in, don't let him in, Sierra's instincts screamed. But she couldn't keep him out without a confrontation. Maybe, if she played nice, he'd just go.

"I didn't expect this to happen, Sierra, I swear." Riley dropped a duffel bag in the hallway. It had clearly been packed hastily; the zipper wouldn't close over the jumble of clothes and toiletries that had been tossed inside. "Mitch took me to see this band—they were *so* good, you should have been there, you would have loved them—and when I got home, all my stuff was out on the lawn. I know I was late with my share of the rent, but only by a couple of days. Well, maybe five days. But Mom knew I'd lost my job, and I was trying to find something new. I've been going to school, and I wanted to find something that used my skills."

Sierra was listening to Riley, but her eyes were on Delivery Truck Man. So far, his behavior hadn't set off any alarms, although she was surprised that he didn't ogle Riley or even seem that interested in her. Instead, he gazed around the front foyer like a connoisseur of Victorian architecture.

"Good thing I was with Mitch, though," Riley said. "When he saw I didn't have anywhere to go, he was nice enough to take me to you."

She shot Delivery Truck Man a smile most men would kill for. He grunted in response and glowered as he shambled over to sit—uninvited—on the couch. Sierra didn't know if he was angry or if glowering was his default expression.

Riley had found a real winner.

"I was wondering if I could stay with you, just for a couple days," Riley said. "We could catch up, you know? And maybe there's some way I could help out." She glanced around the house, at the smooth hardwood floors and newly painted walls. "I've been taking classes in home renovation, but it doesn't look like you need any help with that. Maybe I could work in the kitchen?"

"Riley, you can't stay with me. I live here, at the group home. I don't really need any help, but thanks."

Sighing, Riley frowned down at the floor. Meanwhile, Mitch spent what should have been the date night of his dreams staring around the house as if he was memorizing the floor plan. Now he was gazing up the stairs.

The kids slept upstairs.

Sierra wanted him out of here.

"Where'd you guys meet again?" she asked Riley.

"Me and Mitch? At a meeting."

So he was in recovery too, but he was taking women he met there to bars. Sierra wondered if he was one of those people who couldn't get themselves cleaned up and hated to see anyone else succeed. Either that, or he was a predator looking for vulnerable women. If that was the case, he was in for a surprise. Riley was stronger than she looked.

"We'll figure something out, Riley. Meanwhile, you can stay here tonight." She shot Mitch a dismissive glance and caught him staring at her with a hard, steady glare that was unmistakably hostile.

"Thanks for bringing her." She returned his stare with equal intensity, and when he broke off and looked out the window, she resisted the urge to pump her fist in victory.

As if to make up for his bad manners, Riley lit up the room with a smile. "So where do we sleep?"

"I have a room up on the third floor."

"What about Mitch?"

"What about him?" Sierra shoved her chair back from the table and stood up. "Sorry, but it's not my house, and I don't know him."

Riley's eyes widened. "You don't?"

Without a word, Mitch stood and strode toward the door. With his hand on the doorknob, he paused.

"What are the kids' names?" he asked without turning to look at her.

Sierra thought she hadn't heard him right. "What?"

"You have kids here, right? What are their names?"

Sierra's stomach clenched tight. "None of your business." She shoved back her chair and stood up. "And if you don't get out now, I'll call security."

He didn't need to know "security" was jammed into the waistband of her jeans. She breathed a sigh of relief as the door slammed behind him.

Riley blew out a long breath. "I'm sorry, Sierra." She sat back and brushed her hair out of her face. "I shouldn't have come here, but it just kind of happened, you know? He offered, and I wanted to see you so much. I've really missed you."

Sierra felt the heat of tears at the back of her eyes, but there were more important things going on right now than girlish reunions.

"Who is he, Riley?"

"I don't really know. I thought *you* would."

"How would I know a guy like that?"

"He said he was a friend of yours."

Sierra felt a chill tiptoe its way up her spine like a slow-walking spider with cold, cold toes. "I've never met that man before in my life."

She did her best to slow the questions ricocheting through her mind. How did Mitch know her name? How did he know about her friendship with Riley? Could he be the parent of one of the kids? Nobody should have been able to track them down that fast, but that was the only reason Sierra could think of that he'd want to know the boys' names.

He'd asked that question at the last second. It was a dead giveaway he was up to no good, and the way he'd asked it—he'd sounded a little desperate. And that made him doubly dangerous.

She'd have to look at the kids' files, check out their parents' mug shots.

"How well did you get to know him?" she asked Riley.

"Well enough to be glad he's gone," Riley said. "I only talked to him because he said he was a friend of yours, and that made me feel safe, you know? But he's not, so…"

Riley wrapped her arms around her waist and hunched her shoulders. She was staring down at the floor with a lost expression that reminded Sierra of the little girl she'd been matched with in high school. Riley had been so young and so broken. She seemed to be mending now, but she'd always lived right on the edge of poverty, a paycheck away from disaster.

"Come on." Sierra jumped up, shaking off the dread Mitch had inspired. "Let's have some tea. Tell me what you've been doing."

Sierra heated up two mugs of water in the microwave then dropped in two tea bags—Earl Grey for her and Lemon Zinger for Riley. She didn't even have to ask.

She grabbed a handful of sugar packets, and they sat down at the rickety kitchen table.

Sierra sipped at her tea then fanned the hot liquid with one hand while Riley tore open a sugar packet and poured it into her tea.

"So what have you been doing? You said you were taking classes?"

Riley shifted to the edge of her seat, her face brightening with excitement. "I got into this program called Climb Colorado. It used to be just for single moms, but now they've opened it up for unemployed women too." She opened another packet of sugar and poured it into her tea, and then another. "They teach male-dominated trades to women—construction, home renovation, electrical and plumbing—that kind of thing. I got to do renovation." She preened a little. "That's the most popular choice, and it's hard to get into. My test scores were really high."

"Riley, that's great." Sierra wasn't sure how to ask her next question. Riley wasn't exactly famous for finishing things she'd started. "Are you still taking courses?"

Riley shook her head then peered into her mug. No doubt she had a mountain of undissolved sugar at the bottom of the cup. Sierra got up and grabbed a spoon from the dish drainer beside the sink.

"I'm done," Riley said, stirring vigorously.

"You graduated?"

Riley shook her head again. Sierra felt like she was playing some kind of game—good news, bad news. Good news, bad news.

"I have to do a project. I was hoping to find a job that would qualify, so I could make money and finish my certificate at the same time. It needs to be a whole-house renovation."

"Wow. That's a huge thing to take on."

Riley took a sip of her tea, cocked her head like the judge on a TV cooking show, then grabbed another packet of sugar.

Sierra smiled. Riley had always loved sweets. Even

though she wanted good things for her friend, she was glad Riley was still Riley.

"It is big. I don't have to be in charge of the project, but I have to work on at least four different parts of the renovation—like maybe countertops, flooring, electrical, and drywall."

Sierra cocked a head toward the front room. "Did you hear Mitch's truck start up?"

Riley shook her head.

"Stay here."

Sierra headed for the front window. Brushing back the curtain, she was dismayed to see the truck still sitting at the curb, with the bulky silhouette of Mitch at the wheel.

"He's still out there."

Riley got up and looked over her shoulder as Sierra edged the curtain aside again. The lights had come on in a few neighboring houses. Sierra really didn't want to frighten the neighbors by striding out there with her gun drawn.

"Is there a sheriff or somebody you can call?" Riley asked.

Sierra could just see Sheriff Swaggard pedaling up on his bicycle to take on Delivery Truck Man. "This isn't *Gunsmoke*," she said. "There's no Matt Dillon here. Our sheriff—well, he's not much use."

She glanced back out the window and studied the shadowy man at the wheel of the derelict car. Suddenly the darkness that had seemed so velvety and warm an hour ago seemed deep and dangerous.

"But there is somebody I can call." She let the curtain swing shut and grabbed her cell phone. "I'll call him right now."

Chapter 24

RIDGE HAD SPENT THE WHOLE NIGHT TWISTING AND turning in bed, first on one side, then on his back, then the other side, turning around and around again, with thoughts of Sierra tumbling through his mind. He felt like a pig on a spit.

So when the phone rang, it didn't jerk him out of a sound sleep, only out of a waking dream, one where he and Sierra were out in the barn taking a literal and very pleasurable roll in the hay.

"Ridge?"

It should have surprised him to hear her voice, but it seemed the most natural thing in the world. She sounded worried, though. He sat up, raking his free hand through his hair.

"What's wrong?"

"My friend Riley's here, and I think the guy who brought her is after one of the kids."

He sat up so fast he felt light-headed.

"Which one? Why? Where is he now?"

"I don't know. He's out front, in a big old truck. He won't leave. I could go out there and talk to him but..."

"No. I'll be right there." He reached for the T-shirt and jeans he'd shed hours earlier.

"Thanks." Some of the tension had drained out of her voice, but it was back when she spoke again. "Ridge? Just so you know, he's really big. And I don't know what he might do."

"You got a gun?"

She sucked in a sharp breath. "Um… yes."

"What about Riley?"

She would have laughed except her mouth was so dry she couldn't. "No. Riley does not have a gun."

He struggled to hold the phone to one ear then the other, as he stepped into his jeans and flailed around with a suddenly uncooperative shirt.

"Just sit tight," he said. "I'll be right there."

He finally conquered the shirt then toed into his boots, struggling to seat his heel when one of them went on crooked. He was in the hall in a heartbeat, snagging his Carhartt jacket off the hook. Opening the door, he almost closed it behind him before he realized he didn't have a gun himself. He had no idea what kind of situation he was walking into. The guy in the truck was probably just some citified loser, but Sierra had sounded panicked—and he had a feeling it took more than some wannabe tough guy to scare her.

Dodging back inside, he opened the hall closet and rummaged through the accumulated detritus of a generation of ranchers: scuffed boots, a couple of horse blankets, gloves and hats and heavy socks, all tossed in willy-nilly. No one had cleaned out the closet since Irene had passed. He'd have to clean it out next chance he got. It was damn near impossible to find anything.

With the wide sweep of a breaststroke swimmer, he parted the jackets hanging from the rod and found what he was looking for: Bill's old Winchester and a box of shells. Pocketing the ammo, he tucked the gun under his arm and set off into the night.

Sierra and Riley had moved to the upstairs hall to make it less obvious they were watching Mitch. Sierra couldn't tell if his eyes were open, but he'd turned sideways in the front seat so he faced them, with his back against the driver's side door. His arms were folded across his chest, and his legs were crossed at the ankles. It sure looked like he was watching, but his face was hidden by shadows.

There was no law against a man sitting in his car, and it was still possible he was just an ordinary guy who didn't want to make the long drive back to Denver. She didn't have any proof that he was after one of the boys.

But why else would he want to know their names? And why did she have that itch between her shoulder blades that told her trouble was coming?

She strained her ears for the sound of Ridge's pickup.

Crickets. Just crickets and a faint breeze tickling the trees.

"How far away did you say he lived?" Riley asked.

"Pretty far," Sierra admitted. "He's a rancher."

"How do you know him?"

"He's teaching the boys to ride."

"So he's, like, a cowboy?"

"Sure is."

"Are you, um, *involved*?"

Sierra shook her head. She had been involved with Ridge—*very* involved—for one night. But that night was over and so was their relationship—what little there'd been.

"Can you see me with a cowboy?" She let out a laugh,

praying it didn't sound as fake as it felt. "Definitely not my type."

"Maybe he's mine."

"What?"

"My type."

Sierra turned, stunned by Riley's wistful tone. Cowboys hadn't ever been her own cup of tea, but they'd been as far from Riley's type as a friendly beagle puppy from a pit bull. Riley liked the bad boys, which was one reason she'd never been able to get her life together.

"A guy like that would take care of you, you know?" Riley stared dreamily into space. "Maybe I could get a horse or something. Have a couple of kids. It feels safe out here."

Sierra looked out at the ominous truck parked at the curb and wondered what it was that Mitch "delivered."

"It's not feeling very safe right now."

"Yeah, I guess you're right. And some straight arrow would bore me to death." Riley gave Sierra a sly little smile. "You *sure* you don't like him?"

"I like him a little." Sierra's smile trembled at the corners, but hopefully Riley wouldn't notice she was holding in a secret. "But I don't think he's looking for anybody to take care of."

Ridge saw the battered delivery truck the moment he swung around the curve and passed the municipal building. A couple of lights were on in nearby houses—Ed Boone's apartment over the hardware store and Wayne Elkins's. So he'd have backup if he needed it.

He pulled up behind the truck and shut off the pickup's engine, jerking the hand brake into place. Spilling out of his vehicle with swift moves honed through a lifetime sliding off roping horses, he saw the driver jerk his head up toward the rearview mirror and tense his shoulders. But by the time his target was ready to move, Ridge had already wrenched open the driver's door.

"Son of a bitch!" The guy had been lounging against the door with his legs stretched across both seats. When Ridge opened the door, he nearly fell backward onto the road.

It was lucky Ridge had caught the guy at a disadvantage, because he was broad-shouldered and meaty, with a bald head shaped like a lumpy potato. Flailing to regain his balance, the guy stumbled out of the car and stood to his full height. Six foot four, Ridge figured. Maybe five. Those muscles were clearly honed by a weight-lifting regimen. Bulging veins traced tortuous paths just under the skin.

"What the hell you doing?" the stranger bellowed.

A few more lights flicked on nearby, and a door creaked across the street as a neighbor stepped out onto a darkened porch.

"That's what I was about to ask you." Ridge stood with one hip cocked, holding the Winchester at his side in a casual grip. The big man's eyes flicked to the shotgun and then to Ridge's face. The gaze was appraising, as if he was trying to figure out if Ridge would really use the gun.

Ridge stared the guy down. For a long moment, the confrontation could have gone either way, but evidently he'd put enough steel in his eyes to discourage whatever resistance the stranger had in mind.

The man lifted his eyebrows, grimaced, and wiped the back of his thick neck with one hand. "I dunno. I brought some, um, my girlfriend out here, and now..."

He waved toward Phoenix House. The windows were dark, but Ridge caught the sway of a curtain in an upstairs window and knew Sierra was there.

"You'd better find someplace else to figure it out." Ridge nodded toward the homes across the street. Shadowy men stood in several doorways, all watching. In the darkness, you couldn't tell they were all pushing eighty; all that mattered was their watchful posture and the confident way they held their weapons. A lot had changed since the *Gunsmoke* days of the West, but one thing stayed the same: in small towns, folks stuck together. And everybody had a shotgun in the front closet.

Ed, half-hidden by the shadows under the awning of the hardware store, racked a shell into the chamber of his weapon. The hard clack of the bolt cut through the night almost like a shot.

The man looked Ridge up and down as if searching for a badge and sneered when his gaze lit on his battered Stetson. "You the sheriff here or something?"

"Or something." Ridge touched the brim in wry salute. "You really want to stick around and find out?"

He waved toward Ed and then at Wayne, who racked his own gun at the signal. Down the street, another cartridge slid home.

The outsider curled his lip.

"I don't need trouble. But I'll be back. You can bet on that."

"Fine with me," Ridge said. "Strangers are always welcome in Wynott. Just make sure you stay away from those girls."

"I'm not interested in the girls," the man sneered. "That little blond is a piece of work. She—"

Ridge cut him off. "So, what exactly are you interested in? Little boys?"

Most men would have thrown a punch at that suggestion or at least slung a curse. But the bald-headed man just climbed into the truck and cranked it to life, revving the engine in an empty display of machismo. The engine coughed, sputtered, and nearly died before he got it going again.

As he pulled out from the curb and careened down the street, Ridge heard the creak of a sash opening. A gray-haired woman leaned out of a second-story window across the street.

"Lawd's sake!" Her voice was high and quavering.

"Sorry, Mrs. Carson," he said. "All clear now. Go back to sleep."

"Well, I'll try." She put a self-conscious hand to her curler-bedecked head. "Is that Ridge Decker?"

He ignored the fact that she'd given him Bill's last name. Most people thought of him and his brothers as the Decker boys, and that was fine with him.

"Yes, ma'am."

She rested her elbows on the sill. "You're playing white knight to that girl with all the children, aren't you?"

"Ellie, leave the man alone," groused a creaky voice from inside the house. "Come on back to bed and quit your gossiping."

"That's a mighty big family for a man to take on, is all I'm saying."

Ridge gave her a grin and tipped his hat. The women in Wynott married him off every time a woman under forty turned up. He was surprised they'd linked him to Sierra so fast, though. She must be doing something right to lose her outsider status so quickly.

She'd sure done something right as far as he was concerned. Lots of things. The only thing she'd done wrong was to say she wouldn't do it again.

Climbing back in his truck, he cranked the engine and set off in the direction the wheezing, coughing delivery van had gone. It wasn't tough to track it by the racket it made, and Ridge made sure it swung onto the interstate before he executed a quick illegal U-turn and rode slowly back through town.

He tipped his hat at a few straggling neighbors who were heading back into their houses then slowed as he passed Phoenix House. A light was on in the front room now, and he knew Sierra would let him in if he stopped. She'd be warm and welcoming since he'd helped her out, and he'd get to meet the famous Riley.

But then, the famous Riley would scuttle any chance he had of getting Sierra alone. Plus there were the kids.

He wondered if the noise of the confrontation had wakened them. Probably. That engine had been loud enough to wake a dozen senior citizens. So why weren't the kids out on the porch hoping for a fight or leaning out the windows? When he was their age, nothing would have kept him inside when there was trouble brewing.

He glanced up at the bedroom windows and spotted one small face peering from behind a curtain, but the boy—Jeffrey, he was sure—dodged back into the darkness as he passed.

Tapping the horn, Ridge pressed the accelerator and motored off toward home, trying not to think about the things that could make a bunch of ten-year-old boys hide at the sound of a little late-night excitement.

Chapter 25

SIERRA LET THE CURTAIN FALL BACK INTO PLACE AND turned away from the window, doing her best to hide her disappointment from Riley.

Why hadn't Ridge come inside?

It was just as well, with Riley here. She doubted she could hide her feelings, and she didn't want her friend to know how she felt about the rancher down the road. Heck, she didn't want the rancher himself to know. Although she hadn't been able to define the feelings he'd stirred in her the other night, she knew they were stronger than they should be.

Still, she would have liked to thank him. She was sure she'd hauled him out of a sound sleep, because cowboys always slept soundly, didn't they? They lived pure, wholesome lives, and they always beat the bad guys.

She tilted the curtain again and glanced outside. Porch lights were on all up and down the street, but as she watched they flicked off one by one. The old man who ran the hardware store limped into his house with a gun cradled in his arms. Ed Boone, that was his name. He spent half his time on the bench out in front of his store with a couple of other old men, chatting and watching what little of the world passed through Wynott.

The window next door creaked then slid shut. That was Mrs. Carson, who had brought over a casserole on Sierra's first day. She was apparently the town's unofficial welcome wagon, and probably its chief gossip as well.

Great. She'd rousted the two neighbors most likely to spread the story.

"Isn't your cowboy coming in?" Riley asked.

"He's not *my* cowboy." Sierra tried to smile, but it was impossible to hide her disappointment.

"Oh, boy." Riley sounded more like her old self than she had all night as she gave Sierra a sharp jab with her elbow. "You *do* like him. You like him a *lot*."

"No, I—I just feel bad that he had to come all the way out here."

"The look on your face when he was getting rid of Mitch was definitely not the *feeling bad* look," Riley said, laughing. "It was the *oh-my-God-do-I-have-the-hots-for-you* look."

"Well, sure." Sierra lifted her shoulders in what she hoped was a casual shrug. "I mean, who wouldn't? You saw him."

"Sure did. And *I* wouldn't." Riley tossed her head. "I mean, come on. Did you see that hat? The boots? The guy's a redneck. I mean, he has a *pickup truck*. With a *gun rack*." She shook her head. "Not your type. Not long-term, anyway. But short-term…" She made a happy humming sound.

Sierra did *not* want to continue this conversation, but she couldn't help defending herself. "I don't do short-term."

Riley bit her lip and looked away, and Sierra wished she could take the words back. Riley didn't seem to be capable of a relationship that lasted more than a week, but what had Sierra done with Ridge if she "didn't do short-term"? It wasn't like there was any long-term potential in her relationship with a small-town cowboy.

Maybe she should tell Riley she actually had fallen into bed with Ridge. Maybe it would make her feel better.

"I…"

She couldn't do it, couldn't talk about it. Last night might have been short-term, but it had still been special and somehow sacred. It might be crazy, but the night had been precious and it was hers. It didn't belong out here in the real world.

"There's nothing going on between me and Ridge." The lie made something in her stomach twist. Guilt, she guessed. It would have to pile up on top of the rest of her guilt about Riley. There was plenty in there to keep it company.

From the first time she'd met Riley's family, Sierra had known there was something off about Riley's stepfather. He looked at his daughter too long and touched her too much. Finally, she'd confronted Riley and found out the truth. He'd abused her once. Twice, actually.

Riley had begged Sierra to keep the abuse a secret. She'd cried and raged and sworn she'd never tell Sierra anything about her life ever again if she went to the authorities. Foolishly, Sierra had weakened, worried about what would happen if Riley had no one to share her secrets with.

Riley had claimed it never happened again, but Sierra knew now that the abuse had continued. It hadn't been an isolated incident, something that had happened once or twice and been forgotten. It had been a constant in Riley's life, the dark force that had driven her to rebel in every way she could conceive of: drinking, drugs, bad boys, you name it. She'd spun into a downward spiral that had turned her from a beautiful, intelligent girl into a broken woman who might never be fully healed—all because the one person she'd confided in had failed to step in and save her.

That guilt had driven Sierra ever since—first into law enforcement, in the hopes she could put people like Riley's stepfather away, and then into social work, where she thought she might be able to help children escape their abusers. She was doing that now, but the guilt wouldn't go away. It sat deep inside her, so heavy sometimes it stole her breath.

"Actually, Ridge and I discussed the possibility of a relationship and realized it was better to keep it strictly professional." There. Now, that was true.

"Why not? Are you not good enough for Mr. Perfect Cowboy or something?"

"No, it's not that."

Sierra pretended to examine a tear in the sofa's vinyl cover so she wouldn't have to look at her friend. But she'd already seen the mulish expression that set Riley's chin and thinned her lips. She was not giving up on this line of questioning.

"Well, what is it, then? The sparks are flying off you two like lightning strikes. If I didn't know better, I'd think you were already doing it."

Sierra flinched, catching herself half a second too late.

"Whoa, Nellie!" Riley rested her elbows on her knees and laced her fingers together to prop up her chin. She looked like a kid at story time. "You did. You *did*! I thought your relationship was 'strictly professional.'" She lowered her voice mockingly on the last two words.

"It is."

"Only if you've taken up a new line of work." Riley bounced in the chair again, unable to contain her glee. In spite of all she'd been through, she could still be a big kid sometimes.

"Don't look so happy about it," Sierra said. "It was a huge mistake. I can't start up that kind of relationship here. I'm not staying here."

"You're not?"

"No. I got a job down in Colorado. I start in about five weeks."

"Oh." Riley stared down at the floor. "That's too bad."

"No it's not!" Sierra bounced on the sofa, surprised and a little frustrated that Riley didn't share her excitement. "It's great. It's a really good job. I'll be able to do so much more good work there."

"That's good, I guess. I just think this little town's kind of cute. And it feels so safe."

The fact that Riley felt safe so soon after the episode with Mitch offered a hint of what her life had been like with her mother.

"I guess it's not your kind of place, though," Riley said. "It would be hard to save the world from here."

"I'm not trying to save the *world*," Sierra said. "Just the kids. But this isn't *your* kind of place either." She congratulated herself on the smooth segue. "So what are your plans?"

Riley closed her eyes and gave an elegant, one-shouldered shrug. She was so graceful, so beautiful in her pale, fragile way. What if her life had been different? What if someone had intervened, reported her parents to the authorities, gotten her out of the terrible situation that had ruined her childhood and stolen her soul?

What if she'd had a different mentor, one who knew better than to keep secrets? One who knew it was worth losing Riley's trust to save her life?

"Stop worrying about me, Sierra." Riley gave her an old-style Riley grin, lopsided and childlike. "I'm a big girl now. I really am." She gave Sierra a hard, assessing look. "Actually, I'm not sure you're worried about me. I think you're worried about that cowboy."

Sierra *was* worried about Ridge. She was happy to spend time here with Riley, but she felt as if a part of herself had followed Ridge out of town, over the hills and valleys, around the sweeping turns and straight-aways that led to the Decker Ranch.

She was also worried about Riley, and about Jeffrey and about the safety of the boys now that Mitch—whoever he was—had found them.

She gave her friend a wan smile. "I'm worried about everything," she said.

"Yeah," Riley said. "Big news flash there."

Sierra rose. "Let's go to bed."

She settled Riley on the sofa in her little sitting room and went to check on the kids. Josh and Isaiah slept soundly, Josh lit by a shaft of moonlight. His face was open and relaxed in sleep, and she thought she could see the man he might become if life didn't harden him too much. Isaiah lay straight as a soldier, the covers barely wrinkled.

In the next room, Carter sprawled like a fallen angel, his round face cherubic in sleep. He was the only boy without a roommate, and the soft but endless snores filling the room reminded Sierra why. In the third bedroom,

Frankie was sprawled in a nest of twisted sheets and blankets, his dark hair curling like flames around his face. Jeffrey, as always, was turned toward the wall, his face hidden by the blankets. Even in sleep he defended himself against the world.

Next to his bed sat the pink cowboy boots with the Converse shoes beside them. She stood awhile and watched him. She hoped he was riding Ridge's big yellow horse in his dreams, riding away from his troubled past into a future as golden as the animal's gleaming coat.

She wished she could find golden horses for all of them. For Frankie and Carter, Josh and Isaiah. For Jeffrey. For Riley. Maybe even for herself—but she didn't want to ride away until she was certain, without any doubt, that every one of them had already mounted up and ridden off to some safe forever.

Or did she? Taking that new job was her choice and only hers. She could rationalize all she wanted about doing good in the wider world. Nothing changed the fact that she was abandoning these kids she'd come to love, tossing their fragile futures into the hands of some stranger.

―∞―

Ridge headed to town feeling refreshed and revitalized for the first time in months. Watching the road disappear under his wheels, he looked out at a blue sky that for once seemed to promise good things, rather than another interminable day to be lived through. He was no longer a man without a future.

He knew where he was going but getting there was going to be a challenge. He'd have to jump through a lot of hoops to become a foster parent, and he needed to know what the hoops were and how high he'd have to jump. The only person he knew who had that kind of knowledge was Sierra Dunn.

That's why he'd rushed through his chores so he could head to Wynott to see her. It had nothing to do with the fact that she'd interrupted every waking thought for the past week and haunted every one of his dreams.

As he rolled into Wynott, he realized he'd better think of a few other excuses for other folks too. He didn't want to water the Wynott gossip vine, which burst into bloom at the slightest hint of news.

Breakfast at the Red Dawg was a good start. People had driven farther than twenty miles for Wayne's breakfast burritos. He could always say he had a craving.

Then he bought a few items at Boone's Hardware. He was careful not to even look at Phoenix House, though he was so distracted by its white-painted, gingerbread-frosted bulk just across the street that he couldn't think of anything to buy. A rancher always needed *something* at a hardware store but danged if Ridge could remember what problems had come up this week that might need nailing, mending, rewiring, or screwing.

Screwing… He shoved the ugly word aside. What he and Sierra had done couldn't be described by an ugly word like that.

"So who was he?"

"He?"

Jolted back to reality, Ridge couldn't figure out what Ed was talking about. Sierra was no "he," and nobody could ever mistake her for one.

"Who was who?"

"Guy in the ugly truck last night." Ed rang up the box of screws Ridge shoved across the counter. It was a ridiculously Freudian thing to buy, but hey, screws always came in handy.

"Don't know," Ridge said. "He was making the girls over at Phoenix House nervous, so I chased him away. That's about it."

"How'd you happen to be in town at that hour?"

Fortunately, Ridge had finally remembered what he needed, and it was easy to fake absorption in the task of choosing a latch for Sluefoot's stall. The old horse had mastered most of what Ed carried and needed a new challenge. Ridge figured stall latches were to Sluefoot what crossword puzzles were to people.

Some out-of-towners came in and kept Ed busy, so Ridge managed to make his escape and cross the street to the house without further questions—until Mrs. Carson hailed him from her front porch.

"You calling on Sierra?" she asked.

Ridge quickly shook his head. In Mrs. Carson's generation, "calling on" a woman had implications that could get the whole town talking. "Seeing" was the next step. He didn't know what step he was on right now. Ed would call it "sniffing around." Wayne, over at the Red Dawg, would have a far more graphic word for it. It was a good thing the men weren't in on the conversation, because Ridge would have to punch Wayne for that one.

"Ridge?" Mrs. Carson peered into his face, her brow wrinkled with concern.

"Oh. Sorry," he said. "No. I'm just—just coming by on business," he said.

"Good." She frowned. "All that to-do last night. That

man wasn't our kind. Those boys, they're innocent and deserve a second chance. But I don't hold with grown women who paint their bodies and wear clothes so tight you can see their—well, their *everythings*."

Had Sierra gone a little crazy after he'd left or what? She had a tattoo, sure, but it wasn't visible—unless, of course, she was wearing clothes that showed her *everythings*.

Dang it, he knew he should have stuck around last night.

The thought put a spring in his step as he climbed the porch steps and knocked on the door.

The woman who answered had to be Riley, and he could see Mrs. Carson's point.

She was the palest woman Ridge had ever seen. Gazing at him from the doorway through watery blue eyes, she looked like a ghost. A ghost with a lot of tattoos, wearing a barely there tube top and low-slung jeans that exposed a jeweled belly button between jutting hip bones. A ghost who definitely wouldn't fit in around Wynott.

No wonder Mrs. Carson was concerned. Riley looked like trouble. Heck, she'd already dumped a great big dose of it on Sierra's doorstep. Too bad she hadn't left with the guy in the truck.

"Hi." She seemed to be addressing her greeting to his left boot. "You must be…" She paused, chewing her lower lip.

"Ridge Cooper."

"Right. Ridge. I'm Riley. Thanks for—you know." She edged back a few steps, making room for him to enter.

Hooking his thumbs in his belt loops, he looked her up and down. If she was tough enough to get all those tattoos, why wasn't she strong enough to take care of her own problems? He'd seen how tense Sierra was whenever she talked to Riley. She had enough to worry about with the boys.

He knew he ought to be more tolerant, but something about the girl reminded him of someone he'd known a long time ago—someone who'd brought trouble into *his* life. He had no patience with helpless waifs who waited for the world to take care of them. Other people always paid for their mistakes.

"You're a friend of Sierra's, right?" he said.

She nodded.

He felt words burning in his throat, the heat of his anger building and building, pushing them out before he could think.

"Then why did you lead a guy like that straight to her door? You know she's in the middle of nowhere out here. Why did you let that happen?"

Riley put her hand to her lips, biting her thumbnail while she seemed to seriously consider his question. "I don't know. I didn't think about it."

"Do me a favor," Ridge said. "Start thinking." For once in his life, he couldn't stop talking. "She's here all by herself, protecting these little kids that haven't got anybody in the world but her. She needs people to help her, not more people to take care of."

He knew the words would get hotter and crueler if he stayed with her another minute. Pushing past her, he headed for the office.

Chapter 26

Just as Ridge came around the corner, Sierra appeared at the door of her office.

"Oh," she said. "Hey."

Her eyes met his and for a second he was back in that four-poster feather bed, rolling around naked in a fog of sexual bliss. He knew she was there too—he couldn't say how, but he knew. One blink and the feeling was gone, but it had already warmed him and his bad mood drifted away on a breeze of dreams and wishes.

He took off his hat and pressed it to his chest. She was wearing the leather jacket she'd had on the first time he'd seen her, along with her usual skinny jeans and a lacy top that somehow made the whole outfit look feminine.

And sexy.

For a half beat, he completely forgot why he was there and simply stared at her. It took a while to get his mouth moving, but finally the fog in his mind cleared.

"Hey," he said. "I wanted to talk to you."

Yeah, he was a genius. How could she resist his scintillating conversation?

"Okay. Come to the office."

The office. Did he dare follow her there?

Sure he did. In fact, he wondered if there was time to pay Riley to lock the door and turn out the lights. Probably not.

"That guy didn't come back?"

"Nope. You chased him off for good, I think. Thanks." She sat down on the edge of her desk. "But I'm sorry about that. I probably got you out of bed. I could have handled it myself, but—"

"It's no problem. We take care of our own around here."

He searched his mind for a new topic of conversation, but they'd covered all the easy ones and the air felt unsettled, shimmering with expectation but empty of inspiration.

"Where are the boys?"

"School."

"Good."

He wondered what would happen if he shut the door. Would she be scared? Or would she welcome the privacy as much as he would? He didn't want to risk scaring her, so he eased into the same chair he'd occupied the first time he'd come.

"I almost kept Jeffrey home today," she said. "He had a rough night."

"What's wrong?"

"I don't know. You know how he is. But he threw up last night. Really late—after you left. And he was still awfully pale this morning."

"He saw me," Ridge said. "Last night, when I was leaving, he was at the window."

She sighed. "He was probably feeling sick already." She closed her eyes and tilted her head back, running her fingers through her hair, and let out a deep sigh. Ridge had heard her sigh before, but this was a sigh of defeat. "I really wish he hadn't waited till three a.m. to get sick. I hardly slept at all."

"Did he come and get you?"

"No. I'm a light sleeper." She smiled. "This situation, it's a little like being their mom, you know? I've always got one ear open for trouble."

"How's this situation different from the other ones you've worked in?"

"It's more like a home. Like they're—mine." He could tell she was almost afraid to say the word. "I've always worked in city shelters, where the kids come and go."

"Are you afraid you'll get too attached?"

"Afraid, heck," she said. "I already am too attached."

"But you're still leaving."

"Five more weeks."

"That's a shame. The kids are going to miss you." So was he, but he doubted she wanted to hear that.

"I know." She looked troubled. "We're supposed to keep our distance, be warm but professional. But this little gang's really gotten to me."

"Maybe you should stay."

He held his breath, waiting for her answer. It surprised him how much he wanted her to say yes. Just like that, yes, she'd stay.

But she shook her head.

"The new job's a huge step up. I'll be making policy for the whole state of Colorado, affecting thousands of kids. I can do some real good."

"You're doing real good here."

Her brow creased again. "But it's just five kids. I've always wanted to really change things, and I can't do it from here."

"You could change this whole town. You said it

yourself—give the boys a hometown and revitalize the place, keep it alive."

"It's not the same."

He grimaced. He had to admit she was right. Wynott was hardly the center of the universe. But Bill had changed him and his brothers. Wasn't that a worthwhile effort?

The answer to that made plan B even more important. What Bill had done only mattered if Ridge and his brothers passed on the gifts they'd received.

Sierra sighed. "It's going to be hard to leave. This little group—they're so good together, you know? They fight all the time, but they're like brothers already."

"I know." He put his feet up on the desk beside her so they lightly touched her hip. It felt intimate but not in a sexy way. Just *close.* "Frankie's the life of the party, Josh is the worrier, Carter's the funny one, and Isaiah's the troublemaker."

"Exactly. It's amazing you got that, just in one day." She smiled. "What about Jeffrey?"

"Jeff? He's just a scared little kid now." He took a deep breath before his cautious first step. "But he's got the makings of a cowboy."

"You think?"

"I know." He thought back to Jeffrey's riding, his affection for the horse, his wondering expression when he saw Moonpie.

"Takes one to know one, I guess."

She smiled at him again. He smiled back. There was that feeling again, that time had stretched out, but then it stretched too far and the magic broke. They both looked away.

He needed to say something more about Jeffrey, about how much good it would do him to spend more time around horses, but the chance slipped away somehow. Were there men who knew how to talk to women, how to keep this kind of thing going? Or was it a mystery to everyone?

She stared down at her hands, laced in her lap. "I'm sorry about last night. It's just that I don't know anyone here, and the sheriff…" She shook her head like she was trying to forget a bad dream.

"I'm glad you called me," he said. "There were a few neighbors watching as it was, but if you'd called Sheriff Swaggard, that truck driver would have been eight feet tall and bulletproof by morning, with wings and a tail." He cleared his throat, wondering how she'd take his next warning. "It's a small town, and anything you do here, anybody who comes around, the neighbors are going to notice. In fact…"

He was just about to caution her about Riley's presence when Riley herself walked in and leaned up against the wall beside the bookshelf with her hands clasped like some innocent schoolgirl. Sierra put on the chirpy tone of a party hostess.

"Oh, you guys haven't met. Ridge, this is Riley. We've been friends for a long time. Since Riley was— what were you, hon, thirteen?"

Riley nodded.

"And Riley, this is Ridge. He's my best friend in Wynott, obviously."

Riley gave him a thin smile and a nod. Her fragility probably sparked the same feeling in Sierra that the boys did. He had a feeling Sierra tried to save baby birds that had fallen out of their nests, and pound puppies and crippled kittens.

Maybe men too—the ones who'd lost their direction and couldn't find any meaning in lives derailed by disaster.

"So what did you want to talk about?" Sierra asked.

He wanted to talk about foster kids, about how he wanted to close a circle that had started years ago. He wanted to talk about the rest of his life, but there was Riley, blinking as expectantly as Sierra, and he wasn't about to talk about his hopes and dreams and dumb ideas in front of this so-called friend of Sierra's—the friend who drew a homicidal maniac biker dude to her house, the friend who had set the neighbors to buzzing about the "city girls" at Phoenix House.

He shot a glare toward Riley, but for all her fragility, the girl stood firm. She was like some weird chaperone out of a Tim Burton movie. He probably wouldn't get Sierra alone as long as Riley was around.

This called for desperate measures. He cleared his throat and faced Sierra. "I was wondering if you'd want to go to lunch."

Riley looked up from her perusal of her fingernails. "There's no place to eat around here."

What would it take to shake this girl? "I'm sorry, but I was talking to Sierra just then."

"Oh. You mean a date," Riley said, flustered. "Sorry. I didn't realize..." She clapped both hands over her mouth. "Geez, I'm a goofus, aren't I?" She fled the room.

Great. He'd totally misjudged that situation, which wasn't too surprising since it involved women. Now he could talk to Sierra alone, but he'd already committed to lunch. If he laid out his case now, he'd have nothing to talk about later and it really *would* be a date. Which might be a good thing or might not. As usual, he had no idea.

The two of them stared at each other, each unwilling to restart the conversation. When the old landline phone on Sierra's desk rang, they both jumped.

"Phoenix House," she said. There was a pause while she waited for the caller to speak, but it wasn't long. "He isn't?" She thrust her fingers into her hair, and he wondered again how she managed to have such thick hair when she manhandled it so much.

"I put him on the bus this morning," Sierra said. "Did you check the bathrooms? He wasn't feeling good."

There was more chatter with assenting grunts from Sierra, who was tugging at her hair with increasing viciousness as the conversation continued. "Thank you. We'll find him," she finally said and hung up.

"Jeffrey's not at school," she said. "He didn't come in after recess. One of the town kids said they saw him slip out the gate."

She looked down at her desk and rearranged a few items that didn't need rearranging.

"What are you thinking?" Ridge asked.

"I don't think he was sick last night," she said. "I mean, he was sick. He threw up. But something about the way he acted—I think he was scared."

Chapter 27

"How scared?" Ridge asked.

"He clung to me. He let me hold him. That's not normal for Jeffrey—Jeff." She liked Ridge's idea about names, but she had a hard time thinking of serious little Jeffrey as just Jeff. "It's not normal at all."

"You think that jerk that brought Riley here scared him?"

She wasn't about to let him blame this on Riley. "Maybe just the confrontation."

"Well, he can't have gotten far." Ridge shouldered his way back into the denim jacket he'd been wearing and headed for the door. "Where's his family?"

"Denver."

"So you figure he'd head south? Try to join 'em?"

"No way." Jeffrey would run away from, not toward, the family he'd left behind.

"So where do you think he went?"

She thought a moment. "The ranch." She was surprised he hadn't figured it out. "He's probably thinking he'll steal that magic horse you've got that fascinates him so much."

Ridge dug in his pocket and came up with his truck keys. "I'll drive."

Sierra headed for Ridge's truck without a word of protest. If she had any doubt about which way Jeffrey might have gone, she would have taken her own car to cover more ground, but she knew she was right about the ranch. With Ridge driving, she could play lookout.

Jeffrey had run away before. All the boys at Phoenix House had, and by the time the state sent them to Wynott, they'd run so many times their files actually contained information on patterns in their escapes. Jeffrey tended to stick to the roads, though he'd take off running for whatever hiding place he could find if he thought he'd been spotted.

"What time did recess end?" Ridge asked.

"I think recess is about ten, so it hasn't been long." She scanned the road ahead, praying for the sight of a small, unhappy figure plodding along the shoulder.

Ridge scanned the road too, but every once in a while, he'd shoot her a questioning look, as though he was trying to figure something out.

"What?" she finally asked, irritated.

"What's with Riley?" he asked.

"What do you mean?"

"Who is she? She drags that guy here, causes all this trouble—why do you put up with her?"

"I 'put up with her' because we've been friends for years."

"But how did a straight-arrow like you wind up with a friend like that?"

"I wasn't always a straight arrow," she said. "There's a reason why I help these kids. I know how it feels to be unwanted, to be cut loose before you're ready."

"What were your parents like?"

She shrugged. "My dad, I don't know. He left when I was six. I barely remember him, and what I do remember is all rosy and perfect. I suspect time wore off the rough edges and just left the good parts."

He wanted to put an arm around her. He wanted to tug her over beside him on the bench seat, so they could sit close while they searched the fields for Jeffrey. But she sat so straight, with her hands clasped so tightly in her lap, that he knew she'd push him away.

"What about your mom?" he asked.

"She stuck around, at least. She did her part—bought my school supplies, my clothes. But after my dad left, she got bitter. For a while, when I was around thirteen, I rebelled. I could have ended up like Riley, but I pulled myself out. That's why I thought I could help her."

"Who helps you?"

"What?"

"It seems like you're always helping people. Who helps you?"

She stared out the windshield, unblinking. "I help myself."

He kept driving, one hand on the wheel, the other on the sill of the open window. He rarely put both hands on the wheel, she'd noticed, and he always drove with the window open. That had been fine when they were at the ranch, but she'd actually tried to do something with her hair this morning, and the wind was ruining it.

"Could you roll your window up? It's messing up my hair."

He grinned. "I like it messy."

"I know you do." She immediately blushed. That was the closest they'd come to talking about what had happened between them.

They drove a long time in silence, passing the school

and heading toward the ranch. They traveled a surprising distance before Sierra's prayers were answered by the sight of Jeffrey's slight form trudging through the grass by the side of the road.

Ridge braked and pulled the truck onto the shoulder. At the sound of tires on gravel, Jeffrey took off running straight across what had once been a field of sugar beets and was now an obstacle course. The rows of withered plants seemed to be spaced perfectly for Jeffrey's running stride, while Ridge could leap two rows at a time. Sierra was left to struggle along behind them.

After tripping countless times and falling to her hands and knees twice, she stopped and watched the man and the boy tearing across the field. She had no doubt Ridge would catch Jeffrey. She'd seen the boy run a lot faster.

He wanted to be caught, she mused. Ridge really did have a way with these kids.

When Ridge got to where he could reach out and grab the back of the boy's shirt, Jeffrey simply stopped running. The man and the boy exchanged a few words, and Jeffrey turned to plod back to the truck. After a while, the cowboy draped his arm over the boy's shoulder. Miraculously, Jeffrey let it lie.

When they reached the truck, Sierra dropped to her knees to give Jeffrey a hug. It was like hugging a wooden doll, but he didn't push her away. But when she opened the door to the crew cab truck's backseat, though, he stood stolidly unmoving.

"Get in, sport," Ridge said.

Jeffrey looked up at Sierra then shook his head and returned to immobility.

"Phoenix House is where you live right now." Ridge

set his hand on the boy's thin shoulder. "Maybe someday that'll change. For starters, I'm going to see if you can come out more often and help me with the horses, okay? But for right now, you have to go back. Sierra will keep you safe, and I'll help."

Sierra almost stopped Ridge. Did he realize he was handing the boy false hope? Anything could happen in this kid's life. He could be moved. He could even find a family, though that would be nothing short of a miracle.

But when Jeffrey spoke, she forgot all about Ridge.

"He was there last night." The boy's face twisted with fear. "He came to get me."

Ridge glanced at Sierra, and she nodded, letting him know she'd heard. But she was confused. There was only one "him" for Jeffrey—his father, who had abused him. And Delivery Truck Man was not Jeffrey's father. The father was in jail, where he belonged.

"Who?" she asked.

"Him." Jeffrey bit his lips, as if he wasn't going to let another sound out ever again.

"But who is he? Is he a friend of your father's?"

The child refused to even look at her.

Ridge knelt down on the gravelly shoulder of the road and put both hands on the boy's shoulders. Looking him straight in the eye, he lowered his voice and said, "I will never let him get you. Never. I promise you, it's safe to go home."

Sierra would have stepped in if she'd only known what to say. Ridge couldn't keep that promise. Giving the kid a sense of security was good, but hadn't the cowboy said he believed in telling the truth? What was he going to do—set up a 24/7 vigil outside Phoenix

House? There was no way he could protect Jeffrey all the time.

Jeffrey's normally expressionless eyes searched Ridge's, as if making sure he could trust him. Ridge never looked away, and finally the boy nodded. Turning away from Ridge, he climbed into the truck's narrow backseat and tugged the seat belt across his small body.

"*Never*," Sierra heard him whisper to himself. It was barely a breath, but she wondered how often the boy would repeat the promise to himself in the days to come. Some kids had a bit of blanket from home that made them feel safe; now Jeffrey had a word—and he'd carry it with him like a security blanket for months, maybe years to come, until it wore out.

When would that be? It seemed inevitable that it would wear out. These kids' lives changed so fast, so frequently. But Ridge was a man who kept his promises. She suspected he'd find a way.

She wouldn't want to be Mitch right now.

The other boys were hanging out with Gil in the kitchen by the time Ridge got Sierra and Jeffrey back into the house.

"Hey, look, it's the man from Mars," said Isaiah. "He came back to his home planet."

Jeffrey walked past him without a word. Sierra let him go, waving an admonishing finger at Isaiah.

"Watch it with the name-calling, mister," she said. "You know better."

She turned back to Ridge. "Looks like everything's back to normal here. Thanks."

"That's all you have to say? Thanks?"

"What do you want me to say?"

"Nothing. I don't like chatty women." He grinned and looked so charming, with his five-o'clock shadow and battered hat, that she couldn't help smiling back. "But now that I chased down your renegade kid for you, I could really use that lunch."

"Oh. Lunch." She'd obviously forgotten all about the invitation. He could almost see smoke coming out of her ears as her mind cranked up excuses. "It's kind of late for lunch."

"Dinner, then."

She stewed a little while longer and finally came up with another excuse. "What will Riley do while I'm gone?"

Riley appeared in the doorway so fast she had to have been eavesdropping.

"I left some stuff in Denver. I need to go pick it up," she said. "If I could borrow your car..."

Score one for Riley. Surprisingly, she was on his side for some reason.

"Sure," Sierra said. "I should go with you, though."

"You don't trust me?"

"I trust you," Sierra said. "But come right back. Okay?"

"Sure."

Sierra turned to Ridge. "I have to go wash up a little."

Riley looked so uneasy at being left alone with Ridge that he felt sorry for her. Perching on the edge of one of the chairs, she kept glancing at him and looking away. He wondered what had happened in her life to make her so frightened of men.

"You don't have to babysit me," he said. "If you have things to do..."

"No. Well, yes, actually. I do have things to do." She took a deep breath and straightened her spine. "I'm not just going to get my stuff. I'm going to find Mitch and figure out what he's up to. He lied about knowing Sierra. He used me to get to her. And I want to know why."

"That could be dangerous."

"Maybe." Riley looked him straight in the eye for the first time since he'd met her. "But I don't care. I'm not a total loser, you know. I'd do anything to help Sierra." She glanced down at her feet, the brief tough-girl facade fading. "I'll do it smart, don't worry. I'll pretend I'm on his side, like I'm mad at Sierra for not letting me stay."

"That sounds smart," Ridge said. "But it still sounds dangerous."

Chapter 28

As Sierra followed Ridge into the dimly lit interior of the Red Dawg Saloon, she managed to tear her eyes from his backside long enough to nod hello to a few of her new neighbors. His jeans weren't tight, exactly, but they sure did fit. And he'd gone out to his truck and returned wearing a clean straw cowboy hat.

A clean hat should have been a good thing, but for some reason Sierra missed his bashed-in, stained, scarred, battered old felt hat. It fit better with his face somehow—and his personality. Ridge wasn't about the showy cowboy charm sold by Nashville singing stars; he was the real thing. A working cowboy.

Those Nashville stars might have money and fame and legions of groupies, but they weren't this rugged, or this masculine, or this *hot*. They didn't have that walk, the slight swagger a man could only get from long days in the saddle. Or the quiet self-assurance of a rodeo rider who's been tossed in the dirt by a hundred horses and bucking bulls and walked away every time—well, almost every time—with a tip of his hat. Certainly if you could subdue a bucking bull, you'd be pretty confident about everything else.

She struggled to still the crazy sparrow that seemed to be fluttering in her chest as she slid into a booth upholstered in red vinyl with a few duct tape patches.

Why was she so nervous? She was only here because he bailed her out last night. Period. End of story.

"It's not exactly The Four Seasons," he said, sliding into the other side of the booth.

"I've heard it's the best restaurant in Wynott," she said.

"I don't know. The microwave burritos at the Mini Mart are pretty darn good."

She glanced around and caught several other diners looking their way. Ed Boone, who had been armed and dangerous outside his hardware store the night before, had his deep-set eyes fixed on the two of them and a sly smile on his face. Mrs. Carson, who was having a silent but companionable dinner with her husband, averted her gaze every time Sierra looked her way. A few men at the bar were watching speculatively. Ridge had nodded at them as he walked in, so they must be friends or acquaintances.

"They'll quit staring after a while." Ridge grinned. "Might be a long while, though. You're the most interesting thing to happen to Wynott in a long time."

What did he mean? Interesting to everyone or interesting to him? Or both? Was it a reference to what had happened between them at the ranch? Or just a passing reference to the fact that she was the new girl, somebody a little different.

Why did that matter, anyway? As Isaiah would say, she was being such a *girl*.

As she pretended to admire the Red Dawg's rustic decor, Ridge accidentally brushed her calf with the toe of his cowboy boot. There couldn't possibly be a more innocent touch, but it was like he'd pushed a button that started an old-fashioned Super 8 movie flickering in her mind. She saw snippets of their night together, disconnected pictures of the moments that mattered: their bodies intertwined, his rough hand cupping her cheek, his pale eyes looking into hers and seeing far more than she wanted to reveal. Then things got really heated and she saw the sculpted muscles of his thigh against hers, the bulge of his biceps as he lifted himself above her, the earnest concentration on his face as he closed his eyes and savored the sensation of driving into her, over and over and...

Stop.

She folded her hands on the table—partly to look poised but mostly to stop them from shaking. The waitress had stopped by, and Ridge had said something. What had it been?

She smiled and nodded vaguely, wondering what she was agreeing to. He could have asked her to cut off her left thumb and feed it to Sluefoot for all she knew.

When the waitress gave her an expectant smile, Sierra realized she hadn't so much as glanced at the menu.

"I'll have a cheeseburger," she said. She could see the remnants of one on Mrs. Carson's plate and the fries looked good. "With fries and a Coke."

"Rib eye," Ridge said. "Rare. And a baked potato. Water to drink."

Sierra fished around for a subject that didn't involve herself or Ridge or how they felt about each other.

"So how do you know Mike?" she asked.

"Mike who?"

"Mike Malloy. Your drinking buddy."

He gave her a blank stare.

"The guy that runs Phoenix House, who thought you should teach the kids rodeo."

"Oh. Him." Ridge shook his head. "I actually don't know him. Shane met him in the beer tent at a rodeo once. The guy wouldn't leave Shane alone until he promised to get involved."

"So you're not my boss's best friend after all."

"I never even met the guy."

"That's great." She could hardly hide her glee. If Ridge and Mike weren't friends, she was free to...

Free to do things she shouldn't.

Ridge was watching her as if he could read her mind, so she fished around for a safe topic. Local history should be safe.

"Phoenix House was a group home before, wasn't it?" Sierra said.

Ridge nodded, grimacing. "They called it an orphanage then, but yeah, it was pretty much the same thing." He stumbled over the words, as if this was a hard topic for him to talk about. "The woman running it was nothing like you, though. She was a lot older, for one thing."

Sierra grimaced. She got comments about how young she was all the time. It was her size. It kept people from taking her seriously, and she was tired of it. She'd hit her limit in heel-height, and her posture was straight as a number-two pencil. The only way she could look taller was stilts, and they hadn't come into vogue yet.

She sat back as the waitress arrived, bearing heaping plates of food. Sierra's burger was big and juicy and deliciously messy, which would have been fine if she'd been eating alone.

"Anything else?" the waitress asked.

"Drinks?" Ridge smiled as the girl whirled and headed back to the kitchen.

"What was she like?" Sierra asked. "The woman who ran Phoenix House, I mean."

Ridge huffed out a mirthless laugh. "She sure as hell didn't care about the kids like you do. She was just there to collect a paycheck. She scrimped on supplies, and she never lifted a finger to clean the place."

"You know a lot about it," she said. "Have you always been concerned about homeless kids?"

"Sort of." Ridge toyed with his food, which made it all the more embarrassing that Sierra couldn't help attacking her cheeseburger like a hungry wolf.

"She never should have been given control over kids. Not anywhere." Ridge was staring across the room, his eyes fixed on the wall as if he was seeing the skimpy meals and unwashed laundry himself. "She'd lock the kids in the basement, make them go without meals, you name it. That's what finally got the place shut down."

"That's awful," Sierra said.

"It was. It's so isolated here, you know? There was nobody for the kids to turn to. I think there were supposed to be state inspections, but nobody ever came."

He was still staring blankly into the distance. The term "thousand-yard stare" was usually applied to combat veterans or post-traumatic stress sufferers. But if she didn't know better, she'd say that's what Ridge was doing now.

He seemed to take a lot of things about the home personally. Maybe it was a sad commentary on society that the level of his caring set off warning bells in her head.

Or maybe...

All the questions that had been lurking in the back of her mind since her first trip to the ranch surged to the forefront. Why didn't Ridge have the same last name as his father or his brothers? Why did the three boys look so different? And that picture…

She reached over the table, stopping just short of touching his hand. He jerked in his seat, as if he'd been dreaming and she'd woken him up.

"You seem to know an awful lot about this," she said cautiously.

He shook his head, as if snapping out of a dream. "Yeah, well, I was there."

She didn't know what to say. He *had* been there. *There*.

He'd been one of the kids.

Pieces began falling into place—the way he understood the kids. The way he talked about the place.

She didn't know where to look or what to say. She'd heard how bad the place was back then. Mike had cautioned her that Phoenix House had a terrible reputation to overcome.

No wonder Ridge had trouble with relationships. No wonder he understood the boys so well.

He'd been a foster child himself.

Chapter 29

RIDGE'S DINNER WITH SIERRA WAS NOT GOING according to plan. He'd figured on bringing up his past, but the picture he wanted to paint was of a man who'd experienced the foster system and had a positive outcome—not of a man who'd been through the worst the system had to offer. Now Sierra was looking at him with a mixture of horror and pity that didn't bode well for any rational discussion.

Maybe he should just give up on this. Why did he want to complicate his life with a kid anyway? He was no good with people.

But he *was* good with Jeffrey. The memory of the boy riding circled in his mind—the glow of his smile, the new confidence in his movements. Dammit, he remembered that feeling, that elation when you swung into the saddle and took control of a chaotic world. He wanted to give that feeling to Jeffrey, and maybe some other boys too. Not just once a week, but every day, the way Bill Decker had done for him.

"Ridge, I had no idea you were a foster kid," Sierra said. "I'm so sorry. I hope I haven't said anything stupid. I mean, I had no clue."

He waved away her pity. "I'm fine."

She leaned forward, a french fry dangling from her fingers. "Well, you've done pretty well for yourself. I mean, I had no idea. How did you ever end up a cowboy, of all things?"

"When they shut the place down, they found homes for all the kids but three—the three nobody wanted. Me, Shane, and Brady. They gave us an emergency placement with Bill Decker, at the ranch where I live now."

"And you stayed."

"Best thing that ever happened to me. Bill Decker didn't plan on keeping us for long, but something just clicked for all of us."

"Wow." She sat back, staring at him with a mixture of wonder and pity in her eyes.

He wondered how to make her stop feeling sorry for him. He'd been through hard times, sure, but now he was done with that time in his life. Period. He was who he was, and that's what he should be judged on—not his past.

"Bill must have been quite a guy."

"He was." Ridge pictured his foster father, a wiry rancher tough as a strip of rawhide, with the energy of a Tasmanian devil, the tenacity of a wolverine, and a heart as big as all of Wyoming. "He and Irene treated us like we were their own."

"It must have been an adjustment for you if you'd been in care that long."

"I hate that phrase, 'in care,'" he said. "Nobody 'cared' for me until I got out of the system."

"I'm sorry. I never thought of it that way." She toyed with what was left of her food awhile before she looked up and met his eyes. "So that's why you're so good with the boys."

"I hope so. It's also why I want to adopt one. Or two. Actually, I'd eventually like to take three. That's what worked for me and my brothers." He thought of the conversation they'd had earlier about how well this whole group fit together. "But I could take more."

She stopped as suddenly as if someone had hit a pause button, a french fry halfway to her mouth. Setting the fry down, she blurted out, "You want to be a foster father?"

Maybe the pity in her tone hadn't been so bad. It sure beat disbelief, which was what he was hearing now.

"Yes, me. Why? Is that so unbelievable?"

She gave him a critical look. "It just surprised me. You don't seem like the type."

What did she care what "type" he was? He'd spent time in three foster homes in between his bouts in various state-run group homes, and nobody had seemed to care what "type" those foster parents were. His first placement was with a pair of lazy layabouts who wanted to take advantage of easy money from the state. He'd been six then, and they'd mostly used him to clean floors and bring them beers. His second foster parents were zealots on a mission to save the world by beating morality into the hides of innocent kids. The third family meant well, but they'd expected Ridge to love them unconditionally from day one. They'd given him back to the state three weeks after his arrival.

Obviously, nobody had checked to see what "type" they were.

"You don't think I can do it," he said.

"It's not that. It's just a lot to take on, that's all."

"You care about the kids, right?"

"Of course I do."

"Then aren't you anxious to find real homes for them?"

She took a small bite, chewed, and swallowed.

"Anxious isn't a good word." Patting her lips with her napkin, she looked thoughtful. "Just because they enter into a family living situation doesn't mean they're home free. Foster parents have to have an understanding of the issues these kids face and the difficulties they have adjusting to what we think of as a normal life. These kids can't just blend in with an existing family or create the kind of family most people hope for. It's different."

He just stared at her. Did she think he didn't know this stuff?

"I know you have a good understanding of the problems they face, but you have to make sure this is a commitment you can stick with, because there's no going back."

"I'm a rodeo cowboy, remember? 'Sticking' is what I do. I don't quit."

"For eight seconds."

He wanted to argue, but she had a point.

She pointed a french fry at him. "You're a single man who's been on the rodeo circuit most of your adult life. You're used to change, to being on the road, right? I don't see how you could create a home for a child when you're always on the road."

"I'm not going on the road anymore." He'd been resting his bad hand on the table while he ate, but now he put it out of sight in his lap. This wasn't the topic he'd wanted to discuss.

She nipped off the end of a french fry. "But once they fix your hand…"

Damn it, he was going to have to say it out loud. He didn't mind discussing his injury with his brothers, but admitting defeat here, right in the middle of the Red

Dawg, seemed so public. And that made his situation seem final in a way it never had before.

He lifted his hand from the table and showed how stiff the fingers were. "Can't."

Damn. *Can't* was a word Bill had taught him should never be said. But in this case, it was true.

"You can't bend them?"

She reached over and took his hand, forming the fingers into a fist. They bent all right, but as soon as she let go the hand opened again. He felt like slamming it against the table. The doctors said the problem wasn't just in the hand; he had a neck injury that contributed to the problem. They'd tried to fix it with a spinal fusion, but it hadn't worked.

"Nerve damage," he said.

She was giving him that pitying look again, and he quickly pulled his hand away.

"It's okay. It was time to quit anyway. I was the world champion bronc rider last year and the year before. That was my goal. I made it, and I'm done."

There. Now she was looking at him with some respect. She'd never know that championship hadn't been his final goal—that he'd had to quit short of winning the All-Around.

Quit. That was the other word Bill had outlawed. God, he felt like such a failure.

He knew it didn't make sense. It wasn't his fault. His hand had been caught fast in the rigging, and the horse, a bronc named Twister who'd ruined more than one cowboy, rolled over on him. Accidents happened in rodeo all the time. That day, it had happened to him.

But he still felt like he'd failed somehow.

Sierra reached over and put her hand over his good hand. Did she realize he couldn't eat now? He couldn't pick up a french fry with his bad hand, for God's sake. He shook her off.

"Sorry." She seemed to realize she'd made a wrong move. Picking up her burger, she took a bite and eyed him warily, apparently unaware that the bun was dripping condiments onto her leg.

Wariness beat pity, anyway.

"I'm ready to move on," he said. "It's time to do something new, something that does some good in the world." He remembered what Shane had said. "Rodeo's good for learning toughness and try, and for building up your strength. It's a good world for a young man. But in the end, it's all about buckles and babes, and that's not enough anymore."

He watched her tackle the end of her hamburger, licking up a drop of ketchup that threatened to drip out the back of the bun.

"Do you think you might be moving a little fast?" she asked. "It's a big change. Maybe you should—I mean, maybe it would be good to…" She patted her mouth with her napkin and took a deep breath. "Ridge, you don't seem to have a job. How are you going to support a bunch of kids? The state gives you money, and I know you've got the ranch, but is it enough to live on?"

He grinned. This was one problem he didn't have. "Well, for one thing, I have enough rodeo winnings in the bank to buy the ranch three times over, and it's a big ranch. For another thing, I'm pretty well-known around here as a horse trainer, so I can make a living with that."

"Oh." She bit into another french fry, contemplating

him as she chewed. Once she'd swallowed, she patted her mouth again. He was starting to learn this was a signal that she was about to say something uncomfortable. "But won't you miss rodeo? Guts and glory, adoring women—all that stuff?"

He was starting to understand *her* issues. She didn't understand who he was. She couldn't see past the carefree athlete who lived on the road. She had no idea how disciplined he was, how goal oriented.

"No," he said. "I know what I want. And once I take something on, I don't quit until I've succeeded. You don't have to worry about me changing my mind."

"But there is no success in this. You know that, right? You can't just *fix* these kids."

"Bill fixed me. And my brothers."

She locked her eyes on his. "So you have no lingering effects from your childhood?"

He narrowed his eyes. "Do you?"

"We all do. Bill didn't flick a switch, and neither can you. If he were still alive—and I'm really sorry he's not, by the way—he'd still worry about you, wouldn't he? He'd still be your dad, taking care of you."

Something about that phrase brought a lump to Ridge's throat, but he swallowed it down and moved on. He was a grown man now. He didn't need anybody taking care of him; it was his turn to take care of someone.

He thought of the old man's will. He'd left the ranch to all three of the boys, of course. But he'd left them more advice than money, page after page of close-typed text on how to live a good man's life. Nobody complained. Bill's wisdom had meant more to them than anything. More, even, than their home.

They used Bill's advice every day, so Sierra was right; they still needed him. The job was never done.

"I'm not saying you can't do it," she said. "I'm just saying it's a lifelong commitment, one that's not always easy to deal with."

"I can deal with it."

She seemed to accept that answer—or at least, she went back to her french fries and ate with a little more enthusiasm. He went back to his too, although he sure wished he could have something to drink with it. Sierra was probably thirsty too.

"Hey, I'd go to the bar and get you something to drink, but that's Chrissie's dad." He gestured toward the bartender. "Poor kid's always in trouble. Don't want to cause her more."

"I'm fine." Sierra smiled. "She's a cute kid."

Ridge smiled. Shelley would've been up there at the bar, insisting on some sweet pink girlie drink and complaining about the service. Which would have made Chrissie even more of a wreck, and then she'd have screwed up their food too.

They ate for a while before he spoke again. "Look, I might not be perfect dad material. But I'll respect them, I'll protect them, and I'll teach them right from wrong."

She smiled gently. "You forgot something."

"That too. You know I—care about them." He waited for her to point out that maybe a man who couldn't even say the word *love* wasn't capable of it. Shelley had always gone on about that. But Sierra just nodded. Maybe she understood that what you did was a lot more important than what you said.

"So how do I start?" he asked.

"Well, you'll need to fix up the ranch first."

"What's wrong with the ranch?" He and his brothers knew the house needed updating, but none of them had been there long enough to do anything about it. Still, the place was comfortable. It might not be a mansion, but it was home.

"It has to pass a pretty rigorous inspection before they'll let kids live there. You'll have to bring it up to code. Wiring, plumbing—I'm betting that stuff's as old as the building or close." He had to nod. "And there's one more thing."

He waited for her to finish, but she seemed to be having trouble getting the words out.

"Go on," he said. "What is it?"

She looked wary. "They generally don't approve single men."

He should have realized that. With all the hideous cases of abuse in the papers lately, no man would be trusted with a child on his own. Never mind that the only people who had ever smacked Ridge around as a kid were women. In the minds of most people, it was men who couldn't be trusted.

"Hmm." He thought a moment. "Maybe we ought to reconsider that relationship."

She gave him an eye roll worthy of a sarcastic seventh grader. "I thought you were only good for one-night stands."

"That was a slight exaggeration." Even as he said it, he remembered what Shelley said. *You don't need the things other people need. You think that makes you strong. But it doesn't. It just makes you alone.*

Maybe this wasn't something he could do. He'd

learned the value of family from Bill and Irene, but he'd failed miserably at the only long-term relationship he'd ever attempted. He thought he could be a good parent, maybe even a great one. But husband? That word scared him.

It wasn't right. He knew he could create the right environment for a child. Along with his brothers, he *owned* the right environment. Decker Ranch had been paradise to all three of them, and no state home could ever match it—no matter how many Sierras there were out there.

Not that there were very many. He'd never had a housemother or even a counselor who seemed to care as much as Sierra did. Maybe he'd been right when he'd said they should reconsider the relationship. She was a great group-home manager. Wouldn't she be an even better mother in a real family?

She was just what he needed.

Chapter 30

RIDGE COULDN'T HELP WATCHING SIERRA AS THE flickering candle lit those sparkling green eyes. It certainly wouldn't be any hardship to make those eyes shine every night and wake up to them every morning.

"Quit looking at me like that," she said.

"Like how?"

"Like you're thinking you might use me to get what you want."

"That's not what I was thinking."

Not exactly, anyway. Well, maybe, sort of.

Actually, she'd hit the nail right on the head. But it wouldn't be using her if he genuinely cared about her, would it?

He did his best to shut out Shelley's voice, echoing from the past. She'd pointed out that there was something missing in his emotional makeup, probably because, in her words, he had "abandonment issues." She'd claimed he was afraid of being hurt again, so he never allowed himself to love anyone fully.

He'd had to admit that he hadn't loved Shelley in the unreserved, all-out way some of his friends loved their wives or girlfriends. He knew guys who'd quit rodeo for the women they loved. He'd had to admit to Shelley that he wouldn't do that. He wouldn't give up the job that was the core of his identity just to make her happy. He didn't think he should have to, but that seemed to be the test a man had to pass. And he couldn't see himself ever passing it. Not willingly.

As if on cue, a sharp pain shot from his shoulder to his hand, reminding him that he'd had to give up his life-long passion anyway. So he'd lost the girl *and* the job.

He missed the job. He knew he should miss Shelley too, but all he'd felt was relief when she'd left. He knew she'd deserved better, but even when he reached deep into himself and squeezed everything he had out of his heart, he hadn't been able to give her more.

He realized he was staring at Sierra as all these thoughts swirled through his mind. Some girls would have smiled. Some would have fixed their makeup.

Sierra crossed her eyes and stuck out her tongue, cocking her head to do an uncanny imitation of Sluefoot.

He laughed, and she joined in, launching into a case of the giggles that had everybody in the Red Dawg craning their necks to see what was so funny.

And for some reason, that did it, sure as if she'd flipped a switch. He remembered how Bill and Irene had laughed together, sharing secret jokes nobody else knew. He wanted that, and he knew, in this moment, that he could have it with Sierra. He could actually fall in love with this girl.

Maybe he already had.

For now, they could work together. She could help him figure out what the ranch needed. Meanwhile, he'd do his best to make her see him in a new light, and he'd try to open up his heart a little more.

It would be a stealth courtship. If he succeeded, she wouldn't even know what had hit her.

Shane would laugh at that idea. Subtlety had never

been Ridge's strong suit, but hey, a man could learn, right? Especially if the prize was big enough.

"Tell you what," he said. "I'm going to try, anyway, and see what happens. It can't hurt to fix up the ranch, right? I need something to do anyway. And maybe, somewhere along the way, I'll find a woman who can make it work."

She shrugged one shoulder in a move so casual it had to be faked. "Maybe."

Chrissie arrived, triumphantly bearing a Coke and a glass of water. With a proud flourish, she placed the Coke in front of Ridge and gave Sierra the water.

"How's *that*?" she asked.

"Perfect."

They traded drinks as soon as the waitress turned her back, and then they were laughing again, softer this time, their eyes meeting as they shared their secret joke.

He'd have to get to work on that list when he got home, add some detail. *Bring the house up to code* would be the first addition. And the next would be *Find wife*. Or, maybe, given his shortcomings, *find partner*. Surely there was someone who wanted a family, like he did, but had the same kind of difficulty giving her whole heart. And maybe, just maybe, that person was sitting right in front of him.

He remembered what she'd said after they made love. *I might not ever get married. The boys are all the family I need.*

Maybe she'd been lying, trying to play it cool, but he didn't think Sierra was that manipulative. She wouldn't have said those things if she hadn't meant them.

He was tempted to remind her, to argue that they both

wanted the same things and should be together, but then he remembered what kind of courtship this was.

Stealth.

"So. What do I need to do to the house?" he asked.

The smile dimmed. "You realize you could do all this work and not succeed, right?"

"No. You work hard enough, you get what you want."

She laughed like he'd made a joke then sobered. "You really believe that, don't you?"

"It's worked for me so far. It'll work with this."

"Okay. Can I ask you a question?"

"Sure."

"Why do you want this so much?"

He thought a moment, about what he felt and also what she'd want to hear. He decided she'd want to hear the truth.

"I want to give back. I want to do for someone else what Bill did for me. He showed me you can change someone's life just by giving them a chance."

"Okay." Apparently, he'd passed some test. "I'll get you the requirements for the renovation." She suddenly stilled. "The *renovation*. Oh my gosh." She practically bounced in her chair with excitement. "Sure. You should definitely do it."

"Great." He made a triumphant *X* on his mental to-do list. His foot was in the stirrup; now all he had to do was swing into the saddle and take the reins.

"It's really good that you want to give someone a chance, change lives," she said. "I've got a really good place for you to start."

Uh-oh. He had a feeling he'd overplayed his hand. "Like what?"

"Riley's working on a certificate in home renovation. She just needs to do one project—a whole-house project, with things like electrical, plumbing, all that kind of thing."

Shoot. He didn't want Riley fixing his house. But how could he say no?

"She needs a place to stay too, so it's perfect."

Perfect? Hardly.

Before he could speak, Sierra read his expression. She held up her hands to stop his protest. "Just give her a chance for a day or two. See if it'll work out." She looked down at the table and fussily brushed some crumbs into her hand, dumping them in her napkin. "She's a good person. You'll see. Somebody helped you, remember?"

"I was a kid. Why are you so hell-bent on helping a grown woman?"

"I owe her," Sierra said. "Trust me, I owe her way beyond anything I owe anyone. If you can't let her stay a couple days, I'll have to take some kind of leave until I get her situated. And then they'd have to send someone else to take care of the boys." She folded the napkin neatly and began wiping the table. "I could even get fired. I'll definitely have to break into my savings. I see Riley as family, but I doubt they'll give me family leave to take care of her."

He sighed. There was something about Riley that reminded him of his mother. She'd been the same kind of helpless waif, relying on a series of men to take care of her. When that didn't work out, she'd relied on drugs instead, and eventually she'd lost custody of Ridge and his brother. Ridge had landed on his feet, but he didn't

know what had happened to his older brother. Last he
knew, Tell had disappeared without a trace into the same
underworld that had claimed his mom.

His mother had taken away something more than his
brother when she'd given up her parental rights. She'd
robbed him of a confidence in the rightness of the world
that other people took for granted. It wasn't fair to people
like Riley, but she'd left him with a distaste for weakness.
The feeling was so ingrained, he couldn't get past it.

"Don't think of it as helping Riley," Sierra said.
"Think of it as helping the boys, and working toward
your goal. Really, she's great at this renovation stuff."
She reached across the table and set her hand on his arm.
The touch fired up a whole bunch of neurons, which
carried their message straight to his brain and dizzied it
into submission. That was the only possible explanation
for what he said next.

"It's just on a trial basis, right? For a couple of days."

Sierra beamed. "Right."

He nodded reluctantly then felt his reluctance lift as
a thought struck him.

"Okay. But you're right about the ranch. It's in pretty
bad shape." He tried to look regretful, but he'd never
been much of an actor and he suspected it came off more
like indigestion. "I don't know where to put her. Why
don't you come out and take a look? You can see if it'll
be okay for her."

"I'm sure it's fine."

"I don't know. I'd feel better if you took a look."
He couldn't believe it. He was begging, really begging, a woman to come home with him. Maybe he'd
lost his touch.

He'd tossed out his credit card as soon as the check came, but Sierra snatched it and ran her finger down the columns. She flipped through her wallet and laid out half, plus a couple bills for the tip. "We can look at the house when I drop her off." Her eyes widened. "Oh. I need to be home to let Riley in."

Riley, always Riley. Although Riley was doing the right thing tonight, trying to figure out more about this Mitch character. She'd showed some spine there, at least.

Sierra's phone suddenly blasted out the electric whine of rock guitars—Led Zeppelin, Ridge thought. Heads turned as she fumbled through her purse. When she finally found the poor smashed thing, she bobbled it and nearly dropped it out of sheer nervousness before she managed to answer.

"Riley?"

Oh, great. He sat back, wondering if he should try to get Chrissie's attention and get another drink. Something stronger this time.

Sierra gestured an apology and mumbled into the phone for a while. Finally, she shut it off.

"What's up with Riley?" he asked.

"She's spending the night in town." Sierra shoved the phone into her purse and zipped the bag shut as if she could zip Riley and all her problems inside with it. "She said she's too tired to pack all her stuff, but it sounded like she was at a party."

"Where did she say she was?"

"At a friend's apartment. But I'm not sure I like the friend."

"Why?"

"I could swear I heard Mitch's voice."

He put on his best poker face. "You don't think she'd go anywhere near him now, though, do you?"

"Not after I told her he lied about knowing me."

"It was probably someone else."

"Probably." But Sierra looked troubled, glancing down at her purse.

"Look, why don't you come over? We can do something positive for Riley by making sure I have a place for her."

"Ridge, I'm sure you have something. She's hardly picky."

He shook his head sadly, hoping he looked helpless. "It's pretty bad. I mean, the three of us have been batching it for a long time now, and Bill before that."

"What about Irene?"

"She passed away a few years after we boys moved in. There hasn't been a woman in the house for years."

Unless you counted the girls Brady brought home. But they weren't likely to clean anything or add a woman's touch to anything but Brady himself. He supposed you could count Shelley too, but she'd only been to the ranch a couple times. She liked neatness and order, fancy meals by candlelight, and expensive sheets and towels. The couple times she'd come to the ranch, she'd seemed a little taken aback by the roughness of his lifestyle.

Sierra, on the other hand, seemed to like the ranch. She'd been a little shocked by Sluefoot, but the natural way she talked to the dogs told him she'd be as good with animals as she was with kids once she got used to them. And when they'd walked into the bedroom, and she'd seen Irene's lace curtains and flowered wallpaper, he'd seen a look in her eyes that said *home*. It had scared him a little that night, but now he'd changed his mind. He wanted to see that look again.

Because another thing he'd discovered since coming back to the ranch was that it felt like home to him too. The steady work, the animals, the sense of being home—he'd been surprised to discover he didn't mind waking up to the same sunrise every morning one bit.

The question was, could he wake up to the same woman?

He looked over at Sierra, who was fishing an extra dollar out of her wallet.

"You paid your share," he said.

"This is a little extra for Chrissie." She flushed. "I know she screwed up a little, but this is a big job for a high school kid. And she did the best she could."

Yes. He could wake up to this.

He reached across the table and took her hand in his.

Chapter 31

SIERRA LOOKED DOWN AND REALIZED WITH A START that Ridge had reached out with his damaged hand. The fingers wouldn't curl around hers, but she did that for him, lacing her fingers through his.

She'd seen shame in his eyes when he'd first shown her his injury, and since then, he'd kept his bad hand under the table where she couldn't see it. But now he'd handed it to her, quite literally put himself in her hands. She felt like Androcles in the old fable, holding the lion's injured paw.

The last time she'd visited the ranch—now there was a euphemism for you, *visited*—she'd been drawn by Ridge physically, and her libido had crashed through all her boundaries like a rodeo bull breaking down a chicken-wire fence. But now, she felt like she'd peeled away the secrets of his past, layer by layer, and uncovered a man who'd been shaped by a fractured childhood, just like the kids she cared for.

She could only pray they'd do as well as Ridge had. He represented everything she hoped her boys could achieve—success, fulfillment, a place in the community. But with his injury, that success had been stripped away.

Men tended to define themselves through their work—construction foreman, stockbroker, teacher, rodeo cowboy. Ridge had lost that identity, and he needed to find a new place and purpose for himself in the world. And need was the one thing Sierra could never resist.

A ribbon of desire spun through her veins, spiraling into a tangle of feelings that was so dense and confusing she didn't want to even start to unravel it.

She was going to go home with Ridge. She'd slide into those cool sheets again, watch the lace curtains billow in the breeze from the open window. She'd feel his hands on her again, and she'd ease his pain. She'd kiss him and touch him and take him inside her, giving him and herself the simple gift of losing themselves in the rapture of making love.

She had the whole night off from Phoenix House — a treat she got twice a week, when Gil and his wife stayed over. So she had no excuse.

Or did she? Riley had the car, and she didn't feel right about going in the truck with Ridge. She had to get back to Phoenix House tonight, and she didn't dare leave that detail to anyone but herself. So she didn't just have an excuse; she had a roadblock.

She felt the dull thud of disappointment low in her stomach. There had to be some solution.

The van. She'd take the Phoenix House van. She had permission to use it as a personal vehicle when necessary, so driving it to the ranch wouldn't be a problem. She'd just have to park at the bottom of the dirt road and let Ridge drive her up to the house, but she had a feeling he wouldn't mind.

She could hardly claim momentary madness this time, though. She'd have to go back to the house, get the van, and drive all that way. She couldn't pretend she was going to all that trouble for Riley.

No, she was making this trip for herself. She'd have plenty of chances to stop, but she knew she'd keep right on going, straight to the heart of the Wyoming night.

Sierra followed Ridge's truck through town. Ahead of her was the ranch; behind her were Wynott and Phoenix House and the careful, rational life she'd planned to lead here.

She'd given up on love on her very first day. Sure, it had just been a computer dating profile, but the act had been symbolic, and she'd meant to stick by her resolution. So why had she gone to dinner with Ridge Cooper? And why had she followed him home?

On the surface, she and Ridge had nothing in common. They'd both had difficult childhoods, but his was much, much worse. And they'd overcome them in different ways. Ridge had gone country—or, more accurately, gone cowboy. He'd found a simple way of life that worked for him, one that fit his strengths and made him happy. Sierra, on the other hand, had escaped the poverty of her childhood by excelling in school, earning scholarships and using good grades and intelligence to fulfill the purpose she felt she'd been born to.

At some point in their lives—maybe about the time that picture had been taken of a sulky Ridge on the doorstep of the homestead with his new adoptive family—they could have been soul mates. They were two kids who'd been born into difficult situations, kids whose anger and resentment was about to propel them toward a solution, but they'd chosen different paths. Could those roads come together again?

She was starting to hope so.

Ridge pulled over in front of the old homestead, truck tires crunching on rocks and dirt. She pulled in beside him, and when she got out of the van, she took one look at him and found the answer to her question.

She was here because never ever in her whole life had she had the chance to make love to a man like this. And she'd probably never have that chance again.

In the fading light of evening, Ridge wasn't just handsome, like some of the men she'd met in the city. Sure, he looked good—but his appeal ran far deeper than that. He was masculine from the calloused palms of his hands to the righteous core of his heart, which was appropriately hidden in a hard, nearly impenetrable shell. Dogs and kids and horses got a free pass; he loved them without reservation. But people? Not so much.

And yet he saw something in her that he wanted.

He held open the door to the truck and waved her inside with a courtly gesture. Oh, yeah, the truck. She remembered how embarrassed she'd been as she'd scrambled over the shift lever, but now she just zipped right into her place.

"You ever think about getting the other door fixed?"

He rested his arm on the seat behind her while he turned to back up for a straight shot at the rough road.

"Don't need it most days."

She didn't point out that most days he worked alone. If he wanted to start a foster family, he might want two doors on his vehicle. Heck, he might want a minivan, but she wasn't about to mention that idea. The very thought of a minivan sent most men screaming into the wilderness.

When they reached the ranch house, Sierra looked at the place with new eyes, imagining she was some strict state inspector looking for trouble. And she realized Ridge was right: the house needed a lot of work. It was amazing what a mess a bunch of men could make in ten years.

Women made a nest of a house, arranging every-thing to create a sense of comfort. Men, on the other hand, made their homes into offices, or workshops, or whatever else seemed useful at the time. In this case, the house had been made into a barn.

That was the only possible explanation for the fact that a hoof-pick was in the dishwasher or that the center of the kitchen table held a napkin holder, salt and pepper shakers shaped like cowboy boots, and a pair of pliers.

"Maybe we'll start with laundry hampers in the bedrooms," she said, surveying the pile of laundry beside the front door.

"No way." Ridge looked at her like she was crazy. "You want us tracking all our dirt into the house? We're not heathens. We always take off our clothes as soon as we walk in."

Sierra choked back a laugh. There were women, lots of women, who would pay to help the men of Decker Ranch shed their Carhartts after a long day's work.

He showed her the family room next. Sierra opted not to comment on the well-worn saddle that sat in front of the fireplace, stirrups splayed toward the hearth. The two old rocking recliners that bracketed the hearth were more traditional furnishings, along with an old sofa along the wall behind them. It was draped with blankets and looked like it probably belonged to Dum and Dee.

"The state won't make us replace these chairs, will they?" There was a note of panic in Ridge's voice.

"I don't think so." The furniture was worn and well-loved, but not dirty enough to condemn.

"Bill sat there." He pointed to the one on the right. "That was Irene's. Now Shane uses Bill's, and I sit in the other one."

"So Brady sits on the sofa?"

"Kid doesn't sit still long enough to need a chair," Ridge said. "Most of the time, he's in that saddle, stretching."

"How old is Brady?" Ridge always referred to him as a kid, so maybe he and Shane were raising a teenaged brother. That would make it a lot easier to argue that they were capable of caring for other kids.

"Twenty-two," he said.

She laughed. "The way you talk about him, I thought he was fifteen."

"The way he acts, you'd think he was ten."

Sierra laughed. "I think I'm going to like Brady."

"Everybody does—everybody female, anyways. You might as well join the herd." Ridge rolled his eyes as he spoke, but there was a note of pride in his tone that almost overwhelmed the annoyance.

He showed her the pantry lined with canned goods and cereal boxes, and a quaint powder room off the kitchen. Then they climbed the stairs, and she felt her heart skip up to a happy, anticipatory beat.

Halfway up the stairs, he took her hand. Just putting her small hand in his big, rough one had made her feel warm and ready for anything, so she was almost disappointed when he kept up the pretense of showing her around the house. She barely looked at the upstairs bath, which was clean enough considering three men lived here on and off.

"This is Brady's room." He opened the first door on the right. Sierra jumped backward and let out a little scream.

It wasn't a room; it was a cave. Jeans, boots, and tattered rodeo magazines paved the floor from wall to wall. The furniture was festooned with dirty laundry, and various discarded items, from gum wrappers to aftershave bottles, littered the floor. The bed was unmade and probably had been for some time. It looked more like the cave of some beast than a man's bedroom. Sierra wouldn't have been surprised to see the bones of deer and other prey tossed in a random corner.

Ridge shut the door quickly. "Sorry. Kid's a slob. One of the best bronc riders in the PRCA, though."

"So you call him a kid because he's the baby of the family."

Ridge laughed. "Don't let him hear you say that."

She smiled. "Looks like he's used to having his big brothers pick up after him."

"Don't remind Shane of that fact. He's a neat freak, and that's exactly what ends up happening."

He opened the next room down the hall.

"I guess this one belongs to the neat freak," Sierra said. The room was so clean and well organized it was almost stark. The bed was made with military precision, and every surface, from the old oak desk to the wide windowsill, gleamed.

"Yup. Shane's room," Ridge said. "I was thinking this might work for Riley."

"Well, duh."

She'd been pretty sure the whole "I don't know where Riley should sleep" thing was a ruse to get her to the ranch. Now she was positive, and she couldn't help laughing.

He shrugged. "I just wasn't sure."

"What about your room?"

Now it was his turn to smile. "I thought maybe you could sleep there. Tonight, anyway."

She ducked her head to hide a smile and followed him down the hall.

Chapter 32

RIDGE'S ROOM FACED WEST, SO ITS ROUGH PLASTER walls were blessed by the first hint of sunset. Sierra swept the curtain from the window to reveal a sky streaked with the colors of Black Hills gold, a shimmering pink with coppery highlights. The sun blessed the day as it died, bestowing a richer shade of green on the pine trees and a brighter glow on the aspens' bright gold leaves.

Ridge came up behind her and set his hands on her shoulders. The beauty of the scene seeped into her senses, along with the warmth of his chest against her back and the whisper of his breath on her neck. Somehow, his hands wound up clasped around her waist, but she couldn't have said when or how.

This place was magic. She didn't know what it was that made her feel so safe here—the peace of the prairie or the warmth of the evening sky. Maybe it was the ageless plains or the trees standing sentinel like soldiers at attention. Maybe it was the house: the well-worn floors, the old-fashioned furniture, and the faded linens, or just the feeling that generations of men and women had made this their home.

Maybe it was Ridge, but she didn't want to think about that. If she let herself believe for an instant she might be falling in love with him, she'd have to protect herself from the magic of this moment, and she didn't want to guard her heart tonight.

When she'd followed him home, she'd made up her mind to break through all her carefully constructed fences and promised herself she'd mend them tomorrow. Tonight, she was like a racehorse running wild, pounding past the finish line without slowing down, racing into the distance toward a future where she didn't belong. Her heart beat like hooves pounding on hard earth, pumping energy through her whole body.

She didn't know when she turned around or when Ridge's hands slipped beneath the gauzy shirt she wore. Come to think of it, she didn't know what had happened to her leather jacket. She must have shed it when they stepped inside. Maybe that's what had made her so vulnerable; maybe the jacket was her armor. She'd have to remember to put it back on when she left. Put it on and keep it on.

Right now, she wanted to take things *off*. Resting her wrists on Ridge's shoulders, she let him tug the shirt up over her breasts. She loved the way her skin glowed in the fading light, all gold and mellow peach. She heard his breath quicken when she lifted her arms over her head and tossed her hair back, giving herself to him without reservation.

As he slid the thin fabric up, up, and away, the slip of cotton and lace seemed to float in the air a beat longer than was possible, lofted by the breeze that billowed the curtains. It twisted and danced in a ray of the dying sun as it fell, and she swore she heard a sigh as it settled to the floor.

She sighed too, dropping her arms, draping them around Ridge's neck as he eased her gently onto the bed. With that long, slow sigh she released what little was left of the old, cautious Sierra. The new Sierra reached up and grasped the vertical posts of the big wooden headboard as he pulled off her boots then watched as he worked her belt loose and slipped off her jeans. The denim hung forgotten from his fingers as he stared down at her, his hot gaze licking up her body like flames, setting every nerve alight.

Just when she'd started to feel self-conscious, he sat down on the side of the bed and ran a cautious finger down the strap of her lacy bra with a touch so tender it soothed her fears.

"I had a Victoria's Secret catalog under my mattress when I was a kid," he said in his low, gravelly voice. "Maybe that's why I like a pretty woman in pretty lingerie so much." His voice dropped to a low murmur as he traced the edge of the fabric that cupped her breasts. "Pretty woman... in pretty... clothes..." He ran his fingertips down into the V of her cleavage then up the other side. "You're a fantasy come true."

She didn't have the heart to tell him it was hardly lingerie, just underwear, bought from some regular place like Target or maybe Walmart. It matched, of course, but it wasn't up to her usual standards. She'd worn Hanes Her Way on purpose, thinking it might keep her out of his bed if she were to lose her mind and end up at the ranch tonight.

She said a silent farewell to her mind and let go of the headboard to reach for him, but he caught her hands in his and brought them back to the headboard.

"I like you this way." He smiled a slow smile, and she felt pinned there, bound by his gaze as if soft rawhide tied her to the bed. Twining her fingers around the posts, she felt like a sacrificial virgin. She wasn't sure what it meant that he liked that, but she liked it too. As long as she kept her hands tight around those turned oak posts, she was at his mercy. None of this was her fault. It was him—either him or the devil—that made her do it.

Ridge was evidently dead set on becoming an expert on lingerie in one easy lesson. He took his time appreciating every seam and slip of lace. He traced the elastic of her low-cut bikini and her skin shivered as he swept over the soft dips by her hip bone.

She wanted him to take them off.

She wanted that even more as he traced the high line of her sternum and stroked the arch of each rib. Why did she have so many ribs, anyway? She made a mew of impatience but he kept moving slowly, journeying up over her breasts again and taking a slow dip into her cleavage. She shivered and twisted, still gripping the headboard.

Then he threw a leg over her and pinned her to the bed. Bending down, he kissed her, deep and wild, and suddenly his hands were everywhere, cupping her breasts, squeezing and teasing and moving, always moving, to her hips, to her thighs, to the V between her legs. He caressed her through the fabric until the panties he'd so admired were damp and she wished they would burn right off her body. She was smoldering inside, the heat of her body warming the room as she simmered with a desperate desire to give him everything—her body, her breasts, her bones, her lips, her heart.

No, wait. Not her heart. No.

The heat rushed out and panic coursed in to replace it, panic that left her fluttering and breathless. She let go of the headboard, pulling her legs up under her so she could kneel and put a hand to her heaving chest while she struggled to catch her breath.

"Sorry," she said. "Wait—just—I don't know… Wait."

Ridge sat up too, the heavy heat of his gaze telling her she'd caught him just in time. Another second and he couldn't have stopped. As it was, his eyes were wary, and he wasn't smiling. Not even close.

"What happened?" His hot gaze cooled to warm as he took in her panic—a warmth she remembered, the warmth of the man she knew. For a moment, their need had been so strong it was like they'd been two strangers.

He skimmed his hand down her shoulder. "What's wrong?"

"Nothing. I—I just need a break." She was breathing like she'd just run a marathon. What the hell was wrong with her?

"What kind of break? You hungry? Tired?"

"Just—just a break." What could she tell him? That she was overwhelmed? That he made her feel too much, too fast?

This was supposed to be a fling. They weren't supposed to *mean* anything to each other. But one minute she'd been herself, savoring the pleasure of his touch, and the next she'd melted, and they'd blended together into one, like honey stirred into ginger tea or cream billowing into coffee and blending, inseparable.

If she let that happen, she'd be part of him, and she'd be something less than whole when she left. Jumping fences was fine as long as the racehorse remembered where she belonged when the wild run was over.

And Sierra didn't belong with this cowboy who sat patiently beside her, watching her for signs of skittishness, wondering if she'd try to bolt. She didn't belong in this room, spare and masculine, infused with the scent of cedar and leather and that indescribable blend of clean linen, candle wax, and dust that defined old houses.

She belonged—she belonged...

Had she ever belonged anywhere?

She hadn't. Not really. She'd always been so set on creating her future, she'd never paid attention to the present. She'd never made herself the kind of home she was so set on creating for the boys. Maybe she needed a hometown too.

Funny, she'd never thought of that. But it would have to wait, because tonight she couldn't think.

She'd lost her mind, after all.

Ridge lifted one hand slowly to her face, as if he was afraid she'd shy and run, and gently traced her hairline. That forced her to look at him, and looking at him— well, looking at him forced her to kiss him.

He kissed her tenderly, coaxing her out of her panic. His tongue tangled with hers and they sparred; some- times he was winning, sometimes it was her, but there was a sweet humor to it that made her rise on her knees and kiss him harder, deeper, and he answered with a kiss that rocked her right out of all that foolishness about running and belonging and what she should and shouldn't do.

Ridge didn't know why Sierra had needed a break, but she'd evidently gotten the rest she needed to think things through because she went from willing to wanton in 3.5 seconds. A moment ago she'd been lying there, letting him touch her, responding and reacting. Now she was taking things into her own hands, literally tearing at his shirt and laughing when a button flew off and pinged against the wall. She was throwing off sparks like tinder struck by lightning, and he stood and shed his clothes quickly, before she burned them off.

Then it was his turn. Victoria's Secret be damned; the lacy bra was off in seconds, the panties even faster, and then she was naked, rolling beneath him, twisting against him like she was a cat and he was catnip. The first time they'd made love they'd barely known each other, but now he knew what she liked and he put every bit of that knowledge to use, stroking the secret spots that made her moan and kissing her full on the way she liked it, giving and taking, tangling tongues with no reservations.

But he wasn't fully in charge.

She'd learned a few things herself, and when she reached between his legs and stroked him there, right *there*, he thought he'd die if he didn't take her right that moment. But he closed his eyes. He held back.

The words he planned to write formed in his head: *Find partner*. He was surprised he was capable of conscious thought, but the words were as clear as if plan B were pasted to the headboard of his bed.

Equally clear was the knowledge that he could cross the words off his list because he'd found her. Now he had to win her.

He was winning her body, but he wasn't sure that was supposed to be the first step. He was supposed to win her heart first, but he didn't know a darned thing about women's hearts.

Hell, he wasn't even sure he had one of his own.

Chapter 33

SIERRA REACHED UP AND CUPPED RIDGE'S FACE IN HER hands. He looked down into puzzled green eyes and realized, with a jolt of panic, that they'd lost that playful spark.

"Ridge?" She started to sit up. "Do you need a break?"

"No." He wanted to tell her why he'd stopped. What if he told her he'd seen the future, and the two of them were together in every part of it, for years to come? What if she knew what he was thinking?

She'd run away screaming, that's what. She'd scramble off the bed and throw her clothes on, tossing off some vague excuse while she ran for the door, for her car, for some future that didn't keep her here, with him.

She wasn't ready. And anyway, lists and goals had no place in the bedroom.

"No, darlin'. I'm fine."

He looked straight into her eyes, and she probably saw a piece of his thoughts there, but she let him ease closer, let him kiss her, and then they were lost in lovemaking again.

Lovemaking. That's what they called it, right? And that meant that sex *made* love. So he was doing it right after all.

Now that he'd shut down the whirling tornado in his brain, his confidence came back. His hands stroked her skin, rough on smooth, and his tongue and lips followed, kissing what he'd just caressed. He memorized the gentle geography of her curves and swells, an explorer advancing into new terrain.

Easing her legs apart, he found her sweet and swollen, glistening with her want for him. As he licked and teased, she threw her head back and moaned, erasing everything from his mind but desire.

But she hadn't reached the heights yet. He gripped her hips as she writhed and rose; he kissed and licked, but it was when he said her name that she tensed and lifted her hips as she cried out, formless cries at first and then his name, over and over and over.

When he stopped, she was breathing hard, like a racehorse pushed to the edge of endurance, but rather than roll away, she reached for him for comfort.

Lovemaking.

He lay beside her and held her while she calmed, stroked her hair and kissed her cheek, her ear, her neck while she trembled through the aftershocks.

He could feel her coming back to the real world, leaving the world they'd made together. He hoped they'd truly *made love,* and she wouldn't pull away when she returned to reality.

But she did.

—∿∿—

Sierra scrambled up to a sitting position and stared at Ridge. What the hell had he done? She'd had sex before, good sex, but the feelings he'd filled her with were something new. She had been completely out of control, utterly at his mercy, and yet she felt empowered, not diminished.

Empowered.

How could that be? She'd called his name over and over, wanting him, needing him with a desperation she'd never experienced before. And yet, she felt stronger than she'd ever felt before.

It was her turn now.

Putting one palm on his chest, she pushed him onto his back. She straddled his thighs with her hands on his shoulders and rocked her hips, slowly at first, slip-sliding her center along the length of him, leaving him glistening with her wetness and groaning with desire.

He reached up to grab her hips, but she wasn't letting him take charge again. Not that she'd minded, but it was her turn now. Catching his hands, she laced her fingers into his and pushed them down on the mattress at his shoulders while she lowered herself onto him, just a little, barely letting him inside before she stopped and rocked again. All the while, she watched frustration war with ecstasy on his face, inches below her own.

She thought she might lose it again if she kept playing, so she lowered herself a little more then pulled away, then gave him more, then more, then more, until she had to reach up and grab the top of the headboard so she could hang on and close her eyes and *go,* just *go,* riding, riding to sweet oblivion.

He filled her. He warmed her. And he touched all the right places inside her, as if he'd been made to fit her. He felt perfect, so perfect…

She thought about hanging on to sanity, but then she lost her grip on everything, everything but him. Her body tightened, tensed, and broke all over again. She rose on a dizzy tide of sensation as he thrust one more time and clenched his fists and she knew he'd broken too.

—~~~—

Ridge held Sierra as she slept, but he didn't sleep. He couldn't. He was too busy sorting out the conflicting ideas that were running through his mind like a bunch of ornery bull calves, knocking stuff over and trampling his sensible plan into an unrecognizable mess.

Hell, Sierra had done some trampling of her own. He hadn't had this much taken out of him since his last rodeo ride. Their lovemaking had been anything but gentle, and he felt bruised and battered and worn right down to the bone—in a good way.

For the most part, his plan hadn't changed. He still wanted Sierra to be his partner in plan B. But he wanted her in another way too—a way that had nothing to do with plans or partnerships. She'd suddenly become a whole lot more than an item on a list.

She stirred in her sleep and muttered something he couldn't understand. He closed his eyes and pulled her closer, but instead of snuggling up, she bolted from her pillow like a vampire popping up from a coffin.

"No," she said.

He chuckled as she glanced wildly around the room, as if she wasn't sure where she was.

"You having a dream, sweetheart?"

She fixed her eyes on him, and her look of horror made him feel like *he* was the vampire.

"No." She groaned and fell back onto the bed so hard she bounced. "I wish I was."

She said it under her breath, and he knew he wasn't

meant to hear it—but he did, and he felt his own dream shattering like crystal hitting concrete.

What was he thinking? There was no happily ever after in Wynott for Sierra. She'd made it clear from day one that her goal was to view Wynott in her rearview mirror as soon as possible. If he wasn't careful, she'd run him over on her way out, leave him lying in the dust while she zoomed off to better things in bigger places.

———

Sierra turned her head to see the numbers on Ridge's ancient clock radio glowing red in the darkness.

Midnight. Great. She'd be returning to her apartment above Phoenix House around one.

Gil and Jessie wouldn't ask her to explain where she'd been, though Jessie would smile knowingly. Riley was spending the night in Denver, so Sierra wouldn't have to face her. But her neighbors on Main Street would hear the van pull up. The whole town would be talking by daybreak.

She scrambled out of bed and started gathering her clothes. Where were her panties? What was it about this guy that had her flinging her underclothes in all directions?

"Hey." Ridge sat up against the headboard, the rumpled sheets barely hiding the fact that he was ready for another go-round. "Take it easy."

She had her jeans half on, and when she turned to look at him, her foot got stuck. She hopped twice and fell sideways on the bed. Scrambling up quickly so he wouldn't have a chance to seduce her again, she made another attempt at pushing her foot through the leg of her jeans and fell again, this time on her back. There was that ceiling again. She closed her eyes tight and wished the world would just stop spinning.

"Breathe," Ridge said.

That was easy for him to say. He wasn't looking at himself naked and wishing he could start the whole rumpus all over again. Nor did he know what a bad idea said rumpus was.

No, he was looking at her. Not at her breasts, barely hidden by the lacy bra, but at her face. And his expression scared her to death. It was—it was *tender*.

Lustful would have been okay; even leering was all right. But tenderness set off warning bells that made her want to get in her car and drive to some far corner of the earth where there were no cowboys to look at her like that and make her feel this way. This *much*.

Because he made her want to stay. She had things to do, places to go. She'd always been defined by her fierce ambition, but he made her want to chuck it all and keep her job in Wynott, so she could stay with her little boys and her cowboy, and enjoy a normal, happy life. He made her feel like she didn't have to change the world, like she could let somebody else do that.

And what if everybody felt that way?

"Breathe," he said again.

She did, but it came in short, shallow breaths that sounded like the Tweedles panting. Fortunately, he let go of her arm and didn't make any attempt to touch her again, so she eventually regained her self-control and managed to get the rest of her clothes on without falling down.

He didn't say much as she readied herself to leave, just followed her out of the bedroom and down the hall. He'd put on a pair of jeans and nothing else, so when she turned to say good-bye, she didn't know where to look. She couldn't look at his chest, because it was naked and might get her thoughts spinning back to the bedroom. So she looked at his pants, but that wasn't any better since apparently he'd really enjoyed watching her dress. That left his face, and the minute she met his eyes, she realized that was a mistake too.

The tender expression was still there.

"Thank you," he said.

What was she supposed to say now? *You're welcome* seemed to invite a second showing, and she wasn't about to offer that. But she'd better figure out her exit line soon, because the longer she stood there, the longer he could work his magic on her.

She'd been relieved when this job in the back of beyond turned out to be temporary. But now she felt like she'd stepped into a quagmire of love and attraction. She was crazy about the kids, every one of them, and loved them almost as if they were her own. She was crazy about this cowboy too, and by the looks of things, he felt the same way.

But in four weeks—one short month—she was leaving Wynott forever. She was starting to worry she'd be leaving her heart behind.

The light from the hallway spilled out the door, highlighting the uneven floor of the porch and making the white railing stand in sharp relief to the pure, deep dark of the country night. She looked out into black velvet and felt her heartbeat steady to the chirping of the crickets' faint chorus. The distant call of a night bird added a touch of mystery to the scene, and the grass whispered, stroked and soothed by a gentle breeze.

"It's beautiful here." She stepped outside to lean on the porch rail. "Don't you get lonely, though? It's so quiet."

"It's not quiet all the time. But yes, I do get lonely sometimes."

The crickets chirped a few more bars of their steady symphony.

"I'm—sorry," she said. "I—you're a really nice guy. I just…"

"I know," he said. And she felt like he did. He understood, and he wasn't asking anything of her that she wasn't willing to give. The problem was what she was asking of herself.

"You're welcome back anytime," he said. "You know that. The door's always open."

You're welcome, please, thank you—since when had life's little pleasantries become so loaded with meaning?

He stepped past her, jogging down the porch steps and heading for his truck.

Shoot. Talk about awkward; she'd forgotten she'd have to endure the long, bouncy ride to her vehicle.

Hadn't they bounced enough?

The thought made her smile, breaking the grim mood that had plagued her since she'd woken up next to Ridge. They *had* bounced, and it had felt great, and there wasn't a darned thing she could do about it now.

They jounced down the road in silence for a while. She stared straight ahead, but she could see, from the corner of her eye, that he watched her whenever he didn't need to watch the road.

"I'll get that door fixed," he said. "I can probably get Ben to come out and grade the road too. Make it a little easier for you to get up here."

"That's right," she said. "I need to bring Riley out. Would tomorrow morning be okay for that?"

"Anytime tomorrow, I guess. And you're still bringing the boys on Saturday, right?"

His tone was sharper, and she didn't blame him. She had to admit that it would be cruel to deny the boys their outing just because she couldn't keep her hands off the teacher.

"Sure." She hoped her casual tone covered up her original intention, which was *to heck with the boys, I'm staying away from Decker Ranch*. "But we need to stay on a professional level, okay? On a personal level, I feel like I'm on a roller coaster ride."

"My fault," he said as he pulled the truck to a rocky stop.

"No, it's not your fault at all. It takes two. And I'm really grateful for your help with Riley."

She didn't mention that she was also grateful for the darkness, so he couldn't see her blush, and grateful for the van, waiting at the foot of the drive to carry her back to Wynott. Back to Denver, if she wanted. Back to a city so big nobody knew who you were. That was her kind of place. Here in this little town, everybody knew your business. And her business was getting too complicated to share.

He stepped out of the truck and she crawled awkwardly after him, trying to maintain a little dignity despite the fact that she was scrambling around on all fours. Finally, she slid to the ground, planning to run to the van and go. But he was standing right there, so close she wanted—*needed* to touch him. She leaned against his truck, staring down at the ground.

"So you don't like roller coaster rides," he said.

She shook her head. "Not emotional roller coasters."

She edged past him to climb into the van and sit behind the steering wheel, but his eyes were on hers and although she heard a danger signal deep in her brain, she was still unable to do what she knew she should do—crank the ignition and drive.

He tapped on the window, and like a fool, she rolled it down. He rested his elbows on the edge. She resisted the urge to reach out and stroke the hair on his muscular forearms, brown hair bleached to blond by the sun.

"As far as the drive home is concerned, just watch your speed. Sheriff Jim loves to catch speeders."

She nodded, a little annoyed. She hardly needed driving instructions from him. Why did men always assume women couldn't drive?

"As far as our personal relationship goes, the roller coaster's going uphill right now—not a bad place to be, really."

He straightened, tipped his hat, and headed back to the truck, so she didn't get the chance to tell him again that there wouldn't *be* any personal relationship between them. It would be professional, all professional. She was getting off the roller coaster, even if she had to climb out of the car and jump.

But as she rolled down the road, she couldn't help puzzling over what he'd said. Uphill was the hard part of the roller coaster ride, when the little cars huffed and puffed to reach the top of the hill, right? So what did that mean, *It's going uphill right now*? He said that like it was a *good* thing.

She thought of the last roller coaster ride she'd been on. It had been at Elitch Gardens, an amusement park that had been built in the 1890s and somehow survived despite the fact that it was located in the heart of Denver. She'd regretted her decision to ride the Sidewinder the minute she handed her money to the sunburned teenager who ran the ride. But as the little car began its clattering ascent, the park spread out below her. She watched the families strolling the grounds, the young couples sharing funnel cakes and hot dogs. As they rolled higher, ever higher, she could see beyond the border of the amusement park, where the city's apartment buildings and warehouses gave way to open land, neat squares and circles of planted fields divided by straight, brown roads leading in all directions. The world kept getting bigger and bigger as she rose higher and higher.

Snug in her little car, she'd felt like she owned that world—a happy world, a world where kids rode the Spider for fifty cents and couples snuggled on the Ferris wheel, where teacups twirled laughing children and winning a giant teddy bear was the only ambition that mattered.

When she'd reached the summit, she'd felt her car tipping forward, first a little, then a little more, and she'd wondered, with a thrill of delight, what lay ahead. Whatever it was, however fast they clattered down the tracks, she knew that if she lifted her arms in the air and trusted to the future, her heart would fill with joy.

Is that what life with Ridge would be like? Because she could live a life like that.

She just couldn't live it in Wynott.

Chapter 34

WHEN SIERRA SHUT THE CAR OFF IN FRONT OF PHOENIX House, the little town's silent night seemed even more profound than usual. She heard the scrape of a window being opened, then the bang of a screen door. Her neighbors were on the job, watching the street for trouble and probably hoping to pick up a little gossip fodder as well. The story of her late-night arrival would be a topic of speculation on the bench outside the hardware store by morning.

At least Riley wasn't there to tease her about her long night with Ridge—or to hear her toss and turn as she relived their lovemaking over and over in her dreams.

As it turned out, Riley didn't turn up until nine the next morning—late enough that Sierra had time to put the kids on the bus and pace the floor for over an hour, worrying about her.

"Where have you *been*?"

Riley flashed her a smile. "Umm, Denver?" She set her hands on her hips and cocked her head. The pose exuded an air of confidence Sierra hadn't seen from Riley in years. "You know, where I told you I was going to be?" She grinned and flopped down on one of the two worn chairs by the bay window.

"It's just that I worry," Sierra said.

"I know. But wait till you hear what I found out." Riley wriggled with excitement.

"About what?"

"About that asshole Mitch."

Sierra sat up and grabbed the edge of the sofa. "I knew it! I knew you were with him! I heard his voice on the phone." She narrowed her eyes. "So you *did* lie to me."

"Nope. I was at my Mom's place."

"He was *there*?"

"I invited him over."

"Riley, how could you do that? You know he lied about knowing me." Her eyes widened. "You're not thinking about starting up a relationship with him, are you? Because—"

"Sierra." Riley cocked her head sideways and glanced up at the ceiling, still channeling that fed-up teenager. "I'm not stupid. I know he lied, and I wanted to know why. So I lured him into my web and found out more about him." She did her best Cruella de Vil laugh. "I think he thought I was going to sleep with him or something. He was trying to impress me with all his great accomplishments."

"Like what?"

"Like that he's a major drug dealer down there. *Major*. I got him bragging about how much *product* he moves, all that kind of thing."

"Oh, that's great news."

"So we know he wasn't at that Alcoholics Anonymous meeting where I met him to deal with any kind of addiction. He was looking for me because he wanted to get to you."

Sierra felt a prickle of unease at the nape of her neck, as if a cold hand had reached out to tickle her there. "Why would he want to get to me?"

"I don't know." Riley's confidence seemed to escape from her like air from a balloon, and she slumped in her chair. "I asked him, but he wouldn't tell me. I asked him why he wanted to know the kids' names too, and he gave me some bullshit about friends naming their baby."

"You *asked* him?"

"Well, sure. Why not?"

"You shouldn't have put yourself in danger like that."

"Sierra, I rode all the way up here with him. If he was going to hurt me, he'd have done it then. I think he's after one of the kids."

"I know." Sierra picked at a hole in the ancient couch.

"Do you think one of the kids' parents is some kind of druggie and owes him money or something?"

The chill clutched the back of Sierra's neck then scampered down her spine. "It's possible." She stood. "In any case, there's no way you can go back to Denver now. We need to keep you safe until I get this figured out."

Riley perked up again. "So I can stay here?"

"Even better." Sierra took a deep breath and put on her best Happy-Birthday-Fourth-of-July-Merry Christmas smile. "You're going to stay at Decker Ranch!"

Riley stared at her, her mouth hanging open ever so slightly. "With that cowboy?"

"You bet. *And* he's got a job for you."

"Right," Riley said. "Next you'll tell me he's got sparkly unicorns. If he does, he probably wants me to clean their stalls."

"Nope. You won't believe this. He's renovating the house, and he wants you to help."

That got Riley's attention. "Really?"

"Really."

"He actually wants me to help, or you talked him into taking me on as a pity case?"

"You're not a pity case."

"But you *did* talk him into it, didn't you?"

"Just take a look," Sierra said. "Come with me and see the place. If you hate it, I'll take you back to Denver."

"Really?"

"Really. But I think you'll like it. He has a really nice room for you, with plenty of privacy."

Riley's eyes narrowed and a slow smile spread over her face. "You went out there last night."

Sierra felt herself blushing, so there was no point in lying. "Just to make sure he had a good place for you to stay."

"Yeah? And is that all you did?"

Sierra didn't want to lie outright. "You know I'm not looking for a guy right now."

"*I* know that. But does *he* know that?"

Sierra nodded, feeling like she was back on solid ground. She had told Ridge, in no uncertain terms, that she wasn't looking for love. Riley didn't need to know that was *after* she'd had red-hot, crazy, caterwauling sex with him.

"So you guys are just friends?"

Sierra thought a moment. What was the truth? Was she really done with Ridge Cooper, or was she kidding herself?

They had a strong connection—stronger than she'd ever felt with a man. It had her thinking about love that lasted, love that led to marriage. Over and over, as she'd tried to sleep, she'd pictured the ranch house as it had looked when she'd left. The lights from the windows had been the only sign of human habitation on the wide, night-shrouded plains. The squares of gold beaming light out into the deep, dark prairie night had looked welcoming and warm. What would it be like to live there, to always have a real home to return to, to always have a light burning for you no matter where you went? What would it be like to know where you belonged?

You're welcome back anytime. That's what Ridge had said. *The door's always open.*

She needed to stop thinking about that door. Because no matter how well they meshed when they were rolling around in that big old bed at the ranch, Ridge's lifestyle was so different from hers he might as well be the King of England. They were miles apart.

"Earth to Sierra." Riley waved as if from a far distance. "You and Ridge. What's the story?"

"There's nothing going on," Sierra said. "I mean, are you kidding? He's a *cowboy.*"

"Exactly." Riley laughed. "That would never work."

"So are you ready to go?"

Riley froze like a startled rabbit. "Now?"

Sierra stood, brushing imaginary lint off her black capris.

"No time like the present. Come on, Riley. It's time to cowgirl up."

Chapter 35

A HEAVYSET MAN IN OVERALLS GAVE SIERRA AND Riley a cheerful wave from the cab of some enormous Caterpillar monstrosity as they paused to turn onto the ranch road. Looking ahead, Sierra realized the monstrosity was apparently a grader, because the road's ruts and washouts were all smoothed away.

She couldn't help smiling. It was nice to know there were still men who kept their promises. Not that Ridge would be making any promises to her or anything. And grading a road was hardly a romantic gesture. But still…

She had no trouble coaxing the Jeep up the hill this time. When they reached the top and looked down on the quaint ranch house and barn, she turned to Riley.

"See? I told you it was nice."

Riley hummed the theme song to *Green Acres* under her breath. When Sierra didn't laugh, she fidgeted in her seat and kicked at the floorboards. "I'm sorry. I know I should be grateful that you've found a place for me. And I am, I really am. It's just so—different."

"Just give it a chance," Sierra said. "I didn't expect to like it either, but I love it out here. I wish *I* could live here for a while."

"Yeah, but you have ulterior motives."

"Do not."

"Do too."

They laughed together, and Sierra felt the tension between them easing away.

As they exited the car, the Tweedles bolted from their stations on the porch and performed their usual balletic greeting, swirling around both women, swishing their long, brushy tails. Riley shied away as Sierra bent to pet them, ruffling the thick fur on their shoulders and stroking their silky ears as they took turns lunging for her face, sloppy kisses locked and loaded.

Once the dogs had calmed down, Sierra headed for the house with Riley trailing behind her. She rapped sharply on the screen door. Since the front door was standing open, she stepped inside, the dogs following.

"Ridge?" she called.

The dogs shoved her aside and rocketed past her, furry feet skidding on the hardwood floor of the hallway as they hooked the turn into Ridge's bedroom. Almost immediately, a volley of curses erupted, and one of the dogs appeared a second later, gleefully dragging a white T-shirt. The other dog joined its partner, slipping and scrambling as it grabbed the other end of the garment.

"Dammit, give that back." Ridge bolted out of the bedroom. His hair was wet, his eyes were wild, and he wore nothing but a pair of jeans. He barely wore those, since they were unbelted and hung so low on his hips Sierra was afraid he might lose them at any moment.

"Dum! Dee!"

Sierra and Riley jumped aside as the dogs sped out the front door, enjoying a rollicking game of tug-o-war with the shirt as they ran. Once they reached the yard, they stopped and really put their hearts into the game, bracing their front legs and growling ferociously.

"Dum! Dee! *Dum!*" Ridge yelled as he passed them.

Riley looked at the dogs then at Ridge, then at Sierra. "Dum dee dum dee dum?" she sang in a tentative alto.

Sierra started laughing just as the dogs paused in their growling and the unmistakable sound of tearing cloth rent the still autumn air. But at least part of the shirt held, and the dogs began circling, still growling, still tugging, humping up their shoulders with effort as they moved across the yard in slow circles.

Ridge caught up and grabbed the middle of the shirt with one hand, nearly hauling both dogs off the ground. Still they clung to it until one lost its hold. The loser turned and barked madly as the remaining contestants tussled over the shirt.

Ridge wrapped the fabric around one hand, reminding Sierra he couldn't hang on with the other one. The muscles in his arm bulged while his back and shoulders rippled with every tug.

Meanwhile, the dog laid back her ears and held on, shaking her head furiously as she tried to rip the shirt from his hand.

"Dum. *Dum!*" he yelled.

"Is that the dog's name?" Riley asked.

Sierra nodded, but she wasn't paying much attention to Riley. How could she when Ridge was putting on such a show? Water droplets flew from his hair and trailed down the bunched muscles of his back as he wrestled with his dog.

The dog growled low as Ridge hauled her closer and closer. Soon man and dog were nose to nose, and Sierra was pretty sure they were both growling. Ridge's brows were drawn down and his eyes were fixed on the dog's with a primal intensity that made Sierra a little nervous. If *she* were a dog, she would've given him back his shirt.

Although she might not let him put it on. She'd have to give the dogs a treat later on to reward them for the show.

Actually, she'd have to give them a treat for side-lining what could have been a very awkward situation. She'd been worried about what she'd say to Ridge. What he'd say to her. Whether Riley would be able to sense the tension between them...

"*Rrrrrrrr.*"

Dog and man seemed locked in a battle of will as much as a contest of strength, and Sierra wondered if Ridge even knew she and Riley were there. Riley had retreated to the porch and leaned against the railing, checking her cell phone messages and ignoring the half-naked man and his dog.

Sierra couldn't do that. In fact, she was tempted to join the game. Maybe the dog would let go and she'd be left with Ridge. If she could recapture the energy that had hummed between them in bed, she just might win. Or the battle would end with the two of them rolling in the dirt. She could think of worse outcomes.

No, no, *no*.

She was done with that. Ridge was a friend who was helping Riley and the boys. And she couldn't spend all day waiting for him to reclaim his shirt. Somebody needed to stop this fight or it might go on long enough for her libido to cycle around again. There were a million other reasons she shouldn't act on her impulses, but she'd deliberately insured herself against his charms when she'd gotten dressed, choosing her ugliest granny panties and a mismatched bra. There was no way anyone was going to slip back into last night's amorous mood.

But if this fight kept up, even that wouldn't work. Putting her fingers to her lips, she let out a high, shrill whistle.

Stunned by the sound, the dog let go of the shirt so quickly that Ridge stumbled backward and landed on the seat of his Wranglers. The dog ran to her, and she rumpled its fur as it gazed up at her with a happy doggie grin. If dogs could laugh, that's what Dum was doing.

"Good dog," she said. "Good dog."

"Thanks." Ridge rose and dusted off his seat. "I think." He held up his shredded T-shirt. Sierra took one look at it and started to giggle.

The other dog, who had been watching the fight, trotted over to check out Riley, who stood stiffly as the dog sniffed her thoroughly.

"Hello, Dum-dum," she said.

That sent Sierra off into another round of giggles. About the time she doubled over and grabbed her stomach, Ridge tossed the shirt over the railing and joined her, laughing.

"What? Isn't that his name?" Riley looked indignant, which only made them laugh harder. "You said his name was Dum-dum."

"Sorry. Sorry." Sierra struggled to regain her self-control, but it was a tough fight. "It's…Dum," she gasped out.

"I know it's dumb. It's a stupid name for a dog. It's— ack! What is that?" Riley's eyes were fixed over Sierra's shoulder, her expression a mixture of revulsion and horror that could only mean one thing.

"Sluefoot," Ridge said. "Dammit, how did you get out, buddy?"

Sierra turned to see the horrifying horse coming up behind her, his head tilted oddly, his one good eye fixed on the newcomer. Judging from the determination in his stride, he was sure someone had brought him some treats, and he thought Riley looked like a likely candidate.

"What the hell *is* that?" As the horse stretched his neck toward her, Riley retreated up the steps and both Sierra and Ridge burst into laughter again.

"He's my horse," Ridge said. "He can let himself out of his stall, and he comes when you whistle."

Sierra clapped her hand over her mouth. "Sorry. I was just trying to break up the fight."

"I'm not sure I'll be able to sleep here," Riley said. "I swear, he is *after* me."

Sierra did her best to smother her laughter. "Ridge'll have to put a lock on his stall. I'll add it to the to-do list." She showed him the folder she'd brought with her. "I brought your code requirements."

Riley perked up for the first time all day. "So he really is renovating?"

"Well, yeah, dummy. I told you he was."

"I thought you were just trying to get me out here." She grabbed the folder and started flipping through it. "There's a lot here. When was the house last updated?"

Ridge shrugged and Riley grinned. "Oh, this is gonna be fun."

Sierra hadn't ever seen Riley so happy. As soon as they stepped inside, she was everywhere, tapping the walls, frowning at the floorboards, even picking at paint on the wood trim. "This is probably lead-based paint," she said. "I don't know what the rules are in Wyoming, but in Colorado you have to strip this and repaint. You'll need a mask, 'cause you don't want to breathe the stuff. Pure poison. And I wonder if the insulation is asbestos." Frowning, she looked up at the light fixture hanging from the ceiling. Sierra had never noticed it before. It was apparently from the twenties or thirties. The brass was decorated in geometric patterns and the glass globes etched with matching designs. "That's cool, but if your wiring's the same age as the fixtures, you've got a lot of work to do."

Sierra could feel her jaw dropping. Where had this confident, competent Riley come from?

"How do you know all this?" Ridge asked.

"I took classes at Climb Colorado," Riley said. "I got a certificate in Home Renovation—or at least I will, as soon as I find a whole-house project to do. I know all about codes and how to do the work." She pulled a curtain aside to study the woodwork beneath. "I haven't been able to finish because my job took up my days, so I couldn't get my final project done. But this would work." She turned to Sierra with a bright smile. "This could be my project."

Sierra felt all the pieces of her universe clicking into place, fitting together in perfect harmony, making the random events of the past few days align in patterns as neat and pleasing as the decorations on the old light fixture.

"This is perfect," Sierra told Ridge. "She's just the person you need."

Ridge shot her a doubtful frown.

"See?" Riley said. "I knew he didn't want me here."

"No, really," Sierra said. "Riley, go get your stuff."

"Who says I want to help him, anyway?" Riley said. But she headed for the car to get the battered suitcase that had gone with her from one shoddy apartment to another with frequent stops at Sierra's in between.

"See?" Sierra gave Ridge an encouraging smile. "It's meant to be. You help her, and she helps you."

"We'll see," he said.

"It's a great idea," Sierra said firmly. "She needs a place to stay and a house to renovate, and you need help with your house. She won't feel like she's taking charity, and you won't feel like, um, well, like I talked you into something you didn't want to do."

He didn't look convinced. "I never said I needed help. And you said she'd just be here a couple of days." He nodded toward the bulky folder under her arm. "That looks like a lot more than a couple days' work. And I can do it myself."

Sierra gazed pointedly around the room, at the cracked plaster walls, the damp stains on the ceiling, and the chipped paint Riley had pointed out. "Have you done this kind of thing before?"

He shook his head. His hair was still wet, and droplets of water dripped onto his bare shoulders.

"And you do need the help. Your hand…"

"Forget my hand." He looked positively fierce, and she decided she'd better remember not to mention his injury again. "My hand's fine. I don't need help from anybody. And she just said she doesn't *want* to help."

"I said I didn't want to help *you*," Riley said, appearing at the doorway with an ancient Samsonite suitcase in tow. "I didn't say I wouldn't do the work."

She looked utterly out of place in the old-fashioned
front hall with her cockeyed haircut and her angular,
mismatched earrings catching the afternoon light from
the window. But her eyes glowed as she gazed around
the hallway at the antiquated fixtures and uneven walls.
"I'd love to do the work. This place is a renovator's
dream." She reached over to the window and stroked a
pane of glass. "You want to keep all the original stuff
you can, right? We'll bring it up to date without spoiling
the features that make it special. Preservation. That's
what I really want to do. Like, for historical places."

She tossed her hair back with more spunk than Sierra
had seen from her in years and gave Ridge a sharp nod.
"I'll take a look at this to see what's different from
Colorado. Then I'll check out the house, room by room,
work up a supply list and a budget, and figure out a
reasonable time frame for each job. Sound good?"

Ridge stared down at the floor and heaved a heavy
sigh. "All right," he said. "Let me show you where
you'll sleep. Temporarily."

As he led Riley down the hallway, Sierra stood dumbstruck in the foyer, wondering what had happened to her
needy, fragile friend. Who was this capable, sharp-eyed
stranger who had taken her place?

Most important, why did Sierra feel a little melan-
choly at the loss of the old Riley?

Maybe it was because the new Riley didn't need
her anymore, and that made Sierra feel a little less
capable herself.

Chapter 36

TWO DAYS LATER, SIERRA COULD HARDLY RESIST THE urge to hum as she shrugged into her leather jacket and pulled on her flowered cowboy boots. Everything seemed to be going smoothly between Riley and Ridge. Ridge hadn't complained, and all Riley had talked about when Sierra called was how much work the house needed and how hard she was working. Sure, she was complaining, but there was an undercurrent of pride in her voice as she rattled off terms and talked about insulation and wiring and how to varnish the floors.

The last few times she'd come into town, she hadn't even stopped to see Sierra. Ridge had loaned Riley the old ranch truck, and Sierra would see it parked right across the street at the hardware store. Riley would exit the store, laden with purchases, and drive away with barely a glance at Phoenix House.

Some people might have been insulted by that, but Sierra smothered the little flame of hurt in her heart and reminded herself that this was what she wanted for Riley: a job that made her feel productive and gave her a feeling of wholeness so she didn't need Sierra—or anything else.

Besides, Sierra had her own life to live. And this morning, that life included heading out to the ranch for the boys' second riding lesson. Hopefully, seeing Ridge would be as easy as last time, and they'd be so busy with the boys, they'd barely have a chance to look at each other.

Because if they did look at each other, she knew what they'd each be seeing. That night, those tousled sheets, those bodies twining together in the waning light…

She pushed those images out of her head and stood at the foot of the stairs, hollering up to the boys.

"Come on, guys! The horses are waiting!"

A thundering cavalcade of kids responded to the call, four pairs of running shoes hitting the stairs along with one pair of pink cowboy boots. Jeffrey had been teased at first for wearing "sissy boots," but his response had been silence. For once, Sierra wished the boy would fight, but the teasing had stopped.

The rest of the kids had no problems fighting. Isaiah and Carter had claimed the back-facing rear seat, and Josh was whining that it was *his* turn to "watch where they'd been." Sierra brokered a peace agreement that put a very smug Josh in the rear-facing seat, along with Jeffrey, while Isaiah and Carter looked forward to taking the first rides once they arrived at the ranch.

There was the usual bickering on the long drive, fading to silence as the boys grew bored and maybe a little bit carsick. But they livened up on arriving at the ranch, spilling out of the car and racing around.

Meanwhile, Sierra watched Ridge. She couldn't help it. Things had run more smoothly than usual at the house over the last few days, and that had left her too much time and mental energy to devote to memories of the time she'd spent here the night she'd come for her phone, and the night after dinner at the Red Dawg. And then there was the shirtless tug-o-war game he'd played with the dogs…

She'd decided it was okay to enjoy those memories. They were too good to throw away. Someday, in the distant future, she'd *want* a serious relationship, and she'd be able to judge the contenders by comparing them to Ridge, with his honesty, his generosity, and his hot, hot body that was always ready for action.

Hot, hot… *stop it.*

It was okay to enjoy those memories, but it was *not* okay to look at Ridge, because if she looked at him, he might look back and then he might notice she was staring—and maybe drooling a little.

So she watched the boys as they gravitated toward the parts of the ranch that interested them. Jeffrey went straight for the corrals. Carter and Frankie headed for the hayloft, where they'd built a fort out of the heavy bales, while Josh, surprisingly, was petting Sluefoot and examining his bad eye like a budding ophthalmologist. Isaiah had found an old tractor with its engine exposed and was tracing the path of various hoses and wires.

So she had a cowboy, a vet, a mechanical genius, and maybe a couple of soldiers. Not bad.

She looked around for Riley but saw no sign of her. She worried that the mechanical whine coming from the house might be her friend tearing into something with power tools, but she couldn't leave the boys to find out.

She jogged to catch up with Ridge, who hailed the boys with a whistle as he headed for the barn. Naturally, they started their efforts to imitate him again, driving old Sluefoot to distraction. The old horse pawed at the gate, nodding his head in frustration. Ridge had evidently found a latch that was Sluefoot-proof—at least for now.

"Where's Riley?" Sierra asked.

"In the bathroom," he said. "Or what *used* to be the bathroom. She tore out the tile and now she's cut a god-damn hole in the wall. I sure as hell hope she knows how to put it back together once she's torn it apart."

"How's she doing?" she asked. "Is she paying her way?"

"Yeah, she is." It was a grudging admission. "She's made a big difference already. I'm not sure how, since she spends all her time in town with you. Maybe you could talk to her about it or just send her back here. You can't have that much time to take away from your job."

"Ridge, she's not spending any time at all with me. I haven't seen her in a week. I feel like we're kind of growing apart."

"Well, she's spending it somewhere. When I send her into town for supplies, she doesn't need to spend hours and hours visiting," Ridge grumbled. "With the drive both ways, that makes half the day. Meanwhile, I'm waiting with a hammer in my hand because she can't get home with the nails."

"Sorry," Sierra said. "Does she act like she's drinking or something?"

"Don't think so. She's tired, though. I figured you had her doing side jobs at Phoenix House."

"No, honest. It's not me."

"Well, she's up to something. I'm about to the point where I won't loan her the truck anymore. She'll just have to tell me what she needs, and I'll pick it up."

Sierra knew Riley would have a fit if she ended up trapped on the ranch with no transportation.

"I'll talk to her about it. Believe me, I'll talk to her. She can't lose this chance."

———m———

Ridge watched Isaiah circle the ring. The kid had a tendency to boss the horse around too much, and he was going to find himself in the dirt if he didn't change his ways.

Ridge was tempted to let him learn his lesson the hard way. Lessons that ended with the aspiring cowboy on the seat of his pants tended to stick. But Sierra probably wouldn't approve, so he held up a hand in a "stop" gesture.

"Whoa." Isaiah pulled hard on the reins. He still had his brows drawn down and wore a fixed scowl of rebellion that probably had more to do with life in general than controlling the horse. But Dusty didn't care where the rough treatment came from. The horse pinned his ears, tossed his head, and pranced his front legs, almost rearing.

"Whoa. He's gonna throw me," Isaiah said, tugging the reins harder. "This horse don't behave."

"That's because you're not behaving."

"What?" The kid was instantly on the defensive. "You told me to stop; I stopped. He's the one that's being bad."

"Remember I said to get in his head, work with him, not against him?"

Isaiah shrugged.

"You're trying to steer him like a car. He's not a machine. It's a two-way conversation. You tell him to turn, he'll turn. You don't have to drag him around." He stepped into the center of the ring. "Press on him with your left leg. Just barely, not hard."

Isaiah obeyed and the horse did a reluctant but serviceable side pass toward the rail. His ears were still pinned, and his expression was as sulky as his rider's.

"Now the right. Just a gentle pressure. No heel, just your leg."

The horse stepped right.

"See? He's a flight animal. He doesn't fight pressure; he moves away from it."

"He's a sissy, then."

"No, he's smart. Horses aren't made for fighting, so they've found a way to live where they don't have to."

"What about when wild stallions fight?"

"That's the exception, not the rule. Mostly, horses follow the rules of the herd and live peacefully."

Isaiah muttered something that might have included the term "chickenshit" but Ridge chose to ignore it. "So when you use the reins, they're not like a rope you drag the horse around with. They're a signal, not a weapon. Same with shifting your weight or touching him with your heels. It's a special language, and he knows what everything means, so you don't have to force him to do anything."

Isaiah didn't look convinced.

"It's like if I was standing beside you, and I wanted you to move. I could just touch your shoulder and ask you to move. I wouldn't have to shove you."

"You better not." The scowl darkened.

"Well, that's what you're doing to Dusty, and he doesn't like it any more than you would. Now tell him to walk on and touch him—just touch him, don't kick—with your heels."

Isaiah obeyed.

"Now rein left, but don't pull his head. Just lay the rein across his neck. Keep your hands down."

He went back to the rail and watched as Isaiah and the horse began to communicate better. Soon the kid was riding on a far happier horse, and he looked a little less dour himself. Meanwhile, Josh and Carter sat on the fence like an experienced pair of ranch hands, contributing to the lesson with occasional good-natured insults.

It felt good, having the kids here. The more time he spent with them, the more he knew this was what he wanted. Every one of these boys was having his life changed, at least a little bit, by the horses. He wanted to devote his life to making that change possible.

Sierra stepped up to the rail behind him.

"Look at that," she said. "It's amazing what happens when you get a kid on a horse. Look how relaxed he is and how gentle he's being."

Ridge grinned and nodded. "Yeah, it's like a miracle. All I have to do is stand here."

Sierra didn't catch the sarcasm. She shook her head. "Amazing."

He moved closer, nudged her shoulder with his own. "You're amazing."

She looked down, flushing. "No. You're the one who's teaching them to ride."

"You're the one who's taking care of them every day."

Somehow they'd turned to face each other, and they were standing inches apart. He reached out as if to touch her face then remembered the rules and pulled away.

She smoothed her hair, as if he could have messed it up by looking at her. It made him wonder what she was thinking. With her skin flushed pink and her eyes glowing with feeling, she looked so pretty, he wanted to lift her in his arms and carry her off to the hayloft.

"Thank you," she murmured. And again he had to resist the urge to touch her.

Frankie and Carter had quit their good behavior and were climbing the rail like a couple of monkeys, knocking each other down from the top rail, laughing uproariously, then trying again.

"Hey, quit it. You guys are making Dusty nervous," Isaiah called from the saddle. "He's a flight animal, you know. He's liable to flight himself right out of here and take me with him if you guys don't behave."

Sierra thought back to the day the boys were playing in the junkyard, when Isaiah had talked about how much he wanted to get away from here—*just drive and drive*. Now it sounded like he wanted to stay.

She had Ridge to thank for that.

All the kids loved it at the ranch—Josh and Carter, climbing on the fence and laughing like they hadn't a care in the world; Isaiah in the riding ring, his scowl relaxing as the horse obeyed his commands; Jeffrey—

Where was Jeffrey?

She looked right then left, her heart fluttering with alarm. "Ridge? Have you seen Jeffrey?"

"Nope." He turned to face her, and when he saw her face, his own changed expression. "Don't tell me he's missing."

The flutter in her heart turned to hammering, and for a second, she thought she might faint. "Okay, I won't tell you. But could you help me look for him?" She hollered to the boys on the fence. "Carter. Frankie."

Actually, only Carter was on the fence. Frankie was on the ground, choking with laughter. He scrambled to his feet and ran to her, right behind Carter. Josh, huffing and puffing, followed along behind.

"Have you guys seen Jeffrey?"

"Sure. He was right here." Josh looked around, then grimaced and pushed his glasses up on his nose. "Guess he's not now, though."

Ridge approached with a sour-faced Isaiah, who obviously didn't like having his riding lesson interrupted.

"Quit sulking," Ridge said to the boy. "You were done anyway." He turned to Sierra. "Maybe he's with Riley. You check the barn and the house; Isaiah and I'll check the corrals and sheds. Whistle if you find him." With that, he was off, striding toward the barn so fast Isaiah had to trot to keep up with him.

Sierra was glad to have the boys with her. They swarmed over the barn's interior, climbing to the hayloft and searching the stalls while she thought of all the terrible things that could befall a quiet little boy on a ranch. She bit her tongue half a dozen times, resisting the urge to warn Carter and Frankie about climbing too high, to warn Josh about getting splinters, to warn them all to stay close.

Because losing them, any one of them, would break her heart.

Chapter 37

CARTER AND FRANKIE REPORTED BACK TO SIERRA LIKE little military recruits on a mission.

"He's not in here," a flushed Carter reported.

Josh emerged from the back of the barn with dust on his cheek and his glasses askew.

"We've been over every inch of the place," he proclaimed. "At least I think we have. On *CSI*, they'd make a grid of the place, and each of us would…"

"Never mind *CSI*." She thought of all the grisly missing children's stories she'd seen on television and shuddered. "Let's check the house."

The boys raced ahead of her, taking the porch steps two at a time and slamming the screen door behind them. The sound of the old door slamming reminded her of summer days at her grandparents' old house, and she wished the boys were racing into the house for a different reason, for ice cream or to play some summertime game.

She found Riley in the downstairs bathroom, wearing oversized plastic safety glasses, a mask over her nose and mouth, and a bandanna over her blond hair. She was wielding a crowbar like a weapon, tearing into the wall like it was responsible for every injustice she'd ever suffered in all her twenty-one years.

"Riley?"

Riley shoved the crowbar into the ever-growing

hole she'd made in the drywall and levered out another chunk. She apparently didn't hear Sierra over the rending, tearing noise of destruction.

"Riley?"

Sierra minced over the detritus littering the floor of the bathroom and tapped her friend's shoulder. Riley whirled, crowbar extended. With her goggles and her mask, her weapon ready to strike, she looked like a space warrior from some science fiction movie.

Sierra raised her hands in surrender. "I come in peace!" she said.

Riley lowered the crowbar and tugged earbuds from her ears. Only then did Sierra notice the white wires trailing down her neck and into her front pocket, where an iPod made faint screaming noises.

"Sorry, I couldn't hear you," Riley said.

"Man, she almost *killed* you." Frankie sounded almost happy about it. Sierra knew not to take it personally. Disaster was better than nothing when you were a kid—anything to break the monotony of everyday life.

"I kind of get lost in what I'm doing. Especially during the demo phase." She grinned. "Demolition." Through the scratched plastic of the safety glasses, her eyes glowed as she waved toward the crumbling wall. "What do you think?"

"Well, it's demolished," Sierra said.

"It's *cool*." Frankie and Carter had crossed the littered floor to examine the copper plumbing and electrical wires snaking through the exposed two-by-fours.

"Don't touch anything." Sierra turned to Riley, keeping one eye on the boys. "Have you seen Jeffrey?"

"Jeffrey." Riley's glasses moved slightly, and Sierra

assumed she was wrinkling her brow in thought under the bandanna. "One of the kids?"

Sierra nodded.

"Nope. You lose him?"

Sierra felt her stomach clench. "Yup. Come on, guys, let's keep looking."

All the while, she'd been listening for Ridge's whistle, praying he'd find Jeffrey wandering in the pastures and corrals. As she turned to resume the hunt, the long-awaited sound split the still air.

Relief hit like a tsunami and she almost collapsed on the floor. She hadn't realized how anxious she'd been until the weight of worry lifted.

Frankie and Carter had already shot out the door and were rocketing over the dirt path to the barn by the time she got to the porch. She pounded down the steps and took off after them with Josh right behind her.

But there was no one in the barn. The whistle must have come from outside.

"Ridge!" She put her fingers to her lips and whistled. Even Riley could probably hear that.

But there was no answer.

She looked at the three boys, biting her lip. If she let them out of her sight, she was liable to lose them both. But Ridge could be anywhere. A network of corrals and outbuildings stretched from the barn, along with sheds and chutes and narrow walkways. It had probably started out as something sensible, but it looked like every generation had added on until it was hopelessly convoluted. And Ridge was nowhere in sight. He and Jeffrey had to be in one of the sheds, all of which seemed to face away from the barn.

The boys ran ahead, ignoring the gates and swarming over fences. They called Jeffrey's name, their voices thinning as they moved away from her.

Sierra used gates when she could, her fingers fumbling with the unfamiliar latches, but it was almost easier to use the kids' method and go over, under, and through the fencing.

She was only halfway across when Frankie ran back to her. "We found him." His face was alight with triumph. "He's over in that corral at the side of the barn. He found one of the horses and he got *on*. He's in trouble, huh? He was riding *by himself*."

"Yes, he's in trouble," Sierra said, but she couldn't put any heart in it. She was too relieved.

Somehow, getting through the gates seemed easier once she knew Jeffrey was safe. Carter and Josh joined her at a whistle, and her hands finally stopped shaking. Following the dirt path around the barn, she turned the corner and saw Ridge standing a few feet from a fence.

"Why didn't you answer my whistle?" she said a little shrilly. "I've been…"

He turned slowly and set his finger to his lips, but it wasn't necessary. Her words were trapped in her throat as she saw what was in the enclosure and nearly choked on horror.

When Sierra had set off for the barn, Ridge had led Isaiah through the corrals. The boy gamely clambered over fences when necessary and closed gates behind them when needed.

"Maybe he went to see that horse," Isaiah said.

"What horse?"

"The yellow one. He liked it a lot. Remember he called it *golden*?"

Ridge did remember. Knowing how unpredictable Moonpie could be, he'd put him in the farthest-flung corral this morning, but he knew in a flash Isaiah was right.

Ridge stepped up his pace. As the tallest of the boys, Isaiah had no trouble keeping up. When they rounded the corner of the barn and Moonpie's enclosure came into view, Ridge stopped and put a hand on the boy's shoulder, squeezing slightly to signal silence.

Isaiah had been right. Jeffrey had found Moonpie.

Later, Ridge would cuss himself out for letting this happen—for not watching the boy better, for not realizing right away, as soon as Jeff disappeared, that his breathless fascination with the horse would lead him straight to the sunny corral where Moonpie grazed, out of sight of the other horses.

Ridge had moved the horse only partly to hide him from Jeffrey. He'd also figured Moonpie might calm down if he didn't have the mares to impress, and he'd hoped the horse would get lonesome in the large enclosure so far from the barn. As herd animals, horses hate to be alone, and a period of isolation makes them far more likely to bond with a human.

But right now, the horse wasn't alone. He was calmly cropping the grass on the far side of the enclosure with a boy on his back.

Jeffrey wasn't riding the horse. He was lying on the horse's back, with his arms stretched around the animal's neck, his head resting on its withers and his legs dangling dangerously close to its flanks. For one brief moment, Ridge enjoyed the sight of the boy and the horse savoring the sunshine. If you didn't know the horse was dangerous, if you didn't know the boy was troubled, you'd think you were looking at a scene straight out of a Norman Rockwell painting.

Actually, knowing the truth made the scene even more beautiful. These two troubled souls had somehow found each other, and found a way to take comfort in each other's understanding.

But this was no time to get sentimental. Ridge was in trouble. Big trouble. So was Jeffrey if things didn't go right. And Moonpie was in the biggest trouble of all. A killer horse couldn't be tolerated on a ranch that hosted children.

"That horse is mean, right?" Isaiah whispered. "He might throw Jeffrey. Stomp him, even."

Ridge nodded. He wasn't worried Moonpie would throw the boy. Boys got thrown all the time. Boys bounced.

But Isaiah was right, although he sounded a little too excited at the prospect of watching a stomping. Moonpie bit. Moonpie kicked. And this morning, when he'd been moving the animal, he'd seen a glint in the horse's eye and known Moonpie was one of those horses who saw red sometimes, who were subject to a fear so intense it turned to rage and overwhelmed all their other senses. Ridge had owned horses like that before, and when the red veil obscured their world, all their training, even their inborn instincts, gave way to an urge to crush whatever set them off.

He knew he could help horses like that. He'd had that feeling himself sometimes when he was a boy.

He'd felt like he had no say over his own life, no control, and it seemed like every time he'd found his place in the world and placed his feet firmly on the ground, someone would come along and yank him off-balance again.

He had no doubt Moonpie felt the same way. Ripped from his herd, forced into confinement, he had every right to be angry. Ridge's goal was to make the horse feel safe and convince him that cooperating with humans was his own idea, not something he'd been forced to do.

The big buckskin was doing better. He'd let Ridge lead him this morning, and he'd allowed himself to be soothed back to sanity when a sharp noise had startled him into a bucking, snorting dance of fear. But there was no way to know when Moonpie might decide his truce with humankind was over.

"Stay here," he whispered to Isaiah. "And I mean *stay*."

He moved carefully toward the enclosure, making sure the horse saw him from a fair distance before walking slowly to the fence. Keeping his hands at his sides, he was careful not to look the animal in the eye.

And still, the horse jerked his head up and rolled his eyes as Ridge neared the corral. A warning snort and the stamp of a hoof told him he was close enough.

"Hey, Jeff," Ridge said softly. "Looks like you found a friend."

Jeffrey sat up, blinking, and rubbed one eye with a fist. Had the kid been *asleep*?

He heard the faint piping sound of a whistle in the distance. Sierra. He couldn't answer, that was for sure. A whistle would send Moonpie into conniptions. He couldn't leave the boy, either. He needed to get him off the horse and out of the enclosure, fast.

"Just stay there," he said. "Stay right there."

He couldn't tell if the kid could hear him or not. In any case, he didn't listen. Reaching up and tangling his fingers in the horse's mane, he slid from the horse's back.

So far, so good. The boy stood at the horse's shoulder. If the horse so much as tossed his head, he'd toss the boy. If he reared—well, there was no point in thinking about that unless it happened.

"Come on over here," Ridge said, nodding toward the gate. "Slow and easy."

Once again, Jeffrey ignored him. He seemed mesmerized by the horse and stood silently smoothing its golden coat with the palm of his hand. Ridge couldn't blame him. He knew how magical that connection could be.

But the kid needed to snap out of it.

Just at that moment, a herd of elephants rounded the corner of the barn.

Well, it wasn't really a herd of elephants. It was only three ten-year-old boys and their group mom. But in the tense air of the corral, it sounded like more.

Sierra figured out what was going on and flung out a hand to stop the running boys, but it was too late. Moonpie had seen them, and Moonpie reacted like Moonpie always did: with a scream of rage and a kick of his heels.

Jeffrey cried out as the horse threw his head down and his heels up, plunging twice before he took off to race around the enclosure in a jumping, bucking, flying display of fury. The boy's fingers were still tangled in the animal's mane, and for a second, Ridge was afraid he wouldn't be able to get loose. But his hand was torn away at the first plunge of the horse's head.

Ridge wasn't sure if the horse's hooves hit the boy or if he'd just been jerked off his feet. Either way, Jeff was on the ground, looking a little dazed as he picked himself up. He was still on all fours when the horse completed his circle and raced past, barely missing him with his flying hooves.

"Come on, Jeff." Ridge did his best to stay calm, knowing things would only get worse if he added more panic to the stew of emotions swirling in the air. "Come on over here."

It wasn't until the boy got moving that Ridge realized his transit of the enclosure would bring him to the gate at the approximate time the horse passed it.

"Go slow," he said.

Jeffrey sped up. He'd make the gate before the horse got there, especially since Moonpie had decided to pause in his circuit to display his bucking abilities, leaping in the air with his head arrowed straight down and all four legs stiff and splayed.

Twisting his body, the horse landed and bucked again, rising on his hind legs just as Jeffrey reached the gate, then hitting the ground with a snort and thundering toward him.

"Come on, Jeff." Ridge opened the latch, but Jeffrey didn't so much as look at him. Instead, he paused, directly in the horse's path, and waited, knees bent and arms outstretched, as if he thought he could catch the horse like a thousand-pound fastball.

Chapter 38

SIERRA WATCHED IN HORROR AS JEFFREY STOOD AND waited for the horse to run him over. It took Moonpie just a half second to reach him, but the rules of time seemed to have been suspended, and she watched the horse run at the boy in seeming slow motion, hooves pounding, nostrils flared, long mane flying.

Actually, the whole horse seemed to fly.

But just before he reached the boy, Moonpie faltered, dropped his head, and transformed from a beast of streaming flame into an ordinary horse, old Dobbin walking an ordinary walk toward what seemed, at that moment, like an ordinary boy.

Jeffrey caught the horse around the neck and hooked his fingers in its mane as he had before. He turned to walk beside the animal as if he'd walked that way a hundred times. The two of them, boy and horse, seemed as comfortable as old, old friends as they strolled to the far side of the corral. Jeffrey rested his forehead against the horse's for a moment and stroked his neck, smiling. Then he crossed to the gate and stepped out.

The boys immediately swarmed around him.

"How did you tame him?" Frankie asked.

"Hey, maybe you're, like, a horse whisperer now," said Josh.

Only Isaiah remained unimpressed. "At least *somebody* likes you," he said, "even if it is a stupid horse."

But it seemed nothing had changed for Jeffrey. The face that had glowed with such happiness when he'd looked at the horse was now set in its usual dispassionate expression, and his posture had stiffened. Sierra didn't need him to smile, necessarily. Frowning would have been fine. Any emotion—anger, hate, whatever—would have been better than this closed-off, expressionless look.

It made her want to cry.

He carefully avoided her gaze as he walked from Moonpie's corral to the riding ring, but something about him lit a little spark of hope in her heart. There was just the slightest swagger in his walk—a little extra confidence that said he knew he was special.

In her work with inner-city kids, Sierra had seen many who'd lost their capacity for joy. Rejected by their parents, denied the love of a family, their lives had been unimaginably difficult, but they weren't beyond help or happiness. You just had to find the key—the one thing that made them smile.

Apparently horses were a pretty good bet. They sure worked for Jeffrey. She'd hold the image of him walking with Moonpie forever as a reminder that you should never stop looking for that key.

—◆◆◆—

The trip home was a nightmare, as usual, with Frankie, Isaiah, and Carter lunging at each other until she was afraid the seat belts would rip from their moorings. Only Jeffrey was quiet, of course, though he was rhythmically kicking the back of her seat with his pink cowboy boots. They packed quite a wallop.

She wished *she* had something to kick. Spending the day with Ridge had given her a splitting headache and put her in a terrible mood. Every time she'd turned around, he was patting one of the kids on the shoulder or kneeling down to help one of them solve a problem. Or just standing there, looking handsome and kind.

There was no doubt in her mind the man would make a great father, and she'd found herself falling into reveries about what it would be like to have a family of her own. Her and Ridge and a couple of kids—or maybe more. Some adopted, some not.

But she'd made the decision a long time ago to wait until she'd done her best to make a difference in the wider world before starting a family of her own. She wanted to help more kids in more places. She wanted to get her doctorate and move up in the system so she could change the way the foster system worked.

She knew that was the right thing to do, but sometimes she got tired of waiting for that other life to begin.

Ten minutes passed before she glanced at Jeffrey again. It surprised her to see he was looking back at her, staring at the mirror as if he'd been waiting for her to look.

"He isn't going to let me ride Moonpie again, is he?" he asked.

His voice was raspy with disuse, and a little choked, as if he was holding back sobs. But it was his voice, and to Sierra it was music. She did her best to pretend it was no big deal, but her own voice shook when she answered.

"Moonpie's not ready to be ridden yet."

"I rode him."

"But he's not tame yet, hon." She wanted to pull the van over so she could devote all her attention to this rare conversation, but she was afraid that would spook the boy back to silence.

Jeffrey kicked her seat again, once, twice, three times.

Either he was nervous, he was mad, or he had it in for her right kidney.

"I bet if you work hard at riding the other horses and get really good at it, Ridge would let you ride Moonpie someday," she said.

Jeffrey rested his forehead against the window and stared moodily at the city limit sign that welcomed them back to Wynott.

"I'm sick of someday," he said.

She couldn't think of an answer to that because she knew just how he felt.

That evening, Sierra was working by the window when she spotted Ridge's big white truck at the hardware store. Since Riley had arrived, he'd taken to driving a big Ford with all the latest bells and whistles. He'd apparently had it all along, but chose to drive the ranch truck for some reason. Maybe because, like him, it was work worn and strong, a real cowboy truck.

She put down her papers and walked over.

"I thought maybe you were Riley," she said. "I mean—you're not Riley, obviously, but there was glare on the truck window, and even though you usually don't let Riley take this one, I thought you might have, and…"

"Thanks for coming over to see me," he said with a grin. "You're in luck too—the ranch truck's parked around back, so I guess Riley's here too. As usual."

She followed him into the store, taking a moment to breathe in the old store's unique scent of sawdust blended with machine oil, metal, and wood. On one side of the store, lumber lay in orderly rows, along with all the tools that would help local do-it-yourselfers turn it into fences, porch swings, and sheds. On the other, sacks of grain and corn were piled high on pallets next to fragrant bales of hay and straw.

She roamed the aisles, moving up one and down another until she'd covered the whole store and determined Riley wasn't there. Oddly, Ed wasn't around either. The place was unnervingly empty—so much so that when Ridge stepped up behind her, she spun quickly and knocked a few small boxes off a shelf. One of the boxes burst at her feet, scattering tiny screws all across the aisle.

She knelt to pick them up, sweeping them into a pile with her hands. Her long nails didn't make it easy to pick up the tiny screws and transfer them to the box. Having Ridge watch her struggle with the task made her feel hot and awkward.

"Here."

He grabbed a dustpan from a nearby shelf and knelt beside her. At first she tried to help, but it was embarrassing to pinch one small screw at a time between her nails while he swept swaths of them into the dustpan and dumped them neatly into the box. Finally, she sat back on her heels and watched him work.

"You find Riley?" he asked.

She shook her head.

"Did you ask Ed?"

"I haven't seen Ed either."

"He's probably in back with his wife." He lowered his voice. "Alma's got MS pretty bad. Ed's not doing great either—he had a heart attack about six months ago, but he still does everything for Alma. Most everybody in town thinks they should sell the store, but they keep hanging on. I don't think they have much put away for retirement, and what could the store be worth, really?"

"They seem to do a pretty good business."

It was true. Living across from Boone's Hardware was like taking a master course in American truck models—*Pickups 101*. The trucks that moved in and out generally left loaded up with lumber, tools, and tile to the point that their back ends drooped dangerously low. Ed sold farm and ranch equipment too, and Sierra had seen people fill horse trailers with corral gates, fencing, and feed sacks.

"It's the only place for miles. Serves half of South Dakota and Nebraska, as well as central and western Wyoming. Folks that come here for supplies stop at the Red Dawg, gas up at the Mini Mart. Boone's Hardware keeps the whole town going."

"It would be a shame to see it close, then."

"You bet. The trouble is getting anyone to live out here and work as hard as Ed and Alma always have."

"Don't they have kids?"

"Nope. Had one son, and he died in a car wreck years ago. Sad to see an older couple on their own like that."

He ran his hand along a shelf then stopped and looked at his fingertips. They were surprisingly clean.

"Somebody's been working hard," he said. "It's been a while since the place passed the white glove test. Maybe Alma's having a good day. Hope so. It's been a while since she could help out."

Sierra breathed in the place's homey scent and felt a pang of nostalgia. There weren't many of these mom-and-pop places left. If Ed closed up, all the business would go to Cheyenne's and Casper's big-box stores, where fluorescent lights glared on rack after rack of merchandise and employees bustled around, avoiding eye contact and praying no customers would ask them for help.

But while the place still felt warm and homey, it was also eerily quiet.

"Do you suppose something's wrong?" Sierra asked.

Ridge nodded, then stepped behind the counter and opened a door that apparently led to a back room. "Ed? You here?"

"Hold on!" cried a voice from beyond the door. "Be right there!"

The old man was all aflutter when he hustled out of the door and shut it firmly behind himself. He was a big man, but hunched over from old age so that he had to look up at them from under his bushy eyebrows. The eyes under those brows were sharp with intelligence, though, making it clear there was nothing wrong with his mind. "You folks need something?"

"I should probably buy this box of screws," Sierra said. "I dropped it, and I think half of them are still rolling around under the shelves."

Ed dismissed her with a wave of his hand. "Never mind that, hon. We'll find 'em later. You shouldn't have dirtied up your pretty clothes looking for 'em."

She looked down at her white capris to see twin ovals of dust adorning both knees.

"My Alma would tell you to use bleach to get that out," Ed said. "Presoak 'em, that's what she'd say."

"How is Alma?" Ridge asked.

Ed waved away the question as he shuffled over to take the screws from Sierra and set them on the counter. "Oh, she'd tell you she's fine, but she had a flare-up last week, and she's back in the wheelchair." The old man's rheumy eyes glistened and he seemed eager to change the subject. "So how can I help you folks?"

"We're looking for Riley. You know, the girl who's working on the house for me? I sent her over for some supplies."

"Sure I know her," Ed said. "You bet. She's—"

"You looking for me?"

Sierra spun to see Riley strolling down the lumber aisle as if she'd been there all along. But Sierra had just checked that aisle, and Riley hadn't been there. She was sure of it.

"We sure are." Sierra set her fists on her hips and gave her friend a hard stare. "Where have you been?"

"Here."

"No, you haven't. We looked for you."

Riley looked from her to Ridge, a mulish expression coming over her pretty face. "Why? Did you need something?"

"No, I just wondered where you were," Sierra said. "Ridge mentioned that you were spending a lot of time in town, and I wondered…"

She let her voice trail off as she realized she didn't want to say what she'd been wondering.

"Ridge?" Riley turned her flashing eyes and hard-set jaw on him. "Have I been spending too much time in town?"

"You've been spending a lot of time with my truck," he said. "I don't know where you've been."

"We agreed the truck was mine to use until the job was over. Was I supposed to tell you everywhere I went?"

"No. But…"

"But what?"

"But Sierra was worried about you."

"Worried about what?"

The old store went so quiet, you could hear the old Ben Franklin clock behind the counter ticking away the seconds.

Chapter 39

"I just worry," Sierra finally said.

"You worry about me *here*?" Riley looked hurt beyond words. "What, do you think I've been hanging out in secret meth labs out in the cow barns? Do you think I've gotten my evil drug pusher to drive up to this godforsaken burg to supply me with heroin?" She slumped back against the shelving as if she was too tired to support her own weight. "How bad do you think I am?"

"I don't think you're bad."

"No, but you think I'll find a way to screw up no matter where I am, no matter how hard I try. You're the person who knows me best in the world, Sierra."

"I'm the person who loves you the most too," Sierra said.

"I know." Riley's eyes shimmered with tears. "So how do you think it makes me feel when you, even you, can't trust me?"

She flounced to the back of the store while Sierra stared down at the floor. She knew her friend was strong, and she knew she was trying. Yet still, her mind had jumped to all kinds of terrible possibilities when Ridge said she was spending a lot of time away from the ranch. Riley was right. It was time for trust.

"Looks like your little girl is growing up," he said.

"I guess I'm a better mentor than friend. I can't seem to make the transition."

She picked up the box of screws and it came apart in her hand, spilling screws all over the countertop. Shoveling them off the countertop with the flat of her hand, she caught them and dropped them back in the box, spilling them again in the process.

Ridge picked up the errant screws and dropped them in the box. "You should come out tomorrow and see her."

Sierra shook her head. She was hoping for a quiet Sunday at Phoenix House tomorrow, though that was almost impossible with five active boys around. They always managed to get into some kind of trouble if she didn't think of some kind of activity beyond doing Monday's homework.

"Come on, Riley would like it. Plus I'm working Moonpie. You could bring Jeff."

"I can't leave the other boys." She was happy to have a good, solid excuse.

"Bring 'em along," he said. "My brothers will be there. They'd love to have the boys around. Especially Brady. He's not much more than a kid himself."

"You want them out there two days in a row?" Sierra asked.

"Sure."

She felt herself weakening. Tomorrow would be another beautiful fall day, and she could hardly stand staying inside herself. Getting the boys outside where they could work off some energy would be good for everyone, and it sounded like there'd be plenty of adult supervision. Maybe she'd have a chance to straighten things out with Riley.

"Come on, Sierra. You know you want to. And I want you to meet my brothers."

She'd already spent way too much time with Ridge Cooper. Meeting his family would only make the bond between them stronger, and that was the last thing in the world she needed.

But for some reason, she found herself smiling and nodding.

"Okay. Sure. I'll see you tomorrow."

Her heart fluttered and leaped, and she knew she'd better find out something bad about Ridge Cooper tomorrow. Something that would make it easy to walk away from him.

Because right now, she didn't know how she was going to do that.

The next day, Sierra surprised the boys with the trip to the ranch. She wasn't sure who was more excited—her or the kids.

She couldn't wait to meet Ridge's brothers. Maybe, with these men who'd been through the foster care experience, her boys could find the friends and mentors she'd been hoping to find in Wynott itself. So far, the townspeople seemed to think the kids were nothing but noisy little reprobates. They were right, but they were *her* noisy little reprobates, and she wished other people could see the warm hearts buried under all the swagger that had helped them survive.

By the time Sierra reached the ranch, she'd had about enough. The noise in the van was deafening as the boys acted out scenes from a video game that she sorely regretted buying. She'd thought a plot featuring battles between woodland creatures and barnyard animals would be a video version of Peter Rabbit raiding Mr.

McGregor's garden, but she'd been wrong. It was more like *Pet Sematary* meets *A Nightmare on Elm Street*.

"I'm Mr. Fox, and I'm coming to get you!" Isaiah declared with an evil leer. As he lunged over the back of his seat to the full extent his seat belt would allow, his cohorts burst into loud chicken cackles that quickly degenerated into high-pitched shrieks.

"Guys! Stop! I can't drive!" Sierra's own shrieks produced a brief lull before Carter decided he was a bear raiding the beehives. The resultant buzzing made Sierra want to open the van door and hurl herself under the spinning wheels.

"How about music?" she suggested. She had to shout out the idea several times before it got through to the madly buzzing bees, who agreed to settle down as long as she put on a particularly annoying *Best of the Eighties* CD that the boys, for some reason, found irresistible.

As Madonna sang blithely about what it was like to be a virgin, the boys mimed along into imagined microphones. When they finally reached the ranch, they burst out of the van with a raucous rendition of the chorus.

Good thing there were no state officials around to hear *that*.

But the hubbub they created was hardly noticeable. The normally quiet ranch had come alive in a new way. Two new pickups were parked in the wide circular drive—one a shiny new Dodge with every chrome accessory ever invented, the other a battered Ford hauling a three-horse trailer. A tall, dark man in a black hat was coaxing a gorgeous bay horse with a shining black mane out of the barn, soothing the animal as it jerked its head back and rolled its eyes at the boys' sudden burst of noise.

Man and animal stood poised on the edge of disaster

for a long two seconds as the horse flared its nostrils and danced, shying at the boys and their racket then spooking again at a leaf that blew across his path.

"Easy." The man had a low, soothing voice that reminded Sierra of George Strait crooning a country love song, but the horse wasn't succumbing to his charms.

The boys had calmed a little, except for Isaiah, who was still shouting Madonna lyrics in total disregard of the delicate situation with the horse. Jeffrey looked from the horse to Isaiah then stepped up to the taller boy with his hands on his hips.

"Shut *up*," he hissed into Isaiah's face.

Isaiah looked as shocked as if the horse itself had spoken, but he followed orders and fell silent.

"Thanks, bud." The tall man gave Jeffrey a nod of thanks. "You must be Jeff. You want to lead this guy over to that corral?"

Before Sierra could object, the guy had handed the lead rope to Jeffrey. She wanted to run and grab it away, or at least shout out an objection, but she knew she'd only make matters worse. She could only watch as Jeffrey took the rope and walked the horse to the corral, opening the gate and passing the horse through, then unclipping the rope from its halter as if he'd been a ranch hand all his life. He shut the gate and returned to stand nearby, like a soldier awaiting further orders.

The tall man grinned and tipped his hat to Sierra with a charm that stopped her objections in her throat. "I'm Ridge's brother Shane. You must be Sierra. Am I right? That was Jeff?"

She nodded while the man looked over the rest of her crew.

"And you're Carter, and you're Josh, you're Frankie, and you're Isaiah," he said, pointing at each of the boys in turn.

"How do you know our names?" Josh asked.

Shane laughed. "My brother talks about you all the time."

"Ridge?" Josh looked both thrilled and amazed. "Ridge talks about *us*?"

Ridge stepped onto the front porch, slamming the screen door behind him. "Yeah, I complain about you guys," he said with a grin.

Isaiah shoved Josh. "He probably said Josh was the wimpy blond kid."

"Well, I bet he said Isaiah was the smart-ass black kid," said Carter.

Ridge gave the boys a quelling look. "And I said Sierra was in charge of all of you and she'd take you all back home if you didn't behave."

Another truck rolled up in a cloud of dust, hauling a trailer that was empty, judging from the way it clattered and bounced over the ruts.

"Is that Suze Carlyle?" Shane asked.

Ridge nodded. "She's here to pick up her horse. He was giving her some trouble, so I ran him through some fundamentals again. He was running the barrels all right, but he'd forgotten how to stop."

Sierra watched the new arrival climb out of the cab. Suze Carlyle looked like the quintessential cowgirl in fitted jeans and a white shirt. Graceful and well muscled, with a don't-mess-with-me look in her eye and plumes of long blond hair spilling from a rakishly shaped cowboy hat, she reminded Sierra of the horse Jeffrey had just led to the corral.

"How's my guy doing?" She walked right past Sierra

and the boys without so much as a look. It was kind of rude, really, but Sierra figured there was probably some reason the woman's attention was so firmly fixed on a red horse with a blonde mane that matched her own—or maybe her social skills just needed a little work.

"He's ready to rumble," Ridge said. "You can load him up, but let me go get Brady. He wanted to take a look at him before you take him back."

"Brady's here?" she asked.

"Yeah, let me go get him," Ridge said, but she gave him an airy wave.

"Don't bother. I need to get home in a hurry."

Sierra assumed the man who emerged from the barn was Brady. She could still see the remnants of the boy he'd been in the picture, but he'd acquired a smile somewhere, along with a confident stride filled with youthful energy.

"You're in a hurry? How come?" he asked the cowgirl. "Is somebody waiting for you?"

She flipped her hair and ignored him.

"No, really. You said you're in a hurry. You got somebody waiting for you at home?"

He was evidently hitting a nerve, because the woman was flushing deep red as she strode past him, heading straight for the corral gate. It was obvious she wanted to get her horse and go. Jeffrey stepped up eagerly.

"You want me to get him for you, ma'am?" He waved the lead rope that was coiled in his hand and Sierra's jaw dropped. Another full sentence from the boy who never spoke—and he'd said "ma'am." To a stranger.

Wonders never ceased at Decker Ranch.

Chapter 40

THE GIRL GLANCED AT BRADY THEN BACK AT JEFFREY and sighed. "Sure," she said. "Let's get Ridge or Shane to help too. Trailering's hard for this guy."

"I'll help," Brady said.

"You shouldn't have any trouble with him now," Ridge said. "I fixed that problem."

"You fixed Brady?" Suze smiled for the first time since she'd arrived, and Sierra was stunned at how it transformed her face. "It's about time somebody did that. Maybe he'll behave better once his testosterone level quits clouding his brain."

"He fixed your *horse*." While his brothers laughed, Brady strode over and tried to take the lead rope from Jeffrey, who had just clipped it to the horse's halter. The horse pinned its ears and danced, a bundle of hair-trigger energy wrapped in horsehide. Sierra held her breath, wondering if the boy was about to get kicked or trampled, but Brady backed off and Jeffrey spoke softly to the horse, who calmed down as quickly as he'd riled up.

"Speedo just needs to run," Suze told Jeffrey. "That's what makes him a good barrel horse."

"His name is *Speedo*?" Frankie and Carter staggered around, laughing. Even Jeffrey smiled a little.

"He earned that name," Ridge said. "Nobody ever had to teach him to race. Hard part's getting him to slow down and take it easy when there's *not* a rodeo purse on the line." He turned to Suze. "But you were right. He's getting older. I wouldn't practice hard stops any more than you have to."

While Ridge showed Jeffrey how to safely trailer the horse, Suze climbed into the truck and clipped on her seat belt. Brady hovered nearby, and Sierra thought his confident grin had gone a little shaky at the edges.

"Why don't you stick around a while?" he asked Suze. "I had a great ride on Tornado last night. Don't you want to hear about it?"

"No," she said flatly, checking the rearview mirror.

When Ridge clanged the trailer door shut and gave Suze a thumbs-up, she cranked the engine into a slow rumble and put the truck in gear.

"I'm sure you wore that story out already, telling it to all the girls at the beer tent last night," she said.

"I didn't..." Brady clamped his mouth shut, and Sierra figured he'd realized protesting would be a lie. He might seem like a devil-may-care cowboy right out of a country song, but he'd been raised by the same honorable man who'd raised Ridge, and while womanizing was evidently irresistible, he drew the line at lying. Casting Suze a wounded look, he pressed his worn brown felt hat lower on his forehead and slouched into the house.

"They're in love," Ridge told Sierra as Suze rolled out of the drive. "Hope they figure it out before they kill each other."

Sierra didn't comment. From what she'd seen, Suze couldn't stand Brady, but Ridge apparently saw his little brother through rose-colored glasses. She supposed that's what it was like when you had family. She'd never had any siblings herself; it had been just her and her mother. She still talked to her mom now and then, although the two of them didn't have much to say. Sierra got tired of listening to one-sided rants about how men were dogs.

Shutting down her memories, she brought her attention back to the present. Jeffrey stood by the corral, watching the bay horse with far more fascination than it seemed to merit. The animal was only cropping grass, but Jeffrey seemed entranced.

"How come you talk here at the ranch and not at home?" she asked him.

"Nobody can hear me," he said, as if it was obvious.

"Sure we can. I can, and Ridge and his brothers. What do you mean, nobody can hear you?"

"You said." His little face was solemn. "It's a secret place, where nobody can see or hear us. It's okay here."

"I did say that, didn't I?" She remembered that first day, how she'd told the kids the ranch was magic.

She'd been right.

She walked with him to the barn, where Ridge and Shane were handing out instructions for the day.

"I'll be your riding teacher today," Shane said. "Jeffrey's going to stick with Ridge."

"No fair," Isaiah grumbled, but a glare from Ridge shut him down.

"I teach a little different from Ridge," Shane said. "I have some secret cowboy stuff he doesn't know about."

Isaiah's eyes widened, and he followed Shane willingly.

On a hunch, Sierra followed Ridge and Jeffrey. When she was certain of where they were going, she stopped.

"Wait a minute."

Ridge turned. "What?"

She bent over Jeffrey and pointed toward a corral that was far enough that he wouldn't be able to hear their conversation but not so far that she couldn't keep an eye on him.

"Jeffrey, could you go over there and watch those horses for a minute?"

He nodded and began trudging over to the corral.

"Just watch. Don't touch," she called after him.

She turned to Ridge. "What are you doing?"

"I'm taking him with me while I work Moonpie," he said. "And by the way, you can't come. It'll distract the horse and he's liable to get feisty."

"Feisty? Ridge, that horse is dangerous."

"Not to Jeff. You saw them, same as I did. You telling me there's not a bond between those two? They're just alike. Their only experiences with people have been bad ones. There's something broken in both of them, and it's like they recognize each other."

"Kindred souls."

"Exactly. Jeffrey's never had that. There's a chance he'll never find it again."

She thought a moment. "Can you guarantee the horse won't hurt him?"

Ridge looked irritated. "Of course not. There are no guarantees in ranch life, believe me." He thought a moment. "Except one."

"What's that?"

"If you keep Jeff away from that horse, you'll break his heart."

She looked over at the corral. Jeffrey had climbed

up the fence and was perched on the top rail. The two horses were jockeying for his attention, pushing each other in a battle for the boy's touch.

She could hear his voice in her head. *I'm sick of someday*.

"Don't take this away from him, Sierra," Ridge said. "Let him help this horse. I'll guide him through it, and he'll see that you can recover from the past. It might be the best thing that ever happens to him."

"It might be the *last* thing that ever happens to him," she said. But it was a weak protest. She'd seen Jeffrey's face. The horses had helped all the boys, but for Jeffrey, they'd opened a dark door that had been closed, locked, and painted shut a long time ago.

"All right," she said. "Just let him watch, okay?"

Ridge smiled, and the old cowboy was back—the one who won every contest, who conquered every bronc and bull. Suddenly, she knew exactly how the broncs and bulls felt.

When she returned to the group, Shane had Carter and Isaiah mounted on two horses, playing a game that involved tossing rings onto fence posts from the animals' backs.

"Looks like fun," she said.

"Yeah, they needed to do something more than ride in a circle." He turned and flashed her a smile.

Dang. Ridge's big brother was almost as deadly handsome as Ridge himself.

"Did Ridge take Jeff to work on that damned crazy horse he bought?"

Sierra felt suddenly cold. "You mean Moonpie? You think he's crazy?"

He looked her in the eye and seemed to sense the panic there. "He's fine. Just one more hayburner than we need, that's all. They'll be in the round ring over there." He gestured toward a high-walled enclosure near the back of the barn. "The kid'll be fine as long as you leave 'em be. Seems like the quiet kind, and he's got a way with horses. Reminds me of Ridge at that age."

"Really?"

Shane grinned. "Really. You could hardly get a word out of him when he first came here. Barely talked at all."

Sierra thought about that while she watched the kids for a while, making sure Shane could handle them. After ten minutes, she wondered what it was about cowboys that cast a magic spell of good behavior over her raucous crew of troublemakers.

She drifted away, telling herself she'd go look for Riley, but somehow she found herself at the round ring where Ridge and Jeffrey were working the buckskin horse. The high sides of the ring shut her out, so she just stood and listened awhile. She didn't hear a word from Jeffrey, but Ridge was talking to somebody. She could hear hoofbeats, slow and sort of stumbling, and the cowboy kept saying "That's it. That's it."

Curious, she pressed her eye to a knothole. Jeffrey was walking around the ring with the horse following behind him. At first Sierra thought the boy was leading the horse, but as Jeffrey circled and backed up, moved sideways and executed sharp, sudden stops, she realized there was no rope involved. The horse was simply following him, as if fascinated. Through most of the exercise, it looked as if the horse's muzzle was almost touching the boy's shoulder.

As for Jeffrey, he looked enraptured by what was happening. He had a wondering, dumbstruck look that told Sierra something was changing inside the dark world of his mind.

She'd just crouched down for a better look when the horse stopped and snorted. Jeffrey gave Ridge a puzzled glance, and Ridge turned and looked straight at the knothole.

"Go away, Sierra," he said. "You're distracting the horse."

She started to speak then realized she'd only spook the animal and endanger the child she was trying to protect.

Trailing off to the house, she felt a little lost. She was used to being indispensable, and now nobody needed her—not even Riley.

As if to answer her thoughts, Riley came clomping down from the second floor in work boots that made her pale legs look even skinnier than usual. Her hair was covered in plaster dust and her tool belt hung so low on her hips Sierra feared for the cutoffs that barely covered her butt, but she was smiling like she was glad to see Sierra, and that was all that mattered.

Chapter 41

SHOVING HER SAFETY GLASSES UP ON HER HEAD, RILEY led Sierra out to the porch, where Brady was drinking a beer.

"There's something terrifying about a beautiful woman who can handle power tools," he said.

Riley revved the electric drill in her hand and Brady faked terror.

"Long as you stay out of my way, you're safe," she said.

"No problem there," he said.

Sierra looked from Brady, cool and calm on the porch swing with his beer, to Shane and the boys, who were shrouded in the dust rising from the dry, hot dirt of the riding arena.

"Let's make lemonade."

"Why? Somebody give you lemons?" Brady asked.

"No." She smiled. "Not today, anyway."

Riley shed her tool belt and goggles and hung out in the kitchen while Sierra stirred up a pitcher of Country Time. Their conversation was a little awkward, but Sierra was reassured; they were still friends. The frost between them was dissolving, sure as the sugar was dissolving in the glass pitcher as she stirred.

Maybe the men and boys had a sixth sense for refreshments, or maybe they heard the ice cubes clinking. Shane and his four aspiring cowboys trailed in, dusty and dirty but with smiles on their faces. Just when she'd gotten them all situated with plastic Solo cups of lemonade, Ridge and Jeffrey arrived.

"How's that stargazing, saddle-shedding, bucking, biting son-of-a-bitch working out for you?" Brady asked.

Shane shot his brother a quelling look as he settled on the porch rail. "There are kids here, Brady," he said. "Try to watch your language."

Sierra, perched on the railing on the far side of the porch where she could see the whole group, saw Frankie mouthing the phrases to himself already.

"They got to learn sometime," Brady replied, but he switched off his grin for a second and shot Sierra an apologetic look. She could see why he drove Suze crazy. He was charming in a roguish way that made it impossible to dislike him, and disliking him seemed to be Suze's goal in life.

"Anyway, the stargazing saddle-shedding horse is a wonder," Ridge said. "Either that, or Jeffrey is. Kid had him joining up in about five minutes and just put his first ride on him."

"It must be the horse," Isaiah said. "Because I can tell you, Jeffrey ain't no wonder. He doesn't even talk."

"Do too," said Jeffrey.

"Wait a minute," Sierra said. "Did you say Jeffrey 'put his first ride on him'? What does that mean, exactly?"

"Means he rode him." Ridge grinned. "I told you, the kid's a natural."

"You put him on the back of that horse?"

Ridge shrugged. "It's not like it's the first time."

"But the horse is dangerous."

"Maybe. Or maybe he just needed the right person to help him see the world a little different."

She felt her anger rising and trapped it just before it spewed out. Shoving off the railing, she ran down the porch steps and stalked around the corner of the house. As soon as she figured they were out of hearing of the group on the porch, she turned to face Ridge, who'd followed her just as she'd expected.

She stepped up to stand toe to toe and eye to eye. "I can't believe you did that. We decided together we'd let him *watch*."

"I know horses. And I think we've determined that I know kids pretty well too. The right moment came, so I just went with it. I told you, it would be cruel not to let those two help each other out."

She jabbed a finger in his chest. "You also told me you can't guarantee he won't get hurt."

He looked down at the finger then up at her face, his eyes steady and hard. She took back the finger, but other than that, she refused to back down one inch.

"No, I can't," he said. "I can't guarantee that you won't crash that van on the way home, either. But if we waited around for guarantees, we wouldn't have much of a life, would we?"

"We'd be alive."

"I don't know about you, but I want more out of life than survival." He turned away and headed back to the group, leaving her seething, her anger barely diminished.

She stood apart for a while, watching the aspens sway in the breeze and listening to the cries of the meadowlarks that perched on nearby fence posts. They'd light on a post, preen a little then flit up into the air with a burst of liquid song.

She couldn't stay mad with the meadowlarks around. She wasn't through with Ridge, but he had a point. Besides, she wanted to go back to the group. She didn't have siblings, and the bond between the brothers fascinated her. The whole atmosphere of the ranch made her happy. The place was all about family and animals and children. Not a bad place to be, even if Ridge was being a careless jerk.

When she returned, a couple of Brady's rodeo friends had arrived and were perched on the porch rail trading stories. Frankie was showing Brady a beetle he'd found in the garden.

"Hey, look at that," Brady said. "What kind of bug do you suppose that is?"

Frankie shrugged. "I don't know. Looks like some kind of biting, stinging son-of-a-bitch, doesn't he?"

Brady blanched and slid his gaze toward Sierra.

"Sorry," he mouthed.

Sierra grinned and wandered over to the other side of the porch, where Shane was sitting and leaned on the porch rail beside him. "I think you've got a higher population here than the whole town of Wynott," she said. "I always thought ranch life was lonesome."

"Not here," Shane said. "With Ridge's training business, the seasonal cattle work, and Brady hauling his troublemaking friends here, there's never a dull moment."

She remembered the other night when she'd sat on the porch and wondered how Ridge could live a life so solitary. How he could stand the quiet.

She had her answer now.

"It was quiet the other night," she said. "It was just me and Ridge here, and you could practically hear the earth turn."

"That's rare, feeling the earth move," Shane said. "I guess you really got lucky."

She laughed. She'd labeled him the serious brother too soon.

"Seriously," Shane said, as if reading her mind. "How are you guys doing?"

"You mean me and Riley?" She did her best to stare at him blankly, but his dark gaze didn't waver.

"No. Although I ought to thank you for Riley. She's a wonder with a power saw and a real nice girl. We all like her."

"You do?"

He nodded. "The way Ridge described her, she sounded like a holy terror. But she's a sweet girl under all those tattoos. Doesn't take long to see that. But what I was asking about was you and Ridge."

"It's nothing serious." She nudged a rock with the toe of her boot, rolling it under her foot. "We're just friends because of the boys."

She kept rolling the rock back and forth, back and forth. She hated lying, and this was a lie. Friends didn't kiss. Friends didn't feel all hot and squishy inside every time they looked at each other. And friends didn't have knock-your-socks-off, caterwauling sex at every opportunity.

"That's too bad," Shane said. "You make him happy."

She almost choked on her lemonade. "Me?"

"You and those kids." He nodded toward the porch steps, where Ridge sat surrounded by boys. They were listening intently to whatever he was saying, watching him gesture with his hands.

Sierra remembered those gestures from the first time she'd met him, when he'd been describing cattle work. *Jink left when they zig, right when they zag.* She'd been worried that the gruff cowboy wouldn't be able to handle the kids.

"He's so good for them," she muttered. She'd lost her rock somehow, so she found another one.

"And they're good for him." Shane downed the last of his lemonade in a long gulp and set the cup down on the floor. "I don't know if you know about his—situation."

"His hand?"

Shane nodded. "He told you?"

"Yeah. It's a shame."

"Not really. It got him off the rodeo road, and he needed that."

She swung her head around, surprised. "He did?"

"It's a rough life," Shane said. "I did it myself for a while, and then I took a job managing a ranch up north of here." He straightened the brim of his hat. "Rodeo's one injury after another, and the older you get, the worse the injuries are. It was bound to happen sooner or later, and it's better now, when he's young enough to turn it around."

"I never thought of it that way. It seemed so tragic. He loved rodeo."

"He thinks he did because it's all he knows," Shane said. "But like I said, it's a hard life. You do it long enough, and you get to thinking there's nothing else to life but the next bull, the next bronc."

"And the next buckle bunny?"

Shane grinned then sobered. "He wasn't into that. Got involved with a woman who wanted to tie him up and brand him for good so she could spend his money. Goddamn Shelley." He kicked at the air as if booting the unfortunate Shelley out of Ridge's life. "She was bad for him. Really bad. Figured out where the scars were and cut every one of 'em a little deeper." He gave Sierra an appraising look, as if he was trying to decide whether to confide in her. "I won't lie to you. Ridge is messed up. We all are." He nodded toward the boys. "They will be too, but they're getting a better time of it than we had at that age. You love those boys, and that helps."

She knew he was right. The Decker cowboys' childhoods had molded their adult selves, and the same would be true of her boys. They'd always miss the steady, unquestioning love that came with good parenting.

Dear God. How was she ever going to leave here?

Shane continued, unaware of the storm he'd started in her heart.

"When Ridge came here, he didn't talk."

"Brady mentioned that," Sierra said. "It surprised me."

"That just shows how different he is around you. It wouldn't surprise anybody else. He still doesn't talk any more than he has to. Not to most people, anyway."

"I didn't know that."

"You've changed him, and for the better." He grinned. "Maybe he just needed the right person to help him see the world a little different."

She had to smile. "Point taken."

Shane stood and picked up his cup. "I hope you stick around. He doesn't need another heartbreak."

"Like with Shelley?"

He laughed then shook his head. "No, like with rodeo. He never gave a rat's ass about Shelley. But he loves you and those boys like he loved bronc riding."

He walked into the house without another word,

letting the screen door swing shut behind him. Sierra sat in the shadowed corner of the porch for a while, watching Ridge with the kids and thinking about what Shane had said.

She'd seen Ridge's eyes when he talked about rodeo. She'd seen the hurt, the disappointment, the feeling of failure. Was Shane right? Was she going to hurt him like that all over again?

All along, she'd been worried about her own heart, her own feelings. She'd just assumed that Ridge was like most men—just looking for some caterwauling sex. It hadn't occurred to her that he could be hurt too.

It should have. He was a Phoenix House boy grown tall, with a past as full of loss and sorrow as any of her boys. She should have been more careful.

She needed to explain things to him before it was too late. She needed to explain that there were things she needed to do in the world, that Wynott simply wasn't her last stop.

Once she was gone, some other Shelley would come along and steal his heart. Break it, probably. The thought made her gut twist, but really, she was no better than Shelley herself. Because she was going to break his heart too.

Chapter 42

THE RANCH SEEMED STRANGELY QUIET TO RIDGE after Sierra and the boys left, even though the other two Decker Ranch cowboys were still on hand. Once the three of them had had all the energy of those boys, Ridge thought, and there'd been enough riding and roping and fighting and game playing that the place was never quiet. But now there was no sound but the chattering of the birds and the singing of the crickets.

Part of the problem was that the three of them were sitting around in the family room like a bunch of old ladies. Shane was working on his leather braiding, Brady was stretching his calves in his bronc riding saddle, and Ridge was staring into the fireplace, thinking about Sierra. His brothers kept glancing at him, smiling. It was obvious they'd figured out how he felt about her. Staring into the fireplace wouldn't have been such a dead giveaway if there'd been a fire to look at.

"Nice woman," Shane said.

Ridge nodded. "Saw you talking to her."

"Yup."

Ridge shifted in his chair, irritated. Shane had to know he wanted to know what they'd said, but he was going to make Ridge beg for it.

"What did she say?"

"Not much."

Ridge clutched the arms of the chair with both hands.

It was probably a better choice than putting them around his brother's neck, which was what he wanted to do.

Sensing the tension, Dee got up and trotted over to Ridge, laying her head in his lap. Stroking her silky ears, he shot his brother a hard look. "Well, what did *you* say?"

"Oh," Shane said, as if he'd just noticed Ridge was there. "I told her you were in love with her."

"You *what*?"

"Somebody had to do it," Shane said, unperturbed. "And it didn't seem real likely you were going to get around to it." He set aside the braiding board. "She's leaving in a few weeks, right?"

Ridge nodded.

"Then you'd better get moving. Tell her yourself, man. And then find a way to get her to stay."

"What makes you think I feel that way?" Ridge buried his hands in the heavy fur over the dog's shoulders to steady them.

"I just do. Everybody does. You talk to her. You don't talk to her enough, and you probably don't say any of the right things, but you talk to her more than I've ever seen you talk to anybody. You two love those kids, and you love each other. If you don't do something about it, you're going to lose her."

"She's got a big job waiting for her," Ridge said, "one where she can really make a difference."

"She can make a difference here," Shane said. "Bill did."

"I know," Ridge said.

"Tell her that. And tell her how you feel," Shane urged. "Promise her it'll last."

Ridge nodded, remembering how Sierra wanted everything guaranteed. Maybe his brother was right, but he couldn't help grumbling a little. "I can't believe you told her. You should have talked to me first."

"Can you tell Suze for me?" Brady asked. "'Cause every time I try to do it, I mess it up somehow." He kicked at the floor, frustrated. "She just can't seem to understand that we belong together."

Ridge and Shane looked at each other and laughed, the tension between them broken.

"You might want to try staying away from other women for a week or two first," Shane said. "Just a thought."

Sierra spent a sleepless night thinking about what Shane had said. She lay on her back and stared up at the ceiling, picturing her boys growing up, struggling through the hardships ahead, and then being derailed by some woman's careless cruelty. She felt like she wanted to lunge into the future and kill anybody who might break their hearts.

She thought about Ridge, alone out there on the ranch. She'd thought he was a loner when she'd first met him, but he wasn't. Quiet as he was, he still reached out. He wanted the boys there. And he wanted her.

But she was leaving. She wished she could stay. She loved the boys, and she knew they'd grown to love her. It didn't take long for kids so starved for love to latch on to anyone who seemed to care. If she was honest with herself, she loved Ridge too. She'd never met a man so decent, kind, and caring.

Hearts would be broken all around, and one of them would be hers.

She didn't know how to fix it, but she knew she had to start with Ridge. She'd be honest, and they'd talk it out. Maybe, if she could make him understand why she had to go, they could still have some kind of long-distance relationship. Denver wasn't all that far, really. And although she'd be busy with her job, and he couldn't really leave the ranch…

She sighed. It would take a miracle for this relationship to survive, and she couldn't imagine a happy ending. But she wanted to try.

Ridge grabbed two rope halters and headed for the corral to catch a couple of horses he had in training. They'd arrived green as grass in springtime, but they were coming along well and just needed some finishing.

As he exited the barn, a car pulled into the drive. He squinted, shading his eyes with one hand.

Jeep Liberty. Sierra.

When he felt how high his heart leaped at the sight of her, he knew his brother was right. He was crazy in love with her, and he had to do something about it. He knew she had ambitions that were all about the boy he'd been, and the boys she cared for now. Those ambitions were one of the reasons he loved her, but somehow he had to make her stay.

There was only one way to do that. He needed to look her in the eye, rip out his heart, and hand it over. He had to admit that all his dreams, hopes, and plans depended on her. It was the truth, and he needed to say it out loud.

If he had to do it, he was going to do it his way. When he was a kid watching how Bill and Irene cared for each other, he'd dreamed of finding a woman of his own one day. And in his teenaged foolishness, he'd figured out just how and where he'd tell her he loved her. He knew a place that represented everything that mattered about love—about how it made you feel and how it lasted to the grave and beyond.

It was stupid. It was the crazy dream of a kid who knew nothing about love. But he was going to make it happen, because maybe, just maybe, it would work—and the life that had been denied him, the life he'd thought was a total impossibility, could actually be his.

———

Sierra followed Ridge through the barn and out its back door, leaving the cool, hay-scented shade behind for a sudden splash of sunshine. She blinked and tried to see the ranch through his eyes—the crisp gold spears of autumn grass, the worn gray wood of the corral fences, the half-dozen horses dozing in the sunshine by the rail.

She wondered what this life was like, day after day. It seemed like a rancher cobbled together a living any way he could. Bill had taught riding lessons, run cattle—who even knew what that involved?—and trained horses, all while raising three spirited boys.

He sure had a nice place to do it in, though. This sheltered valley, ringed with craggy rock formations and trees on one side and sloping gracefully toward a faraway mountain range on the other, was the most peaceful place she'd ever seen. It was a place where time seemed to stop, where everything was done just as it had been fifty, even a hundred years ago.

She envied Ridge, really. Anytime he wanted, he could just get on a horse and ride. She imagined racing a horse up over that rise, heading for the distant mountains. Here, a woman could live a life shielded from the ugliness of the outside world. Instead, Sierra had chosen to dive right into the ugliness in the hopes that she could pretty it up a little.

"Come on," Ridge said, waking her from her reverie. He waved her over to a nearby corral, where he was lifting the latch on a crooked wooden gate. "I was planning on riding today. Now you can come too."

A swirl of fear spun in her chest, taking her breath away. Daydreaming about horses was one thing. Actually climbing on top of one was another matter entirely. Secretly, she was a little afraid of perching so high up and trying to control an animal that outweighed her by hundreds of pounds.

"I don't really ride." She took a step back toward the safe haven of the barn.

"You'll learn." He opened the gate to a sun-drenched corral. It was a warm day, and the horses were a sleepy lot, standing in relaxed poses, some with their eyes closed.

Ridge put her on Dusty, the lesson horse he used for the boys, and once she figured out how to relax and enjoy the rhythm of the horse's gently swaying walk, she felt like the world and all her troubles faded away. There was just her, the horses, and Ridge, who rode beside her on a handsome bay named Spiff. Riding meant they both watched where they were going rather than looking at each other, and that made it a little easier to talk.

It also made it easier for her to fall even harder for Ridge. She'd seen him handle horses during the boys' lessons, and admired his ease with the animals and his instinctive understanding of their needs. But she'd never seen him on horseback. It transformed him.

She should have known. She'd seen how the boys

changed when they rode, how they straightened their shoulders and looked so much more capable, so much more in control.

Ridge looked capable all the time. On horseback, he looked like he could rule the world.

It reminded her of that first day when he'd walked into Phoenix House looking like he'd just come off the Chisholm Trail. His face, with all its hard planes and angles, was the face of a sheriff or a lawman. But his eyes, pale and hard, were the eyes of an outlaw. It was that strange dichotomy, of the good man and the tough guy, that had grabbed her right from the start.

And his body? It was a thing of beauty on solid earth, but on horseback, he moved with a grace that seemed almost supernatural, rocking in rhythm with the horse and controlling the animal with the slightest shift of his weight, the faintest tightening of the reins, or an almost imperceptible nudge of his heels.

At first, she worried she'd need to perform similar feats of control on her own horse, but it didn't take her long to figure out that Dusty would simply follow Spiff wherever he went. It was a relief to know she didn't have to learn any of those subtleties, but watching Ridge made her want to learn. She'd love to be able to befriend these huge, gentle creatures, to move in sync with them through this wide-open land.

"Where are we going?" she called to him.

"You'll see," he said. "You'll like it. It's magic."

Sierra almost groaned. As far as she could see, everywhere Ridge went turned into magic—the barn, the bedroom, and now this shining landscape. She was almost afraid to follow, but what could she do?

It was all Dusty's fault.

Chapter 43

RIDGE WAS PLEASANTLY SURPRISED WITH SIERRA'S riding ability when they set off down the trail that bordered the tree line to the south of the ranch. She might not have much experience, but at least she didn't jerk on the reins or kick the horse too hard. If anything, she was a little too timid in her cues, and Dusty took full advantage, pausing along the trail to snatch up occasional bites of grass. It took a couple of sharp words from Ridge to make him straighten up and behave himself.

As they entered the timbered area beyond the pastures, the constant wind that whipped Wyoming's open spaces died down to a gentle rustling of the trees. The trees were so dense that they blocked the light, creating a forest surprisingly devoid of undergrowth. Only the trail was open to the light, so flowers and ferns flanked it like a deliberately planted border.

Sunlight filtered through the regal tops of the trees, creating an ever-changing kaleidoscope of bright light and dark. This had always been a magical path to Ridge, and he turned in the saddle to see how it affected Sierra.

She was leaning back in the saddle with both hands on the horn, her head thrown back and her eyes dreamily scanning the treetops. He couldn't say much for her riding form, but at least the beauty of the scene wasn't wasted on her. It was a good thing he'd given her a gentle mount. Otherwise, she'd be staring at the tops of the trees from the middle of the trail, where she'd be lying on her back.

He couldn't blame her for mooning over the scenery. The majesty of the tall trees looming over the narrow trail was a reminder of how big the world was and how small human beings were. Yet God took the time to touch every detail along the everyday path, leaving little hints of grace all along the rugged road.

The trail started to descend, and he turned to make sure she'd awoken from her daydream and was paying attention to the trail. As they rode, the chatter of birdsong was punctuated by the sharp cries of jays and crows. Another sound floated toward them on the wind—a faint metallic tinkling.

"What's that?" Sierra asked.

"You'll see."

As they rode on, the trail opened slowly to the sky. Dark pines petered out and were replaced by golden aspen with pale, graceful trunks and bright leaves that shimmered in the sunlight. The metallic sound grew louder, making it seem as if the leaves of the trees were actually forged of gold.

As they entered a small round clearing, the wind rose and the sound lifted with it like the ringing of a thousand tiny bells. Ridge knew where the sound came from, and he wasn't given to flights of fancy. Yet even his practical mind conjured up a fairy court every time he heard it.

The wonder on Sierra's face told him she'd come up with an equally fanciful explanation. Gradually, as she looked around and spotted the tiny metal ornaments glittering in the trees, comprehension dawned on her face. But she was still struck with wonder at the strangeness of it.

He'd never shared this place with anyone but his family. Not even Shelley had seen it. It was a family secret, but looking at Sierra's face, he knew he'd made the right choice.

"Who did this?" She slid from the saddle and gazed wonderingly around. The surrounding trees were hung with every sort of wind chime, from cheap dime-store novelties to pricey bronze tubes, from mass-produced gift-shop treasures to unique works of art. Most were corroded, some tangled, but the sound was pure magic.

"It was Irene's," he said. "We call it the Chime Grove."

As always, he felt as if Irene herself was there, enjoying her creation. "She loved this spot. Dad brought her here when they were first married, and he gave her a wind chime for a gift. He thought she'd bring it home, but it sounded so perfect right here that she hung it in one of the trees."

"It does sound perfect." Sierra slung Dusty's reins over a branch and wandered around the small circle, reaching up to stroke the little noisemakers as she spotted them among the leaves. "There must be a hundred of them."

"Close," Ridge said. "Every Christmas and birthday, Dad would give her another one. And us boys would pick them up too. Once we got older and started traveling with the rodeo, we bought one everywhere we went."

"That's so sweet." She fingered a worn gold-plated bucking horse silhouette with chimes hanging from its feet. A weight at the bottom was marked "Rapid City 2010." As she let it go, the chimes tinkled in tinny harmony with the rest. "She's been gone a long time, right?"

He nodded.

"But you still buy them."

He nodded again then dismounted and led Spiff around a little, as if he needed to find just the right spot to leave him. The truth was, all he had to do was drop the reins and Spiff would stay put. But the conversation was straying dangerously close to emotional territory, and he preferred messing with the horse to looking Sierra in the eye.

Because this was the one place he'd ever allowed himself to cry. After Irene passed, he'd come here often to grieve. He often thought he wouldn't trade his two years with Irene for a lifetime with any other mother. Still, it seemed unfair she'd been taken so soon after he and his brothers had found her.

"We still buy them," he said. "Still put 'em up."

Sierra strolled around the periphery of the grove, her steps light, her fingers gently stroking the branches to make the ornaments chime. As she completed the circle, she came to a stop in front of him. With every chime in the circle ringing, she seemed like some elfin princess who'd called up magic with the touch of her fingers.

"Do you think she's still here?"

Gazing up at the sky, so blue beyond the gold of the leaves, he searched for the truth. "I think she's here in our heads. Whenever I have a question or a problem, I come here and feel her presence. Somehow, I know what answer she'd give. Sometimes it's advice; other times, it's just a kick in the patootie."

Sierra laughed.

"Her words, not mine," Ridge said ruefully. "We keep this place for her, and she's here when we need her. But she knows when we come here just to be alone."

The magic held. Sierra didn't balk as he took her in his arms, didn't pull away as he kissed her. And she didn't stop him when he moved his hands over her body.

He broke the kiss reluctantly to return to Spiff. Quickly untying a few knots, he pulled out a blanket that had been rolled up and nestled under the cantle of his saddle. With a flourish, he shook it out, letting it flutter to rest in the soft grass in the center of the clearing.

And then, without a word, he swept Sierra into his arms and laid her gently on the blanket.

Sierra loved Ridge's strength, loved the feeling of being picked up and swept away, carried off to his grassy bower. But she knew, deep down, that making love with him again would strengthen the bond between them to the point where it wouldn't break. She'd leave here at the end of her contract. That was a hard, cold fact. But maybe it wouldn't be good-bye forever.

He was right. There were no guarantees in life. And that meant anything could change, at any time.

In the meantime, she'd enjoy what she had. The kind of love they shared wasn't something to be smothered in fear. It was something to be celebrated.

She kept her arms laced around his neck, so he had to drop down into the grass with her. She'd noticed eye contact was hard for him. He'd even avoided it just now, when they were talking about Irene. He was probably worried she wouldn't want to have sex if she thought his mother was watching.

The thought made her smile, but she swallowed the laugh and kept her eyes on Ridge's.

This time, he looked back. It was a look that told her he was giving her everything he had—or at least, everything he could. After a childhood like his, she understood there were memories that were hard to share. But the way he looked back at her, honestly and without reservations, told her he'd trust her with them someday if she stuck around to listen.

Sitting up, she smiled at him then bit her lower lip, wondering how to start. She'd never been the kind of girl who had sex outdoors, but the occasion seemed to call for a brazen attitude, a wantonness beyond what was usual.

It didn't take her long to make up her mind. Grabbing the hem of her shirt, she pulled it over her head in one smooth motion. Then, rising to her knees, she peeled off her jeans. She had to sit back down and kick up her heels to finish the job—which included kicking off her flower-bedecked cowboy boots.

Even on the worst days—especially on the worst days—Sierra wore beautiful underthings. Pretty bras and panties were her little secret. Now Ridge was in on today's secret, which was a pink satin bra decorated with off-white lace that traced the edges of the bra and the waistline of the panties. The outfit wasn't immodest; in fact, it looked like something that might have been in some ladies' trousseau in a steamer trunk bound for the Continent.

But Ridge didn't seem to mind the fact that it was old-fashioned or even that it covered most of her breasts. He was still struck speechless.

She had to admit that if she'd known she'd spend part of her day naked in an aspen grove, this was the outfit she would have chosen. The pink contrasted with the golden leaves and yellow grass, and the smooth satin was a nice contrast to the slightly scratchy green blanket Ridge had provided. It was apparently wool.

"What is this, army issue 1942?" she asked.

He flushed. "It's all I could find that was clean. We used it camping." His brow furrowed. "We could go back to the house if you'd rather. I know it's not..."

She stopped his apology with a kiss. "This is perfect, Ridge. Perfect."

Chapter 44

THE ASPEN GROVE REALLY WAS THE MOST PERFECT SPOT
Sierra had ever seen—especially for a lovers' tryst. The
little wind chimes danced in the wind all around her and
Ridge, creating a curtain of sound that seemed to shut
out the rest of the world. As he kissed her, one of the
straps of her bra slid off her shoulder. Part of the cup
peeled away with it, revealing one pink nipple that was
obviously aching for his touch.

She didn't make any effort to cover up, so Ridge took
full advantage of the situation, peeling the strap away from
her other shoulder. Ducking his head, he licked and sucked
at each swollen nipple in turn while his fingers squeezed
and stroked. Sierra's breath came fast and hard, and when
he moved his hand down to trace the edge of her panties,
she gasped and squirmed, hiking her hips up to let him
know she wanted more. More? She wanted everything.

"No rush," he murmured. "No hurry. Let's take our
time."

That was easy for him to say. He was the one with
his clothes on.

She reached up to rectify that situation, but he pulled
her hand away.

"This is about you," he said. "I can wait."

"I'm glad somebody can," she said with a gasp as the
back of his hand brushed the tip of one breast.

He kept playing, kept touching until it was almost a

torment, and then, finally, he slipped his hand inside her
panties and found the hot, wet welcome waiting for him.

Maybe now he'd get the message.

But no, he was still sweeping his fingers over her
skin, sliding up and around her curves, skimming over
her ribs and belly, alternating between sweet torture for
her breasts and then her sex, and each one ached for him
as the other reveled in his touch.

If he'd ever had any doubt as to how much she wanted
him, those days were over now. She found herself twisting her body to reach his hands, moaning as he caressed
her breasts, and then she was clutching the blanket in her
fists while he stroked between her legs, and oh yes, this
was a man who knew what he was doing. She supposed
some women might wonder where he'd learned it, but
she didn't care. Their life together began when they met
that day in the closet, and anything that happened before
that was just preparing them for this moment.

His fingers slid inside her and found some magical
place that seemed to render her boneless in an instant.
And then he was kneeling between her legs, and then
she was bucking and moaning, almost weeping with the
wonder of it. The stroking of his fingers, the touch of his
lips, and the talents of her tongue were going to drive
her over the edge.

Just then, she found it—the edge, and she slipped
over it, and there in the middle of the woods, to the
music of a hundred tiny chimes, she rose and rose and
then crashed in an orgasm so wild she thought she'd
rise up into the trees and hover there, happy and sated
forever, floating on the gossamer wings of something
that sure felt a lot like love.

Sierra in the throes of lovemaking was the most beautiful thing Ridge had ever seen. He'd always dreamed of bringing a woman here, into this magical space, and now he lay beside the one he'd chosen, the one woman in all the world he knew he could love, and looked up at the sky. The aspens seemed to lean inward, almost as if they were protecting them, and the golden leaves shimmered like old-fashioned pirate coins dangling from the supple branches.

Her breathing slowed and she squeezed his hand, letting him know she was back in the real world.

"It's like they're protecting us," she said, looking up at the trees. "The trees, the way they lean in. They make it feel safe."

"It is safe." He pulled her close, and she propped her head up on one elbow. One hand nested in her hair; the other one busied itself unbuttoning his shirt, and this time he didn't mind.

He didn't mind one bit.

Once the two of them were naked, he sat up and grabbed his jeans, flipping through his wallet to find a condom. As he put it on, he watched Sierra stretch and stare up at the sky. When she turned back to him, her smile was almost wicked.

"You ready?" she asked.

"Do I look ready?"

She laughed. "Maybe the question I should ask is 'are you willing?' Because you've been ready for a while."

"It feels like I've been ready ever since we met."

"Well, I would have been a little taken aback if you'd tried this in the closet."

"I know," he said. "But I was never so grateful for an electrical outage in my life."

She laughed, and he kissed her, and then their bodies were writhing together under the sun. He fitted himself to her, and though it was nearly impossible, he held back, stroking slow and easy, giving her the full length of him in a push and then easing out, only to push again.

She was with him all the way, wild for him in a way he'd never experienced before. He did all right with women—he had enough experience to know that—but Sierra wanted him in a new way. It was as if she needed him, as if she were starving and he was the one thing that could sate her hunger.

She stroked his back and rocked him with her hips then whispered in his ear, "I want to be on top."

She rolled with him as he moved, and somehow, without the usual awkwardness, they'd managed to flip her to the top without pausing in their lovemaking.

She flexed her muscles to ride him, and he remembered feeling those muscular calves the first time they met, playing chicken in the closet.

She kissed him, and when she sat back up, he rose with her without breaking the kiss. Face to face, they fell back into her rhythm of rising and falling, rising and falling. Then the kiss broke, and they were looking each other straight in the eye while the sensations intensified. He was slowly losing his mind, or at least his ability to think, and he suspected she was too. But they never lost eye contact.

It was like nothing he'd ever experienced. Usually he'd closed his eyes or turned his head or somehow evaded sharing *this*—his thoughts, his emotions, the overwhelming passion he felt for this woman and she for him.

He'd always used sex to stave off feeling rather than to share it. Oh, he'd shared sensation and pleasure, even desire. But never love.

With Sierra, it was different. There were no barriers between them as her gaze grew hotter and hotter, and finally she arched back and came, crying out to the sky. It was the most beautiful thing he'd ever seen—but he only saw a second of it because then he too was suddenly in a world of swirling sensation that made him shout with joy so loudly that the birds stopped singing.

They lay side by side in the sudden silence, their fingers linked together, their hips touching. Filtered by the aspen leaves, the sun cast a golden glow over Sierra's pale skin, making the shadows of leaves and branches dance and chase each other over her curves. He wished he had the time to follow every one of those shadows with his fingertips, stroking her body the way the shadows did.

Maybe he did have time.

Maybe he had a lifetime.

Sierra could have laid in that grove forever, staring up at the sky with Ridge, watching the trees sway above them. But she wanted to know him better—not just his body, but his mind too.

"What was it like, growing up as a foster child?"

"You don't want to know about that," he said.

"No, I do. I'm not trying to pry. I want to understand the boys better."

He turned to face her, and she saw the tough cowboy give way to the tender man she'd seen the other night. He had a shield he kept in place ninety percent of the time, a tight lid on the part of him that still held the hurt he'd suffered as a boy. She knew he needed that shield, but he'd dropped it that night at the Red Dawg when he'd given her his injured hand. And he was doing it again now.

"It's hard," he said. "When you don't have parents, you look at the other kids, and it's like they're all golden, every one of them. Even the meanest, nastiest bully is everything to someone. Someone cares if his clothes are clean and his hair's combed. If he skins his knee, somebody helps him up and fixes it for him. But we just had to get up and keep going on our own."

"I try to do those things for my guys," she said softly. "I know it's not the same, but I try."

"And that's good," he said. "That's more than a lot of foster kids get. But even when you do your best, you're not their mom."

"I love them," she said.

"But they're not *yours*. And you're not *theirs*."

She flinched, but she knew she shouldn't. Where was that professional distance she was supposed to keep?

"I'm not trying to hurt you," he said. "But you said you wanted to understand."

She nodded, and he seemed to lapse back into a haze of memory. "When you're a kid, you don't understand that it's not your fault. You wonder why you don't shine the same as other kids, why you're not first in anybody's heart. Why your parents chose drugs over you, or worse yet, just walked away and left you like trash for other people to pick up. You don't know it's the luck of the draw, and you think you must be flawed somehow."

She nodded.

"There were two kinds of us," he continued. "There were the ones who tried like hell to matter to somebody—like Josh—and there were the ones who pretended they didn't care, like Isaiah."

"Which kind is Jeffrey?"

"The person Jeffrey was supposed to matter to didn't just stop caring. That person hurt him and would hurt him again if he could."

"You're right." She'd flinched every time she'd read Jeffrey's file, unable to imagine the kind of people who would hurt a child that way. But Ridge hadn't had to read a file to know the answer.

Had he suffered the same kind of childhood as Jeffrey? Was that the bond that seemed to draw them together?

"Jeffrey doesn't talk because he doesn't trust himself," he said. "He's afraid that if he starts, he won't be able to stop."

She stared resolutely down at her lap, afraid that if she met his eyes, he'd stop talking. And she needed to know these things. To love her boys better, the way they needed to be loved. And maybe to love Ridge too. This man needed to be first in somebody's heart. With her mother so distant, she had nobody but Riley to care for, and she knew it was time to let Riley go.

But a man like this, so damaged and difficult? All of her heart wouldn't be nearly enough. Her whole life was about helping people, but could she help Ridge?

She could. She could love him enough to stay with him. She could help him create a life so complete, so *right*, that his dark past would recede behind their shining future.

And for herself? She could have the family she'd always longed for: a patchwork family, with kids from every culture and background plus a few of her own. She wouldn't just be a replacement for their mothers, a temporary fix; she'd be the real thing. And they'd be golden.

Maybe someday…

She remembered Jeffrey's words in the car on the way back from the clinic.

I'm sick of someday.

Well, she was sick of someday too. She was sick of trying to change the world when she couldn't even deal with the changes happening around her. Sick of giving all she could to others and never taking anything for herself.

She was sick of working so hard to help others attain the good things in life—love, a home, a family—and denying those things to herself every single day, even though she wanted them with all the depth of her being.

Chapter 45

RIDGE REACHED OVER AND TOUCHED SIERRA'S CHIN, lifting her face so she could look in his eyes. And when she did, she saw the pain he'd suffered while he waited for his own someday—the hurt, the healing, and the courage it had taken to survive. His eyes held a solid determination under the tenderness, and she sensed a tensing of his whole being as he looked into her eyes.

"Sierra." He said her name as if he were tasting it, as if he were saying it for the first time. "What do you want out of life?"

Funny he should ask. "I don't know," she said. "I thought I did, but now I'm not so sure."

"What's changed?"

She thought a moment. What had changed? Just one thing that mattered.

"I met you," she said.

"That changed me too." He pulled her close, so her head fit just under his shoulder and her cheek rested against his chest. Together, they watched the little gold and silver ornaments glitter as they swayed in a gentle breeze. "Before I met you, I never expected much more out of life than survival."

She nodded. She'd known that somehow—that he was just moving from one day to the next, with no real goal in sight.

"I knew I was lucky to have my brothers, to have had

Bill and Irene. But I never thought I'd have a family of my own."

"Why not?"

"I didn't think I knew how." He thought a moment, his thumb gently stroking her shoulder. "No, that's not it. I thought I was my father's son. My mother told me once that men in my family were born without a heart, and I believed her."

"And now?"

He chuckled, pulling her closer. "You and your little band of outlaws showed me different. I never knew there were so many ways to love somebody."

"I know," she said. "I can tell you love them."

"And you," he said. "I love you."

She tilted her head up, and those gray eyes looked into hers. They were soft now, all their crystalline hardness gone.

He was right. He had changed since they met. And so had she.

She rested against his chest again, tucking her head under his chin, so he couldn't see the tears gathering in her eyes. "I didn't mean for that to happen. I'm only here for a few more weeks. I'm so sorry, Ridge."

"Sorry for what?"

"The last thing you need is for someone else to leave you."

"Then don't."

She sighed. "I have to. But I thought maybe we could see each other now and then. I could come up on the weekends once in a while. And maybe you could come down to Denver."

He somehow managed to put his arms around her and

pull her away at the same time. Now he was looking into her eyes, and she knew he could read the storm of emotions there as clearly as he could read the Wyoming sky before a rain.

"That's not what I want," he said. "And I don't think it's what you want, either."

"What do you want?" She regretted the question as soon as it left her lips. She wasn't sure she wanted to know what Ridge wanted. She wasn't sure she was ready.

"I want you to marry me."

She opened her mouth then closed it, then opened it again. She must have looked like a horse mouthing an uncomfortable bit.

"I know it's sudden. I know it's soon. But I love you, Sierra. I love you so hard it hurts, and I need you beside me every day." He squeezed her hands, and those honest gray eyes were fixed on hers. "We can make it work. Say yes."

She couldn't speak. She wanted to, if only to tell him to wait, but she couldn't get a word out.

"I know you want to make a difference in the world," he said. "But can you really do that from some high-rise in Denver?"

"That's where all the decisions are made."

"Really? That's where they decide that Isaiah should be put in charge of something to channel his bossiness into something constructive? That Frankie needs to hang on to that old hat, even if it is a menace to public health, because it was his grandfather's? That horses hold the key to Jeff's heart? You don't change the world with laws and rules and policies; you change it with love. I know that, because you changed me."

"But I've tried to make a difference here," she said. "I wanted to make this a hometown for the boys, remember? And the neighbors just look at me sideways and turn the other way. I don't know how to do it."

"I do," he said. "I know these people. Brady said Isaiah was really interested in that old tractor engine over there. So how about we let him work with Ben Sanders a couple afternoons a week?"

"Ben Sanders?"

"He's the mechanic in those garages in town. Fixes cars sometimes but mostly heavy equipment for the oil fields. And Josh seems to be interested in medicine."

"I thought maybe he could be a vet someday."

"Vet, heck. He could be a doctor. But we could start with the animals. I could have him shadow Doc Harrison once in a while on his rounds. Carter seems like sports might be his thing, but he also likes military stuff. He could talk to Phoebe Niles's son when he comes home from his deployment. And then when Mike goes back to the military, maybe Phoebe would enjoy having him around once in a while. He reminds me a lot of Mike when he was that age."

"Why didn't you tell me all this sooner?"

"I've only just gotten to know the kids and figure out what would work. Besides, I was too busy talking you into spending time with me."

She bent her head and began plucking fuzz from the old blanket as if it was the most important thing in the world.

"You might not be able to save the world from here, Sierra. But I think you could save this little town. And who knows what could come after that? You could write about it. Make it a book. That way, you could have that influence you want."

"I've always wanted to do that someday."

"Do it now. You don't have to compromise, hon. You can save the world *and* be happy. You just have to say yes."

She stared into the distance, her mind spinning as she watched popcorn clouds drift across an indigo sky. An airplane sliced through the blue, leaving a white contrail like a tear in the blue of the sky. She watched it fly, a silver speck in the great blue bowl of the sky.

Ridge was right. She was just one person. There was no guarantee that she could change the world. But she knew she could change this man, this town, these kids.

"Yes," she said.

"Yes?" He looked so startled she wondered if she'd done the right thing. Maybe he hadn't expected her to say yes. Maybe he'd been playing with her, or maybe he thought he had to propose to get her—well, not to get her into bed, because he already had that, so…

He leaned into her, and she suddenly found herself on her back on the blanket, and then he was kissing her with a new tenderness but somehow, at the same time, with a new power—a possessiveness that should have irritated her but only made her feel like she'd finally found where she belonged—and who she belonged with.

Chapter 46

SIERRA HUNG UP THE PHONE IN THE OFFICE, JUMPED out of her chair, and let out a whoop. Her job at Phoenix House hadn't been filled. She could stay. She could stay with her boys and marry her cowboy and live a life she never even could have imagined a month ago.

The tiny office seemed too small to contain her joy, so she headed out to the front porch. Leaning on the rail, she looked up and down the street and saw Wynott with new eyes. This was her town. These were her people.

This was her hometown.

She paced from one end of the porch to the other. She needed to tell somebody. Ridge would be out in the corrals, messing with his horses. But Riley—she glanced across the street. Sure enough, the battered ranch truck was parked behind the hardware store.

Did Riley park in the back to avoid her, or what? Was she hoping Sierra wouldn't see the truck? Sierra was pretty sure Riley had forgiven her, and she'd seemed fine at the ranch the other day, but she should go over there and check.

She waited for a truck to pass then ran over to Boone's.

"Hi, Ed. Is Riley here?" Sierra was bouncing on her toes, barely able to contain her news. She'd resisted the urge to tell anyone about Ridge's proposal and her answer; there had been too many logistics to work out. But now that she knew she still had her job, she felt like hollering from the rooftops.

"Sure is. She's back there with Alma," Ed said. "She's a ministering angel, that girl is. Been a gift from heaven for us, that's for sure."

Sierra had heard Riley described many ways, but *ministering angel*?

That was a new one.

"The way she helps out in the store is one thing, but it's what she does for Alma that really makes me grateful," Ed continued. "There's some times a woman needs another woman when she's ailing and can't help herself, you know? Riley's given Alma her dignity back."

"Wait a minute." It sounded like Riley had news of her own to share. "So Riley's been helping you here at the store and nursing Alma too?"

"Just in her spare time," Ed said. "I know she's working for the Decker boys out at the ranch, but she always seems to have a little time for us, and I appreciate that. It's good Ridge's so flexible and all about the truck, so she can be here when we need her."

"Well, that's—that's great." Why hadn't Riley told anyone about this?

"She's like the daughter we never had." He leaned across the counter, resting his elbows on the scarred linoleum surface. "Alma just can't wait till Riley's done with the Decker job and can move here for good. We don't use the upstairs anymore since Alma got so bad, so she'll have plenty of privacy, and she'll be here if Alma needs her. Yup, that girl's a blessed angel. No doubt about it."

He gave Sierra a serene smile. Much as she wanted to mirror that expression, she just couldn't. She felt like one of those surprised cartoon characters, like her eyes were bugging out of her head and bouncing on little springs.

"Aw, did I spill the beans?" Ed looked down at the counter and shook his head. "Alma always said I couldn't keep a secret in a ten-gallon bucket. Riley was probably going to tell you all about this at some special dinner or something. I know she's awfully proud of finding her place here in Wynott. She said you didn't think there was anywhere for her to work here." He grinned, as proudly as if Riley was his own daughter. "Guess she proved you wrong, now, didn't she?"

Sierra nodded, smiling, but she felt a little stunned. This was so sudden, so unexpected. Who would have guessed that Riley would end up selling hardware in a small town in Wyoming?

"Well, she'll be out soon as she gets Alma settled," Ed said. "Then she can tell you herself."

Sierra wandered through the aisles, pretending she was shopping when really she just needed some time to digest the news. Why was she feeling a pang of loss when her friend was finally setting out on her own, just like Sierra had always hoped she would?

She turned to see Riley standing behind her like an apparition.

"How do you do that?" she asked.

"Do what?"

"Just appear here, out of nowhere?"

Riley laughed. "There's a door back there, in lumber. It goes to Ed and Alma's place."

"Ed was just telling me about your—plans."

Sierra did her best to sound happy. Why was that so hard? She should be jumping up and down, hugging her friend.

"Sorry," Riley said. "I was going to tell you, but

somebody just can't keep a secret." She gave Ed a pointed look.

"I'm sorry, honey. It just spilled out."

"I'm just glad to hear the good news." Sierra pretended to examine various nuts and bolts, wondering all the while what was wrong with her. It was hard to cover up an emotion when you didn't even know what it was.

Riley looked as puzzled as she felt. "What's wrong, Sierra?"

"I don't know. I'm happy for you, but I feel like everything's changed."

"I know," Riley said. "I don't need you anymore."

The words hit Sierra like a dagger. But then again, this was what they'd worked for. The whole point of mentoring someone was to teach them to make it on their own. Maybe she'd forgotten that goal along the way. She looked at Riley, standing there with her tool belt draped around her waist, and felt her own grin widening to mirror her friend's.

"You *don't* need me, do you?"

"Not as a mentor, I don't," Riley said. "But I could use a friend. You're not going to lose interest now that I'm not all helpless and needy, are you?"

"No. It was never about that."

Riley arched a disbelieving eyebrow. "It's always about that with you."

"No, it's not."

"You think? The work you do? The way you love those boys?" She lowered her voice. "Heck, even Ridge is a project for you." She thumbed carelessly in the direction of Decker Ranch. "He came from a broken home, just like the boys. Just like me. I mean, he's hot and everything, but you feel safe because he needs you. That's what attracted you to him. You want to fix him."

Was that true?

On the surface, it seemed like a no-brainer. Sierra was, in a way, addicted to fixing people. And Ridge definitely was, in some ways, damaged goods. But deep down, she knew their relationship wasn't that simple. There was something more between them—something inexplicable. When she was with him, she felt like she was home.

Maybe that's what everyone was looking for all along—the boys, Ridge, and Sierra herself. Everybody wanted to belong somewhere.

And so far, the only one who'd succeeded was Riley.

In any case, this wasn't the time to tell Riley her own news. She'd give Riley this day to celebrate her own victory. God knew she'd worked hard to get here.

"Maybe you're right about Ridge. I don't know." Sierra put an arm around her friend. "I just know that I am so, so proud of you."

Riley smacked the nearest shelf and lifted her fist in a victory salute.

"There! I did it!"

"Did what?" Sierra asked.

"I got you to say you're proud of me." She was beaming, practically lighting up the room. "From the first time I met you, you seemed like the most put-together, amazing person I'd ever met. I wanted to be just like you, but I knew that would never happen. So I decided the best I could do was to make you proud of me. And believe it or not, for all those years I screwed up so bad, that was still the goal I was always trying to reach."

"And you're there," Sierra said. "*So* there. I should have said it sooner, Riley. I was always proud of the way you fought."

"Even when I lost?"

"Nobody wins every fight." She looked around the hardware store, noticing how tidy it was. Neat, hand-written labels marked each section, and the white-glove test would work anywhere in the place. "You've really made a difference here already. So what's your goal now?"

Riley grew serious. "I want to get Alma into town more often. I think physical therapy could really help her, and Ed hasn't had time to take her. And I want to computerize the inventory. Half the time Ed doesn't know what he's got in stock and what he needs to order."

"Pretty ambitious," Sierra said.

"Well, at least I don't think I'm going to be able to fix that cowboy," Riley teased. "Now *that's* ambitious."

"I don't know," Sierra said. "Maybe the really big job is fixing me."

Chapter 47

Sierra was preparing for a long night with the kids when Gil turned up at the house.

"You got the night off, sugar." He flashed a shopping bag from Target. "I went down to Cheyenne today and got a new Xbox game."

She lifted her eyebrows. "You want to play that so badly that you're taking my night shift?"

"I figure you probably have places to go, cowboys to talk to."

"What makes you think that?"

He grinned his toothy Gil grin. "You bought four bridal magazines at the Mini Mart this morning."

She knew she should have gone to Cheyenne for those. But she hadn't recognized the young man behind the counter, so she'd taken a calculated risk.

"Go on," Gil said. "Looking at all those frilly dresses for a few hours will do Ridge Cooper good." He turned and headed for the TV room.

Sierra felt her shoulders relaxing and a smile spreading across her face. She wasn't going to argue with him. Although she sincerely doubted she and Ridge would spend the gift of a surprise evening together looking at magazines.

There was no sign of Ridge when she reached the ranch, but the big white truck was parked in its usual spot, so he was around somewhere.

She grabbed the bridal magazines. She'd taken the time to dog-ear a few pages, marking the most hideous, over-the-top wedding dresses she could find to see if she could scare Ridge.

She tried the barn first, but it was empty of both horses and cowboys. The only sounds were the cooing of doves in the rafters and the occasional flutter of wings.

She stood there awhile, enjoying the soothing dimness and savoring the way the sunlight angled in through slits in the roof where storms had blown the shingles off. Breathing deep, she absorbed the scent of hay and horses, old wood and dust. This quiet place would be a part of her world someday, and though it was as different from her old world as any place she could imagine, she loved it already.

But she was on a mission. Stepping out of the barn, she called Ridge a couple times.

No answer.

She called his name again as she entered the house. He was probably in some far pasture, doing whatever it was cowboys did. That was another thing she'd have to learn someday.

So she had the house to herself. That wasn't such a bad thing. She could check out Riley's improvements and daydream about living there someday.

She thought about fanning the wedding magazines out on the coffee table, but then it occurred to her that one of Ridge's brothers might stop by, or some of Brady's rodeo friends. No, it would be better to keep their plans private until Ridge wanted to tell his brothers about it, so she headed upstairs to his bedroom.

Sitting on the bed, she tried to picture him as that sulky boy in the photo. It was obvious he hadn't stayed sulky long, since he'd accomplished so much in rodeo. She picked up the old composition book he'd shown her, where he'd written down his plans for the future, and flipped through the pages. The first few were devoted to boyish drawings of horses, with body parts carefully labeled. Then came a long list of cowboy and rodeo terms. That was pretty interesting. She'd have to go back to it later. The next page was the list of goals she'd already seen, and the page after that was a new list.

Plan B, it said at the top of the page. The handwriting looked more mature and less faded. Ridge could have written it just yesterday, for all she knew.

A fierce little claw of guilt clutched at her subconscious. She was snooping, in a way. But didn't she have a right? She and Ridge were going to get married. They'd have to work out new goals, shared ones. Maybe they'd develop their own plan B, or maybe this one would work for both of them. She needed to know, right?

The little claw clutched a little tighter, but she kept reading.

1. Clean house.

Well, that was a goal they could share. Ridge had actually come a long way with it, but there was still work to be done.

2. Talk to Sierra.

She smiled. This *was* a recent list. She wondered what he'd wanted to talk to her about that was important enough to put on a list. Marriage? Or something more mundane? She'd have to ask him.

The next item was *Bring the house up to code*. That solved the mystery of what he'd wanted to talk to her about. He must have written out this list before their dinner at the Red Dawg, when he'd broached the idea of taking in foster kids.

That was what had brought them together. The kids. Sometimes, she'd thought he cared far more about the kids than he did about her. In fact, at that dinner, she'd felt like he was romancing her as a means to an end.

She remembered telling him about how much work the house would need and how challenging the kids could be. He hadn't let any barrier stand in his way. Even when she'd told him the state usually didn't allow single men to be foster parents, he'd gone ahead and started working toward his goal. He couldn't have known then that the two of them would actually get together and solve that problem—though the thought had definitely crossed his mind. She'd seen it, clear as a shooting star, arcing through his dark eyes that night at the Red Dawg.

But though that was what brought them together, it wasn't the reason he'd proposed. There was more to their relationship than that. She loved him, deeply and purely, and he felt the same way about her. She was sure of it.

So why was that little claw clutching at her again? This time it wasn't guilt; it was fear.

And the next line made it tighten up and twist until she could barely breathe.

Find ~~wife~~ partner, it said. And then, in parentheses, it said *Sierra?*

It wasn't the question mark that got her. It was the parentheses. It was as if she was being considered as a possibility, as someone who might, maybe, solve his problem. Someone who was handy, who might suit his needs and help him get to that goal he was so hell-bent on reaching.

Now it was anger that clutched at her heart.

Because Ridge Cooper always achieved his goals, didn't he? He always stuck to the back of the bronc and finished out the ride. What was it he'd said about rodeo? *It was time to quit anyway. I was the world champion bronc rider. That was my goal. I made it, and I'm done.*

When he wanted something, he made it happen with a single-minded intensity that mowed down everything in his path. Including her.

She wasn't the love of his life. She was only a part of the plan.

If only it hadn't started the way it had, in that old-fashioned bedroom. If only he hadn't been so tender that day in the grove, that sacred place where the breezes stroked the wind chimes that had been placed there with so much love by his family.

She'd realized he was a little reticent when it came to romance, but she'd figured it was a function of his loveless upbringing, or maybe just part of being a cow-boy. In reality, every shred of romance he'd managed to force out had been a lie. He'd been working toward a goal. And while a cowboy might think the means justi-fied the ends, she could never forgive him for leading her on.

She stood up, smoothing out the comforter to erase all traces of her sitting on the bed. It was time to leave Ridge Cooper behind—Ridge Cooper and all the mo-ments they'd shared together.

But she couldn't, could she? She'd called and backed out of her upcoming job in Denver as soon as she

accepted the permanent position as manager of Phoenix
House. So she was trapped here in Wynott. She'd have
to see Ridge all the time. See him, hear about him, and
probably hear about whatever new floozy he found to
further his goals.

To hang on to her own sanity, she needed to change
the context of every memory she had of the times they'd
spent together. What she'd thought was lovemaking had
actually been sex. Good sex, great sex, probably the best
sex she'd ever have in her life—but with no real emotion
behind it. The moments she treasured weren't romance.
They were cold calculation on his part and foolish fantasy on hers.

It wasn't all his fault. She'd seen what she wanted
to see and turned her back on reality. She'd wanted her
someday *now*, and she'd been eager to believe she'd
found the place she belonged. In a way, she'd been as
guilty as Ridge. She'd offered him a way to reach his
goal; he'd offered her the family that, deep down, she'd
always wanted.

Closing the notebook, she picked up the wedding
magazines and tossed them in the wastebasket under the
desk. They landed with a very solid and satisfying *thunk*.

Chapter 48

RIDGE SAW SIERRA'S CAR THE MOMENT HE CAME around the corner of the barn. He'd been working Moonpie half the morning and actually getting somewhere. It seemed as if Jeffrey had broken through some barrier in the animal's mind, and the horse was more willing to trust.

The second he saw the car, he started off at a run. He'd longed to see her, but she'd been scheduled to work the whole day and most of the evening. She must have gotten Gil to cover for her.

He'd thought about her all day—about her and the life they'd build together. The one thing he'd wanted most, all his life, was the kind of love he shared with Sierra. He'd have a home, a family.

He'd be golden.

He ran into the house, jogged through the front hall, the kitchen, and the family room. No Sierra. She must be upstairs.

He ran up, two steps at a time, and there she was, sitting on the side of his bed. She didn't see him at first; her face was turned toward the window, and he wondered if she was taking in the view in a new way, seeing the landscape that stretched beyond the ranch house as home.

He hoped so.

He just watched her for a few seconds, loving the way the light from the window picked out the paler strands in her blond hair, the way it highlighted her cheekbone and silhouetted her strong profile. He loved the way the dim light emphasized the softness of her skin. He loved everything about her, especially when she was here, where she belonged. The ranch might be a foreign land to her, but it brought out the best in her in every way.

His heart swelled with love and the certainty that a happy future lay before him. He'd never believed that, even when he'd started conquering the big bulls, even when he'd won his championships. He'd never believed it until now, and at this moment, his heart felt big enough to hold all of Wyoming.

And then she turned. And she wasn't smiling. Her eyes were dull and dim, her lips drawn into a grim line.

"Hey," he said. "What's wrong?"

She shook her head as she rose, her lips tightening to hold in her thoughts.

She glanced down at the old tin pail he used as a wastebasket, and quickly up again, as if she hadn't meant to give herself away. He crossed the room in a single stride and picked up the bundle of magazines that filled the battered pail.

"*Elegant Bride,*" he said. "*Bridal Seasons, Bride Magazine, Here Comes the Bride.*" He flipped through one of them, looking at the models in their white dresses.

"You'll throw every one of these girls in the shade. You know that, right? You're going to be the prettiest bride in the state of Wyoming."

She didn't smile.

He looked down at the stack of magazines in his hands then back at her face. He didn't think Sierra was the type to care much about clothes, but he'd heard women turned crazy when it came to weddings.

He set the magazines on the desk. "Couldn't find anything you liked?"

She stood, and he reached out, took her hands. She shook him away, and he saw tears in her eyes. What was going on?

Glancing down at the bed, he saw something even more telling than the bridal magazines: his old composition book, open to plan B.

Shit.

He tried to remember exactly what he'd written. He knew her name was in there somewhere, as a goal to be attained. He knew that wasn't a bad thing—to love someone and want to win them—but he'd learned enough about women to know they misinterpreted things. They thought differently from men once you entered emotional territory.

"I'm sorry, Sierra," he said. She didn't answer, just stared back at him with disbelief written all over her face.

"You're *sorry*?"

He nodded. "I just don't know how to do this. I screw it up every time. I don't know a damn thing about love, and I do stupid shit like writing it down on a list."

She sat back down on the bed and looked at the composition book again. He wanted to snatch it out of her hands, take away the evidence of his own stupidity, but he knew enough to hold himself back.

"I knew it. That's what kills me. Remember that lunch at the Red Dawg? I told you not to look at me that way—like I was a means to an end." She picked up Shelley's stupid cowboy book, which he'd left beside the bed. "Did you get ideas out of this? Did I fall for lines from a romance novel?"

"No. That was Shelley's. She left it here. I might have a lot of flaws, but I'm not a liar. Everything that happened between us was for real. Everything."

"I'm sorry, Ridge. Maybe you believe that. But I think you want to succeed so badly that you don't know your own heart. I'm here now, the perfect answer to your problem. But what happens when that other woman turns up, the one you really love?"

"I'll never love anyone but you."

"No, because you'll never let yourself. You'd stand by me because you're an honorable man. I know that." She swiped at her eyes. *I will not cry. I will not cry.* "But once you make your goal, you'll realize that what you thought was love was just—I don't know—determination."

"It's not," he said. "I love you, and I always will." He knelt down, taking her hands in his. This time she didn't pull away.

But she wouldn't look him in the eye, and he knew he'd lost her.

~~~

Sierra could hardly stand to look at Ridge. He looked demolished. Maybe he believed he really loved her.

But there was no way he could know. He'd made up his mind to be a foster parent, and he was a man who always accomplished his goals. Hang on to the back of a bull for eight seconds? Check. Win a world championship before he turned thirty? Check.

Find a partner so he could adopt foster kids, like the dad he so admired?

Check.

She sat frozen by indecision, staring at the pictures on the far wall. Ridge on a horse. Ridge on a bull. Ridge with Bill Decker, with Irene. God, she loved this man, but what kind of situation was she getting herself into? What if she married him, and he only loved her for the kids? He'd get tired of her someday, and then what would she have? A sad, loveless marriage and a heart full of regret for the things she hadn't done.

She swallowed and blinked hard, doing her best to put up that professional shield that had been her greatest weapon. All the time she'd worked in Denver, her ability to shut down her emotions had been her best professional strength. Wonder Woman had her golden bracelets, Spider-Man had his webs, Batman had the Batmobile, and Sierra Dunn had her impenetrable shield of professionalism.

But she'd dropped it here in Wynott. Something about this small town had charmed her and broken through her defenses. She'd fallen for the kids first and then for Ridge. Then she'd fallen for the life she could have here on the ranch, and in the quaint little town.

She so wanted Ridge's love to be real. It was the best she'd ever had. It had convinced her, finally, that there were good men in the world.

But that was the problem. She'd seen what she wanted to see, and she'd ignored the truth.

"I can't do it, Ridge," she said. "I'm sorry. I can't."

"You know, it's the same old problem," he said. "You always want some kind of guarantee. You want a guarantee the horse won't hurt Jeff, or you won't let him ride him. You want a guarantee Riley won't screw up again, or you won't let her loose. Now you want a guarantee that I love you just the right way."

"Those things matter to me."

"I know that. But sometimes you just have to gamble and make the leap, you know?"

She didn't answer. She couldn't, because he was right. It just wasn't a leap she could make.

She turned and left the bedroom, then headed down the hall toward the stairs. She couldn't help touching the doorframes as she passed the bedrooms, running her palm over the round finial at the top of the stair rail, stroking the smooth wood of the bannister. She wanted to memorize this place, to hold it in her heart forever.

Because even though there was a fatal flaw in her love affair with Ridge, it was the closest she'd ever come to the real thing. She had a feeling it would be a long time before she handed over her heart again— maybe never. So she needed the memories of her time with Ridge to treasure, to turn over in her mind for a long time to come.

She knew he'd followed her downstairs. She just needed to make it to the door, to the porch, to the car, without turning around. Because if she saw his face, she might relent, and she knew that would be wrong.

"What about the rodeo?" he said.

She stood in the doorway, still as a frightened deer. "I'll take them," she said. "I'll take them by myself."

Chapter 49

SIERRA HADN'T FULLY APPRECIATED THE COMPLICA-tions inherent in taking a gang of boys to a small-town rodeo until she and Gil pulled up in the parking lot and it was time to open the van's doors. She could see the Ferris wheel spinning as a backdrop to a temporary midway filled with rides and food stands, and she knew the boys would scatter like a covey of quail the moment the doors opened.

"Wait!" she hollered.

Everybody froze. She had that holler honed to perfection.

Spinning in her seat, she fixed each one of them with a stern stare, pointing to each boy in turn. "We will follow the rules."

Point.

"We will stay together."

Point.

"We will be well behaved and orderly."

Point.

"There will be no talking to strangers beyond the polite necessaries."

She narrowed her eyes and addressed the whole group.

"Now, what are the polite necessaries?"

The boys rolled their eyes and chanted in toneless unison, "The poh-lite necessaries are yes, ma'am; no, ma'am; yes, sir; no, sir; thank you; and you're welcome."

"And what do we never tell people?"

"Who we are, where we're from, why we're here, or anything personal."

"And why is that?"

Their tone livened considerably as they bounced in their seats and shouted, "'Cause we're secret agent men from the planet Zorg and revealing our true identities could cause discovery and *death*!"

Sierra doubted Mike would approve the death part, but it heightened the stakes in the game and that kept the boys serious about playing and winning.

"Okay. Our mission today is to study local culture."

The boys groaned. She grinned. She might have a broken heart, but she still loved these boys, and they still made her smile. They would, for months or maybe years to come.

Maybe, in that way, Ridge had done her a favor. He'd made her stay, and she couldn't say she was unhappy about that. She hadn't seen him since their confrontation, so maybe she'd be able to heal in time.

"What does studying local culture mean?" she hollered.

"Something boring, probably," Isaiah muttered.

"No!" She upped the volume even more. "It means we have to cheer for the good guys, eat till we bust, and figure out why these men in funny hats want to strap themselves onto wild animals and ride until their brains are scrambled and their bones are broke. Ready?"

"*Ready!*"

The van's doors slid open and the kids hit the dirt parking lot running.

—⁓—

Sheriff Swaggard thrust his thumbs in his belt loops and made his way through the crowds at the Carson County Rodeo and Fair with his very best cowboy swagger. The Rodeo and Fair was the biggest event that ever came near Wynott, and every year he waited for something important to happen—a challenge that would demand all his skills as a lawman and a protector of the public. One that would let him shine. One that would make him a hero.

Not that he wanted anything bad to happen. It would be terrible if the Ferris wheel stalled, leaving some young girl trapped at the top so he'd have to climb up and rescue her. It would be tragic if some carny took off with somebody's baby, and he had to track the miscreant down and shoot him, catching the infant in his arms as the kidnapper fell to the blacktop. It would be a shame if there were a bomb threat, and he had to clear the fairgrounds while preventing panic and maintaining order.

He didn't want those things to happen, but they ran through his dreams every night, like old-time silent movie reels. He knew he was born to handle disaster with the calm courage represented by the star he wore so proudly on his chest.

But nothing ever happened. Every year, the folks of Wynott and the surrounding countryside came to the fair and had a good time. Sometimes a bull rider would get gored, but then the pickup men played hero and whisked him out of danger on their highly trained horses. Sometimes a fight would break out at the beer tent, but somehow the whole thing was always over by the time he even got there. Sometimes a fan would get a little too excited and try to climb onstage with one of the country music acts, but the bands always had their own security.

That was the other thing. The band security guys, the pickup men, even the rodeo clowns—they got respect, and that respect translated to some very good times with some mighty fine women. But Jim always missed out on that part of the fun too.

Not this year, though. This year, he could feel something tingling in his bones. He could tell his luck was about to change, and he was going to prove he was the one to turn to when things went wrong.

He tipped his hat at a group of young ladies who were perusing the Native American jewelry booth under the grandstands. They giggled and moved away, probably because the sight of such a respectable lawman reminded them to be embarrassed by their tight jeans and tiny tops.

"Excuse me, Sheriff?"

He turned to see a big, beefy cowboy heading his way.

"I could use some help."

Sheriff Swaggard gave a sharp nod. "That's what I do, sir." *Kind of like Superman.* "Now how can I make your attendance here at the Rodeo and Fair a safer and more enjoyable experience?"

The cowboy stared at him a minute, going kind of cross-eyed. Jim knew that sometimes his vocabulary was just too advanced for the average yokel to understand, so he dumbed it down a notch.

"How can I help you?"

"I'm looking for my son."

There. Hadn't Jim just dreamed about a missing child only two nights ago? He took out his pocket-sized notebook and flipped to a blank page. Pulling a pen out of his pocket, he looked up at the cowboy.

The man had muscles like one of those wrestlers on TV. It looked like his head was shaved under that cowboy hat, and he had a bunch of tattoos. It was really something that a tough customer like that needed Sheriff Swaggard to help him, but that's how things worked. The law had certain powers.

"When did you last see your boy, sir?"

"Oh, hm." The cowboy looked confused for a minute. He was probably distraught. But after a little hemming and hawing, he came up with an answer.

"It was about a month ago."

"A month!" This kid hadn't gotten lost in the crowd around the Ferris wheel or slipped away in the grandstands, then. This was a runaway.

"Yep." The cowboy's face reddened, and he looked away for a minute, probably overcome with emotion, and who could blame him? He hadn't seen his kid for a month. Jim didn't have any kids, but he suspected you'd miss one if it were gone that long.

"How old is the child?"

"About—ten?"

Jim squinted at the cowboy. He didn't sound sure of his own kid's age. That seemed kind of strange, but then, it was the mother's job to keep track of birthdays and that kind of thing. This guy was probably too busy providing a living for his little family to take care of details like that.

"And where did you last see him?"

"He's at that Phoenix House place," the cowboy said. "His mom and me got divorced, and she went and put him into foster care while I was away fightin' in Iraq." He showed some kind of military tattoo by way of proof.

Jim couldn't tell what it was supposed to mean, but it had a shield and an eagle, so he just nodded.

"I went over there to pick him up and found out they're here at the rodeo." The guy took off his hat and scratched his head, squinting in the harsh sunshine. Sure enough, his head was bald as a basketball. Maybe he'd been Special Forces or something. "So I thought maybe you could help me find him."

"Sure thing." Jim clapped the guy on the back to reassure him and was stunned when the guy's face reddened and those WWE muscles tensed like he was about to turn into the Incredible Hulk.

He reminded himself the man was a soldier. Probably had PTSD from all the stuff he'd done in the Special Forces, that was all. Evidently his condition was well under control, because already he was smiling at Jim. He even gave him a little punch in the arm, like a buddy would.

There weren't any Special Forces guys in Wynott. In fact, the only military man in town was Phoebe Niles's son, Mike, and he was gone so much, Jim never saw him. But military men and lawmen had a lot in common, and Jim had no doubt he'd have lots of friends in the Special Forces if he lived in a bigger town.

"Now here's the thing." The soldier put a friendly arm across Jim's shoulders and tugged him over by the potato skins stand, where they couldn't be heard by the passing crowd. "You know how vindictive a woman can be when it comes to divorce and child custody and all that."

Jim nodded, though he really didn't know much about women at all, vindictive or otherwise. There just weren't enough of 'em in Wynott that would give a man a chance.

"Well, my ex sent the kid to this Phoenix House place, and the woman that runs it—you know her?"

"Sure do," Jim said. "Sierra Dunn."

The cowboy chuckled. "Doesn't sound like you like her much."

"You can bet your Noconas on that," Jim said. He'd noticed the man's boots right away—expensive Noconas with lizard-skin uppers. He'd thought about getting a pair like that himself sometime. When he had the money. Which he'd never make working here in Wynott.

That's why he needed to do something courageous, something to make himself stand out.

"Well, Miss Dunn really has it in for men," the soldier said. "She's one of those feminists—you know the type."

Jim nodded. He sure did.

"There's no way she'd hand the kid over to me without all kinds of paperwork and probably even a court proceeding."

Jim nodded.

"But…" The big man actually started to tear up. Nearly cried, right there on the midway, just thinking about his boy. "But I just want a moment with my boy. I just want to talk to him, you know? So if you could help me find him, you could help a soldier spend a little time with his son."

"You bet," Jim said. "I appreciate your service, sir, and I'll do whatever I can to help you reunite with your son. I'm sure he's real proud of you, and I'll bet he takes after his old man too."

"I sure do thank you, sir." The soldier looked like he was about to cry. Jim couldn't believe it. A real Special Forces soldier brought to tears by his love for his son. He could see the headline now.

Well, he couldn't really see it. He wasn't much for writing or that kind of thing. But he could see his picture right underneath it, holding the kid while the soldier — well, maybe he ought to let the soldier hold his own kid.

"And you'll make sure that Dunn bitch doesn't know a thing about this, right? Or that boyfriend of hers?"

Jim recoiled a little. Of course, that kind of language was probably used every day in the army. But there was something else...

"How do you know she has a boyfriend?" he asked.

The soldier blinked and then blinked again. Then he smiled. "Doesn't that type always have some man on a string?"

"They sure do."

Not only was this soldier a brave fighter for his country, but he also knew a thing or two about human nature. Jim held his notebook at the ready and clicked his silver ballpoint into readiness. "Now, how about you give me a description of your son?"

Chapter 50

SIERRA HAD BEEN LOOKING FORWARD TO THE RODEO with Ridge. He would have taken the boys behind the chutes and introduced them to some of the cowboys, and he would have explained how the different events worked. Maybe he even would have been able to keep them interested through the roping events, which made them restless and whiny.

The bucking events were better. Once each cowboy had managed to jam his heels into position, loud rock music would blare over the loudspeakers for however long he managed to stay on board. Watching cowboys twirl and spin—and sometimes fly—to the strains of Bon Jovi and Metallica was pretty entertaining.

But watching the kids was even better. They whooped, hollered, stamped their feet, and generally made themselves obnoxious, but the crowd couldn't have cared less. All the grown-ups around them were acting like kids anyway.

Once the rodeo was over, she divided the kids into two groups. One group would go ride the Cyclone and check out the midway with Gil; the other half would stay with her and stuff themselves with fair food. Then they'd switch.

By this point, she was exhausted. She hadn't slept well the night before, and keeping the kids in line with only Gil to help was tough. That had been one of Ridge's greatest charms: his effortless ability to keep the kids happy while keeping them in line. It was a balancing act, and he did it very, very well.

But she wasn't changing her mind. When she married, it would be for love and love alone.

But you do love Ridge, a little voice inside her said.

I only think I do, she answered. *Because it's convenient. And what about him, with his list and his parentheses?*

You know he loves you too, the little voice said.

She slapped that sucker down and got back to business, which at the moment consisted of a turkey-leg eating contest between Isaiah and Carter. She wasn't sure how the food races would work out later on, but for now, they kept the kids laughing and happy, and gave her a little time to think.

You're making a mistake, the voice said.

"Hey, hold on, guys." There was no line at the turkey leg stand, so she was able to watch the kids while she got her own.

"Okay," she said. "Start again. This time, I'm racing too."

There. Now she'd gotten Ridge out of her head as well as out of her hair. Because when you really went to town on a turkey leg, there was no room for anything else.

Sheriff Swaggard passed by, resplendent in his khaki uniform and matching Stetson. She shot him a cheerful wave with one greasy hand. They were at the fair, after all. It wasn't the place or the time for old grievances.

Apparently, Sheriff Swaggard felt the same way, because he sat down across the table and laughed along with them as they ate, declaring Carter the winner.

"You can tell he's a fast eater," Isaiah said, poking his friend in the stomach. "It's all right there, just lookin' at you."

Sierra started to admonish Isaiah for his rudeness—miraculously, it would be the first time that day—but the sheriff laughed, slapping his knee. "You got that right. Going to be a linebacker someday, aren't you? And you, you're going to play basketball."

Both boys nodded enthusiastically and joined the sheriff in a lively conversation about sports. Sierra didn't know a thing about football or basketball, but apparently Carter knew an impressive number of statistics. Better yet, Isaiah passed judgment on every basketball player in the NBA, decrying their moral failings in such colorful terms he had the sheriff red-faced with laughter.

Why had she been so worried about him meeting the boys?

She was glad to see him take an interest in the kids as people, not potential perps. The kids seemed quite impressed by Jim's uniform and asked lots of questions about catching bad guys. But Jim suddenly seemed to be in a hurry.

"What about the other kids?" he asked. "They misbehave or something? Get stuck at home?"

"Oh, no. They're with Gil, doing the rides and the midway."

"Yeah, lucky ducks." Isaiah pouted.

"You'll get your chance," she said. "We're switching off halfway through," she explained to the sheriff.

"So the other three kids are…"

"Frankie, Josh, and Jeffrey."

"Jeffrey," the sheriff muttered. "Okay, then." He

rose, tugging his belt up and tucking in his shirt, all the while staring at Sierra. It would have made her uncomfortable, but Jim seemed oblivious to the rather personal nature of his adjustments.

"Let me ask you a question," he blurted.

"Sure," Sierra said.

"You're pretty crazy about these kids."

She grinned. "That's not a question."

"No." He edged to the end of the table, signaling toward the boys. Sierra followed. "If one of their daddies showed up, you wouldn't keep them apart, would you? If you thought they loved each other, and they'd be happy together?"

Sierra chewed her lower lip a moment. "What makes you ask?"

"Just wondered. I have a friend who's got a boy this age, and they just adore each other. It got me to thinking."

"The short answer is no, of course, I'd never keep a good parent from his child. But all my kids have families with serious problems. Most of their fathers are incarcerated, and the ones that aren't, should be."

"You don't say."

"That's why they're here, Jim. If one of their dads showed up, I'd have to call you for help." She figured this wasn't the time to tell him about Mitch and how she'd called Ridge.

"Well, thanks for clearing that up." Jim tipped his hat. "I'd better be going. It's a big crowd here, and there's almost always some kind of trouble."

"Really?" Sierra looked around at the revelers. "It seems pretty orderly."

"Oh, there's always something," the sheriff said.

After racing through a dessert of funnel cakes and lemonade, Sierra wondered how the kids were going to manage any of the rides in the midway. There was no roller coaster, but there were plenty of spinning, twirling, vomit-inducing rides to shake them up and, unfortunately, empty them out.

And here was Gil, half an hour early. She'd been counting on that half hour for digestive purposes. But he looked worn to a frazzle by Frankie and Josh and...

"Where's Jeffrey?"

The look on his face was answer enough.

"You lost him."

"Hey," Isaiah said. "Don't be too hard on the guy. Kid's so quiet, you never know where he is."

"Sierra, I'm sorry." Gil looked like he was ready to cry. "He just disappeared. One minute he was there, and the next—just gone. I'd just introduced him to the sheriff, along with these other guys. And now I can't even find the sheriff to get help."

"It's okay, Gil. I'll find him. Can you watch the kids? Maybe you could take them to the arcade?"

"Sure. They've got a real race car you can drive on a virtual track."

The kids cheered, and Sierra handed Gil the cash she had left.

"I hope you find that kid," Isaiah said as they left.

"Thought you didn't like him," Carter said.

Isaiah shrugged. "He might be kinda quiet, but at least he never says anything stupid."

Sierra waded through the crowd, looking left and right, scanning the distance even as she watched the crowds flowing past her. She searched for Jeffrey, and also for the sheriff. Gil had said he was right there. And there was something about that question he'd asked…

As she headed past the sideshow tent, a big, beefy guy in a huge cowboy hat stepped in front of her and blocked her view. Frustrated, she stepped up her pace and passed him, shooting him a dirty look as she nearly toppled a lady pushing a stroller.

He shot the look right back, and she felt her stomach flip over.

"Mitch," she said.

"The one and only." He leered at her and a shiver of revulsion shimmied up her spine. "Where's your little band of Indians?"

She kept on walking. She didn't need to have a conversation with Mitch. Unless…

"You missing somebody?" he asked in a mocking tone.

She turned slowly, her mind skittering through various scenarios, hoping to find one that might lead to a good resolution.

She widened her eyes and put a hand to her chest. "Yes, and I have to find him. He doesn't have his inhaler!"

"What?"

"He needs his inhaler. If he has an asthma attack, he could die!" She didn't know why Mitch wanted Jeffrey—she didn't even want to think about the possibilities—but she hoped like hell he wanted him alive.

"You got it?"

She nodded, clutching the oversized purse where she'd stuffed all the essentials for their trip—sunscreen, wipes, a small first aid kit, and an inhaler. The inhaler was Josh's, but Mitch didn't need to know that.

"Give it to me, then," Mitch said.

"You have him?"

Mitch made a grab for the purse and she whirled away. A couple of cowboys paused.

"You all right, ma'am?"

She nodded without looking at her would-be rescuer. "Okay so far," she said.

Looking doubtful, the cowboys blended back into the crowd, leaving her with Mitch again.

"You touch me or try to take this bag, I'll holler so loud, they'll hear me in the next county," she said.

He shrugged. "What do I care?"

"Take me to him," she said. "Let me give it to him and make sure he's okay. Or I'll scream, I really will, and the sheriff will come."

"The sheriff won't help you," Mitch said, his voice clear and cold as ice water. "The sheriff's a friend of mine."

Sierra didn't like Sheriff Swaggard much, but she definitely couldn't see him palling around with a drug dealer from Denver. She thought of the question he'd asked, about dads and sons. There was something going on here. She wasn't sure what it was, but she'd flounder around until she figured it out.

"Oh," she said. "I know. You're Jeffrey's dad, right? I understand how you feel. You want him to be with you."

She knew darn well this wasn't true. Jeffrey's dad was in jail, and she had no idea how Mitch fit into the picture.

He stared at her, his little piggy eyes judging her in every way—including ways that made her very uncomfortable.

"You *are* his dad, right?" She squinted at him. "Because if you're not, I can start yelling right now. But if you're his dad, it's okay."

Good God, she sounded simpleminded. She was pretty sure she was on the right track, though.

"It must be hard, being separated from your son," she said, pushing a little further and hoping, praying, that he wouldn't push back.

"Yeah. Right." He started off across the parking lot and Sierra followed, his broad back a hulking beacon as they made their way through the crowd. With the rodeo over, young families were heading home. The next rodeo started at eight, and it would draw a whole new crowd.

They finally reached the old delivery truck, parked on the far side of the parking lot. The sun glinted off the side as if it was a mirror. If Jeffrey was in there, he was one step from heat stroke. Somehow, Sierra had to get him out.

Mitch shoved a key into the padlock on the back door of the truck and raised it an inch or two.

"Hold on," he said. "You really got an inhaler?"

Sierra rummaged in her bag and finally found it, holding it up so he could see it.

Mitch snatched the bag away. "That's all you're going to give him."

He raised the gate about a foot. Sierra wished she hadn't looked at the sun reflecting off the side of the truck; the glare in her eyes made the dark interior of the truck totally impenetrable. She couldn't see Jeffrey—or anything else for that matter.

"Kid musta passed out," Mitch muttered. "Go on in and see if he needs it."

Sierra paused. Getting trapped with Jeffrey in Mitch's truck wouldn't do anyone any good. She knew where he

was now. She'd memorized the plate and run through a
description in her mind. She knew there were cowboys
watching the entrance and exit, taking money for parking. Mitch wouldn't even make it out of the lot if she got
the description to them.

But as she turned to run, Mitch grabbed her belt at
the back of her jeans and tossed her, hard, into the dark
cavern of the truck's delivery box. Skidding across the
rough wooden floor, she slammed into the back wall as
the door came down and darkness descended.

"Jeff?" she said. "Jeff, are you in here?"

If he was, he wasn't answering.

Chapter 51

RIDGE PLOWED THROUGH THE CROWD, PANNING THE blur of faces. He couldn't remember the Grigsby rodeo ever drawing this many people. Finding Sierra in the midst of all these vacationers and thrill seekers was going to be practically impossible. But he had to find her. Had to. He'd been pulling into the Mini Mart to gas up the ranch truck when he'd spotted a familiar delivery truck parked at the pumps.

He'd pulled in to confront Mitch, determined to make sure the man drove out of town. He'd done it once, and he was sure he could do it again. But as he'd pulled in, the truck had pulled out. The station was choked with fairgoers and kids, and Ridge had been trapped. By the time he made his way out of the lot, the truck was gone.

He hadn't been able to see the driver. Maybe it wasn't Mitch. But Ridge had no doubt it was the same truck, and he seriously doubted it had come to Wynott twice by pure coincidence.

Plowing through the crowd, he craned his neck, scanning the crowd for Sierra—for that messy blond hairdo, those sharp green eyes that saw straight into his soul.

And then he saw it. A cowboy, tall and lean, with wire-rimmed glasses and a handlebar mustache, walking toward him with a kid tossed over his shoulder.

Not just any kid. Jeffrey.

It wasn't a cowboy Ridge had ever seen before. Not

a neighbor or a friend, but a stranger. Not Mitch, either, but maybe a friend of his. Ridge couldn't see Jeffrey's face, but his body had the limp, hopeless look of a kid who'd fought long and hard and had to give up, and the cowboy was carrying him like a sack of potatoes.

Ridge had been angry in his life. He'd lost his temper more than once. But this got him riled up beyond anything he'd ever experienced. Balling his fists, he speeded his steps, shoving a young couple aside in his haste to get to the boy.

As he approached, he realized he couldn't just clock the guy. Jeffrey might get hurt. The best plan would be to grab his boy first then hit the guy. Hit him and hit him and trample him into the dirt, the way Twister had trampled him all those weeks ago.

But then the man grinned and hailed Ridge with a big, friendly wave.

"Hey," he shouted. "You lookin' for this guy?"

Jeffrey stiffened, and to Ridge's surprise, he fought the cowboy as the man tried to put him down. Ridge was pretty sure the kid landed a hard right on the cowboy's jaw, but the man just laughed a little and set Jeffrey on his feet.

Ridge looked at Jeffrey and realized Sierra was right; the horses had worked a miracle. He'd forgotten how stiff and expressionless the boy's face had been the first time he'd come to the ranch, but he was reminded of it now. What he was looking at now was a boy who'd regressed even further. It looked for all the world as if the kid couldn't see what was in front of him.

Not that he was looking in front of himself. He was looking at the ground. Ridge stepped closer, and the boy's eyes traveled up from the tips of his boots, past his jeans and his belt buckle, and got to his face before there was any sign he recognized him. Even then, there was only a slight widening of the eyes and then a quick move toward him.

But instead of grabbing Ridge around the waist, the way most lost boys would, he stepped behind him and grabbed onto the back of his shirt. The only sign of emotion was the strength of his grip; the carefully tucked-in shirttail was twisted in his fist in no time.

"Where was he?" Ridge's voice was raspy, partly from emotion but partly, he realized, from disuse. Without Sierra and the boys around, he rarely had a reason to speak.

"Found him in the trailer with my roping horse, Dice."

"In the trailer?"

"Hiding out. Didn't pick a very good spot for it, though. Dice is no pussycat, and the kid somehow got clear to the front, right under his hooves. Lucky he wasn't killed."

"Sorry," Ridge said.

The cowboy shook his head. "Dice is a handful even for me. He hates dogs and kids and anything under his feet, 'specially if he can't see it." He cast a puzzled look at Jeffrey. "How'd you get past him?"

Jeffrey's grip on Ridge's shirt tightened. "His foot hurts."

"His foot?"

"The right one, in front. It hurts a lot. That's why he's mean."

"Yeah, okay." The cowboy gave Ridge a quizzical look. "The horse doesn't limp or anything."

"He doesn't want you to know," Jeffrey said. "He wants to do stuff right. It's just that, sometimes his foot hurts so much, he can't stand it."

"You got any idea what's wrong with it?"

Jeffrey shrugged.

"Guess there's a limit." The cowboy turned to Ridge. "You think he's right?"

"I'd bet on it." Ridge reached back and put an arm around Jeffrey as best he could. The boy felt stiff as a board under his hand, as if he'd turned to stone. "Look, I've got to get him back to his mom. Anything I can do for you, just holler. I owe you one."

"Not if he's right about Dice, you don't. I've been trying to figure that one out for months. He's always been a good roping horse. Just all of a sudden got mean." He paused, eyeing Ridge. "You're Ridge Cooper, aren't you?"

Ridge nodded. He hated this part.

"You sure could ride 'em. Sorry about what happened."

"Thanks."

Ridge walked in silence for a while, giving Jeffrey a chance to realize he was safe. Once he felt the boy's shoulders relax a little—a very little—he stopped and knelt down, letting the crowds flow around them.

"What happened?"

Jeffrey shrugged and looked away.

Ridge tightened his grip on the boy's shoulder. "Sorry, but that's not good enough today. I need to know what's going on. Where are Sierra and the other boys?"

Another shrug.

Ridge sucked in a deep breath. *Patience.*

"Look, you're safe now. Whatever scared you, I'll

protect you—but I can't do that if you don't tell me what's wrong."

Jeffrey glanced right then left. When he looked back at Ridge, his eyes were glossy with unshed tears.

"I saw him."

"Who?"

"Mitch."

"Okay. How do you know Mitch? What does he want?"

Jeffrey shrugged again. "My dad worked for him. Like, selling stuff."

"Drugs?"

Jeffrey nodded.

"Did he threaten you?"

This time, the nod was quick, exaggerated, and very affirmative. "He said if I talked, he'd kill everybody I cared about."

Shoot. The kid had probably seen a drug deal, maybe something worse, and the guy had threatened him not to talk about it. Jeffrey had taken the threat so much to heart that he did his best not to talk at all. Ever.

"I get it. That scared you."

"Not then. But now it does." A single tear overflowed and slid down his cheek. He dashed it away with the back of his fist. "He saw me with Sierra. He looked at her and he made a gun with his finger." The boy demonstrated, pointing his index finger and cocking his thumb like a trigger. "He pointed at her, and he shot her."

"Tell you what," Ridge said. "I'm going to hoist you up on my shoulders, and you tell me when you see anybody. Sierra, the other kids, Gil—or Mitch."

Jeffrey's face reddened and the tears spilled over. They were silent tears, which struck Ridge as a terrible thing. No child should ever learn to cry without making a sound.

"He'll see me," the boy said in a hoarse whisper. "And he'll see you, and he'll track you down and find you and shoot you because of *me*."

"Jeff." Ridge shook him gently and smiled as best he could. "You saw that night. You were looking out the window. Remember? I came to Phoenix House, and Mitch was there. Do you remember what happened?"

Jeffrey just looked at him, unable to speak, his mouth stretched shapeless by the intensity of his fear.

"He turned tail and *ran*. And that's what he'll do if he sees me here. But this time?"

He shifted Jeffrey toward him to make sure the boy was listening.

"This time, I'm going to chase him down. And I'm going to tell him that you *are* going to talk, as much as you want, and he can't stop you. And if he tries, you'll talk to the police, and he'll go to jail. Because you know what?"

Jeffrey just looked at him, but at least he looked a little more like himself. The flush had faded, and his lips just trembled the slightest bit.

"Because he's more afraid of you than you are of him. Because you know things about him that could put him in jail for a good long time. And when this is over, you're going to tell me all about them, and we'll decide together what to do. So don't you be scared of him. Not now, not ever again."

Jeffrey nodded. When Ridge hoisted him to his shoulders, the boy's hands gripped his hair and hung on so tightly it hurt.

He didn't complain. He just started walking.

Sierra sat in the back of the van with her back against the wall and her knees raised in front of her. Resting her forearms on her knees, she stared at the faint shard of light that slipped through the cracks in the van's door and wondered how the hell she'd ever get out of here.

She'd felt her way around the entire perimeter and crossed the floor in a careful, methodical grid pattern, assuring herself that Jeffrey wasn't in the truck.

That meant that Jeffrey was probably still out there at the rodeo, with only Gil to protect him. No shame on Gil, but the man was in his seventies and had the muscle tone of Jerry Garcia. He was hardly a match for Mitch.

She hadn't found any tools in her search of the truck either. The temperature was approximately ninety outside, so it had to be over a hundred degrees in the box that held her prisoner. She was going to be roasted like a chicken if she didn't get out of here.

She'd hammered on the walls of her prison for a while, but despite the satisfyingly drumlike resonance of the truck's metal sides, no one responded. She'd tried shouting too. Shouting and shouting.

No one had answered.

She was resting now, and trying to stop sweating. She probably should have conserved some energy, but she'd figured *someone* would pass by and hear her. But the truck was parked in the far corner of the lot, and nobody had been anywhere near it when Mitch had thrown her inside. It might be some time before she had a chance to escape.

But she *would* escape. She would *not* let Mitch kill

her or rape her, or use her to get to Jeffrey. He might outweigh her by a hundred and fifty pounds, but she would kick his ugly big behind before she let him hurt her or any of the kids.

It was really hard to do all that from inside the pitch-dark, super-heated confines of a delivery truck, though.

She wondered if he'd done anything with her purse. Hopefully, he'd put it in the truck, so the police could track her by her cell phone's GPS if she went missing long enough.

Although they'd probably find her mummified body curled in a fetal position inside an abandoned delivery truck.

No. No they wouldn't. Someone would pass by sooner or later. It just sucked that he was out there stalking Jeffrey, and all she could do was sit here and listen, as hard as she could, for a possible savior.

She had no sense of time, sitting there in the darkness. She might have been in the truck for an hour, maybe two, maybe four. It felt like four, but there was still sunlight coming in through the cracks, so it was still daylight.

She was starting to feel sick from the heat. Little sparkly flowers danced in front of her eyes, and her stomach was rebelling against all the junk food she'd ingested just before she'd seen Mitch.

The dense darkness inside the truck was starting to spar-kle more and more, and the top of her head felt even hot-ter than the rest of her. It felt like her brains were cooking, and maybe they were. It was hot enough in there to cook an egg, she was sure. Brains were a lot like eggs, weren't they?

Don't think like that.

She headed over to the door of the truck, even though the slightest movement made the sparkling even worse.

She wanted to be by the door in case Mitch opened it for any reason. She leaned against the door. If she passed out, she'd *fall* out when the door opened.

Or if she died.

Well, that was morbid. She'd better find something else to think about, like what she'd do when she got out of here. Not *if* she got out. *When*.

First of all, she would never again compete in a turkey-leg eating contest. That was number one.

Second, she'd stop worrying about petty bullshit and *live*. She'd stop trying to change the world for people she didn't even know and start loving the ones she did. The idea of never seeing Frankie or Josh or Carter or any of the other boys again was almost unbearable.

And Ridge?

Whatever happened between them from here on, she needed to tell him she loved him. Had she ever told him that?

Despite the airless heat, a chill rose along her arms. She hadn't. She'd never told him she loved him.

He'd told her. He'd asked her to marry him. But she'd never even told him she loved him.

Why?

Because he hadn't asked.

He hadn't asked about her motives or whether she was capable of being a decent ranch wife—which she probably wasn't. He hadn't asked for anything. While she'd been parsing his reasons and second-guessing the feelings he'd laid before her like gifts on a blanket, he'd never even asked her to say she loved him.

What the hell had she been thinking? He was the best man she knew, and he wanted to marry her. He asked for virtually nothing in return. Quibbling over the reason *why* was just plain stupid. If he didn't love her for the right reason now, she'd see to it that he did before their first year of marriage was up.

Because right now, she didn't even deserve his love. And he loved her anyway.

The darkness shimmered in front of her eyes. Turning, she tried to see the shafts of light she'd noticed before, and she couldn't. Was it dark outside? Or was she going blind, like a cave bat?

She needed to get out of here. She might as well yell. Opening her mouth, she did her best to holler, but what came out of her parched throat was a feeble croak.

People must be looking for her by now. Ridge would be looking for her if she'd let him come along. Would Gil call him? She didn't know. But she had to get out of here. Because if she didn't die of thirst or heat or starvation, she'd die of regret.

She never would have believed there was a darkness deeper than the inside of that truck, but it seemed as if an even blacker dark was closing in on her, flowing inward from the edges of her vision until just a pinhole of consciousness was left.

Just before she gave herself to that darkness, she thought of Ridge and the ranch and that stupid horse, the one that came when you—came when you—*oh*.

Why hadn't she thought of that sooner?

She put her fingers to her lips, sucked in a deep breath, and blew out a keening, piccolo-pitched whistle, praying the sound would carry to every corner of the fairgrounds.

And then she slumped to the floor and let the darkness come.

Chapter 52

RIDGE WAS CONFUSED.

He knew Sierra was upset with him, but had she seen him there with Gil and the kids and walked away? Would she really leave Gil with the kids and sulk somewhere just because he'd come and joined them? He'd found Jeffrey, after all.

But she hadn't returned to the arcade where she'd left Gil and the boys marooned, and she wasn't answering her phone.

"Why don't you try calling her?" he asked Gil.

"I don't have a phone. Lemme use yours." Ridge shot him a look, and he flushed. "Oh. Yeah. It would look like you were calling, wouldn't it?"

"Do you have the keys to the van?" Ridge asked.

Gil nodded.

"Then how 'bout this. You take these guys back to the house. Jeff and I'll stay here and see if we can find her. If she's at the house, give me a call and let me know, okay?"

"I want to stay with you and Jeffrey," Isaiah said. He and all the other boys were in full-out whining mode, and Ridge couldn't blame them. Their fun day at the fair had turned into a dull campout in the hot sun. Carter had thrown up twice, and Josh was looking a little green around the gills. Apparently, they'd eaten an awful lot of fair food. He was surprised Sierra had allowed that, but maybe, as a city girl, she wasn't aware of the ill effects of too much turkey leg, barbecue, and funnel cake.

"I'm just taking Jeff for right now, okay?" Ridge patted the boy's shoulder. "There's a good reason, but I can't explain right now. It's complicated."

"It's always complicated when it comes to that kid," Isaiah mumbled. "I'm gonna quit talking. See how you like it when *I* get complicated."

Ridge suppressed a grin. Isaiah would never make it as the strong, silent type.

He walked the group to the van and made sure they made it out okay, feeling a little forlorn as he watched the gang take off and leave him and Jeffrey in the waning light. It was probably stupid to keep on looking for Sierra, but he felt like something was wrong.

For one thing, Sierra wouldn't stop looking for Jeffrey until she found him. She just wouldn't. For another, she wouldn't refuse to answer her phone. She wasn't childish like that.

So she must still be on the grounds, looking for Jeffrey. Somehow, she'd lost her phone or maybe it was turned off and she didn't realize it.

He'd turned away and started back toward the fairgrounds when a high, thin sound pierced the air. A whistle, loud and long.

"Sierra." He and Jeffrey said it together, and then the two of them took off running toward the sound.

The whistle led Ridge and Jeffrey to the far side of the parking lot. It didn't take long for them to notice a scratched, scarred delivery truck parked in the far corner. Ridge put a finger to his lips, signaling Jeffrey to keep quiet, then had to smother a laugh when he realized how unnecessary that was.

They ducked low and eased closer, moving from one parked car to another. As they neared the truck, Ridge heard a familiar voice.

"I'm sure sorry we couldn't find him. But I really think you ought to come on back to town. I've got the power of the law on my side, so we can get all this straightened out."

"I'm not up to dealing with that woman tonight," said another voice. "The shrapnel in my knee's hurting like a bitch, buddy. I'm going home."

Ridge stopped, glanced down at the boy beside him. The kid had gone still as a scared rabbit.

"*Mitch*," he whispered.

As the boy's hand tightened on his, Ridge tugged Jeffrey behind a horse trailer and knelt down on the flattened grass of the makeshift parking lot.

"You remember what I told you?" he whispered.

Jeffrey swallowed hard and nodded.

"I think he might have Sierra. I have to find out, and that means we need to face him, okay?"

Another nod.

"Just remember, you've got the goods on him. He's the one who should be scared."

Tightening his grip on the boy's hand, he stepped forward.

"Sheriff."

"Ridge Cooper." The sheriff hardly looked happy to see him until his eyes lit on Jeffrey. "Well, look here. There he is now! Son, we've got a real surprise for you!"

He turned to Mitch, who was climbing into the cab of his truck as fast as he could.

"Hey!" Jim grabbed the door handle. "Hold on, buddy! Here he is."

Mitch started the engine.

"Hey! Your kid's here, buddy!"

Jim hung on like a sideways bronc rider as Mitch struggled to swing the door shut. Meanwhile, Ridge grabbed Mitch's sleeve and hauled him out of the driver's seat, throwing him on the ground a little harder than he'd intended.

Not much harder. It's just that he hadn't intended to knock the air out of the guy's lungs. He'd wanted him to be able to talk.

But that was okay. He was willing to hang on while Mitch coughed and hacked, struggling to get his breath back.

"Now take it easy," Jim said. "We don't know for sure he's a criminal or anything. It's just he says that boy's his son, and I'm starting to have my doubts."

"His son?"

Ridge turned around, but Jeffrey was gone. Panic set in for a second before he saw the boy scrabbling around on the floor of the truck cab, setting all kinds of junk on the seat.

A lipstick. A little packet of Kleenex. A roll of Lifesavers. A cell phone. And a very familiar leather purse.

Ridge stared at it a moment before he realized what it meant.

"Open the truck," he said to Mitch.

The guy stood, swaying a little, and started back to the cab of the truck, but Ridge grabbed the back of his shirt and hauled him backward.

"Open the back," he said again.

"I don't have to open anything for you," the man said. "I'm outta here."

Jeffrey stepped up to Mitch, holding Sierra's purse in front of himself like a shield. The kid was red-faced again, Ridge noticed, and he trembled all over as he looked up at the big man.

"You better open it," the boy said. "Because if you don't, I'm gonna talk and talk and talk 'cause you can't stop me. I'm gonna tell the sheriff everything you did. I'm gonna tell him…"

Mitch leaned toward the truck cab again. Ridge started to grab him again, but he was only reaching for the keys.

"I'll open it," he said. "I'll open it. Just hold on, kid."

Jeffrey folded his arms over his chest and looked on as the man staggered around to the back of the truck and unlocked the padlock on the overhead door. Ridge gave the handle a yank, boosting the door up on its rollers, and barely managed to catch the unconscious woman who tumbled into his arms.

The walk-in clinic in Grigsby was busier than usual. Sierra wasn't the only case of heat stroke to come from the rodeo, but she was definitely the most severe. She lay on a cot, her face pale, and closed her eyes while a nurse expertly started an IV.

"She just needs fluids," the nurse said. She was a portly middle-aged woman with a motherly face. Ridge made a mental note to find out who she was and to find out whether she might want to volunteer at Phoenix

House in her spare time. "Don't you worry, we'll have your wife fixed up in no time."

He cleared his throat, wondering if Sierra would notice the slip. He'd told the admitting clerk that they were husband and wife, just in case they wouldn't let him stay with her. She'd barely regained consciousness on the drive to the clinic, so he wasn't sure she'd be able to make rational decisions.

She reached over and tugged his sleeve.

"It's okay," she said. "It sounds kind of nice, actually."

He took her hand and squeezed gently then patted it with his other hand, worried he might have hurt her. She looked so small and fragile under the bright lights.

But at least she was alive. He'd never forget how she'd tumbled into his arms when he'd pulled up the truck door. How limp she'd been. He'd been afraid they were too late to save her. And now he could barely speak. Had he heard her right? Had she changed her mind?

"I just hope it can still come true someday, even though I was an idiot," she murmured. Her voice was hoarse, probably from shouting for help, and her words trailed off as she closed her eyes. She flipped them open again, looking a little panicked as she turned to Ridge. "I love you," she said. "Did I ever tell you that?"

"Sure," he said. "I think so. I knew it, anyway."

"That's not good enough." She squeezed his hand so hard it hurt. "I love you. Love you so much. You're the best man I know. The best I ever knew."

He smiled. "Thanks. I'm not sure what that says about the men you've known, but I'll take it."

"Please do," she murmured.

"Okay." He paused. "Are you in your right mind?"

She laughed. "I'm living in Wynott, Wyoming. How could I be in my right mind?" She saw by his face he was serious and sobered. "Yes. I'm feeling better. Really. You don't have to worry."

"Good." Sliding out of the orange plastic chair he was sitting in, he knelt on the shiny linoleum floor and took her hands in his.

"You already did this," she said.

"You said no."

"I said yes. And then I got stupid and doubted things and screwed it all up." Tears sprang to her eyes. "I'm sorry, Ridge. I was selfish and stupid."

"You're neither one of those things. You got scared, that's all."

"So we're good?"

He shook his head solemnly. "Nope. Every time you say no, I have to ask again. So here we go. You ready?"

"Sure." She looked down at her hospital robe. "I'm even wearing white."

"Good." He cleared his throat. "Sierra Dunn, will you be my wife?"

The nurse walked in, took one look at them, and screamed. Ridge jumped up, ready to grab her if she fainted, grab Sierra if they were being attacked, grab whoever needed grabbing. But the nurse grabbed him instead and seemed intent on shoving him down to the floor.

"No," she said. "You go on. I didn't mean to interrupt." She leaned out the door. "Sadie! Carol! You gotta see this! That good-looking cowboy's *proposing* to the little blond girl!"

By the time Ridge got his nerve back, he had an audience of three nurses and a doctor.

"Go on," the original nurse said. Her name tag said *Mary*. "Ask her again. I'm sorry."

He looked down at the floor, gathering his courage for the third time.

"Sierra Dunn…"

"Yes." She sat up, almost dislodging her IV as she reached for him. "Yes, yes, yes. Now come up here and kiss me."

He stood up and shot the audience a look. The two newest nurses and the doctor skittered away, but Mary just beamed. So did Sierra, and she looked so pretty, Ridge kissed her, gently, and eased her back down on the cot. When he finished, Mary was gone. He sat down on the edge of the cot and held Sierra's hand.

"Sleep," he said.

"After that I'm supposed to sleep?"

"Definitely. I'm going to kiss you like that every night when we're married."

"Promise?"

"Promise."

She was almost asleep when she suddenly struggled to sit up, her eyes wide and panicked. "Hey. Is Jeffrey okay?"

"He's fine," Ridge said. "Better than fine. Jim called and found out Mitch had all kinds of warrants on him—so many that the Denver police came up and got him. Jim was strutting like a bantam rooster while he waited. Mitch has enough paper on him that they'll be able to hold him until Jeff's ready to go talk to them about whatever it was he saw. And I think he'll be ready soon."

"That's good," she said. "Really good."

"Here he is now," Ridge said.

She looked alarmed, and he realized she'd thought he meant Mitch—or the sheriff. But it was Jeffrey who walked into the room, accompanied by Mary.

Sierra's face lit up. Ridge kind of wished she'd smiled like that for him, but part of the reason he loved her was the way she loved her boys. It was the thing that had drawn him to her in the first place. He knew what a difference that kind of love could make in a boy's life. Just knowing somebody thought you were worth caring about made the world a better place to live when you had no one to call your own.

The boy edged over to the bed. It was obvious that the medical setting made him nervous. Who knew how many emergency rooms he'd seen in his young life? Or how often he'd been forced to lie to doctors about walking into doors, falling down the stairs, and all the other timeworn lies kids told to save their parents?

God, the world was a screwed-up place. Sierra thought she could change it, but Ridge didn't see how you could. For him, it seemed ambitious to believe they could even change their little corner of it, but he was willing to try.

That just went to show how much Sierra had changed him. Before he'd met her, he'd been convinced that all he could do was ride broncs and bulls, take the beatings they dished out just as he'd taken the beatings his parents had given him before he was taken from them all those years ago. He'd always believed his only real talent was stoicism—the ability to cover up the pain no matter how much a blow hurt. He'd gotten pretty good at covering up emotional pain too.

So had Jeffrey. Ridge had assumed his refusal to speak had its roots in the same kind of pain that made Ridge quiet and unwilling to engage with people. But as it turned out, Mitch had ordered the poor kid not to talk, threatening to kill anyone Jeff cared about. That hadn't been a problem until Sierra came along and the poor kid had something to lose. Talk about a mixed blessing.

Right now, the kid was leaning against the side of the cot and beaming down at Sierra, the love in his eyes as clear as the sun rising on a bright spring morning.

"I'm glad you're alive," he said.

"Me too." She smiled.

"I sort of saved you," he said. "I found your purse and stuff."

"Sort of?" Sierra struggled to sit up, accepting Ridge's help so she could sit up and dangle her legs over the side of the cot. "Sort of? Heck, you saved me for sure. Nobody ever would have opened up that truck if you hadn't said something." Her expression softened and she smoothed the boy's hair. "You *said* something. I'm so proud of you."

"I'm not scared to talk anymore," Jeffrey said, sitting beside her. "And I'm not scared of Mitch."

"We'll talk about Mitch sometime, okay? But right now, let's just wait." She cupped his cheek with one hand and pulled him close—a mushy mom-type gesture some little boys shied away from, but Jeffrey closed his eyes and leaned into her touch, a beatific smile on his face.

Like so many foster kids, he'd been starved for love. He might have been hungry, tired, and hurt too, over the years, but Ridge knew that lacking love was the worst of the pain he'd been through. He knew firsthand the empty ache it caused, the deep, dull pain that never really went away, that couldn't be relieved by any kind of medicine.

Only someone like Bill, or Irene or Sierra, could heal it. And there was no more valuable thing you could do for the world than to lift a child out of a loveless life.

Jeffrey opened his eyes and reached out. Eyes tearing, Ridge sat down and put an arm around the boy. The three of them sat motionless for a moment in a family tableau—one that Ridge knew would be a reality as soon as he and Sierra and the state of Wyoming could make it so.

Acknowledgments

Okay, guys, this is going to be a long one. As many readers know, breast cancer brought a screeching halt to my normal life just as I began this book. I lost my hair, but I didn't lose my mind (or my life!), thanks to the following people:

My friend Mary Throne, who inspired me to go get that mammogram. She was always there for me despite her own struggle and her day job as Super Woman. She's an inspiration as well as a friend.

I drew on a deep well of love from my friends through every difficult day. Thanks to Kate Wright and Ellen the Superchicken for the eggs, and Colette Auclair for the marvelously tasteless get-well cards. Thanks to Elizabeth Roadifer for the lovely and tasteful get-well cards. (Colette and Elizabeth, you need to talk. Really.) Thanks to Mary Gilgannon and Jeana Byrne for the good advice and the sharp red pens. Thanks to Amanda Cabot for the most generous (and beautiful) gift ever, and to Laura Werstak for leaping into action with funny animal videos, gifts, and a friendship that never wavers. Also, thanks to Wendy Soto, Jeran Artery, and Mike Bleakley, Mike and Chris Shay, Laura Macomber, and Cie and Samantha Patterson for the love and friendship that warmed me every day. Thanks to the kids — Alycia Fleury, Scott McCauley, and Brian Davis, for being there. And thank you to my parents, Don and Betty

Smyth, and my sister, Carolyn Smyth, for not freaking out too much and staying supportive from start to finish.

Another huge thank you goes to my agent, Elaine English, for her help navigating the challenges of working—and living!—through cancer.

As for my publisher, Sourcebooks—I am so glad we found each other. Everyone in this organization has been nothing but supportive, despite the inevitable delays my illness caused. Thank you to editor Deb Werksman and everyone else for believing in me.

To anyone going through the breast cancer ordeal— it's long, it's hard, and it's different for every one of us. Chemotherapy in particular is full of surprises, many of them unpleasant and all of them inconvenient. But you will survive, and you will be stronger for it.

Last but definitely not least, I am grateful every day for the support of my husband, Ken McCauley. Being a caregiver is at least as hard as being a patient, but his support and understanding never wavered. Always and forever, he is the love of my life and the inspiration behind all my heroes. Mwah!

About the Author

Joanne Kennedy's lifelong fascination with Wyoming's unique blend of past and present inspires her to write contemporary Western romances with traditional ranch settings. She is the author of *Cowboy Trouble*, *One Fine Cowboy* (nominated for a RITA award for best single title contemporary), *Cowboy Fever*, *Tall, Dark and Cowboy*, *Cowboy Crazy*, and *Cowboy Tough*. Her fascination with literature led to careers in bookselling and writing, but at various times, Joanne has dabbled in horse training, chicken farming, and bridezilla wrangling at a department store wedding registry. She lives with two dogs and a retired fighter pilot in Cheyenne, Wyoming. The dogs are relatively well behaved.

Joanne loves to hear from readers and can be reached through her website, *www.joannekennedybooks.com*.